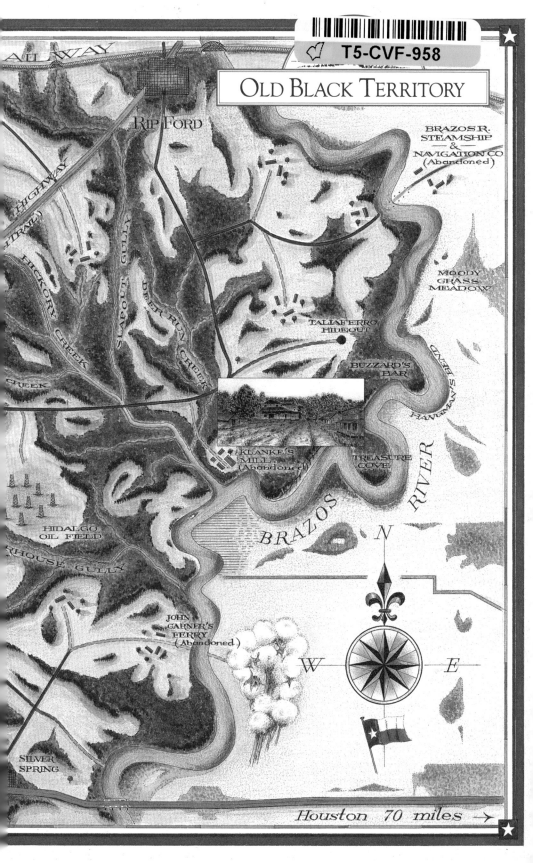

OLD BLACK

OLD BLACK

a novel by

Doug Briggs

Illustrated by Edsel M. Cramer,
Monique L. Jouannet, and Jean-Claude Louis

BEVERLY PUBLISHING COMPANY
Houston

OLD BLACK is a Beverly Book, published by
arrangement with Margate Press, Ltd.

Limited Edition

The text of this book is set in Adobe Caslon;
display is calligraphy by Jean-Claude Louis.
Printed on acid-free paper.

For information about permission to reproduce text or
illustrations from this book, contact Beverly Publishing Company,
P.O. Box 800788, Houston, Texas 77280
Telephone (800)955-2665
Internet address: www.oldblack.com
Email address: bev@onramp.net

Library of Congress Catalog Card Number 97-72767
ISBN 1-881287-12-2

PRINTED IN CANADA

To Cindy and Jim,
and to the memory of their mother,
Dolores; it was she who had the genes.

Author's Note

I recently read a novel by a best-selling author in which a pre-WWII wooden-hull Navy patrol boat sprinted across a thousand miles of open ocean in a time-span that mandated an average speed above fifty miles an hour. This was only one of numerous implausible events and situations that undermined an otherwise worthwhile story, one that the author strongly implied was authentic.

Writers of realistic fiction have an obligation to satisfy their most critical readers' expectations of credibility. Respectful of that obligation, I took care to keep *Old Black* faithful to reality on material points . . . except for one recurring circumstance.

The flag race will be seen in some youth horse shows, but not in those sanctioned by the American Quarter Horse Association.

Because Jim Bradley is, fictitiously, a member of the American Quarter Horse Youth Association and the imaginary Old Black is a registered Quarter Horse, they often compete in AQHA shows. Lacking the insight provided here, readers in the know would have to wonder why a non-AQHA event is encountered in every horse show in the story.

There is no scarcity of official AQHA performance classes in *Old Black*, but it is the flag race that best pits the individual capabilities and shortcomings of Jim Bradley and Old Black against their nemesis in timed events, the hotdog on his racehorse. This is why the flag race appears in the story at all, and why it is the final and most decisive performance contest. Circumstances that will be evident to the reader dictated that it occur in an AQHA show.

Readers who might otherwise be put off by this departure from reality might overlook it, given these considerations.

A note on events at the Houston Livestock Show: Prior to the addition of the Astroarena to the Astrohall complex, performance events of the various horse shows were held in the Astrodome. Today they take place in the Astroarena.

Doug Briggs

A typical western saddle

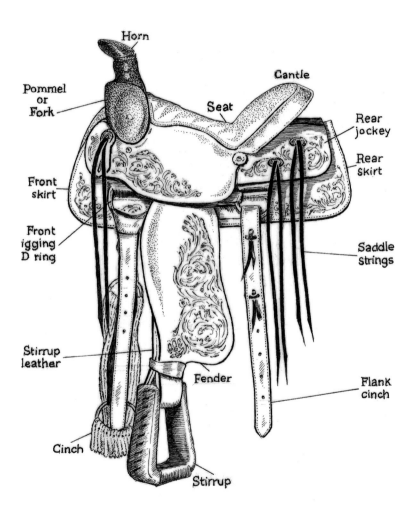

Horn

Cantle

Pommel
or
Fork

Seat

Rear
jockey

Rear
skirt

Front
skirt

Front
rigging
D ring

Saddle
strings

Stirrup
leather

Fender

Flank
cinch

Cinch

Stirrup

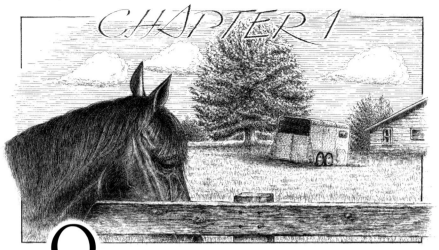

On this particular Saturday morning, no two creatures on earth could have had more opposite outlooks on life than Jim Bradley and Old Black. It was Jim Bradley's general nature to be cheerful and happy. He looked forward to all but the most routine events with keen anticipation, never seeming to notice that the joys derived seldom measured up to his great expectations.

Today, however, Jim was surpassing even himself. He was as outlandishly happy as a boy had a right to be. He felt like a string of firecrackers about to go off, like a skyrocket with a burning fuse. It took deliberate effort on his part to keep from acting silly.

The event responsible for Jim's rip-roaring spirits was that today he was going to get a horse. Well, he *might* get a horse today. He and his father were going to look at one. He had been promised a horse for his tenth birthday, only two weeks away, and Mr. Bonner, the horsemanship counselor in his 4-H Club, had told him and his father of a fine youth horse that was for sale right now.

George Bonner was a small man—but a man never seen as small by his students—and he was thin and wiry. Although he was about seventy, he had the vitality and looks of a man a dozen years younger. Through a half-century of training horses, he had accumulated a boundless knowledge of horses and horsemanship. In South Texas, the name George Bonner was legendary among western horsemen.

For two decades he had taught a horsemanship class to youths in the 4-H Club. He had a quick and intense nature, and although he was a stern disciplinarian, Mr. Bonner had a way of creating a secret conviction in his students: "He's hard, but he *likes* me!" His classes were always full, for his program returned big rewards— knowledge of horses and life in general, horsemanship skills, and the companionship of enthusiastic classmates. Youths who were unruly and indifferent to learning elsewhere often became eager achievers under his hand, reflecting the age-old idolization of strict but fair masters by the creatures subject to their discipline.

It was Mr. Bonner's way to stroll about as he spoke in a distinct voice, but at a level that made his students sit up and pay close attention in order to hear. To reinforce the belief of each one that they were the main object of his attention, he would often lock eyes compellingly on a student, then casually use his or her name in his discourse.

Every class had a few minutes of philosophy woven into it. At the last meeting Mr. Bonner had spoken on the art of winning and losing: "You will encounter every human condition in the show ring. This applies whether the ring contains horses, dogs, cats, beauty contestants, or Little League ball players and their coaches and parents. As competitors, we must be gracious winners as well as graceful losers. Arrogant, haughty winners can be more trying than bad losers."

He had paused for a long time, his penetrating eyes stopping an instant on every one of the thirty-odd pairs of eyes before him. Then he continued, "I am speaking not only of our personal conduct at horse shows, but equally of the show ring that is life. Dale Carnegie was right when he preached that if you *act* enthusiastic, you'll *be* enthusiastic." He struck out vigorously with a fist and was pleased at the gesture's impact on the class. "The poor loser in the arena who acts angry will *become* angry. Retorting to another's provocation with angry words will not only further infuriate our adversary but will kindle the fires of anger in ourselves."

THE HORSE THAT JIM AND HIS FATHER WERE going to see was a Quarter Horse named Old Black. Although eighteen years old, he was the world champion calf-roping horse. Like Jim Bradley, Old Black was by nature bright and happy; he had never known any other disposition. But he was not bright and happy today, and had not been so for weeks. While Jim was going to great exertions to keep his jubilation under control, Old Black was as forlorn as a horse could be this side of his deathbed.

The reason for his dejection was that his lifelong rodeo career had, only a few weeks ago, come to an abrupt end. He simply could not fathom why his master, Buck Jones, had abandoned the rodeo circuit and suddenly hunkered down at the little home place.

"CIRCUMSTANCES," MR. BONNER HAD SAID to Jim and his father, "sudden and unexpected circumstances have arisen that make a splendid horse available right now. He's a Quarter Horse gelding named Old Black, and a rare find for a youth's first horse. Although he's getting along in years, he still performs in—gosh, close to a hundred rodeos a year, calf roping and team roping. That's testimony enough that the horse is more than up to the performance demands of our youth events.

"For what my opinion is worth—probably no more than its cost to you, Jimmy—Old Black would be a prize at this stage of your adventure with horses. Yes, a prize." Jim's father believed Mr. Bonner's opinions were worth a lot, and he had listened closely. The opinion came at a good time, for Mr. Bradley had been having some anxieties about finding a suitable horse for his son.

Bonner explained that he had known the horse and his owner for more than a decade but had felt obligated to closely inspect the horse before mentioning him to the Bradleys.

"I went to see him yesterday," he said. "It's a pity he wasn't gelded sooner. No doubt his neck would have been much keener." Bonner's disregard for that fault was displayed by a fleeting sour expression and a shrug of his shoulders. "Not surprisingly," he said with a wry smile, "the horse has experienced a few wrecks in the arena. There is a knot on one knee—from an old injury, completely healed—and a few scars here and there."

He waved the blemishes away with the back of his hand. "They are purely cosmetic defects. The horse seems as sound as can be. Buck says he is, and I would take Buck Jones's word to the bank. You can never tell about the health of a horse, though. I bought a cutting horse for ten thousand dollars some years back and a week later there he lay in his stall: dead as a doornail from a twisted intestine.

"I would not be put off by this horse's being eighteen years old. He's in superb shape, the physical condition of a horse of fifteen—no, even less. You occasionally see a man of seventy who you would take to be a decade younger, by his looks and vigor. The same goes for horses. Another thing in Old Black's favor is that he's been owned by Buck since he was a weanling. A horse could not find himself in more considerate hands."

He tapped his forehead with a finger and his eyes narrowed in a meaningful look. "This horse has something else, too, a quality that is all too rare in men as well as horses: sagacity." He looked at Jim and considerately added some words the boy would be more likely to understand. "He has wisdom, Jim, and keen judgment. Yes, indeed. Along with sagacity, he has a remarkable athletic aptitude and a ferocious determination to apply it. *Ferocious* determination, and I do not speak idly. The devices that horse has been known to employ to shave the barest fraction of a second to win a roping. . ." He held his hand before his eye with thumb and forefinger a hairsbreadth apart.

Mr. Bonner cleared his throat significantly. He placed both hands on Jim's shoulders and looked him square in the eye. "But he won't halter, Jimmy. He's a doer, not a looker. Even in his prime Old Black would have had tough sledding in the halter arena. So if you're looking for a halter horse, you'd best look elsewhere."

His hand went to his chin and he was silent for a moment. "Old Black has some Flying Bob in him—boy, did it show! How that horse could run! Buck says he isn't as fast as he once was. But he's fast enough, if you look at what he's been doing to the cream of the crop—clipping their fleeter tailfeathers with his cunning moves and stealing one purse after another, that's what. When he learns what our games are all about, he'll discover on his own what it takes to win." He closed one eye and shook his finger for emphasis. "That is what I meant by sagacity, Jimmy." He handed Matt Bradley a sheet of notepaper on which he had written the name and phone number of the horse's owner.

Matt thanked Mr. Bonner for taking the time to inspect the horse, and for his thoughtful opinion. They would look at Old Black this very Saturday, the day after tomorrow, he said.

IT WAS ALL JIM BRADLEY COULD DO to keep a grip on himself, to act normal while his father attended to what Jim felt were wholly needless tasks before their departure. Jim had already washed every last dish, had wiped off the table and stovetop more than once, had neatly folded the towels and placed them in a tidy arrangement on the counter top. Since he could find nothing else to do, he stuck his hands in his pockets and moved about with his notion of acting normal, a contrived casualness that had a stiff and awkward air about it. Matt had to restrain himself from laughing out loud, but he considerately got a move on and they were soon on their way.

Jim had been nervously chatty during the first few miles of the drive clear across Houston to where they would find Old Black, then he fell silent. Now he sat looking out of the window, on his face a thoughtful expression, his eyes squinted as he often did when concentrating. "I'm glad I get to go to 4-H, Dad. I really like Mr. Bonner. He teaches us all kinds of things that people need to know."

"I like Mr. Bonner, too, Jim," Matt said. "He's an exceptional man. We could use a lot more Mr. Bonners, but the country, the world, is dirt poor when it comes to his kind. Weren't we lucky you got in his class?"

Jim nodded. He looked anxiously out of the car window for a time, then leaned forward to stare at the road ahead. "I'll sure be glad when we get there," he said.

THE MAIN REASON FOR OLD BLACK'S present state of despondency was that he had never before been idle for very long. Ever since he was big enough to pack a cowboy and a forty-five-pound roping saddle around, all his years had been spent on the rodeo circuit. Because an exceptional mount is essential if a competitor is going to make it to the pay window often enough to make rodeoing a profession, most cowboys took good care of their horses. There could be no higher calling than that of a rodeo roping horse under Buck Jones, and his care of Old Black was exemplary.

Fifteen years ago Buck was only an also-ran in the rodeo game. He was making a living, but just barely. Then his young gelding that he called Black—because he was coal black with only a white star on his forehead—became mature enough to be started on roping calves. After two seasons with Black under him, Buck was among the top fifteen calf ropers. He finished their third year in the top ten.

"Funny thing about Black," Buck once told his friend Charlie Sommers when the young horse was still learning the ropes. "He knows when it's for real and when it ain't. The difference between how he worked when we were training and when he walked into an arena with a real audience and real competitors was amazing.

There's no question that he knows we've got to *win* this thing."

Now that Buck and Old Black had been together forever—at least as *forever* applied to the *horse*—they were much more than just a cowboy and his mount. They were real pals with a genuine harmony between them. Even during the short periods when they weren't on the circuit, camped out here at the old home place or somewhere else, Buck spent a lot of time with Old Black. He stood by chatting amiably as the horse ate his evening feeding. Each morning Buck exercised him on a long rope; he bathed him often, hosing him down and then letting him air dry as he exercised. Buck rubbed Old Black down with his hands, which he said brought out the coat's sheen, and massaged his legs with Absorbine.

If the setting permitted, when Buck was working on his truck or repacking the wheel bearings on the trailer, Old Black was left loose to hang around like an attentive dog. To give the horse a break on a long haul, Buck would find a place on the roadside with grass and trees where he could let Old Black out of the trailer to stretch his legs. Buck would break out his old canvas director's chair and sit reading under a tree while the horse grazed nearby, staked out on a rope.

It was Buck's way to talk to Black when they were together. Sometimes he explained what he was doing. He might lay out their plans for the weeks ahead, discuss where they were going, describe some features of that part of the country that he thought Black would like to hear about, tell him of old friends they would get to see. During the past year Buck had talked with mounting enthusiasm about retiring to a place in the Texas hill country. Old Black always liked it when Buck talked to him.

Suddenly, though, like snapping off a light, their rodeoing had ended. Buck had told many a friend, "We'll see you in Austin," but Houston had been their last performance. And in the weeks since, they had not budged from the old home place.

Now Old Black was penned up in a corral that was ankle deep in mud when it rained and a craggy hardpan when it dried up. His shelter consisted of a leaky lean-to that was sultry and airless when he sought relief from the blazing sun. At least it was a sound windbreak from the biting winds that still swept in from the north now and then. The weather often switched from hot to downright frigid this early in the spring. On cold nights, Buck always dressed Old

Black in his stable blanket and took it off in the morning.

Much of the time, Buck was strangely absent from the place. More than once he did not return at all in the evening. On those occasions a man came over to feed Black and top off the concrete water trough. But even when Buck was there, he seldom came out to the corral more than once a day. In the evening he let Black out for exercise and then fed him. While Black was eating, Buck would give him a rubdown with a soft old burlap sack, then scrape any mud from his coat with the currycomb, follow that up with a good brushing, and finish with an invigorating leg massage with Absorbine.

All the while, Old Black would study his master eagerly for a smile; he would listen for an encouraging word, but Buck had little to say. And there was no more talk about retiring to the hill country. Occasionally Buck would ask him, "How's it going, Black old pal?" But it seemed spoken with forced enthusiasm. Buck also avoided looking the horse in the eye, reinforcing Old Black's growing misgivings of some rift in their relationship, an alienation. It seemed as if the lifelong fellowship between them had just evaporated, and it made Old Black ache to his very bones, his suddenly very old bones.

No doubt many horses had never experienced loving, compassionate care, an intimate companionship with a human being, so they couldn't miss what they'd never known. Old Black had never known anything but the happiest relationship with Buck, and so its abrupt disappearance left him with a crushing sadness.

It was because of these things that on this Saturday morning Old Black stood morose and downcast, his legs astraddle and his head hanging despondently. His great face was a picture of sadness that only a truly great face can express—ears askew, with his lower lip sagging feebly, grotesquely displaying his lower teeth. One lifelong quality of Old Black had always been his quick, keen, sparkling eyes. There was no sparkle in them now, only a dull despair accented by lifeless, drooping eyelids.

Old Black sniffed with contempt at the smelly pen. It was a world away from the invigorating blend of aromas that wafted through the rodeo horse barns, and which now tormented a far corner of his mind—fresh bedding straw, savory alfalfa in the hay rack, Absorbine and alcohol and black salve, hoof dressing, leather, saddle soap, neatsfoot oil, clean sweat . . . And then, at feeding time, the mouth-watering aroma and delectable taste of Omolene topped off with a scoop of Animax.

To escape the sight of his dismal stockade, Old Black tramped listlessly to the fence, the toes of his hoofs making trails in the dirt. He hung his head far out over the top rail and wearily inhaled the clammy, stagnant air. Although a few puffs of cloud trudged inland from the Gulf on light airs aloft, nothing was stirring on the ground.

His dejected gaze fell on the faded yellow horse trailer that had hauled him to so many rodeos. The trailer had always stood proudly erect on its four wheels and jack stand as if it, too, was eager to take to the road. It did not look eager now, or even roadworthy; it leaned wearily over a flat tire on one side and down on the hitch in front. The places on the fenders where the paint was worn away had always been kept burnished to a satiny sheen by people and animals squeezing by in the crowded contestants' parking lots. Now that luster was gone, grown over with young red rust.

Now and then, Buck and Old Black used to drop in to this place on the east side of Houston. Buck jokingly called it "the ranch," although it was scarcely an acre of ground. On it was a sound, neat little house, a garage for Buck's pickup, and a small corral. One end of the corral was made up of a tack room connected to a three-sided lean-to that sheltered the horse from weather.

Their visits to the place never lasted long before Buck would back his pickup to the nose of the trailer and busily begin hooking up, a sure sign they were going to a roping. The cue would send Old Black prancing around and snorting excitedly. Then Buck would stride pretentiously to the corral, wearing his big, vee-shaped grin, and shout merrily, "Hey, Black. Let's you and me go rodeoing, old boy." But all a sudden, the things that Old Black loved to do seemed to be of the past.

As Old Black stood enduring his miserable existence, a gleaming red pickup truck appeared around a bend down the road. Attached to it was an elegant matching horse trailer. When the rig finally registered on his aimless gaze, Old Black cast off his anxiety in an instant. His head came up alertly on a splendidly arched neck and a fine gleam replaced the melancholy in his eyes. They focused intently as the sight floated closer.

Old Black's neck craned and his nose reached out, nostrils flared, tasting the air to pick up the very first delicious scents. His ears twitched and turned until they heard the faintest sounds of what would become a familiar melody. Then they perked strongly to the exquisite harmony of the big Dodge V-10's rich, throaty dual exhaust, eight tires singing on the hard road and the sweet sighing of the windstream.

As the handsome rig swept past, Old Black stared high headed and wide-eyed at a pair of horses' tails flowing merrily in the trailer's wake. When the speeding rig's turbulence tumbled over him, providing a welcome refreshment in the still air, he sniffed greedily at the fragrances swept up from the roadside—of clover, winter grass and wildflowers. Then he detected the faintest delicious scent of the horses.

Even the smell of the truck's exhaust was a pleasant intoxicant and suddenly the air was a rare delight to breathe. Inhaling deeply, Old Black stared with malignant envy as the sounds waned, one by one, until the sight was a silent, receding mirage. His glistening eyes stared even after the last glimpse of those lucky horses—off to a special someplace—had vanished into the shimmering morning haze.

If ever a horse had thought, Old Black was probably thinking. Behind his shining eye may have been a vision of himself on a road to a special someplace of his own, sailing along in his own trailer. However long the road might be, even when it led to Canada, Old Black keenly savored the rides in the cozy little trailer that Buck Jones often claimed had hauled him the equal of six times around the world, over half-way to the moon.

Old Black would watch as Buck, talking all the while, stowed his saddle, tack and other gear in the forward compartments, as he stacked hay and feed in one of the two horse stalls. Then Buck would open the door to the other stall, and when the loose end of the halter rope landed over Old Black's neck he would eagerly scramble inside. First there would always be the slow twists and turns, the stops and starts and sounds of close traffic until the rig got strung out on the open road. That was when the symphony of the highway began to build, a hypnotic melody of tires singing on pavement, the pap-pap, pap-pap, pap-pap of rubber slapping the tarred cracks, the whine of the windstream blending with the purr of the engine and the hum of the exhaust. Soon it became a lullaby, sending him off into a delirious doze.

The symphony of the highway sometimes fell to a hush as the rig cruised softly along on new-fallen snow, with snowflakes gently brushing the trailer above Old Black's ears like the sound of a gentle breeze in the trees. Snow meant cold, and cold meant that Old Black would be wearing a warm stable blanket in his mobile cocoon.

The symphony of the highway could become a crescendo as nature's big drum section boomed out with thunderclaps, spectacular light shows dancing about as other sections of the orchestra joined in with shrieking wind, rain pounding on the trailer's steel skin, and the sharp hiss of water jetting from under the tires.

Old Black had heard all the symphonies of the highway and loved every one of them. At the end of every road would be a clamorous rodeo grounds, a special someplace alive with cowboys and horses. Inside a big barn would be a clean, straw-bedded stall of his own to loaf around in, and dozens of other horses to socialize with. Sounds of all kinds would merge into another familiar sonata— livestock bawling, cackling, lowing, bleating, and whinnying; radios blending every station within range; loudspeakers that droned on and off; a harmonica crying in the stall down the aisle . . .

It could be that a cranny of Old Black's mind recalled the soothing chant of a rodeo announcer, his voice taking on an excited edge as he reminded the audience that Buck Jones and Old Black held the fastest time on record. At the Houston Astrodome just weeks ago, the announcer spoke with pride to the packed crowd as Old Black walked briskly through the gate carrying Buck to the roping box. "I was there to see it, folks, at Butte, Montana only two years back, when this very same cowboy riding this very same horse set the world's record time in calf roping. It's a record that still stands!" Old Black didn't mind one bit having to stroll around a few minutes to let the applause die down before Buck rode him into the box.

Most of all, Old Black savored those tantalizing capsules of raging action that would come soon after Buck got him set up in the roping box. The tingle of anticipation began when the string barrier was set and he could feel Buck settle down deep in the saddle and place his weight just so in the stirrups. Old Black would feel a final tug on the cinch—Buck making sure it was tight. Then Buck would shake out a loop and Old Black would hear the rhythmic swoosh of a few test swings swirling above his head.

With his weight poised on hind legs that were set like steel beartraps, Old Black's forefeet would start tapping out nervous little dancing steps until the gate that restrained the calf flew open with a *bang!* In a second the calf had its head start, causing the string barrier to come clean. At that instant Old Black catapulted from the box and thundered like a cyclone on the calf's heels. The lariat's song rose swiftly to a sweet wail, and then the music and the loop sailed away toward its target.

In an instant he'd get his cue to stop, and stop he did, planting his hind feet in the ground and rolling back to concentrate all his twelve hundred pounds on them. With his forefeet off the ground, every muscle, sinew and tendon in his chest would be standing out sharply. During that famous slide, Old Black's tail was in the dirt with the loam of the arena pouring like dark seafoam up and around his haunches and roiling behind in a turbulent wake. With his head held as if he were standing in a halter class, Old Black's expression was grim with resolute determination—eyes afire, nostrils flared, and lips clamped tightly together.

In contrast to Old Black's furious action, Buck was a picture of composure. During his dismount, he stood suspended for the fleetest moment in the right stirrup, his leg bent, his upper body straight as a soldier at attention with chin tucked, a pigging string in his teeth and his eyes fixed on the calf. At exactly the right moment, he appeared to just step off, like a trainman's seemingly casual departure from a moving locomotive. Lean and wiry and a fast sprinter, Buck was in a dead run the moment he hit the ground.

That was always when the applause began, and Old Black knew part of it was for him. After sliding to a stop, it was his job to keep a taut strain on the rope all the while Buck was on the ground. He was not to drag the downed calf, though, as some horses did, a hindrance to the roper and treatment of the calf that could draw a fine.

Old Black's reverie might have drifted back to that night in Butte. The sensational run had brought the audience to its feet even before Buck had finished tying the calf. From the stands came a roaring of cheers, whistles, and applause that did not abate even one decibel when the announcer tried to be heard over the pandemonium, "Ladies and gentlemen . . . ."

Finally he was able to say, "Ladies and gentlemen, ladies and gentlemen and all you young folks in the stands, you have a special memory to take home tonight. You might have suspected, like I did, that all of us here just might be witnessing history in the making. Entry number nineteen, Buck Jones, riding Old Black, has just set a new *world's record!* Time: six-point-eight seconds!"

Again the commotion surged from the stands and continued as if it would last all night. At the announcer's urging, Buck paraded Old Black around the arena, shaking many an outstretched hand and waving his hat to the people up high. A thousand hands reached out to touch the champion's glistening, sweat-soaked coat as, filled with spirited pride, he pranced close along the rail.

CHAPTER 2

Even after they began calling him *Old* Black, he and Buck could be the team to beat when they showed up at a calf roping. Buck was a crack shot with a loop and he had a quick release. Old Black was uncannily savvy and had that mysterious assortment of abilities that all truly great athletes possess, along with the unyielding determination that is often called "heart."

As age honed the edge off the horse's speed, he compensated by trying all the harder. He became faster out of the box, passing the string barrier the barest fraction of a second after it had disarmed. Old Black had a keen understanding of what the whole job consisted of and shrewdly made tiny adjustments in the part he played in it.

Over the years of that evolution, the aging athlete gradually developed a distinctive running style. His rather large feet tore up the arena dirt as his legs churned like the vanes of a windmill in a storm. With ears laid straight back, his neck craned as far as could be and his nose extended, he looked like he was reaching for the finish line at a racetrack.

The highly animated effort that he expended, accentuated by the rain of arena dirt filling the air, gave the illusion—and it was only an illusion—that he was moving in slow motion and not covering much ground. It was a display of gritty determination that warmed the hearts of many observers while a few saw it as downright comical. The fun-loving cowboys always looked forward to Old Black's performances.

Buck had begun to get some ribbing about it, but since he was aboard during Old Black's runs, he had never observed the spectacle and was unaware of how dramatically Old Black had enhanced the entertainment feature of calf roping. The important thing—

astounding as it seemed to some of the other contestants—was that Buck's position in the lineup of money earners kept creeping up. He was a familiar face at rodeo pay windows.

One evening when Buck and some other cowboys were gathered at the Dinner Bell Cafe in Austin, the subject turned to Old Black's style of locomotion. The renowned rodeo clown and cowboy Willy Plattner, sometimes referred to as The Professor due to his learned airs, suggested that the horse be anointed with a more suitable name. He rose, raised his mug of root beer, and quoting loosely from Cervantes, proclaimed in dramatic tones:

"It is not fit that so famous a knight's horse, and so good a beast, should want a known name. I declare that he should have the name Rosinante de la Mancha, a name in my opinion lofty, full, and significant of what Old Black has become since he was a plain jade, before he was exalted to his new dignity, being now, as Buck Jones believes and the record book attests, the best calf-roping horse in all the world."

Buck reacted to the proclamation with rollicking hilarity, laughing heartily and slapping his thigh until his eyes swam with tears. Like most rodeo cowboys, he liked to be in cowboy company, but he let the others do the talking. He might even have had a tinge of shyness, though he thought of himself as only a good listener. "I never learned anything from hearing myself talk," he liked to say.

Buck was quick to respond when illnesses or hardships fell upon his friends, always ready to lend a helping hand. Nobody had ever known him to have anything but a cheerful outlook. Once he was asked if he ever got mad, or down in the dumps. Observing that many eyes were on him waiting for a response, he answered thoughtfully:

"Well, now, I don't know what I'd have to get steamed up about. Imagine a fella my age that didn't ever have to work, didn't have to go to a job every day, carrying a lunch bucket and punching a time card. Nobody seems out to do me any harm. And we're in the money more'n we're out, me'n Old Black. So why would we have cause to be down in the dumps? Neither one of us has ever been seriously sick or been in a wreck, a *bad* wreck, either out there," he nodded toward the arena, "or on the road, either. And I don't have any family to worry over."

Feigning a sinister tone, he added, "The only person I ever wanted to *kill* was whoever it was that dropped that box of roofing nails on I-70 west of Denver, giving me five flats at once." His expression was merry again and he laughed at the memory. "But it was almost worth the trouble to see the look on the guy at the filling station when I rode up on Old Black and asked if he fixed flats. He said real quick, 'Not on horses, I don't.'"

The group's laughter intensified when he concluded with a twinkle in his eye and the huge, patented smile, "I have something to give thanks over every time I ride into an arena. Under me is a convicted, habitual purse snatcher that goes by the alias of Rosinante la what's-his-name. See, he's perfected this here sleight-of-hand act, a trick to keep you guys making fun of him and whooping it up while he picks your pockets. It would keep old Ebenezer Scrooge whistling and singing all the way to the bank."

THE GLEAM OF REMINISCENCE HAD NOT left Old Black's eye when he heard the screen door of the house squeak open and slam shut. His ears flicked and twisted, listening acutely for the sound of Buck's bootsteps on the porch. If the sound moved to the right, he would soon hear the door of Buck's Dodge Ram slam shut and the big V-8 engine come to life. If the sound traveled the longer distance on the porch to the left, he was coming to the corral.

Maybe something was up, because morning wasn't feeding time and the sound of Buck's bootsteps clomp-clomped off to the left. The horse's eyes, ears, and nose concentrated intently on the corner of the house where Buck would first come into view. When he did, Old Black watched with sorrow as Buck limped painfully along the path to the corral.

IT HAD BEGUN AS ONLY A MINOR DISCOMFORT that came on just before the Houston rodeo, a strain of some kind, Buck thought, or old age setting in. But the pain deep inside his leg had rapidly gotten worse. Examinations and tests had ruled out every ailment in ascending order of severity until he finally learned it was bone cancer. Only this Wednesday past they said they had to operate immediately. He would lose the leg, if not his life. "You're going to have to give me a few days, Doc," he said. "Until Monday. I have a loose end to tie up." He said it with such finality that the doctor only nodded.

Buck had a premonition that he could be in serious trouble some time before the final diagnosis. As insurance, he began studying how he might find Old Black a home where he would get good care, an environment where he could get some action, but not too much action.

Disregarding a few bumps and scars, Old Black was sound in every way. Many a rodeo cowboy would pay a big price for him, but this option was out of the question in Buck's mind. In the first place, in a few years Old Black should be retired from full-time rodeo competition, even under hands as caring as Buck's own. In the second place, although most rodeo cowboys took good care of their horses, a few abused them with overuse, even rented them out to other contestants. If the horse stayed in the rodeo business, there was no telling what kind of hands he would eventually fall into.

No, he wanted a more promising future for Old Black. But what scheme could guarantee the future care and treatment of a horse? Even the most carefully selected person you might *give* the horse to could sell him, or give him to someone else who might not be so caring. Buck vaguely remembered a news item about a lady who had provided for her cats in her will. She had bought a country home for them, had established a trust fund for their care with good pay for the caretaker. But the caretaker became better paid by keeping all of the money and dumping the cats.

Buck ached inside to think that Old Black could even end up in one of those stables that rent horses, where they plod all day over the same trails to nowhere, get yanked around until their mouths become as hard as saddle leather. That very fate befell a celebrated racehorse in California, Buck recalled. He was a gelding and, of course, no use as a breeder, so when he was no longer fleet enough to win races he was callously sold to a riding stable. When the horse's dismal plight was discovered, somebody more caring than his previous owner rescued the horse and gave him a new and honorable career: leading the pre-race promenade of racehorses at Hollywood Park racetrack.

The dilemma was rarely far from Buck's mind, and he constantly pondered what to do until the perfect solution popped into his head. Many rodeos are combined with all-around livestock shows and other events that are seldom seen by the fans who come to the rodeo performances. Among them are the youth horse shows, where kids show their horses and compete in a variety of performance contests. Some of the events were hell-for-leather affairs against the clock. They required good horses and excellent horse-and-rider coordination to win or even place.

Weekdays, rodeos are held in the evenings. During the day, the arena is used for livestock judging and events like the youth horse shows, so the cowboys often killed time during the day by sitting in the stands and spectating. They always enjoyed the youth horse events, having gained a real respect for the young contestants and for the horses they rode. Buck knew that some of those kids, the ones with well-heeled parents, owned horses that cost more than top-bred, professionally trained cutting and roping horses. The larger youth shows today awarded more than ribbons and trophies; some handed out fine silver-and-gold-inlaid belt buckles, and the big ones even presented winners with trophy saddles.

Buck concluded that being a youth's mount would be the best retirement career for Old Black. There was no question in his mind that once he got the hang of it, Old Black could stand up there with the top horses in *any* timed performance event where raw speed wasn't the primary denominator. And he'd be a natural for the other events, like reining, western pleasure, and western riding. The trick was going to be getting Old Black in the right hands.

He looked up his old friend George Bonner, who taught horsemanship in the 4-H Club program. When Buck explained his thoughts, Bonner said without a moment's hesitation, "Put that horse in the right kid's hands, Buck, and you couldn't give him a better future. Most of these kids take good care of their horses."

Bonner knew that Old Black competed in rodeos all year long, usually in team roping as well as calf roping. As a youth horse he would compete in hardly more than a dozen shows a year, and the pleasure riding he'd get would be no more than exercise. He would also be packing a lot less weight, with never a 250-pound calf or an 800-pound steer on the end of a rope.

"The kids think their shows are pretty demanding for a horse," Bonner said. "But believe me, youth shows are just off-season workouts compared to what Old Black is used to. What I don't understand is why you're parting with him, Buck."

Buck didn't want to discuss his physical problems with anyone. He most definitely did not want sympathy. But Old Black's future was more important to him than his own feelings, so he had prepared himself to explain his situation to George Bonner. This he did, and Bonner only nodded considerately. He promised to give it careful thought and call Buck the next day. When he did, he spoke of some current and former class members he thought might be prospects. He focused on a boy who had been attending his weekly classes for over a year.

"Jim Bradley—he must be around eleven. I doubt if he's ever missed a class," he said to Buck. "He knew little about horses when he came to us. He's eager to learn and studies everything he can get his hands on about horses. He's become a good little horseman with a nice feel for a horse's mouth—a light, sensitive hand. He's the only young rider I allow to ride Jupiter. The boy is very considerate of others and he calls his elders Mr. or Mrs. He's a joy to have in the class."

Bonner paused. "Not that calling people sir and ma'am is relevant to the subject, but it speaks of character, especially today. More on point, Buck, he's almost as good a judge of Quarter-Horse conformation as some doing the judging. I took my class on a field day to see the stallion class at Houston this year. Jim Bradley picked three of the horses that placed, out of maybe sixty head in the arena!"

He speculated that Jim Bradley was the ideal nominee for Old Black. "And Old Black's the ideal candidate for Jim Bradley!" Further, he recalled that the Bradley family owned a farm somewhere west of Houston, though he had no idea of whether they were planning to get the boy a horse. But he said he would see Jim and his father or mother in class this very week and bring the subject up with them.

He ended with some reservations. "Buck, those of us who work with these kids can teach them how to care for horses, we can create an environment in which they can discover the practical aspects of handling and training horses, and we can introduce them to competitive sportsmanship and discipline. But the kids who benefit the most learn the practical side of horsemanship from a wise old horse. The games become obvious to the smart horses— they learn the strategies on their own, if their riders don't interfere too much. But what do too many parents do? They go out and buy the child a flash horse that should be in the hands of a professional horseman. I am not too worried about that in Jim's case, however," he added with a negative shake of his head.

"But I do have one real concern, Buck. This boy has such a keen eye for horses, he might be put off by a horse of Old Black's age and, uh—" he groped for some nicety, but in vain, and so came right to the point. "I haven't seen Old Black in at least a couple of years, but I'm sure he couldn't have become any prettier. As I see him in my mind's eye, Buck, he would never have done well in the halter arena. But if Bradley's planning to get the boy a horse, and if that's not too strong an objection for Jim, he could be the perfect horse for the boy. I owe it to the Bradleys to drop by and look him over. Then I'll speak to them, and let's see what happens."

OLD BLACK SENSED THAT SOMETHING was definitely up. For the first time in ages Buck was in good spirits. He was even whistling a tune. The horse, alert now, stepped briskly aside as Buck opened the corral gate. Buck smiled and talked as he rubbed Old Black's face and scratched his chin. Leaving the gate open, he limped across the corral, still talking softly to the horse. He headed for the tack room with Old Black following closely and emerged with a red nylon halter. When he held it out, Old Black eagerly thrust his nose into it. Buck passed the headstall over his ears and buckled it on the indentation made by many bucklings.

Old Black knew where he was going and was anxious to get there. There was a time when Buck would have commanded him to walk obediently at his side, but lately he had come to allow harmless breaches of discipline. Buck released the short lead rope, allowing Old Black to break into a bucking gallop. Out of the corral he went, stopping as soon as he came to a place where the ground was covered with bunch grass.

Leaning against the corral fence, Buck watched as Old Black sank to his knees and rolled over on his back. His legs thrashed as he squirmed about, massaging and scrubbing his back against the coarse grass. He craned his neck to the ground and closed his eyes at the exquisite scouring feeling as he swung his head in large arcs across the bristly turf. He wriggled his body violently, rubbing himself first on one side, and then rolling over and vigorously scratching the other. Finally, he scampered noisily to his feet, and standing with his legs spread wide apart and his head held low, he shook himself long and mightily. Out of a great dust storm of his own creation he strode, and followed his master back into the corral.

Buck removed the halter and tossed it on a nail in the tack room. Then he began scratching the horse's neck, talking in apparent good spirits all the time. The horse placed his forehead hard on the cowboy's chest and began rubbing up and down. The misery of his existence only minutes before was completely forgotten.

Buck went into the tack room and emerged with a currycomb and brush. The horse stood still and erect as Buck worked away at his coat. The blissful feeling of the brush along his spine caused Old Black to extend his neck in a long arch with his head turned askew. Buck smiled and said, "That feels good, don't it, old boy?" He continued with a steady stream of cheerful, animated conversation as he worked, concluding the brushing with another half-dozen hard, slow, blissful brush strokes down the horse's spine, withers to tail. Finished, he jammed the brush and currycomb together and disappeared back into the tack room.

Old Black's amazement was intensified as Buck came out carrying the saddle blanket and bridle, a sight that tantalized him with a wave of lively anticipation. Buck flung the saddle blanket onto the top rail and approached him with the bridle in his hands.

"Surprised, ain't you, Black old boy?" he said, laughing, and talked to the horse as he worked. Old Black took the bit eagerly and when Buck reached up to fasten the throatlatch he lowered his head in a display of cooperation. Buck passed the reins over the horse's head and left them lying on his neck.

Buck went back into the tack room and reached for the heavy roping saddle that was resting on its rack. He drew a finger across the seat, making a track in the dust that had collected. He frowned, picked out a clean burlap bag and wiped away the dust, following that with a good brushing down with a soft horse brush. From a plastic-capped coffee can he removed a rag, damp with neatsfoot oil, and buffed the saddle to a high shine. Then he carried it to the rail where he deftly swung it up beside the blanket.

Standing back a way, he gave Old Black a good examination. The rare joy of having a bit in his mouth was a strong tonic to the horse; he stood bright-eyed, alert and full-chested; his feet were planted firmly under him. There was no trace of the miserable old animal that had stood on this ground less than an hour earlier. Here stood a champion.

"You're still a doggone good-looking horse to my mind, Old Black," Buck said with sincere conviction.

He stepped in front of the horse and took his big jaws between his hands, causing Old Black to snort with satisfaction. His eyes gazed lovingly into Buck's and his ears perked and twitched ever so slightly so as not to miss a sound from Buck's lips.

Buck reached for the horse's forelock and combed it with his fingers. Then he began rubbing and scratching Old Black's ears. The horse took a small step forward and lowered his head to make his ears more accessible.

"Ahh, that feels good, don't it Black?" Buck said.

Every feature of Buck Jones's face had been shaped by decades of carrying a pleasant expression. Even with his present desperate concerns, his expression gave no clue to the anguish he felt inside. But his eyes did, and the horse looked steadily into them.

Buck spoke to him softly. "This ain't at all what I had figured out for me and you, old pal. I have to tell you we've been dealt a bad hand—not to complain, mind you, since this is the first bad hand we ever got." The horse's tender, penetrating scrutiny drove the cowboy's eyes down. A wave of anguish, tangible bone-aching anguish, swept through Buck's being, and he felt a chill. He stopped talking for a moment and absently watched his booted foot crush dirt clods, his jaw muscles working the whole time.

He looked back into the horse's eyes and said, "But it's a real bad hand, Black. Dang it, what with all the purses we've won, we have a real good stake saved up. I was thinking of a place for us somewhere in the hill country, like Bandera. I always liked Bandera. A little spread on a nice cool creek. Plenty of shade, no bugs or mosquitos to pester you. I could keep a few momma cows, and take in some horses to train on the calves." He looked up at the horse and for an instant his eyes were brighter. "What's more, Bandera is not too far off the beaten path. Some of the boys could drop in on us and stay awhile now and then. But . . ."

His eyes narrowed and his expression hardened. Angrily, he bent down, picked up a clod of dirt and threw it at the fence, where it exploded in a black puff. His shoulders drooped and he shook his head wearily. "Nope. This ain't near what I had planned for us, Black."

The horse pressed his face lovingly into Buck's chest. Buck took the big head in both arms and hugged affectionately, but only a moment. Then he moved back a step and began rubbing and scratching the underside of Old Black's jaw. A passable example of the old Buck Jones smile brightened his expression.

His voice was now much milder. "We've squeezed the best there was out of our years together, old buddy, so we can't start whinin' now. You've sure held up your end of the deal all these years, partner, and by golly I promise that now I'll hold up mine. I'll miss you, that's for sure. But mainly I don't want to have to worry about how you're getting on. I have a plan for you, Black," he said, rapping his knuckles on the wood rail of the corral. "I got a plan, and if the Man upstairs will just allow us this one break, undeserving as we are—"

They both heard the tires crunching on the gravel driveway and turned to see a car come to a stop. Through the glare of the windshield Buck could make out the figures of a man and a boy inside.

"They're here, Black," he said.

"They're here, Black."

CHAPTER 3

The photograph of Buck Jones in the Houston rodeo program had prepared Matt Bradley to meet a lanky, broad-shouldered cowboy about six feet tall, stiff in manner and wearing a stern expression on his long, sharply chiseled face.

The man who now approached him had the same spare but strong build, but the stern expression must have been his working mask. The face Matt saw shone with friendliness, from his sweat-stained hatbrim to his chin. A huge, vee-shaped smile displayed both rows of teeth and drew his eyes into a merry squint. His jaw-line and even his ears were in harmony with the whole amiable countenance.

How that photograph could have captured any stuffiness in this man, Matt could not imagine.

Although he was limping and using a cane, he moved at a lively gait, his free arm pumping energetically. His face positively radiated an agreeable nature, an impression strongly reinforced by his body language. Buck thrust out a muscled, calloused hand.

"You must be Mr. Bradley. I'm Buck Jones and I'm mighty proud to meet you." He spoke in a strong voice that was warm and pleasant, and he had a way of tucking his chin to the side as a sort of visual exclamation point.

Matt Bradley's occupation was flying business jets, a profession that had exposed to him the inner workings of about every species of man mixed up in business or politics; they ranged all the way from solid gold to downright felonious. As the pilot and therefore a non-participant in the business dealings to which he was exposed, he was a mute observer, as unnoticed as a picture on the wall.

The unnoticed observer observed intently, discovering much to despise in an environment where men must be ready to protect themselves from each other at all times. He was often surprised by businessmen who, when away from home base, revealed deplorable character faults that they managed to keep hidden from their associates, friends, and families. Matt had evolved from a trusting soul into a man who rarely took anyone at face value.

In spite of his acquired defenses, he now had a strong intuition, a gut feeling, that he was meeting an outstanding individual, a man whose character was strong right down to the core. George Bonner's words came to mind: "I would take Buck Jones's word to the bank."

Matt liked the way he thrust himself toward you during a greeting. And his handshake was more than a hand*clasp*; his grip was not a contest of strength, but it was firm and steady and projected an uncommon warmth.

Matt said, "Good to meet you too, Buck. An honor, actually. And call me Matt. Meet my son, Jim." Buck had noticed the way the boy stood back a mite, politely waiting to be introduced by his father, all the while stealing anxious glances at the horse standing in the corral. Now he stepped forward eagerly, leading with his arm extended straight out. Buck took the small hand in his own.

Little Jim Bradley warmed Buck all over with a big happy smile that crinkled his eyes and showed a mouthful of teeth. Buck noted, too, that Jim's bright eyes were not staring at Buck's boots; they were not fixed on his belt buckle, nor were they searching the horizon beyond him. No, Jim's friendly eyes looked right into Buck's own. A good sign. So was the strong grip delivered by so small a hand. Buck reflected on Mr. Bonner's words of esteem for the boy. "Howdy, Jim," he said, tugging his hand gently all during the greeting. "I'm real pleased to meet you. Mr. Bonner paid you some fine compliments, and George Bonner is the tightest man with good words that I know."

"Hi, Mr. Jones," Jim said. He hesitated a heartbeat and continued in a small, clear voice, "Mr. Bonner told me and Dad some good things about you and Old Black, too." His tone and the inflection of the words hinted that he was sharing a small secret, but that doing so would not offend any parties to it. About eleven years old, Buck recalled George Bonner saying, but the overall impression projected a maturity beyond that age. After the formal introduction, Jim respectfully stepped back a couple of paces.

Out of the corner of an eye Buck watched as Jim's gaze settled firmly on Old Black. The boy fetched his red bandanna from a back pocket and at the same time swept his hat off with the other hand. Still looking at Old Black, he wiped his brow, then began wiping the sweat from his hatband. His dark brown hair was worn in a conventional haircut—or at least what was a conventional haircut once upon a time. It was the kind worn by his father, and the haircut that Buck had worn for at least the past forty years.

The more he saw of Jim Bradley the more he liked him, Buck decided, still watching as the boy placed his hat back on his head just right, in the casual motion of one who wears a hat often. It was a quality hat—Buck had noticed the Resistol label inside—not new, but well cared for. It fit, and he wore it well. Boot-cut Wrangler jeans that had a shade of the darkest, featureless blue washed out and a sharp crease ironed into them gave him a snappy look. He wore a plain, wide leather belt whose buckle, interestingly, was decorated with a mounted cowboy and a calf on the end of a rope. His trim frame was topped off with a striped two-tone blue western shirt, crisply starched and ironed. He was right at home in his cowboy boots too, which definitely had not been bought at a department store. What wear they showed was only the enhanced beauty of considerate use and they glistened from a fresh shine.

Since talking with George Bonner, Buck had been turning over in his mind all the scraps of information he possessed that could influence the "adoption" of Old Black by the Bradleys. The father must have a good notion of buying his boy a horse, Buck considered, or he would not be taking him out looking. Bonner was certain to have described Old Black fair and square, good and bad—probably describing the bad most diligently. So Old Black's faults could not be immediately disqualifying; Bradley would not have brought Jim to see the horse with any intention of disappointing him.

Going on first impressions, Buck theorized that Jim, rather than his father, would be the real decision-maker today. Buck's greatest concern was Old Black's age. Dad might worry that the horse could die while Jim was still young, breaking his little heart. But young people, Buck mused, lived in the here-and-now. What was here today would be here forever. Bonner said this kid was a fair hand with a horse. He had to have ridden some good ones and some not-so-good ones on his way to becoming that fair hand. It wasn't likely, though, that he had ever been astride a horse of Old

Black's capabilities, a horse that would show little Jim Bradley what it felt like to have a sure-enough can-do performer under him. And from what George Bonner had said about the boy, and from his own limited impression, Buck figured Jim Bradley would go for a horse with real performance ability over a flash horse, regardless of how skilled he was at picking pretty horses.

Jim rolled his eyes at his father in an inquiring manner.

Mr. Bradley nodded and said, "Buck, the night Jim and I went to the Houston rodeo you didn't have a go-around. When we discovered this week that we were going to meet you, we were sorry we didn't get to see you and Old Black in action. Jim brought along his program with the picture of you on Old Black in it. It would make both of us proud if you would autograph that picture for us."

Buck's modest agreement put Jim into action. He scurried away and came back with the program, open at the right page. Buck took the pen Matt offered and, careful to put Jim's name first, he wrote: "To Jim and Matt Bradley from your pals Buck Jones and Old Black."

Examining the inscription with conspicuous awe, Jim confided that Buck's autograph would prove to the guys at school that he had met the world calf-roping champion.

Buck chuckled and said, "Your friends must be easy to impress, Jim. Even so, we best go meet the champion." He took Jim gently by the shoulder and turned him to face Old Black, who was watching them intently from where he stood in the corral fifty paces away.

"There's the champ, Jim. But first I should explain something about championships. The record book says Buck Jones and Old Black hold the fastest time on record in the calf-roping event. But setting the world record time doesn't make a cowboy the champion. The cowboy who earns the most money in an event during the year is that year's champion. I've never won the calf-roping championship. Got fairly close a couple of times. Roy Cooper was one of the top guys to beat for the longest. Then when it looked like I might finally have a chance, Joe Beaver just set up shop in first place, then along comes Fred Whitfield like a house afire, Mike Johnson, Troy Pruitt . . . ." He shook his head and grinned. "Boy! Competition is tough in calf roping.

"I thought I should set your mind straight on the championship angle. But I ain't bashful about saying that I'm mighty proud to be holding the world-record time. Only one team can own it at a time, and somebody has to beat me and Old Black to get us out of the way. So far, nobody has.

"With Black it's different. They don't set championships for horses the way they do for the cowboys. So you can say Old Black *is* the world's champion calf-roping horse, because by golly he holds the record."

Buck made a face. "That calf in Butte—that's where we had our record run—he had me beat, truly beat. It was Old Black that pulled our fat out of the fire." He began walking toward the corral.

Jim looked up at Buck and asked excitedly, "What happened, Mr. Jones? What did Old Black do? Could you tell us the story?" He glanced at his father and was encouraged by his approving smile. His eyes eagerly returned to searching Buck's face.

"Oh, sure, Jim. Sure enough. I love to tell *that* story. It's almost like living it all over again." He stopped walking and stood facing Matt and Jim. "If it was only a regular run where everything went according to Hoyle, but was just blazing fast, there wouldn't be much to tell. But this wasn't going to be a regular run. Nope, a couple of disasters were lurking in the wings." His eyes fairly gleamed and they narrowed as he looked off in the distance, back to the scene in Butte.

He hitched up his jeans. "You know calf roping, right?" he asked, looking from one to the other. Although attending to both father and son, his focus was still tipped in Jim's favor.

"Okay. The run started out good. Old Black broke from the box so close on that calf's heels that I just *knew* we'd broke the barrier, but Old Black knew it had come clean even if I didn't. The calf was a flyer but he ran straight away, an easy target. I had a loop on him about two jumps out of the box. Old Black put a hard stop on him and when he hit the end of the rope he turned a complete backflip—landed flat on his side. I was afraid he had the wind knocked out of him. He was stretched out flat as a pancake, not moving a hair."

Buck held his arms out with his palms thrust toward the ground, his fingers extended wide. "Not moving so much as a hair. It looked bad, because you can't tie a calf without flanking him to the ground first. If he's down, you have to make him get up.

"No sooner had I worried about getting him up than he *got* up. He stood there a split second looking kinda cross-eyed. I'm only a couple of strides from him and I'm already congratulating myself for a fantastic run.

"But I'd started counting my chickens before they hatched, Jim, tempting fate, and *that* is bad business." With a strong, crooked finger he shot Jim right between the eyes. "Don't ever tempt fate by crowing, even to yourself, that you have something done up when there's still loose ends. Old Man Fate hears that stuff, and he just might decide to teach you a lesson."

He smacked himself gently in the chest with a fist. "Fate had heard me crowing! In a split second the calf is in a dead run toward me but off to my right. He's put too much slack rope between us for me to reel him in. I'm trying to cut him off, but he's angling away and it looks like he's going to be just out of reach.

"That thought was barely a flash in my mind when the rope twanged tight as a fiddle string and was sailing through my hand like it was on a Tulsa winch in high gear. It blistered my hand through my glove—that's how fast that rope was moving." As he spoke, Buck examined his right palm, stroking it with the fingers of his other hand.

"Then—" he paused and his head came up, the burned hand forgotten. As he looked upon Old Black, his grim expression relaxed into a smile. He took a deep breath and sighed. "Then, there's the calf right in my lap and, plop, down he goes. I tied him as quick as I ever made a tie and up went my hands. Considering all that had happened, I didn't have a real good feel for the time, but I thought it just might be the fastest run I'd ever made."

His exuberant expression suddenly darkened and he looked at Jim with an intense look. "I was worried about that tie, though. I knew I hadn't made a sure-enough good tie, but I wasn't about to spend an extra second on it. See, most any cowboy would gamble on getting a no-time for even a long shot at first place. The chance of a super-fantastic time was right there in my hands and I wasn't going to blow it on tying practice." He studied the ground, squinting at the memory. "Yeah, I was really worried about that tie!

"As I walked back to Old Black I was tempted hard to look back and see if the calf was trying to kick loose, but I didn't—you always want your compadres to think you don't have a worry in the world. The way Old Black was standing there leaning against the rope and glaring at the calf told me *he* was satisfied with the situation. I knew he would keep the calf's attention on that noose around his neck. Even so, I was all butterflies to take a look without seeming to. Black gave slack while I was climbing aboard. Still I didn't look up. As he walked along, I tried to look like all I was

28

interested in was getting the coils in my lariat just so, but I was peeping at that calf from under my hatbrim." He laughed and looked again at Old Black.

The action was a living picture in Jim's mind. He looked upon Old Black as Buck talked, marveling that such a horse was standing there before them.

Buck's face was glowing and Matt Bradley noticed that his eyes shone with genuine affection as he gazed at the horse. He wondered again about those "circumstances"—made more mystifying by George Bonner's failure to explain them—that made it necessary for Buck Jones to give up Old Black. "The tie held," Buck concluded with a sigh of relief, "and it was record time. World record time. Boy!"

He put a hand on Jim's back and nudged him in Old Black's direction. As they walked, he explained, "I didn't get to see Black's part in the show that day, since my back was to him and I wasn't exactly standing around being a spectator. It's a shame I had to miss the sight, but the boys described what he did. I can see him right now in my mind's eye. He saw that calf get up, and at the first inkling of slack Old Black took off backwards like a rocket."

When they arrived at the horse, Buck patted his neck and reached up and scratched an ear. He looked at Jim and said, "I'd give anything to have seen it, or better yet to have a film of Black taking that stitch right in the nick of time. They said he just shot back like thunder.

"It looked to them like he was going to run out of backup room, though, with all this taking place so close to the box. Well, Black might have been out of room, but he wasn't out of ideas. He stole the critical yard that I needed with a quarter spin at the end of his run that put the calf right in my hands. That kind of maneuver is hard for any horse to do wearing a neckrope—a neckrope is required by the rulebook. Yep, I'd give anything to have seen it." He shrugged and made a gesture of resignation. "They say you can't be in the play and see it too."

Buck picked up the reins from Old Black's neck and brought them over his head. "Old Black was a champion before that day in Butte, though, Jim. It takes a champion to get off the floor and win by a knockout. That's why I have to say Old Black is the true owner of the calf-roping record. Not Buck Jones by a long rope." There was no mistaking that he meant what he said.

He led Old Black out of the corral onto the grass with Jim following. He released the snaphook that held one end of the rein to the bit, so that the full length of the rein could be used. Then he extended his rein hand and made a clucking sound, sending the horse walking briskly in a circle around him. "Whoa," he said when Old Black's left side, his "near" side, was directly in front of Jim. He jiggled the reins and the horse collected himself at attention.

Jim took his time with the overall inspection. Buck watched as the boy's practiced eye went over every inch of the horse from nose to tail. Then he stepped up, grasped the left foreleg near the shoulder between both hands, and brought them down slowly, feeling muscle, bone, tendons, the knee and its knot, and continuing down the lower leg to the ankle, then the pastern and foot.

He pushed against Old Black, just above his leg. When he felt the horse shift his weight to his right leg, Jim patted the back of the left knee and the horse promptly raised his foot for inspection. Jim held the foot up with his left hand while the other fished in his shirt pocket and came out with small red hoof pick. He deftly inserted its flat blade under the compacted soil and in one brisk motion the hoof came clean of a large pad of dirt.

Buck's eyebrows went up and he pursed his lips in surprise at the thoroughness of the examination. Nodding his approval, he said to himself, "This little tyke knows what he's doing. I'd hate to be the guy trying to slip a ringer over on him." He approved, too, of the way Jim gently placed the foot back on the ground, rather than just dropping it, the way some people did after examining a foot.

After inspecting the near hind leg, Jim moved to the horse's rear, reaching out and picking up Old Black's tail as he went. He walked without looking back until the hand holding the tail felt the end of its travel and he turned around. Holding Old Black's tail up and off to each side as his inspection proceeded, he gave the horse a long and meticulous examination from behind.

When he was finished, he dropped the tail and moved back to Old Black's side, nodding to Buck on the way. Buck bobbed his head in acknowledgement. He placed the rein in his left hand and put the horse in a walk in the opposite direction, stopping him with his right side in front of Jim. Now Jim examined Old Black's off side as methodically and as thoroughly as he had the other. Finished, he stepped in front of the horse and stood with his arms crossed in a studious stance. He inspected first Old Black's head, spending some time looking at his ears, eyes, jaws, nostrils, and mouth. He took a step back and scrutinized the horse's chest, legs, and the set of his feet. Finally, stooping slightly, he took a step to his right for a new look, then moved a little to the left and looked briefly from that viewpoint.

EMOTIONAL PREJUDICES CAN INTRODUCE complex and delicate biases in one's perception of "beauty." They can be conspicuous, obscure, or even subconscious influences, and the extent to which they can tamper with one's ability to see a subject objectively can be remarkable. An example is the wife who adores her husband and remarks on his good looks and quick wit, although he may be seen by others as decidedly homely and dull.

Matt Bradley, standing well behind his son, saw in Old Black a reasonably typical example of the Quarter Horse breed, a tough and astute old campaigner, well-behaved and obedient. There was no doubt that he was capable. Matt liked the intelligent glimmer in the horse's eye, his way of holding his head thrust proudly forward. He showed an outstanding shoulder, chest, and forelegs, Matt thought.

And George Bonner was right, he decided. His neck is too cresty for a gelding. A smaller head would definitely improve his appearance, and with any more arch to his face he could be said to have a Roman nose. The standards of today called for a longer hip, and Matt thought he would prefer straighter hind legs instead of Old Black's tendency to stand with his hind legs almost camped under. Finally, there was no question that his feet were too big for appearances' sake, even if that was not a physical defect.

He thought of Mr. Bonner's diplomatic way of putting it: "He won't halter, Jim." And that brought to mind an old saying about a horse so homely that it couldn't win ninth place in a nine-horse class.

At that very moment Buck was stealing a look at Matt, hoping to get some bearing on his appraisal of the horse. His spirits were brought low by what he presumed to be a look of disapproval.

Matt discarded the thought of the unlucky horse in the leg-endary nine-horse class and his full attention returned to Old Black, standing so majestically before him. His silent descent into dark humor in the presence of this horse caused him to scowl in private admonishment of himself. Buck glimpsed that expression, too, and his anxiety deepened.

Matt strolled around casually until he was behind Buck. From this position he could watch Jim in action. Jim stood with his thumbs hooked in the waistband of his jeans, oblivious to everything but the horse. He's a good judge of horses, Matt thought. And even though Old Black was not a halter prospect, he was in a class far above the fabled ninth horse. He was not one bit ugly; he simply was not a real good looker. It is said that beauty is as beauty does, and clearly Old Black had *done* beautifully during his entire lifetime. How many halter champions could say as much? Matt began looking at the whole horse rather than picking out individual and unimportant defects in appearance. He liked what he saw: a horse that anybody who knew horses would be proud to be astride.

JIM BRADLEY BEHELD A DIFFERENT HORSE from the one seen by his father. He saw a horse standing squarely and presenting a fine overall profile, one that stood easily yet prepared and confident with a downright defiant thrust of head. A decent-looking head it was, too, with his short ears perked directly forward, his eyes daring as they looked straight ahead. Jim saw a mouth clamped firmly shut, resolute.

Sound feet supported short, well-sprung pasterns. He saw straight forelegs with fine flat bone and strong square knees. Powerful forearms flowed smoothly into Old Black's massive chest.

Jim very much liked the way the horse's forelegs were spaced well apart and tied into his chest with a deep inverted "vee" of muscling.

His long, sloping shoulder and good bone arrangement would allow a smooth, easy trot and lope. And he has good withers that keep the saddle positioned, else he sure couldn't be a roping horse, Jim said to himself.

The hip Jim observed was perfect, even if it was not as long as judges like today. A modern long-hipped Quarter Horse might be faster on the racetrack, but would not be as capable at maneuvers like spins and reverses, actions that demanded the horse to exert enormous power while balanced on his hind quarters.

Jim applauded Old Black's tendency to keep his hind legs under himself. He saw the stance as one that prepared him for action from a standstill, far removed from the defect called "camped under." The posture was definitely an asset in a performance horse, causing Jim to reflect on Mr. Jones's description of how Old Black did a quarter spin with a calf on the end of a rope.

He approved of the horse's broad, well-muscled hind quarters, more typical of the Quarter Horse of old. His feet were, well, *big*, especially by current conformation standards that call for a foot that is downright dainty. How, he had wondered more than once, could the size of a horse's foot, without its being deformed, become a legitimate standard of conformation?

With show judges today wanting to see a gelding's neck as feminine as a mare's, this horse's neck *was* on the cresty side for a gelding. But what was wrong with a male horse looking masculine? He did have a nice, clean throatlatch. As for the knot on his knee and some other scars, Jim noticed that none were recent and all were completely healed. The scars from those old injuries would not even be a factor in the halter arena, he recalled from the official AQHA rulebook. Nevertheless, now that he had seen the horse, he was in complete agreement with Mr. Bonner: Old Black won't halter. But that was of no concern to Jim, because he had no intention of standing Old Black in a show ring—he wanted a *performance* horse.

Though halter classes were judged strictly on judges' opinions of appearances, certain performance classes were run against a clock that measured time in hundredths of a second. Difficult feats over complex courses had to be performed as fast as possible, where prettiness and prissiness were of no consideration whatever. If the ugliest horse ridden by the shabbiest rider turned in the fastest time, they were the winners and that was that.

Jim also liked the broad nostrils that would give Old Black lots of breathing air when he needed it. The big jaws gave his head a powerful appearance, and when he gazed into the horse's eyes— widely-spaced, dark yet luminous deep down, intelligent, *mysterious* eyes—Jim felt shivery. There was a magnetism in them. Before he knew it he was taking a step forward, and he saw in each of those big eyes a perfect miniature image of himself, as if he were seeing himself through them.

He stepped closer, raised his hand slowly and began to scratch under the horse's jaw. Old Black's gaze softened as the boy's fingers continued their gentle rubbing. Jim's strokes became slower and longer, from the horse's throat to his chin. Old Black half closed his eyes and gently buried his muzzle in Jim's chest. In that moment a bond was forged between a little boy and a big Quarter Horse that would never be broken.

Now Jim could see himself on Old Black, bent low in the saddle, tearing up the flag races, keyhole races, pole bending, barrel races, stake races . . . . He could feel the envious eyes staring upon them in the western riding and reining classes. His vision shifted to obscure adventures down along Hickory Creek. He saw phantom cattle thieves and outlaws in full retreat with himself and Old Black streaking hot on their trail.

CHAPTER 4

"If it's all the same to you, Jim," Mr. Jones said, rousing him from his dreamy adventures, "I'll show you his way of going from the saddle." He led the horse to the corral rail where the saddle and blanket rested. After a few deft movements Old Black was saddled and Buck was mounted. He rode up to Jim and stood the horse still for a few seconds, then turned him directly away and walked about twenty yards.

Then, without a pause, cued only with the slightest movement of Buck's upper body, Old Black executed the smoothest rollback Jim had ever witnessed. The maneuver was performed with nonchalant grace, in perfect time with the cadence of his walk. Hind feet moved rhythmically, precisely, like a soldier doing an about-face. So delicate was his balance that his forefeet floated scarcely off the ground until he stepped out in the opposite direction.

Mr. Jones stopped the horse facing Jim and stood him there no longer than it took him to raise a hand to his hat. Then, from a standstill, he did a rollback with the timing accelerated just enough that the horse stepped out of it swinging away in a trot. Next, Buck displayed Old Black's easy, rocking-chair lope. The rollback in the lope was more of a slow spin with a hint of a leap coming out of it, but it retained every element of its precision at the walk and trot. Buck stopped Old Black directly in front of Jim and dismounted.

He laid a hand on Jim's shoulder, gazed at him with a sincere look and said, "Jim, I've never seen a more professional examination of a horse. I couldn't have done near as good."

Jim grinned self-consciously.

Matt Bradley had seen him inspect a hundred horses and he knew how good he was at it. But it was Old Black's performance that had impressed Matt. His movements approached dressage. Old Black had revealed a rare *handsomeness,* a mature elegance. He thought of the former Houston Oiler quarterback George Blanda, who'd played with distinction for the Oakland Raiders well into his forties. He was then the oldest active player in pro football and a splendid example of mature elegance. Heavyweight boxing champion George Foreman came to Matt's mind and lingered there—a superb, *elegant* old champion. Some athletes do not so readily give in to age, and Old Black is one of them, Matt concluded.

"He's all yours, Jim. Take him for a test drive," Buck said. He stood out of Jim's way, holding the near stirrup for him. Jim moved briskly to the horse's side. As he grasped the stirrup leather and strained to reach the big stirrup, Buck's hand deftly took the little booted foot and guided it home. His hand then went to Jim's seat and boosted him up. Jim grasped the horn and swung easily into the big roping saddle. The saddle seat shone like a mirror, he noticed as he swung into it.

Jim looked around. Suddenly, the countryside was visible for a great distance. All morning the boy had been looking up, way up, at tall men, at a tall horse. Now some instinct from the legions of horsemen over the centuries seemed to invade him as he sat with pride on Old Black, looking down on his father and Buck Jones.

Buck began taking up the stirrups. After making the adjustment, he instructed, "Put your weight in the stirrups and stand up, Jim." Jim extended his toes, grasped the saddle horn, and stood as tall as he could. Buck shoved his hand between Jim's seat and the saddle. "Stirrups are still a shade long, but that's all the take-up there is," he said. "You'll just have to grow an inch, old pal."

He moved a step back and instructed, "He has a good, soft mouth, Jim. Ride him with a slack rein. All Black needs is a notion, an idea of what you want him to do. You could ride him without a bit in his mouth, just using leg signals and weight changes."

Buck held imaginary bridle reins in his left hand, his fist about a foot from his chest. "Lift the reins an inch," he said, demonstrating. "That untracks him, tells him to wake up because you're about to ask him to go to work." Jim raised the reins and Old Black collected himself, lifting each foot and placing it down just so. His head came up and his nose extended. His ears became busy. Jim's rein hand moved forward with the horse's head extension.

"Good," Buck said, nodding his approval. "I see *you* have a feel for the bit, Jim. Now he's untracked and ready for action."

Jim did have a feel for the bit. For those who did not have their own horse, there were horses to ride on special 4-H days, good soft-mouthed horses. Jim never missed a chance to ride, and he welcomed criticism. For his age and amount of experience, he was a fair hand with a horse. Try as he might to hold it back, Buck's compliment brought a big smile to his face. Buck instructed him to apply some pressure with his left leg. "And put a bit more weight in the right stirrup."

He did as instructed and Old Black moved briskly to the right, stopping when Jim released the pressure. An unabashed smile spread across his face.

"That'll come in handy when you want to close a gate. Now we're going to back up," said Buck. "When I tell you to, lean back slightly with your rein hand steady. Your body movement will send a signal to the bit. Then squeeze your legs. So you just lean back and grip. To stop him, relax your legs and lean forward a bit. Go."

Old Black marched backward briskly on Jim's command until stopped with a shift of his weight. This time there was no hiding the smile that broke out from ear to ear on Jim's face. "Boy, Mr. Jones, he can really scoot backwards!"

"Old Black can *run* backwards. That's what got us the record at Butte. Now let's go forward. I don't imagine that this is necessary because I can see already . . . When I say 'go,' lean forward the least amount and extend your rein hand a bit. You don't have to say anything to get him to move out. When you want him to stop, just lean back enough for him to feel it, or say 'Whoa.' Go."

The horse stepped right out at the signal. In a few yards Jim leaned back ever so slightly and Old Black stopped.

"Fine, fine, Jim. Old Black understands your kind of language. Why don't you and him just spend some time getting acquainted. You can ride him anywhere on the place. You don't need me and your dad standing around making you nervous." He turned to Matt, "Coffee, Matt?" Matt nodded and followed him into the house.

THEIR CONVERSATION HAD BEEN NO MORE than small talk by the time Buck got up to top off their cups. Matt was looking out the window, leaning one way and then the other to keep sight of the horse and rider outside. Buck wondered about the direction of Matt Bradley's thinking on the subject of this horse for his boy. He was still worrying about Matt's expressions as he'd watched Jim examine Old Black.

Maybe Bonner was wrong in believing that Bradley wasn't like the "too many" parents who went for flashy horses, letting ability and sense take a back seat. He felt good about the boy's feelings, though—Jim liked what he saw, and he'd get off of Old Black with his first good impression magnified beyond the point of no return. But how much did the father figure into the selection? Would he go so far as to cast a veto? At this stage, even a decision to *delay* making a decision would be disastrous.

The pure fact was that this man and boy represented the highest form of deliverance for Old Black—higher than Buck had ever dared to hope. They were the answer to his prayers. Buck was tormented to his soul by the grim realization that nowhere on the horizon was there another prospect of a decent home for the horse. This coming Sunday evening, Buck had promised his doctor, he would walk into that hospital. Today, he would gladly give Old Black to the Bradleys. But he knew if they didn't decide to *buy* the horse, they wouldn't take on a gift horse. On one hand, Buck saw a paradise for Old Black; on the other was Death Valley. The conflicting prospects were pure torture for him.

Asking direct questions—like "Well, how do you like Old Black, Matt?"—would be too forward, he decided. It might even cause him to begin expressing his objections, which were not as threatening as long as they remained in the thought stage. As for clever prying, Buck's mind did not work that way.

After sinking heavily into his chair, Buck thought he read approval in the father's eyes as he watched the scene outside the window. His dread eased a bit. And he asked himself why, if Matt Bradley disliked Old Black's appearance as much as he had indicated earlier, was he allowing Jim this lengthy performance evaluation? To relieve his mental anguish, he asked a lame question about the Bradley ranch.

He had chosen the right avenue of conversation. Matt Bradley loved their farm and liked to talk about it. "It's not far from Brentwood. Not a big place, only a hundred and twenty acres, but it's the biggest hundred and twenty acres you ever saw." He grinned at the boastfulness of the statement, pushed his chair back and threw one leg over the other in a relaxed, open way. "At least it seems so to us," he said. "It's called the old Rosenbaum place because that's who settled there over a century ago. It's been in the family ever since, until we bought it. We spend almost every weekend there. Well, Jim and his mother do; sometimes I'm flying. Our only close neighbor is a wonderful old black couple who've lived their whole lives within a few miles of the place. Jim just worships them—all of us do, for that matter. Oscar supervises our two hands—and fine hands *they* are, too."

Matt described a large expanse of the best bottomland pasture in Winchester County that spread out at the foot of a high hill. Patches of trees and larger areas of dense, old-growth woods broke up the place, so it looked a lot bigger and provided the livestock with plenty of shade. Stretches of cedar trees and yaupon bushes formed good windbreaks against the north winds in the winter. On top of a high hill near the west property line, a rambling old farmhouse, flanked by a big barn, looked out over the surrounding countryside. They had about seventy momma cows on the place.

The most extraordinary feature on the ranch, Matt explained, was a creek that meandered just inside the north property line. Cold spring water flowed between deep, craggy white limestone banks along this stretch of Hickory Creek, a narrow rushing torrent here, a broad course there. Beneath the darkest waters were pools cut deep into the creekbed. Both banks of the creek were forested with huge trees—pecan, oak, ash, walnut, hickory, sycamore, cottonwood. Delicate ferns and white-flowering dogwood trees grew along the limestone banks.

"A few centuries back the water flow must have discovered a fissure in a limestone arch that formed a low dam across the creek," Matt explained. "The water patiently worked away at that fissure until it carved the opening that's there today. It made a natural bridge, with the water tumbling through the hole below it." He grinned. "I guess if the Colorado River could cut a mile-deep Grand Canyon through Arizona, Hickory Creek could cut a hole the size of a barrel through a ten-foot-wide slab of limestone."

Interest was clear on Buck's face. "Sounds like you had a streak of luck, finding that place and having the sense to buy it."

"Luck was on our side all the way. We bought it at the bottom of country land prices about six years ago. It was so run down and overgrown with weeds nobody would look at it, so we got it cheap, way under what it was really worth even then. It didn't seem so cheap to me, though," he laughed. "In fact, the thought of going into such debt almost made me back out. It scares me now to think that I almost passed on it. The man I fly for sort of pushed me over the brink. He said if I was stupid enough to pass that place up, he might have to start looking for a pilot with some sense. He was responsible for me making up my mind.

"It needed a world of work, and we've put a world of work into it. At the time we bought it, though, we didn't know that we had so much to work with."

Matt focused again on the scene beyond the window. Speaking haltingly, consumed with pride, he said, "You ought to see that kid work. Ten years old now, and he'll work right alongside of me from daylight to dark. He was only four when we bought the place, and he worked like a little man all day long. Not only does he never complain, but he's as eager to go at the end of a hard day as he was in the morning. Those poor little fingers took many a lick from a hammer when he was learning to drive staples and nails. He'd yelp, yank off his glove and stick his smashed finger in his mouth, but a big smile would erupt when it came out. He wanted me to know he could take it. He had several blue fingernails on his left hand for I don't know how long. What a little worker—loves to see things accomplished and to know he played a part in them."

Buck's head bobbed up and down, expressing his understanding. It was easy to see where Jim got the strength to deliver the handshake he did. A hammer that was comfortable in a man's hand is a clumsy maul in a small hand like Jim's. Little hands get strong quick when they're wielding hammers and doing other farm work. "By the time Jim shook my hand, Matt, I knew that you have a good 'un. It just oozes out of every pore in his little body. Ten, huh? I'd guessed eleven, or even twelve. I'd bet my bottom dollar he does real good in school, too, don't he?"

"Yeah, he does. And his teachers love him. He wants to do everything right, and when he doesn't, when he makes some little mistake, it really bothers him." Matt decided not to bend Buck's ear with the example that came to mind. It was a project in second grade that had earned Jim a C, which was as bad to him as a stern reprimand.

The assignment was to make a little four-page booklet on a famous person—Jim had chosen an artist. He had made a cover by folding a sheet of rose-colored construction paper in half and bound the folded page inside the cover with a pink ribbon tied in a bow. On the cover was a picture of the subject of his project, a noted painter of western art. He carefully printed the words on the cover, painstakingly wrote in cursive an introductory narrative that began on the first page and concluded on the third. On the second page he had pasted a picture of a painting by the artist with the title and a description carefully printed below it. The last page was to be left blank.

He was as proud of that booklet as he could be, but the C it received, instead of the A he'd been sure of, was a crushing disappointment. The teacher had not explained the deficiency in his work. It was noticed by his mother when she found him that evening, sitting at his desk with the booklet open before him, searching in vain for its flaw. She sensed his depression and asked him what was wrong. He responded by closing the booklet so she could see the cover, with the big, bold C written in yellow crayon.

His face was red when he looked up, his eyes asking "Why?" Right away she saw the error. The opening sentence said, "Texas artist Joe Rader Roberts is one of America's great temporary western painters. . . ." Norma laughed heartily. "*Con*temporary," she said. "Oh, Jim, this is just precious. Don't feel bad, Darling," she said, mussing his hair playfully. "Anyone could have made that mistake. But I'm surprised Mrs. Mitchell—" Mrs. Mitchell was sick that day, he said; they had a substitute teacher.

He got his A in art that year. Mrs. Mitchell had later taken him aside privately and shared a good laugh with him over the mistake. She let his mother have the original, but she wanted a copy of the booklet. Jim never forgot the difference between "contemporary" and "temporary." Mrs. Mitchell had laughed when she said, "Artists are terrified of becoming temporary."

Jim had ridden up and was just outside the window. He waved and trotted away. Buck noticed that Matt's eyes were a little misty when he said, "Buck, can you imagine a ten-year-old kid who never once in his whole life really deserved a serious rebuke? That's him."

Buck glanced at Matt and saw an expression that was dead serious. He said, "No, I didn't know any such kid ever lived. He had to steal a watermelon or get into somebody's orange grove, throw a rock through a window—he had to get into *some* mischief in his life. Chop down a cherry tree, like George Washington?" He laughed softly. "Didn't he do any of those things?"

Matt only shook his head and was thoughtful for some time. Buck did not seem to have anything to say, so Matt went back to talking about the farm.

"The strangest thing, Buck, was that nobody seemed to see

anything special about that stretch of creek. It is positively *spectacular!* The day we first went to look at the place, we couldn't stop talking about that creek. It was dark and quiet and peaceful in the forest, and so cool. Jim saw his first deer that day, a doe that bounded away without a sound. The real estate agent apparently didn't know anything about the property, just sat down on a rock when we decided to take a look in the woods.

"It was a year before we discovered the unique, priceless nature of *our* stretch of Hickory Creek. Jim and I were exploring upstream and discovered the springs that feed it. Beyond them is a dry creekbed—at least until we get a heavy rain, then it's a roaring river—parched dry, with only weeds and willows growing on the banks. We scouted it out downstream, and a quarter mile below us the water dives back under the ground; below that place the creek is dry again." He shook his head again.

The sober expression of his wonder faded and his face became merry. "It was our good luck that the place was in such awful shape that other city slickers wouldn't even look at it. There were weeds in the bottom ten feet tall. They had stalks like small trees, but they were weeds—you couldn't see a fence on the place for the weeds. And when you did find one, it was falling down."

As he had so many times before, Matt thought over the circumstances that put the old Rosenbaum place on the market—at just the right time. He glanced at Buck and resumed watching Jim through the window. "The last owner died on the place," he said. "He was very old, a descendent of the first settlers from Germany. He just lived in the house there on Social Security. Didn't have an animal on the place, so it was completely neglected for at least a dozen years. The property was put up for sale by his heirs, relatives who probably had never seen the place. But you would think the agent—" He left the subject up in the air and became pensive, quiet.

Buck had been observing Matt throughout his account; his expression of interest had become meditative. Speaking with a note of reverence in his voice, he asked, "Matt, did you ever consider maybe it was meant to be? Have you ever thought that the Man upstairs might have arranged that special place for the Bradleys? You came so close to *not* buying the property, but something provoked your boss into jabbing a spur in your flank to get you to move. And who made the place so gosh-awful looking nobody else would go far enough into it to find that creek? How come the agent didn't advertise that feature? He probably didn't know about it. And on top of that, the place was a steal. Go back over every detail in your mind and you'll probably find too many chips had to fall in place for it to be a coincidence that you came to buy it. The first chip was that it was for sale. The second was that you had to find that out. Then you go from there. How did you learn it was for sale? Had you been looking for a place?"

"Funny you'd bring those things up, Buck. I've never spoken to anybody but my wife about them, but yes, I sure have thought about the whole series of events. Starting with the springs breaking out eons ago, the Rosenbaums buying the strip on the other side of the creek maybe fifty years ago, which gave us both sides—all the things you mentioned. I shiver when I think of how close we came to deciding we couldn't afford the place.

"And no, we weren't even looking for a farm. My boss has a big ranch, and I guess he feels like everybody should have a place in the country. His ranch foreman heard that the old Rosenbaum place was for sale, and told him about it, said it was way underpriced for a quick sale. He told me to go see it and I did, thinking *he* was considering it as an investment. I came back raving about the creek, the woods, the bottomland and everything else and he said, 'Then, dammit, *buy* it!' It's the only place we ever looked at. Yeah, I do think about all the coincidences that put us on to that spectacular property."

Buck was considering another strange turn of fate in the phenomenon of the Bradley Ranch: that Old Black figured into the design. He spurred Matt on to describe other features of the place he wanted Old Black to be calling home. "That bottomland must be some fine pasture, huh?"

"I don't guess there *is* any better soil for pasture, Buck. The grass down there is Bermuda, kept well fertilized. In the winter I usually plant peas or vetch for grazing. One small field that borders the creek gets flooded every few years, so it's not fenced in. It produces several hundred bales of clover hay every spring and Johnson grass hay all summer. There's a grove of great big pecan trees way down in the bottom pasture—*big* trees, almost a hundred feet tall. We get sacks and sacks of pecans off them in a good year."

Buck was not considering the pecans produced. His thoughts were on the deep, cool shade Old Black would find under those pecan trees on a hot summer day, of the abundance of lush pasture grasses and cold, sweet spring water. There would be clover hay in the winter to go with the peavines, the vetch. Then he thought of raw winter nights with freezing rain, cutting winds, and took comfort in the barn Matt had mentioned. Old-time barns where hay was stored were the snuggest places you could hole up in on a cold winter day.

Buck smiled inwardly and melted back into his chair. Another genuine plus in Old Black's favor surfaced in his mind: Bradley's barbed-wire fences and their hazard to horses—the reason why so many horse farms had expensive rail fences. "There's got to be a lot of bob-wire fences on a place like you're telling me about. And you're lucky, because Old Black knows all about bob wire.

"Once we holed up for a few days at a buddy's place in Dripping Springs. One morning I called to Black down in the pasture and he didn't come. I could see him down in the bottom by the fence, just standing there. 'Why don't he come?' I'm asking myself. Then I got in the pickup and drove down to where he was standing. The fence was old and fairly run down, and he had a leg caught up in it. Most horses would have panicked, maybe cut their leg to pieces. But Old Black just stood there patiently waiting for me to come get him loose."

Buck returned to his imaginings. Cows! Old Black was right at home with cows; a horse needs company. He could see Old Black on top of the hill, his head high and his mane and tail blowing in the wind, surveying his domain and the surrounding countryside.

Old Black was going to live at the Bradley's little piece of heaven on earth, Buck Jones concluded with finality. For Old Black's sake, he was not going to let this chance get away. But he had to handle the matter carefully. If pressed, Matt Bradley might back off. He drew his bandanna from a back pocket and wiped the sweat from his forehead. Then he wiped away at his hatband as he worried over how he was going to close this deal. Buck Jones was the farthest thing in the world from a salesman, and so he descended into dark, solemn deliberation.

CHAPTER 5

Matt Bradley was having some serious thoughts of his own. He had seen the magnetic attraction between Jim and Old Black before Jim ever got on the horse. Jim was hooked, that much was for sure. Matt asked, "Buck, how long would you give a horse of Old Black's age and condition to live—if he wasn't pushed too hard?"

Buck looked studious. "I'd like to be able to throw out a magic number, but there isn't one. I've known of a lot of horses that were still in good shape at twenty-five and more. The top calf roper in Amarillo last year was riding a twenty-seven-year-old. Doc Reynolds's daughter has one barrel-racing horse that's twenty-two and another twenty-six." He grinned wryly, then said, "The horse Stonewall Jackson was riding when he got shot at Chancellorsville lived to be thirty-six, but I guess that's pushing it about to the limit. Old Black's a young eighteen, and with no more to do than pack Jim around in those games, my guess is that he has, oh, eight, ten spry years ahead, at least. But I'd hate to be held to anything. They were talking up at M.D. Anderson about a doctor that was famous for his books on how to live to a ripe old age. Sold millions of those books, then keeled over dead at forty. You just never know when the candle is gonna burn out."

Matt's attention intensified and he looked at Buck for a long moment. M.D. Anderson: the world-famous cancer hospital. He wondered what Buck Jones would be doing listening to gossip at M.D. Anderson. He thought about Buck's limp; he recalled seeing a wince or two, just the barest display of pain as Buck moved about. Then there was George Bonner's reference to "circumstances," which he'd left dangling in the air. Matt believed he might be onto the mystery of why Buck Jones was selling his horse. A sorrowful ache swept over him like a wave.

Both men became absorbed in their own thoughts and a silence came over the room. Buck played with a salt shaker, pressing a line of circles in the red and white checked oilcloth. He set the salt shaker down firmly and looked up at Matt.

"I wish my first horse had been one like Old Black. Don't I ever! Instead, I got a little paint pony that everybody thought was so pretty. He had two gaits, a lazy walk and a dead run. No mouth at all." He laughed heartily. "I learned one thing from him, though—how to stay on a runaway horse bareback! I traded a calf I'd raised for Chico—that was his name—when I was eight. I had him for five years, and just having him set me back a mile in horsemanship. You know how it is, you like what you have, and as dumb as Chico was I thought he was smart because I didn't know any better. He got out of the pasture one day and got killed by a truck. I cried my heart out.

"But today, my only memory of Chico is how sorry he really was. If my first horse had been one like Old Black, I would have been a dynamite horseman by the time I was as old as Jim is." He swallowed. "And after having a horse like Black, nothing but a top-notch horse could ever get my eye again." Buck was comfortable, now, talking to Matt Bradley, and Matt was listening with keen interest. Buck went on:

"I read Willie Shoemaker's book about his life as a jockey. What he said about *class* horses has stayed in my mind. I don't know it by heart, but Shoemaker said he couldn't explain in so many words the difference between a dang good racehorse and a *class* racehorse, but he said you know for sure what a class horse is when you get on one. And you don't want to ride anything but class horses ever again."

Buck screwed up his face in an intense expression. "Maybe a million people read those words, but only the very few that had ever been on a class horse could truly understand what he was saying. Black's a class horse. If I was still roping and lost him, I believe the idea of having to find another horse—well, it would just do me in."

He had been concentrating on the salt shaker as he spoke. Now he looked at Matt, squinting his eyes in a way that expressed how desperately he wanted to be understood. "Matt, I ain't all that fantastic a roper—ain't even in the same league with guys like Roy Cooper, Dee Pickett, Troy Pruitt, Fred Whitfield, Joe Beaver—I could keep right on naming better all-around calf ropers than me. I can throw a good loop, accurate and fast. But when it comes to the whole piece of work, Old Black plays a bigger part in it than I do. The starring role, you might say. When Black was a tyke he just naturally took to roping. I didn't have to train him, he just picked it right up.

"It was the same way with team roping. After the barest introduction, he says, 'Okay, boss, I know what you're up to. Let me show you what I can do.' He can head and he can heel, but he likes heading better. And he's quick and strong, so we head. Yep," he said with a bob of his head and a note of finality, "when it comes to the whole piece of work, Old Black plays the biggest part. I doubt if I could ever find another roping horse that could take me to the pay window often enough to justify me being on the circuit."

Matt suddenly realized that he had been a spectator at no telling how many rodeos, but knew nothing of the sport as a profession. "Do you like the rodeo life, Buck?" he asked. "Can a cowboy make a decent living at it?"

Buck said, simply, "Yeah . . . yeah." Matt watched him for a long time. He began to think that was it, the sum of Buck's answer. But Buck was turning the question over in his mind. Finally, he said, "Yeah, I like it and it's a good living. It's like I never had to have a job. Rodeoing is the best thing that could have happened to me for a career, and it's all I've ever done since I was eighteen. I've never had a boss or anybody else to find fault, to have to please. And not once has Old Black given me any back talk."

Matt chuckled before he realized Buck was serious.

Buck squinted significantly at Matt out of the corner of an eye. "Some horses can be crabby, some just have off days. I've seen guys get plumb irate at their horse for doing something stupid. Now and then you'll see a real knock-down, drag-out fight between a cowboy and his horse. But never once has there been any sass or the *least* amount of holding back by Old Black." He squinted his eyes thoughtfully. "And you know, I never thought of it quite that way before telling it out loud to you just now."

Buck began shaking a finger and nodding his head as if he had made a big discovery. "Funny, when you were describing Jim I must have thought you were making some allowances for him being a kid, that he must have strayed over the line now and then, and you didn't see those forays as out of line because boys can be boys. I guess what led me to hear one thing while you were saying another was that *I* was a good kid, but still did some things I shouldn't have. I got some harsh words and more—but not as much as I deserved if everything had been found out!" He laughed until his eyes were slits as the undiscovered misdemeanors paraded through his mind.

"Now, though, when I consider that Old Black hasn't done one thing, ever, that deserved a harsh word—and that's as rare in horses as it is in boys—now I'm beginning to understand your description of Jim. I'm more *able* to see it now, like I was able to understand what Shoemaker was saying while I'm dead sure a lot of other people couldn't."

They both fell silent again. Matt examined in his mind the usual father-and-son relationship, where the father is expected to instill good qualities in his son. In his own case, he thought, the son was passing good qualities up to his father. He was doing it without intending to, without even knowing it was happening. Matt could recall more than once making adjustments in the way he conducted himself to more closely coincide with Jim's high expectations.

He had often considered that if heredity played a part in Jim's development, he had inherited the genes from his mother. As for that, he reflected, Jim's mother was as pure in thought and deed as her son. Jim had been mighty picky when he chose a mother, Matt mused with a silent chuckle.

Buck was reproaching himself for not having given enough recognition to Old Black for his conduct. His comments to Matt Bradley made him realize how long he had taken the horse for granted. He was sadly behind on stepping up to Old Black and telling him man-to-man what a good job he always did.

Buck knew first-hand what it meant to deserve praise and not get it. He had been raised by an uncle and had sensed his obligation for being welcomed into Uncle's house. So Buck the child tried to do the best job he could on everything. He was about ten years old when his uncle asked him to cut the weeds in a two-acre pasture. It would have been a big job for a man, but Buck was a good hand with a weed cutter and he had cut that field before.

Each morning he went to the field early, wearing a wide-brimmed straw hat and carrying his water bottle and a hand file to sharpen his weed-cutter blade with. He came in for lunch and went right back out to the field and worked late. It had taken Buck six days to cut the pasture the first time, and by the time he was done, the weeds he had cut first had grown back enough to spoil the appearance of the whole job. This time he cut the field in three days. It was a swell-looking field too, when Buck finished, and he took his uncle out to see it. Uncle thanked him civil enough but had no other comment. Buck knew his uncle *appreciated* his work, but his failure to even mention what a fine job he'd done had hurt him deeply. Now he felt that he had done the same thing to Old Black.

Interrupting Buck's thoughts, Matt said, "It would seem to me that the rodeo life would be a bit lonely, away from home so much of the time. That would be hard on a family man, but I don't suppose too many rodeo cowboys are family men."

"Oh, no, Matt. It's not one bit lonely. We travel a lot, sure. But for the most part, you see the same guys at the rodeos." He stopped for a moment and became thoughtful before continuing. "You couldn't rub shoulders with better men in any other line of work—the solid friends you have in this business. You couldn't be lonely being around real pals all the time. And then, I always had Old Black. . . ." He paused for only a second.

"As for the family men, I'd guess that more rodeo cowboys are married than aren't, and a lot of them have kids. Shoot, I bet the family men on the rodeo circuit do a better job on the family side than your average guy. Many of them have sidelines, like training horses, ranching, teaching horsemanship to kids like Jim, some run rodeoing schools. One is a famous hunting guide. And you probably know about Andrew Meridith, who is more famous for his statues than his cutting horses. He's from around Brentwood."

Yes, Matt knew Andrew Meridith, a black sculptor whose western subjects were being compared with the works of Frederic Remington. Meridith had grown up poor, but it was evident when he was very young that he had exceptional artistic talent. Somehow, he had by more than one miracle received support and encouragement when he needed it most. As a young man he had persisted with his art through a dozen lean years. Then he had come to the attention of a famous Italian sculptor who took the young artist under his wing and became his mentor. His apprenticeship under the great Italian put a superb finish on an outstanding talent. His work became noticed and Meridith was on his way.

Matt explained that they were acquainted, that Jim and Meridith's daughter, Alexandra, went to horse shows together. Jim had spoken of having long conversations with Mr. Meridith as he watched the artist at work. His studio was a room in the barn that housed his horse training arena.

Matt was thinking of how happily Jim had tagged along with the Meridiths to horse shows as a spectator, never complaining about not having a horse so he could compete. . . . *wishing*, but not complaining. Then he realized Buck was talking. ". . . and nowhere could you find straighter people than the run-of-the-mill rodeo cowboy. Not a one of them is out to get your job, either, like it happens in shops and factories. *Beat* you. Yessiree, they'll beat you if they can. But it's all on the up-and-up and right out in the open. And you're trying to beat *them*." He grinned at a recollection.

"I've got many a useful piece of advice from cowboys I was competing against. Charlie Sommers came up to me once and said that he noticed this little thing. If I would change it and do it a way he showed me, he thought it might shave a little bit off my time. I did change it and before too long I'm beating him once in a while. You can't say much more about a man than that. And they are all over the place in this game. Yeah, I like it." His head was nodding gently.

"And, sure, you can make a living at it if you have some talent, a doggone good horse, and you work like the dickens improving your skills." Now Buck seemed as eager to talk about rodeoing as Matt had been about his farm.

"There's a whole pack of rodeo cowboys earning over a hundred grand a year." Buck jiggled his chair around to allow his legs to stretch out straight. He placed the heel of one boot on the toe of the other and studied them as he talked. "Most cowboys compete in more than one event—like me and Black do team roping along with calf roping. Your all-around champion today, the top money earner during the year, has to pull down something like two-hundred thousand to win all-around. Well, me and Black ain't in that league, but I thought we might break a hundred this year, with such a good start at San Antone and Houston."

His expression was gray for only an instant. Then he crossed his long legs and turned a pleased expression on Matt. "But anyway, me and Old Black turned out okay for two old boys that never had to take a job, that didn't work a day in our lives. Just had fun all the time," he said with a wistful smile.

Buck realized that he should get off the subject before Matt Bradley asked why he was quitting. It was time to play this thing out before it got awkward. Buck was sure Jim would not want to give Old Black up for anything now. He got up and grinned at Matt. "Let's go see if Old Black has bucked your boy off yet."

Jim had been practicing the keyhole race, as well as he could without chalk lines on the ground. As the men emerged from the house, they saw Old Black with Jim aboard flying directly away from them. They watched the horse go into a beautiful slide, reverse, and thunder out of the rollback. Jim was bent low over his neck, hanging on to the saddle horn. He gently slowed Old Black to an easy lope and rode up to them. Then he leaned back and Old Black parked himself. His father put his hands in his pockets and smiled his approval of the exhibition.

Buck said, "You're just what Old Black's been needing. Too bad I didn't know you before now, Jim; you could have been exercising him. By the way, I saw how light you was on the bit when you asked him to stop. Did you see that, Matt? Jim just kinda leaned back and Old Black put on the brakes."

Matt nodded. He had noticed many things. He saw the radiance on Jim's face and the apparent affection he had for Old Black already. He had also discerned some other things that were not to be seen with the naked eye, intuitive feelings that arose from his conversation with Buck. Elation hit Buck with a shock when Matt said, "Jim, what do you think? Will Old Black do?"

The boy's entire upper body thrust forward in the saddle with unrestrained eagerness, a consuming intensity on his face. "I want Old Black, Dad, and Old Black wants me, too." He was on the ground now, talking to the horse and rubbing his neck. When Jim reached up to rub his ears, the horse lowered his head obligingly.

Matt shot Buck a significant look. He said softly, "Yeah, Buck. You'd have been way ahead with an Old Black instead of that paint pony. I suspect so. Thanks for sparing my boy the experience."

"I TOLD YOU SIX HUNDRED, RIGHT?" Buck asked as he made a small heap of the tack and grooming tools he'd taken from the tack room. Matt Bradley nodded. "Well, to make sure there was no mis-representation, that includes the saddle, bridle, hock boots, ankle boots. And here's his breast strap. Jim will want to use it, for sure. Here's some currycombs and brushes, his halter and stable blanket. We'll put all that stuff in a tow sack. There's about half a sack of Omolene—that's been his feed for years. And here's almost a full bag of Animax. I add about half a coffee can of it to his feed."

Matt was making a stop sign with his hands. "We'll pay for those things, Buck. I don't believe you've even asked near what the horse is worth. We were going to look at a young gelding priced at nineteen hundred, with no saddle and very likely no sense."

Buck grinned and said, "A sorry couple of horse traders we'd make, Matt. Me trying to talk my selling price down and you trying to jack it up." He stepped into the tack room where there was a telephone extension. He made a call, spoke briefly and was talking as he emerged. "I've got a guy coming over with a good trailer. Delivery is included, too." He was moving briskly, getting things done. "We better get Old Black ready to travel," he said.

Matt opened his mouth to protest but Buck ignored him. He turned to Jim and described the feeding procedure. "Old Black's ate Purina Omolene all his life. One reason is because Omolene's the hands-down, best-selling sweet feed in the country, you can get it any place, and Purina dealers turn their stock over fast, so you never run into stock that's not fresh. For another thing, it's the best that money can buy, but it ain't expensive. Give him this bucket filled to this line once a day, starting out. Then adjust accordingly, whether he's gaining or losing weight. Purina Animax is a high-protein supplement, and a working horse needs it. Give him half a coffee can with his feed. Bear in mind that a horse needs more feed when he's getting used hard than when he's idle."

Buck cautioned him sternly against getting the horse fat. "For the first time in his life, he'll have all the good, green grass he wants. A horse could live just fine on nothing but grass when you're not using him. You need to see a trace of ribs" he stepped over to the horse and put his hand on the last few ribs on that side. "You need to see a trace of ribs along here. Just a trace. That's his perfect condition. When you don't see that trace, he's fat. Please don't get him fat," he pleaded. "It could be the death of him, just like it is for people. If you make a mistake, make it on the skinny side. Okay? Fine. Help me carry this stuff out to the driveway, Jim."

On one trip to the driveway Matt encountered Buck going in the opposite direction. He noticed the first big complacent smile he'd seen on the cowboy since they arrived. Then he looked closer and wondered whether it was sweat or . . . tears running down Buck's face.

The morning had been a trying one for Buck Jones, physically and emotionally. Now he moved about with such evident difficulty that Matt took charge of readying the horse for the ride to his new home. When Buck attempted to carry the saddle, Jim insisted on lugging it to the car. "I have to get used to carrying it, Mr. Jones," he said, staggering along under the load. His father helped him carefully stow it in the car's trunk. Jim used the saddle blanket as padding to protect the saddle from scuffs.

Buck's eye fell on a wooden peg in the tack room that held several coiled lariats. He removed them and examined each carefully, then handed one to Jim. "Take this lariat, Jim; it's a genuine Classic MoneyMaker. They don't come no better, and it's made right here in Texas. This one's good and broke in, too. And being a thirty-five-foot heeling rope, it's five foot longer than your ordinary lariat. You should keep it on your saddle all the time. You never know when a lariat might get you out of a jam of some kind—Shoot, Jim, in the right situation it could even be the difference between life or death. If you work at it, you'll pick up the knack of throwing a loop in no time."

The trailer had arrived. The driver of the big-cab pickup truck, introduced as Garner, took Buck aside and spoke briefly to him. A light, playful punch on Buck's shoulder ended their exchange and Garner returned to his work. He took up the halter lead rope and led Old Black to the open door of the horse trailer. There he placed the halter lead around the horse's neck and secured it with a loose knot. Instinctively, Old Black moved briskly forward. He placed one forefoot gently on the wooden floor of the trailer and tapped it lightly several times as if he were testing it for soundness before entering.

Then, Old Black suddenly backed up a couple of steps and craned his neck until he was looking squarely at Buck, who was standing a few yards behind him. He stood there staring for five or six long seconds. Then his head swung around in the other direction and he looked at the little yellow trailer that he had ridden in as far as six times around the world. No one spoke. Turning his head once more toward Buck, Old Black stood for a long interval, pouring a melancholy, inquiring gaze on his lifelong friend.

Jim watched, not comprehending Old Black's reluctance to depart, but instead interpreted the actions as a bid farewell before setting off for his new home. His observation could not have been farther off the mark.

After seeming to evaluate the message in Buck's returning stare, Old Black turned back toward the trailer he was expected to enter, his neck drooping as he did so until his nose was almost touching the floor. Then, with reluctant obedience, he trudged inside. Buck Jones ducked his head slightly as if looking at the ground. When he sensed that the attention of the others was on the activity at the trailer, he turned away and quickly wiped a shirt sleeve by each eye.

Garner passed the canvas-covered butt chain behind the horse's rump and hooked it in place. After closing the trailer door, he secured the safety bar and checked his work. Waving a quick goodbye, he climbed into his big-cab Dodge pickup. Matt and then Jim shook hands with Buck.

Buck hobbled along slowly, following as the truck pulling the trailer, with the Bradley car right behind it, crept over the driveway's humps and dips. Once on the road, the tune of the tire sounds rose quickly as the rig picked up speed. Buck responded to arms waving from the car's windows.

He moved to the old sycamore tree by the roadside and leaned wearily against it, watching as the procession that was carrying his old pal to a new life flew away down the road. It disappeared from sight and sound down a dip and when truck and car climbed back into sight there was not a sound to be heard from them. Buck watched the silent caravan as it began to dance vaguely with the heat waves in the distance before it disappeared forever around the far bend.

He kept looking down the empty road for a long time, and then he slowly turned toward the empty corral. The gate stood open, adding to its deserted air. The whole world seemed deserted. He sensed the descent of a black mantle of depression and threw it off forcefully. A lifetime looking at the bright side served him now.

"This is exactly what we wanted, wasn't it Black?" he asked aloud. "Isn't this what I asked the Man for? If we couldn't keep the old times going, we couldn't have come up with a better deal for you. Nope, not by a long rope." Buck forced a smile. The act brought on the real thing and the smile spread across his face. His eyes slowly acquired a gleam of deep contentment.

"I'll miss you, old pal," he said softly. "But I won't be worrying about you, and a fella can't ask for no more than that. You'll miss me, too, for a while. But you'll be having such a high-ho time you won't be pinin' over me for long."

Buck got a mental picture of Old Black standing saddled in the shade of the pecan trees down in the Bradley's bottom pasture, contentedly munching on a mouthful of grass. He saw the boy sitting on the ground nearby, leaning against the huge trunk of a pecan tree, talking to his horse as they both rested in the cool shade. Black always liked it when you talked to him.

Buck exclaimed, "By golly, Black, ain't this something? And if you think they like you now, wait till you and Jim start cowboyin'. You're fixed for life, Black," he said, emphasizing the words with a sideways jerk of his contented, weatherbeaten face. He hobbled vigorously toward the house, talking as if Old Black were walking along beside him and listening to every word. "Ain't this something! I asked the Man upstairs if maybe He couldn't deal us a new hand. And what did we get? *A royal flush!*"

Buck felt the presence of something in his hand. Only then did he look at the check that Matt Bradley had given him in payment for the horse. It had a lot of small writing at the bottom that he couldn't make out. From a shirt pocket he took his round, metal-rimmed glasses and from his back pocket came his bandanna. He wiped the glasses, then his eyes. The check was for one thousand dollars. At the bottom was written on two lines, very small: "For Old Black, $600—saddle, bridle & etc: $400—Total: $1,000 + a thousand thanks and good wishes."

Buck chuckled softly and resumed walking up the drive toward his house. A smile played on his face as he slowly tore the check into tiny pieces that he let fall to the ground. Then he made a lively motion, extending a hand palm up in the direction they had gone. Vigorous thrusts of his outstretched hand punctuated his words as he spoke in a voice that was strong and happy. "And a thousand thanks to you Matt and Jim. You boys sure can make a feller understand how useless money is when something mighty dear is at stake!"

CHAPTER 6

It had been agreed that Garner should lead with the truck, setting the pace until they turned off the highway onto League Line Road. Matt would take over from there and eliminate the need for tedious directions. Now, as the truck slowly made the turn onto the gravel road, Matt tapped his horn and waved as he passed it up. He kept his speed to a crawl so the tires wouldn't throw rocks in the truck's path; it was only two miles to the lane that led into their place.

Since leaving the city behind, Matt and Jim had been observing with growing satisfaction how the countryside had greened up since Tuesday's rain. Now, driving along slowly, Matt could see the plant growth on the roadside. "Just look how green everything is," he said. "The clover along the road has really come alive!"

Jim had noticed it too, he said. "And the road isn't dusty, either. I'm glad Old Black doesn't have to eat our dust. I can't wait to see our bottom pasture. It had a pretty good start last week."

"It sure did. Matter of fact, the grass was ahead of where I expected it to be, considering the shortage of rain this spring. And the clover, it was a foot tall, wasn't it?"

Jim picked up a binder from the seat. It was a daily scheduler in which Matt and Jim recorded just about everything that went on at the farm—rainfall, the first sprigs of green growth in each field, grass height, leafing of trees, new calves on the ground, the occasional calf born dead or the cow that died giving birth . . . . With the book open in his lap, Jim said, "The clover was thirteen inches tall last Saturday morning at nine-twenty."

"It might be ready for baling by next weekend, Jim, so we best put that in our plans. Rufus and Duffie can take a day off during the week so they can help with it."

Jim turned back and watched the truck as it followed them into the lane. He was relieved to see Garner taking it easy over the bumps. "Gee, Dad, I hope Mrs. Jackson is outside," he said. "I'll keep a lookout. If I see her let's honk. I can't wait to show them Old Black." Ruby and Oscar Jackson, an elderly black couple, were the Bradley's nearest neighbors; they were also very close friends of the Bradleys—revered by Jim. "Won't they be amazed? I bet *Mr.* Jackson will be the most amazed. And Alexandra! Ha! *She's* the one that will be amazed."

The Jackson's house was large and suffering from creeping dilapidation. One day while Jim and his mother were visiting and picking out a Thanksgiving turkey, Ruby had leaned back with her fists planted firmly on her hips as she surveyed the house. She declared with a big laugh, "This old house is getting decrepit, but so is the people that lives there."

The house was once the headquarters of the big, productive Richter cotton farm, but that was back when cotton was king, before synthetic fibers arrogantly elbowed cotton aside in the fifties. Eventually, consumers rediscovered the comfort of cotton and welcomed it back with open arms. But by then farmers had deserted cotton in favor of soybeans, and the idle gins were already rusting away. Once there were four cotton gins in Winchester County; now there was one. Mr. Jackson had told Jim about the good old days when Klanke's Mill was operating. Mr. Klanke was a man who treated everyone fair and square, he had said. It was a shame the ginner who'd survived was the bad guy. Unchecked now, with no competition, he charged growers stiff prices, short-weighed them, and stole a big part of their valuable cottonseed.

About two hundred yards off the county road, a left fork in the lane led off toward the Jackson's house. Jim leaned forward with his right arm on the dashboard so he had a clear view past his father; he looked anxiously but in vain for a sign of Mrs. Jackson. He said at last, "I don't see anybody, but Mr. Jackson's pickup is there." He gave up looking when his father turned to follow the lane to the right, past the old Richter barn. In another hundred yards they arrived at the gate to the Bradley's ranch.

Almost before the car came to a halt, Jim was getting out to open the gate. Matt Bradley jerked his head toward the truck behind. "Tell Garner not to bother closing the gate. It can stay open until he leaves." Presently Jim was back in the car and the procession crept up the lane toward the Bradley farm headquarters.

RUBY JACKSON STOMPED HER RUBBER BOOTS several times as she climbed the steps, then crossed the big porch and entered the second of the three screen doors that opened onto it.

"Oscar," she said while undoing the ribbons of her bonnet, "Mr. Bradley just drove in. They was a truck pulling a stock trailer tagging along behind." She had indeed been outside, working in a place in her garden that was not visible from the lane.

"Hmmm," said Oscar, between meditative puffs on his pipe. "Could you see what was in it?"

"No, the sides was solid. But when it made the turn I seen they was a tail hanging out the back."

"Hmmm. Maybe Mr. Bradley bought that bull he's been talking about, that poll Hereford of Mr. Tiemann's."

Ruby Jackson shook her head. "Wasn't Mr. Tiemann hauling it. He would've brought it, wouldn't he?"

Oscar nodded his head thoughtfully. He rocked gently in his rocking chair for a few moments and said, "Yep. He would've brought it over. I'll be going over there anyways tomorrow morning and I'll find out what it is. I'm itchin' to know."

Oscar and Ruby Jackson were both well into their seventies. They were two truly contented people and had lived remarkably productive lives. Even though Oscar's cash income had never topped six thousand dollars in any year, they had raised eight children and put all of them through college. One daughter, now a school teacher, was married to Andrew Meridith, the sculptor.

For thirty years Oscar had sharecropped on Mr. Richter's place, growing cotton on halves. The enterprising couple also raised hogs, turkeys, and chickens. Then there was Ruby's immense and fruitful garden, where she'd been working when the Bradley caravan passed.

Oscar was the overseer of the Bradley ranch. He visited the place daily and provided occasional supervision to the two elderly black men, Duffie and Rufus, who worked there full time.

The Jacksons had a clear view of several hundred yards of lane beginning at their own, curving past the Richter barn, through the Bradley gate and up the hill almost to the headquarters. It was a rare coming or going that went unnoticed by Ruby or Oscar.

Never was a visitor unnoticed by Matt's dog Sam, a female Rhodesian ridgeback who lived full time on the farm. Today as always she met Matt at the gate, her tail wagging with glee, and loped along with the car, looking up at him all the way until he parked in front of the house.

When Matt emerged from the car Sam was there, head down, her body arched in flagrant delight. Her entire hind end was swinging with the momentum of her tail. "Sam, old girl, you're the perfect example of the tail wagging the dog." He engaged in dog talk while he massaged her head between his hands, patted her, and scratched her neck and chin.

Sam was as obedient and playful as could be with Jim and his mother, Norma. But she stuck to Matt like a cocklebur, except when he was operating machinery. On those occasions, he would say, "Sam, I have to go to work. You stay at the house." And she would sit down with glum obedience and pout at his departing back. Once he was gone she would find a shady spot and fling herself on the ground, sphinx-like, stern displeasure showing on her face.

The ridgeback, similar in appearance to a large hound, was bred in South Africa as a big-game hunter and guard dog. Sam was lean, hard, and quick as a snake. Her sleek, tan coat glowed with a hint of gold. True to the Rhodesian ridgeback breed, she had a large, expressive head with a wide, prominent brow.

Running his fingers down the puppy's spine, Matt had explained to Jim, "The term 'ridgeback' refers to this strip of hair that grows forward. See how the rest of her hair falls down and back, like on other short-haired dogs." The band of reverse-growing hair extended from Sam's shoulders and ended like the tip of a broadsword at her tailhead. When she was aroused, the hair along the "ridge" stood straight up, resembling a Mohawk haircut and conveying a well-deserved look of ferocity.

Sam denied entry onto the Bradley place to all but a privileged few—Rufus and Duffie, Ruby and Oscar, and Mr. Richter. Even people she knew who came calling when the Bradleys were not there were intruders, and Sam confined them to their vehicles.

One night Sam "treed" two youths who came lurking about. They were rescued from the barn loft by Duffie and Rufus the next morning and released to the sheriff, much wiser about the dangers of a night raid on the Bradley farm. Sam's fame as a vicious guard dog had spread, as all news does in the country, and only a thief from afar would dare set foot on the place.

The most memorable occasion involved a laborer who had worked for Matt a few days helping build a machinery barn. He had gone out of his way to play with Sam, and must have presumed that his introduction to her was binding. One evening Ruby saw the man's pickup sneaking quietly up the lane, its lights out in the waning twilight. She interrupted the feeding of her turkeys and went to the house to alert Oscar and call the sheriff. Minutes later they saw the pickup careening wildly back down the lane.

On his rounds the next morning Oscar found the seat of the man's overalls on the ground, stiff with blood and a few shreds of his hide still stuck to it. Sheriff Martinez had returned the piece, a back pocket with the man's wallet in it, to him with a warning smile.

Sam's already fearsome fame became more widespread, as was proper, and the tale was amplified with each telling, which certainly did no harm. In the version that came back to Matt, in addition to the seat of the man's pants, a glove was found with fingers still in it.

Sam was inclined to be friends with all of God's creatures and presumed the feeling was mutual. But some wild creatures misunderstood her yearning for harmless sport. More than once she returned home fumigated by a skunk who declined to play. Once she had tried to engage an armadillo in games, barring its escape route by jumping around the pathetic animal every time it tried to run away in a new direction. The frustrated armadillo frantically dug a hole and disappeared into the ground.

GARNER EMERGED FROM HIS TRUCK LIKE A TOURIST, head up and turning left and right. He spread his arms to the refreshing breeze that almost always flowed over the hilltop. Tugging at his driving gloves, he walked slowly to a place where he had a clear view. His attention was drawn first to the spectacular vista off in the northeast. A big smile covered his face as he turned to Matt Bradley, his thumbs stuck in his jeans pockets. His mouth worked as if to talk, but he seemed speechless.

Finally, he said, "If I ever seen such a sight this side of Austin, I can't remember where it was. I wonder how far it is over thataway where the land goes out of sight?" An arm took in a series of ridges

61

that rose one beyond the other, green pastures decorated with patches of woods. Each ridge was less distinct than the one before it until the last one lay in a blue haze.

Garner turned to his right and waved his outstretched arm over the wide forest beginning where the flat of the bottom began its rise a short distance beyond the Bradley fence line. It was a mature forest of huge trees rising, rising up a long slope until the distinctly clumpy treetops of the Baumberg woods collided with the sky a half-mile away. "Ain't that something? Those woods must be working alive with deer." He was right about that.

He turned back to his left, where his original fascination with the more distant scene had caused him to overlook the near view, below. Now he looked down on the broad slash of green woods embracing the banks of the creek snaking through the flat. "Look at that!" he exclaimed, his eyes following the line of the creek to the bottomland pasture dotted with cows. He saw the grove of huge pecan trees, then his gaze rested on the darker green of the clover field.

Suddenly, he seemed to remember what he was there for. Smacking his hands together, he strode briskly to his trailer, released the safety bar, opened the door, and unhooked the butt chain. At the signal of a pat on the rump, Old Black moved backwards, feeling with a toe first for the end of the trailer floor, then cautiously for the ground before committing himself. Then he backed swiftly out of the trailer. With his head high he turned rapidly left and right and sniffed the air. He stepped about in a lively manner, staring wide-eyed and trying, as Garner had, to see all the scenery at once. Presently he began neighing, delivering a long, musical series with a couple of brisk snorts as a finale.

Jim looked at his father and laughed. "He likes it here already."

"Who wouldn't?" said Garner, handing the halter rope to Jim.

"How would you introduce him to the place, Garner?" Matt asked. "Ride him around and show him the boundaries?"

"Naw, I would just walk him through that there gate and let him loose to discover on his own. Maybe he'll come when you call him. But *I* sure wouldn't," he laughed, "once I got my nose in that green grass. Right now he'll just set out to investigate the place, and visit those cows down there."

Jim looked inquiringly at his father, who nodded. Then he walked the horse, impatiently prancing sideways, through the big gate that led from the hilltop to the bottom. The men stood leaning on the gate, their arms on the top rail.

Garner looked sideways at Matt and said with an air of confidentiality, "I wasn't surprised you'd have a showplace, Mr. Bradley. Anybody that could afford to buy Old Black for his boy to ride in kid shows . . ."

"You figure Old Black is too much horse for a boy?"

"Oh, shoot no!" Garner exclaimed. "Old Black ain't too much horse, if you want your boy to win everything in sight. But to put out what *this* horse must have cost for a boy's mount . . . Well, it just seems like things are getting awful dicey when a horse for a kid will bring more than a professional rodeo cowboy can afford to pay for it.

"Now, for rodeoing, that's another matter. Any pretty good calf roper could boost his earnings a lot with Old Black under him. So a lot of cowboys could afford to pay what Buck must have been asking."

Matt said, "How much was he asking?"

Garner cocked his head to one side and stared at Matt with a puzzled expression. "You tell *me*—you bought him! I never did hear that Buck actually set a price, but I know he turned down twenty-five thousand from Terry Fergerson—Terry's a calf roper, but he's not even in the running with Buck. Cashier's check, too, and Buck turned it down flat. Little over a week ago. Terry showed me the check before he went over to Buck's with it, said he'd scraped up every dime of his own, plus begging and borrowing. He said that was the way to buy something you really want, slap down a cashier's check for the *most* the seller might get from anybody else and he'll keel over every time. Buck didn't keel over, though. That's why I'd give a pretty penny to know what it took to buy him."

Matt decided to let Garner keep his pretty penny and said, "Garner, it took a lot more than money to buy Old Black. Something a whole lot more valuable to Buck Jones than money, and I'm just beginning to find that out. Thanks for what you told me." He gave Garner a look of sincere gratitude.

Jim had led Old Black a hundred feet or so from the gate. He unbuckled the halter and glanced at his father. At Matt's nod, Jim removed the halter. Old Black stood still for several seconds as Jim stroked his neck; then Jim stepped back. Old Black's head went up high on an arched neck and swept the whole scene, craning first one way, then another. His ears twitched and turned, trying to focus on every sound. Through flared nostrils he sniffed the stream of lovely scents that flowed across the hilltop. Then he began to trot around in an animated way, knees high as he pranced excitedly, his tail up like a semaphore flag. Soon he reversed his direction and broke into a slow, bucking lope, moving in a semicircle.

When he was facing down the hill, he stopped momentarily and with head high and neck in a fine arch, he surveyed the scene far below. Then with a snort and a series of squeals he put his head down low to the ground and charged downhill. After a few strides his head came up and his nose reached way out. With his tail held high and streaming out behind, he fairly flew down the hillside. Down, down he went at top speed until he reached the flat, where he gradually allowed his momentum to dissipate from a dead run to a fast lope. His head came up high to allow a better view of the surroundings and he galloped easily along the perimeter of the bottom pasture. The cows were watching the sight, a spectacle they had never seen before, but they displayed no alarm.

Garner turned away from the scene chuckling. "Well, I'll let Buck know Old Black's new home is a dilly. Yes, sir, a dilly if ever there was one." He was striding toward his truck before he finished, talking over his shoulder. He waved and climbed in. The Cummins diesel roared to life and Garner's pickup was rolling away.

Matt and Jim stood at the gate looking down on the bottom. Jim's shining eyes saw nothing but Old Black. Matt saw a sea of beautiful emerald green. He was astonished at the difference a fine rain and four days of sunshine had made. He was anxious to get down there for a close look.

"HERE COME THAT TRUCK BACK, OSCAR," RUBY SAID, holding the screen door open and watching the rig descend down the lane from the Bradley barn. She stepped out on the porch for a better view.

Oscar heaved himself up from the rocking chair and came to her side. "Hmmm," he said through teeth clamped on his pipestem. He and Ruby examined the truck and trailer carefully as it made its way in their direction, then around the bend at the barn and along the lane where it was in full broadside view for some time as it rumbled along. Oscar took his pipe out of his mouth with a brisk motion and said, "Ain't anybody from this end of the county."

THEY BEGAN CARRYING THE SADDLE, tack and supplies to the feed room in the barn. It had been called the "feed room" because feed was all they ever kept in there, bags of cattle range cubes and stacks of bagged protein supplement.

Built into one wall were two saddle racks, meticulously handmade long, long ago and notched and pegged into the wall structure by a skilled craftsman. Frequent and prolonged use at some time in the distant past had softened the corners and tool marks, enhancing their beauty. Jim grabbed a cloth feed sack and whipped it across the rack nearest the door to remove the heaviest dust accumulation. When he saw what a fine surface lay below the dust, he began rubbing the rack more diligently. A soft sheen of varying hues appeared and inspired him to pay closer attention to the places that were not so easy to get to. The ancient surface brightened to a fine burnished glow.

His father appeared, holding the saddle. "That's a rack fit for a fine saddle, and we have a fine saddle to put on it," he said. "Strange, as many times as I've been in here I never noticed how well these racks were made—like furniture, don't you think, Jim?"

Jim sure did, and called his father's attention to a row of handmade hardwood pegs for hanging tack. "These look like the pegs in the chifforobe Mom refinished." The handmade chifforobe had been left in the house and discovered when the Bradleys took possession. His mother considered it a genuine treasure. It had a row of drawers alongside which was a clothes closet with wooden pegs for hanging clothes. Now Jim was comparing the tack room pegs to his recollection of the pegs in the chifforobe. His close inspection of the old piece of furniture had been inspired by the discovery of some Confederate money under the ancient newspapers that lined the drawers.

"See, Dad?" He ran his fingers over a peg and pointed out the details. "They're flat here, and toward the end *here* they taper off. The ends are all carved the same. These pegs are just bigger than the other ones. I bet the same man made them that made the chifforobe. When we go in the house I'm going to look at those pegs real close."

Over each saddle rack was a curved rack for saddle blankets, slatted so as to allow the blankets to air dry. They were made with the same skillful attention to detail as the other objects in the tack room. Standing on an overturned five-gallon pail, Jim cleaned one blanket rack well before placing Old Black's saddle blanket on it. Then he hung the other tack on pegs.

About four feet from the floor a shallow shelf had been fitted between the wall studs and ran from one end of the room to the other. Here Jim placed Old Black's brushes and curry combs, and the two bottles of Absorbine. As he was arranging them, his father returned with the Omolene feed and Animax supplement.

Across the small room from the tack woodwork were three large wooden feed bins. Matt lifted one of the hinged lids and saw a fine homemade scoop lying in the small amount of old feed inside. "We'll have to clean these out before we put feed in them," he said.

Jim stood back to survey the newly appointed feed room. Years of foot traffic on the broad, tight-fitting floor planks had left the wood grain beautifully sculptured. One door led into the barn; the other opened to the outside. "It looks swell with a real saddle and some tack in it," he said. "I'm going to start calling it the tack room."

Jim caressed the deep tooling in the leather of his saddle. "Dad, I sure appreciate Old Black. And getting this saddle and bridle, and all the other things to boot! I'll work real hard to make up for him and everything else."

His father said, "Jim, your appreciation is taken straight to heart. But remember that the horse is actually *re*payment for all the years of work you've put in on the farm. You've earned Old Black already several times over, and your mother and I very much appreciate everything you've done. A grown man would have had to hustle to put in the work you have."

As they walked across the graveled span between the barn and the house, Jim stepped over to the fence. Standing on a rail so he could see the bottom pasture better, he felt a thrill as his eyes found Old Black, right at home among the cows and grazing contentedly.

He stood there for many minutes gazing and dreaming. His eyes followed Hickory Creek as far east as it was visible, much farther than he and his father had ever explored. What lay beyond?

When Jim reached the house his father was changing into overalls. "Let's go down and check out the fields," he said. "Would you check the rain gauge?"

"Sure, Pop," Jim said. He used "Pop" when he was feeling particularly lighthearted. "You should've seen Old Black just now. All of a sudden he decided he wanted some action so he went to bucking around and then raced against himself like he was on a racetrack. Then he just went back to grazing. He sure likes it here."

In less than two minutes Jim was out of his room in jeans and work shirt and work boots. Without stopping he ran out the back door to the post that held the rain gauge.

"Over three inches!" he exclaimed. His father took the tube and looked at it closely. "Wonderful. While I'm writing that in the book, will you get the pickup out?"

Again the boy scooted off, emptying the glass tube as he went. They kept an old pickup in one of the large stalls alongside the barn. Jim loved to drive the truck and the tractors, which he was allowed to do only under careful supervision.

He drove the pickup out of the lot and waited for his father with the engine running. Matt crossed the porch with "the book" in his hand and strode out of the picket gate. He was always amused by Jim's appearance, propped up on a cushion so he could see and another behind him to keep him in touch with the pedals.

Sam sailed over the side of the truck and landed lightly in its bed. She stood peering around the cab on Matt's side, looking at the road ahead. When Matt closed his door, Jim put the truck in gear, let the clutch out smoothly, and crept down the long hill in low gear.

Jim looked slyly at his father and said, "We sure are lucky we got Old Black on *this* weekend. You know why?"

Matt looked thoughtful. "Why?"

"Because Monday is a holiday. We get to stay today, tomorrow and Monday—I sure hope you don't have a flight. Boy! I still can't believe it. A horse of my own. And a world's champion! But I'd like Old Black just as much if he wasn't a world's champion. You'll see, when you ride him, Dad. Even Jupiter doesn't handle like Old Black."

Jim stopped the truck as soon as they reached the level bottomland. The instant Matt's door opened Sam sailed out of the truck's bed. Matt got out smiling at a sea of green, fast-growing Bermuda grass. He stooped and ran his fingers through the luxuriant growth. "Those thunderstorms gave us tons of nitrogen," he said.

Jim knew, from an exploration in the encyclopedia with his father, that the air was three-fourths nitrogen. He also knew that unlike phosphate fertilizer, which was dug from mines, air was the earth's only source of nitrogen. Lightning, said the encyclopedia, was a primary producer of nitric acid, which was brought to earth by rain for use by plants and soil organisms.

Matt took in the whole farm in an arc of his arm. "Just look what that nitrogen did for everything, Jim, and it was free." His eyes took in the clover field. "I can see from here that the clover has grown a lot. Let's go look."

Sam had run on ahead and could be heard sloshing around in the creek. A large splash told them that she had jumped into a deep hole from her favorite high-dive place on the bank. Barring encounters with skunks, Sam never needed a bath because she played in the creek almost every day.

The clover was knee high. Several times Matt bent down and swept a hand through the lush growth, then he jerked an entire plant out of the ground. After examining the buds at the tips of the stems, he held it at arm's length against the sky. He tore off a handful of the top and wrung it in his hands, then put it to his nose and took a deep breath. Satisfaction glowed on his face as he passed it to Jim.

Now he pulled up another plant and beat its roots on the ground to shake off the dirt. He scooped up a handful of loose soil and smelled of it. Nodding, he handed the dirt to Jim. The boy sniffed; it was a pleasingly pungent odor laced with a rich smell of decay.

"Look at this," Matt said, pointing out the big whitish globs attached to the roots. "Those are nitrogen nodules. This is an example of a plant extracting nitrogen from the air and storing it up. The nodules will decompose in the ground when this crop of clover dies back. Then the nitrogen will be used by the Johnson grass that follows. Organic farming," said Matt.

His voice took on an urgent edge. "This clover—" he looked at his watch, glanced at the blue sky, decorated with only a few high, sparse streaks of cirrus clouds. "This clover is ready, and we're not going to get any rain during the next few days."

Matt was right at home up there in the sky; he had developed a strong knowledge of meteorology and a feel for developing weather as if his life depended on it, which it did. He claimed that weather forecasters could go to bed after making their forecasts without worrying about whether they were right or not, but going up there and sticking your nose in your forecasts will put a keen edge on them.

"This clover's ready right now, Jim. We can't wait until next weekend to lay it down. With a head start on curing this afternoon and a sunny day tomorrow, it'll be ready to bale Monday morning, as soon as the dew is off." His guess was that the big high-pressure ridge that lay over the southern half of Texas meant there wouldn't be more than a light dew. He turned and strode from the field.

Matt's first observation tour on arriving at the farm almost always included a general inspection of the cow herd and a check for any new calves. But today he only glanced at the herd and said, "Jim, I'm going to get the tractor hooked up to the mower right now. I'll have this clover on the ground in no time. Drive me up to the house."

Sam came running up just as they were getting in the truck. Jim reached down to give her a pat, but just as he bent over her she shook vigorously, covering him with a spray of water. He was laughing and wiping his face with his bandanna when he got in the truck.

MATT WAS TURNED AROUND IN THE tractor seat, watching closely behind as he eased the big diesel back to the hay machine. Straddling the machine's shaft, his hands a foot from the end to keep them out of the way of the mating parts, Jim held the spline where it would meet the tractor's shaft. Once they were mated, Matt crawled down from his seat to finish making the hookup.

Then he walked around the big New Holland machine that did a three-in-one job, giving it what he called a "preflight inspection." The cutter bar mowed down the crop, then it was fed between two long rollers that crushed the plants every few inches to allow the sappy stems to dry as fast as the leaves—the crushing process was called "conditioning." The machine then left the conditioned crop in a loose, fluffy windrow, allowing air circulation to assist with the sun's curing warmth.

Matt would not allow Jim to ride on a tractor with machinery behind it. He guided his son a few steps away from the sound of the idling tractor and said. "I'll be at this until maybe five or so, Jim. What do you plan to do?"

A smile stole across Jim's face. "I thought I would saddle up Old Black and ride over to the Jackson's."

Matt nodded in agreement and squeezed his shoulder. Then he turned to Sam, lively with the anticipation of playing some part in the goings on, patted her on the head and said, "I have to go to work, Sam. You stay up here." The dog's whole being slumped as she sat down in something of a huff. He boarded the tractor again, and a big puff of blue smoke belched out of the exhaust stack as he accelerated away from the barn. With her head down in dejection, Sam trudged to the shade of a peach tree by the barn, plopped down and glowered at the departing tractor.

Old Black did not come as promptly as Jim had expected. As much as the horse liked to pack a rider, he also loved fresh spring grass. Jim walked down to the pasture with a halter to get him. He led Old Black next to a fallen tree trunk and used it as a platform to mount from. Once astride, Jim leaned forward ever so slightly and squeezed his legs; he smiled as Old Black stepped right out. Because he had no reins and only one lead from the halter ring, he signaled for turns by using leg pressure and by changing the balance of his upper body. After a few practice turns, Old Black was responding as if wearing a bridle.

Jim rode by the clover field to show off his bareback-riding skills. It was some time before Matt noticed, for he was concentrating on the edge of the previous cut, but as he was making a turnaround he looked up and saw them. He waved. Jim could see the big smile on his father's face as he turned his attention back to his hay cutting.

Just how he was going to get the forty-five-pound saddle on Old Black had been nagging at Jim's mind as he rode up the hill. Up at the barn, he stood the horse just outside the tack room. While giving him a good brushing, he noticed that the floor of the tack room was a good two feet above the ground. He dropped the reins on the ground and said, "Stand," to ground-tie him as Mr. Jones had instructed. Then he ducked under the horse and entered the tack room.

With the offside stirrup tied up with a saddle string to keep it from falling and banging Old Black's leg, the height advantage and a burst of strength combined to get the horse saddled. It would not be long until he would be skillfully swinging the saddle up onto the horse, instead of using brute lifting force.

When he was finished with the cinches the horse exhaled audibly, releasing air he had been holding in. Jim was expecting this, and he quickly took up another inch in the main cinch. He stepped up and looked the horse in the eye. "I outsmarted you, Black, didn't I?" he said. "I learned that in 4-H."

He sprang back into the tack room and emerged with the breast strap and lariat. The lariat went over the saddle horn. After attaching the breast strap he untied the offside stirrup and let it down, then led Old Black back to the tack room door and mounted from there.

Once in the saddle, he used the lariat loop on the pommel to secure the rope, and he was ready. From horseback it was no feat at all to move Old Black sideways to close the tack room door.

And now, sitting tall, he could see the Jackson's yard and their front porch, always out of view behind the hill. Down there was the wooden bridge over the draw, and beyond that the Bradley gate. He rode around the barn and stopped at the highest spot on the hill, at the pasture fence. A spectacular scene lay before him. He had seen the view from the top rail of the corral and from the tractor, but that was nothing compared to this.

There was his father on the tractor, creeping through the clover field, leaving green windrows in his wake like huge fluffy tubes; Jim saw that he had cut almost half of the field already. His eyes roamed over the Baumberg woods, then off to the northeast to ridge beyond ridge. He stayed there, peacefully playing with Old Black's mane and absorbing the beauty of the scenery. The sight was enhanced by his total contentment at being astride his own horse. He patted Old Black's neck, turned him around and they headed down the lane.

Already, Old Black had exceeded his highest expectations of any horse he might ever get. And as for a saddle, they had talked about a used one for sale at Brentwood Produce. It wasn't a real good saddle new, and it had seen some abuse. But Jim wouldn't have complained about getting it. Instead, though, he had this *fine* roping saddle that anybody would be proud of. He examined it as Old Black carried him along at an easy walk. The sunlight brought out the colors in the deep, rich leather that long use had burnished. Where the leather was stretched over the curved shape of the pommel, the brown became almost a burnt orange in the sunlight. It seemed that he could see deep down into it.

The big saddle horn with its rawhide-covered edge that had brought down countless calves was a handful for Jim. The scuffs in the leather covering of the horn were agreeable evidence of its years in the rodeo arena. The elaborate hand tooling on the saddle leather felt elegant under his fingertips.

He grasped a pair of saddle strings and ran them through his hand, then turned to look behind the cantle for the strings there. They were quite long, two pairs on each side. He figured he could tie his jean jacket or rain slicker back there.

For the first time, he examined the lariat closely. It was in good shape, not frayed anywhere, but definitely not new-looking. He recalled with a mild feeling of superiority that a few of the kids in the shows rode with brand-new lariats that could never have roped anything. The hard lay of the rope felt good to the touch.

As Jim approached the gate he considered how he might get back on after dismounting to open it. He definitely was not going to arrive at the Jackson's leading a horse he could not get on without using their porch as a platform. He figured out that he would just climb up on the gate with the horse standing close by and get on that way. Though he was using props now, it would not be long before he would be boarding unaided. Some of the most innovative ways to get aboard big horses were invented by small riders.

"Mrs. Jackson," he shouted as he arrived at her front porch.

"Out here," came her voice from the garden behind him. "And look at *you!*" She dropped her hoe and came at a fast walk. "Look at you on a fine horse. Oscar, come quick!" she shouted. Then she bent slightly at the knees and waist and repeatedly slapped both hands against her thighs. "My lands, Oscar! Would you come look at this cowboy that done rode up." Ruby laughed roundly as she threw her hands high in the air and begged, "Please don't shoot, mister outlaw, you can have all my money!" Now a very curious Oscar moved cautiously out on the porch.

"Well I swear if it ain't old Jimbo on a great big horse," he said, straightening up and grinning broadly. "Hmmm—and a mighty fine horse it is. And that saddle, Ruby. It ain't no kid saddle, that's a real cowboy saddle."

Jim sat smiling, not yet daring to say anything. Oscar came down the steps and walked up to stand by Ruby at the horse's side. They looked up on high at the rider, and the rider looked down, way down, on them.

"Do he kick?" asked Ruby cautiously, keeping a lot of distance as she walked behind Old Black.

The question loosened Jim's tongue. "No, ma'am, he don't kick. He's a Quarter Horse, and he's used to being around people in rodeos. His name is Old Black and he's the world's champion calf-roping horse."

Ruby's eyes opened wide with wonder. "World's champion, you say? Well, he sure do look like a world's champion. Jim, you got you a mighty swell horse, ain't he Oscar?"

"Uh, *huh*, Ruby. He sure do," Oscar said with feeling. Oscar himself was once a good calf roper who had won many a jackpot roping. He saw much to appreciate in Old Black, and in the handsome roping saddle and the fine lariat. "Jim, where did you find such a horse as this? A world's champion, huh? And this roping saddle? Can I see that lariat?"

"Sure, Mr. Jackson," Jim said. He unfastened the strap and handed the lariat to Mr. Jackson. "We bought him from a rodeo cowboy named Buck Jones. Him and Old Black hold the world record time in calf roping."

"A rodeo cowboy, eh?" Oscar felt the rope and let it glide through his hands. "Boy, Jim, I never had such a rope as this. Hmmm. Been a long time," he said, mostly to himself as he stepped away from the horse. He shook out a loop and took a few practice swings, looked around and spied the tree stump that Ruby used as a chopping block to de-head her turkeys at Thanksgiving and Christmas. Oscar made a few swings, then let his loop fly. It settled neatly around the stump. "Ha!" he said as he snatched up his slack, "I ain't plumb lost my touch."

"Gosh, Mr. Jackson!" Jim said, a look of genuine appreciation on his face.

Ruby chuckled. "No, you ain't lost it, Oscar. Yes, sir, Jim. How I used to swell up proud when he won a jackpot roping. Even when he didn't win he look good. He had a fine horse back in them days."

Oscar smiled up at the sky in recollection. He gave the rope a deft flip, then another, and it came clear of the stump. As he coiled it up, he said, "Yep. Old Banjo was a top-notch calf-roping horse. He didn't look like much, but boy howdy could he rate a calf." He handed the lariat back to Jim. "That's a nice long lariat, Jimbo."

"Yes, sir. It's a thirty-five-foot heeling rope. Mr. Jackson, would you teach me to throw a loop?"

"Sure I will. Ain't nothing to it but practice, practice, practice. That's all they is to it after you get the basics down, the way you hold the loop, how you swing it, and how you throw it. Once you get that down, it's all practice. Sure, I'll show you, Jimbo. Now, how'd you find out about this fine horse?"

Jim explained.

Oscar looked straight at Jim and said, "But how come a rodeo cowboy could afford to get shut of a horse like this? And his saddle and all the rest that I see here?"

Jim's expression became thoughtful. His father had confided to him that he believed Buck Jones was seriously ill, forcing him to give up rodeoing. "I think he was quitting rodeoing and going where he couldn't have a horse," he said.

"How old is—you said his name is Old Black?"

"He's eighteen. Just turned eighteen, calendar. Registered, too. We got the papers."

"He sure don't look eighteen, Jimbo. He could pass for twelve in my book. A mighty fine horse. Well, it's about time the Bradley ranch had a horse on it. What's your daddy doing? Did I hear the big Ford start up?" Oscar was examining the heavily tooled leather breast strap, Jim noted with satisfaction.

"He's cutting the clover field. Cutting it for baling Monday."

"Hmmm," said Oscar. "I'm surprised it was ready. But that fine rain we got—it ain't soft down in the bottom?"

"No sir. We walked even in the lowest place. It's kind of springy, but not a bit soft for a tractor."

"The rain must have soaked in good for thunderstorm rain. Thunder? Wooeee! Thunder that shook the house. And lightning! You should've seen it—I watched more than one tree take a lick. It never did come a sure-enough flood rain, though. Even when it come down the hardest I could still see the top of your barn. But it kept it up all day long Tuesday. The creeks didn't even come up too high. A good soaker, it was, and just what we needed. So your pa's cutting that clover. Hmmm."

Ruby had gone into the house, evidently to attend to something on the stove. She came out with a wooden spoon in one hand, the other balled up in her apron, wiping it. "Jimmy," she said, "I almost forgot to tell you, Buddy's coming tomorrow to stay the whole day. He'll want—"

"Sure he is," Oscar interrupted. "Glad you mentioned it, Ruby. Buddy will sure want to see your horse."

Ruby continued, "I know he'd be thrilled to go for a horseback ride. Will he ride double?"

Jim was puzzled a moment, then brightened. "I believe so, Mrs. Jackson, because Buck Jones, the man that had him, said he sometimes served as pickup man for the bull riders and bronc riders. I believe Old Black will do most anything. I'll see if we have work to do in the morning. If we don't, I'll come over as soon as I can." He thought a moment and added, "Will you put a dishtowel in the pear tree when Buddy gets here?"

THE DISHTOWEL-IN-THE-PEAR-TREE SIGNAL dated back to the

Bradley's first month of farm ownership. Ruby, knowing how hard it was to get a telephone in the country, invited them to use her phone any time, and to receive calls on it as well. The signal that Mr. Bradley had a call to return was a dishtowel hanging in the pear tree by the porch, which was visible from the Bradley's porch—"Ruby's telegraph," Matt called it.

The Jacksons were on an eight-party line that was often busy. When Matt first came over in response to the signal, Mrs. Jackson led him to the phone. She picked it up and heard chatter even before the receiver reached her ear.

Without a moment's delay she said, "'Mergency. Mr. Bradley needs to use the phone. 'Mergency. Get off the phone." Then she hung it up, tapped her foot a few times, picked up the receiver and waved it past her ear before handing it to Matt. "There," she said. "A clear line for you, Mr. Bradley."

Matt had turned away from her to hide the smile brought on by her abrupt action. While dialing he said, "You didn't have to do that, Ruby. I wouldn't mind waiting."

"Lordy, if you waited on people around here you better set down with your lunch and the paper. They can talk all day. And someone is prob'ly waiting for them to get off so *they* can tattle away a few hours."

RUBY RETURNED HER SPOON TO THE kitchen and came down the steps to the yard. "Git down off that horse and talk to me while I hoe a little bit, Jimmy. I don't get to talk to you enough, you be so busy all the time working."

Jim climbed down, dropped the reins on the ground and followed Ruby to her garden. She had not stopped talking, assuming that her invitation would be accepted. She picked up her hoe; Jim took it from her and began hoeing the young weeds at the place where she had left off.

"Lordy, what a gentleman you is. Duffie or Rufus or any of those men would stand out here and talk and never offer to do any hoein'. Well, don't think I mind if you do. I'll just stand around and watch an expert." She laughed. Jim laughed too. "Well, what did you learn in school this week, Jim?"

Without hesitating, he said, "A lot. My history teacher, Mrs. Edmonds, is real good. She makes things interesting. This week we learned about Pompeii and Herculaneum—in Italy—two cities that were buried by a volcano eruption."

He stopped and leaned on the hoe as he talked.

"That was in the year seventy-nine. Only seventy-nine years after Jesus was born! Pompeii and Herculaneum were seaside resort towns a little way south of Naples, sort of like Galveston is to Houston. Except that most of the people that lived there were—" Jim frowned and resumed hoeing with considerable vigor. He grinned sheepishly and said, "I forgot about hoeing. The people that lived there were rich. When—"

Ruby interrupted sternly, "Phooey on that hoein', Jimmy. That can wait—those weeds ain't even youngsters, yet. You come over here and sit with me on this stump." She sat down and patted the ample space still available. "You can tell me all about them towns that got covered up by melted rock from that volcano—Come on, now," she said with authority. "Good boy," she nodded as he sat down. "I seen some of that on TV, happenin' in Hi-waya. But they wasn't no towns in the way. Imagine, rocks gettin' so hot they *melt* and run like cane syrup and burnin' up everything in the way. Uhhh, *uh.*" She shook her head.

Jim sat down beside her. She patted his leg and said, "I got a chance to sit and gab with little Jimmy and we gonna hoe? No, siree. We gonna *gab.*" She looked at Old Black, standing with his reins on the ground. "Ain't you afraid he'll run off? You can tie him to the porch railin'."

"He's ground tied, Mrs. Jackson. When the reins are lying on the ground like that he'll stand right there."

"Trainin'," Ruby said, expressing her approval with a vigorous nod. "I guess you'd expect a world's champion to have trainin'. Now tell me about them Eye-talian towns that got erupted on."

Jim cleared his throat. "Well, it started in the morning on a day in the summer, when there would have been a lot of people on vacations there by the seaside. There wasn't any lava, no melted rock like you saw on TV, running down on the towns. But rocks and ashes rained down until they were sixty feet deep over Herculaneum. The town was buried. They were about ten feet deep in Pompeii. Only rooftops stuck out there. Everybody left in both towns was killed, burned and suffocated by the hot ashes."

"Every last person that lived there was killed?" she asked, her voice expressing both sorrow and astonishment.

"Oh, no. A lot of the people in Pompeii got away—but about two thousand out of twenty thousand got killed." He looked puzzled. "We didn't learn how big Herculaneum was, but I think it was

about the same size as Pompeii. Most of the people in Herculaneum were killed.

"Well, over the hundreds and hundreds of years since that happened, everybody forgot about that volcano eruption and the towns that were buried by it. Then in the seventeen hundreds, about the time Ben Franklin was running his printing shop—Boy! Mrs. Jackson, there's a man that didn't waste a minute: Ben Franklin. At my age he was working in his brother's print shop and reading classic literature at night. His life is worth reading about."

"Do you have a book about Ben Franklin?" Ruby asked.

"Sure do. *Benjamin Franklin* by Chris Looby. It's a good book, with a lot of pictures."

"Could I borry it, Jim? I'd like to read about Ben Franklin."

"Why, sure you can. Oh, I know you'll like that book. I'll bring it next week. I won't forget, either. Well, it was about two hundred years ago that farmers and well-diggers started finding signs of the towns that had been covered up. So they started digging. Today they've been restored so you can walk around in them. Especially Pompeii. Imagine, Mrs. Jackson, digging up a town that was covered up when some people who had seen and listened to *Jesus* might have been alive!"

"Ummmm, uhh!" Ruby exclaimed. "You mean that for a fact? Do somebody know for sure about this? They ain't just makin' something up, like that time they put it on TV that a man got out of his Buck Rogers rocket on the moon?"

"Oh, yes. It's real history. They've been digging steady since the nineteen-twenties."

"Well, now," said Ruby in a tone of acceptance, "that's during my lifetime."

"Our teacher showed a videotape about Pompeii. They even found bodies that had been made into—like mummies, by the wet ashes that covered them up. Some of them were gladiators still in their chains. The houses they uncovered are *fine* houses with pretty pillars and courtyards, and statues and fountains around here and there. Some of them even had running water. But we couldn't figure out how it got there, through pipes or how. The teacher didn't know and the books and videotapes didn't say how they made the fountains spray water or how the bathtub water came in."

"How long ago was it when the volcano erupted?" she asked.

"Well, almost two thousand years—not even a hundred years short of two thousand years."

Ruby laughed a big, rollicking laugh. "Shoot, I know people right around here that ain't got runnin' water or indoor toilets to this day. The Rosenbaums, they didn't have any, did they?"

Jim laughed with her. "No," he agreed. "They had an outdoor toilet. Well, they did have water piped to a faucet in the closed-in back porch, where Sam sleeps, coming from the tank filled by the windmill. That goes to show how far ahead the Italians were."

"No, Jimmy. It just shows how backwoodsy some of us still is." She laughed and slapped her thigh. Ruby was having a good time with her history lesson, her gab session with Jim.

Jim laughed with her, causing Oscar to get up from his chair and peek through the screen door. Seeing them sitting on the stump, talking animatedly and laughing, brought a contented smile to his face. He returned to his chair chuckling with pure pleasure.

Jim went on. "Pompeii had a big stadium for sports, like lion fighting, and men fighting each other to the death. They even found some of the gladiators' swords and other things. The stadium was round so everybody had a good seat.

"They also dug up shops and stores, like a pottery shop, bakeries. In the shopping center they found fruit and other things like loaves of bread—they were preserved by the charring and ashes—things left by people when they ran away."

Ruby laughed. "Don't tell Oscar about that burnt bread or he'll claim it was some of my toast. I always forget the toast in the stove until you can smell it burnin'. Tell me where it was again, Jimmy."

"Pompeii. And I won't talk about the burnt bread."

Ruby was watching him with intense interest. "You so smart, Jim, to know what you know. Even Pam, my daughter that's Alexandra's momma, she's a teacher and she say you so smart." Jim blushed, but Ruby kept right on. "Pam say if she had a roomful of kids like you and Alexandra, she could plow through so much learnin' it would make your head swim. But she have to poke along so slow that the smart kid or two gets bored stiff."

She waved her arm in the air. "All them rich people in them towns that got buried. See what bein' rich got 'em? Nothin'. Rich is what me and Oscar is. And you folks, too, Jimmy." She laughed a deep laugh that made Jim laugh too. "They would sure cackle down at the First National hearin' me talk about how rich me and Oscar is, never makin' over six thousand dollars in any year of our lives. But if we got erupted on tomorrow morning, we would go to our maker satisfied that we were worthy human bein's that lived rich, happy lives. Didn't need no seashore, no house with, uh—no house with those posts and, uh—wha'd you call that fancy yard they had?"

"Courtyard," he said. "Their houses were built in a square with a courtyard in the center. There were no windows on the street. Everything opened to the courtyard."

"Yeah, courtyard. Maybe they thought rich was havin' a courtyard. But rich is never having to go to bed worryin' about some wrong you did to somebody, about some ugly thing you said to somebody, even if he deserve it. You can't ever take back an ugly word. If somebody deserve an ugly word from you and he don't get it, he's hurt worse, because now he's worryin' about why you didn't tell him off. Why you turned the other cheek."

She held up a warning finger, wagged it back and forth and shook her head, frowning significantly. "Now I ain't talkin' about robbers and such. You don't turn no cheek to them. I'd as soon shoot a robber as I'd step on a cockroach. I would, too, with Oscar's shotgun. But I'm just talking about plain old hateful people, like Old Man Skinner and all them crooked laws we had around here so long. Skinner can't hurt nobody no more, and his hateful old words ain't goin' to harm nobody that don't pay no 'tention to 'em. And those laws that used to torment us on the roads, giving us fines for nothin', they's off on regular jobs, now that Sheriff Mike took over.

"The rich people that got smothered to death that day so close to Jesus's time. They couldn't take none of their fine things with 'em, statues and fountains, not even that scorched bread they found. You goes out of this world lookin' like you come in, nekkid and without a penny to your name. But you goes out with the report card of everything you done when you was here. If that report card has mostly good things wrote on it, and the bad things ain't too, *too* bad, you'll go to Heaven. And they ain't nothin' on the good side of your report card of life about havin' a courtyard, neither. It's what you *done*.

"But they's more to it than that. If you do good things and don't do bad things you has a more peaceful time while you're here. Every night you git a good night's sleep without no tossin' and turnin'. You can say 'hello' to ever person you meets and mean it. And they ain't never anybody goin' to be sayin' bad things about you. Nobody on God's Earth can say one bad thing about Oscar Jackson, and I hope I can say the same about old Ruby, too.

"Me and Oscar believe that if we live our lives like we was lookin' over each other's shoulder, then we goin' to do good, ain't we?—to make each other proud." She looked straight at Jim. "We sure wouldn't do nothin' to bring hurt to the eyes of the other one lookin' over our shoulder, would we?"

He shook his head. "No ma'am. And I sure wouldn't want Mom or Dad seeing me do something I shouldn't do," he said, speaking softly and with sincerity.

"Good boy," she said, and looked down at him with genuine warmth. "They won't see you do nothin' bad if you don't do nothin' bad. Just play like your momma and daddy is watchin' every minute, not suspicious like, because they wouldn't have no notion of you doin' bad. But they's lookin' to see how proud you're makin' 'em." She laughed and put her arm around him. "I'd like you to think old Ruby's lookin' over your shoulder, too, and bein' so proud I could bust wide open." She laughed roundly at that wonderful idea and gave him a strong hug. Jim hugged her too, and they sat quietly for a time.

CHAPTER 7

Jim rode up just as his father was driving the tractor out of the hayfield. From high up on Old Black, he could see right across the big, fluffy rows of new-mown clover laid out neatly over the stubble ground and stirring lazily in the light breeze. Already, the clover was wilting fast and its delightful aroma was strong in the air. Old Black's nostrils were detecting it, too, Jim noticed. He petted the horse's big, muscular neck and said, "I'll bet you haven't seen a fresh-cut hayfield for a while. Smells good, don't it boy?"

With the tractor parked just outside the field, Matt closed the fence gap and asked, "So what did Oscar and Ruby have to say about Old Black?"

"They liked him a lot. And, Dad, did you know Mr. Jackson was a roper one time?" He described the events of his visit. "He said he'd be over to see you in the morning. He was amazed the clover was ready to cut."

Oscar Jackson's failure to notice that the field needed mowing was not a sign of neglect of his duty. All farm matters were decided by Matt Bradley. Most farmers cut hay so as to produce the most bales per acre, which *seemed* reasonable but it definitely was not.

From the County Agricultural Agent, Matt had obtained a stack of booklets on every aspect of raising cattle. One of the thickest was a manual on making hay put out by Texas A&M University. From it he learned to his surprise that the protein content for each variety of grass peaked at a certain stage of development, when it was still growing; as soon as it peaked, the protein content rapidly declined. He followed the book and sent off samples to Texas A&M for analysis. Sure enough, his hay tested very high in protein.

In their gatherings at Richter's store, farmers who had seen Matt making hay gossiped about his methods. Old Man Skinner called him a "briefcase farmer" who cut his hay way before it was ready. "Where he gets six hundred bales off that coastal field, it would make almost a thousand if he'd give it another couple of weeks."

Skinner had a strong dislike for Matt Bradley and often made the claim behind Matt's back that he had welshed on a deal between them. Before Matt had any haymaking equipment, Skinner, who was a dairy farmer and needed plenty of hay, had approached Matt about cutting his hay on halves. Skinner would cut and bale and he would stack Matt's share in the Bradley's barn.

After the very first cutting, Matt received signals that he was being swindled by Skinner. Oscar was reluctant to criticize the conduct of white men, but Ruby was not. Oscar had evidently told her that Skinner had put barely a hundred bales in the barn and took away over twice as many. Further, Oscar noticed that Matt's hay came from the outside edges of the field, where the weeds would be most plentiful. Ruby confided that intelligence to Matt.

Mr. Richter had also, in his diplomatic way, put Matt on notice that Skinner was to be watched very closely. "I would be there anytime he does anything," said Reinhard Richter, holding up a fat hand and rubbing thumb and forefinger together. But Matt could hardly be there when Skinner baled. Also, since he did not have any cows during that early period while he was getting the farm in shape, he figured he was not being injured too much by the loss of hay. At least he was getting the fields mowed.

But an incident the following spring was the last straw. Skinner cut the clover field and got his "half" baled and hauled away. But instead of baling and storing Matt's pitiful share in the barn, Skinner hurried over to another farmer's field and got his lion's share of *that* hay safely harvested. Then it started raining. Matt was not able to be at the farm the following weekend because of flight duty, but Jim and Norma described the clover hay lying in soggy windrows. When Matt did arrive a week later, Ruby was waiting for him. She came running down her lane, waving a dishtowel.

"Mister Bradley," she said indignantly, "you should have seen the beautiful hay Old Man Skinner hauled off your place by the wagonloads! Wagons stacked almost to tumpin' over with the prettiest clover hay you ever laid your eyes on. He could have finished, but he never come back before it come to pourin' down rain. And the creek come up over your clover field, mixing all kind of weeds and dregs with the hay that man done left in windrows. And doggone if he don't come back and bale that trash that Oscar would have burnt. And that black old mildewed mess is what's in your barn. Less than a hundred bales. Oscar say you better get that stuff out of there or it might burn your barn down."

On seeing the ugly, smelly mess, Matt decided on the spot to take the bales out in a field, break them up, and when the hay dried out to burn it. He said nothing to Skinner about the matter, but was astounded that Skinner could look him in the eye at Richter's store and engage him in idle talk with such an awful fraud standing between them. Skinner was a worse man than Matt had imagined.

Reinhard Richter had guardedly mentioned that Old Man Skinner was bragging about how he was cleaning up on the Matt Bradley deal; "harvesting Bradley" was the term Skinner had boastfully used. Matt nodded his understanding but said nothing. He had learned, too, that Skinner had struck similar arrangements with two other "briefcase farmers" from Houston. Thus encouraged, Skinner had bought a new tractor and hay-making equipment. He evidently believed that all farm owners from the city were devoid of any agricultural business sense, ignorance that would allow him to become the hay king of Winchester County, but Matt was leading him into a trap.

Matt had quietly assembled a vibrant little company in partnership with his co-pilot, Vincent Tedesco. The company owned several small businesses and was doing very well. They had just sold off one of the companies, leaving Matt with a respectable amount of cash and a note that would provide additional income for several years.

He explained to Norma that before stocking the farm with cattle, he wanted to spend a considerable sum on the machinery needed to make hay efficiently and to plant winter pastures. The balance from the business sale was hers to put in their investment accounts. Norma Bradley knew her husband, knew that he would have thoroughly investigated his equipment needs; she wholeheartedly approved of the plan.

One weekend Matt had driven the pickup to Houston to haul

tree trimmings from their home to the farm, where he could burn them. The trimmings were heaped high in the pickup bed, then tightly tied down in a compact mass. Matt and Jim decided that on their way to the farm they would swing by Richter's store to get some of Mrs. Winklemann's homemade porkskin cracklings, delivered fresh and hot every Saturday morning.

Old Man Skinner was at the store when they pulled in. Nosey as always, he came out to investigate what they might be hauling. When Matt and Jim emerged with their precious cracklings, Skinner asked what they had in the truck.

"Hay," said Matt.

Skinner looked perplexed. "Hay?" He looked closer, scowled and dug into the mass. "Awful sorry-looking hay, to my way of thinking. By the way, I noticed that your coastal's getting ready for cutting. I'll be getting on it in a week or so."

"Oh, no," Matt said, turning to caress his "hay." "It's not all that sorry. In fact, it's better than the last hay you put in my barn." He then turned to face the contemptuous man and smiled broadly. "Mr. Skinner," he said pleasantly, "this afternoon, Winchester County Tractor Company is delivering a new Ford 5000 tractor and hay-making equipment that I bought. I'll be doing my own hay-making from here on. Have you left anything on my place? A rake, pitchfork, hay hooks, anything?"

"Well—no—" said Skinner, speaking hesitantly. His mouth hung open in bewilderment, as if he couldn't comprehend Matt's words.

"Then you have no reason to come on my place," Matt said mildly. "If you want to visit, of course you're welcome, but call Mr. Jackson beforehand to make sure I'm there. Otherwise, the dog—" Matt left unsaid what the fearsome dog might do.

Out of the corner of his eye, Matt saw the image of Reinhard Richter's head pressed close to the screen door of his store. Everyone in the north end of the county would hear this conversation now, one that would be embellished with each telling.

Skinner was so contemptuous of city farmers that he could not believe they had sense enough to discover he was taking up to three-fourths of each crop, and the best hay in the fields on top of that. He hardly acknowledged to himself he was doing it. But almost anybody who had accumulated the financial means to buy a farm was intelligent enough to soon see through his outrageous notion of "halves." So it was never long before he lost the haying arrangements he cultivated.

"His crawfishing out of a done deal left me in a helluva bind," he whined to Richter and the small gathering in attendance one evening. "Now I got all that equipment I don't need, and I still have the payments."

"Why don't you sue him?" asked Richter, hardly able to keep a straight face.

Skinner's eyes shot sideways at Richter, looking for signs that he was being played with. Richter seemed to be innocently weighing bags of cracklings, so Skinner continued his wailing. "Everybody *knows* his lawyer is the county judge. And how would any papers ever get served in this county against a city slicker who broke every campaign contribution law there is to get a Meskin—a nigger-loving Meskin—elected sheriff?" He held up a hand with two fingers tight together. "Martinez is like that with the constable, so your papers would sit in his office until they grew a beard."

Reinhard had no idea how a person might get that done, he said mournfully, adding piously, "I just turn the other cheek to all this oppression and pray for the good old days to come back, when you could buy the sheriff and constable off with fifty bucks and a side of bacon." Skinner's eyes narrowed in a mean expression. After a few seconds he slowly turned and poured a penetrating, suspicious look at Richter, who was now busily stocking shelves. Still unable to decide if he was being played upon, he sniffed and stalked from the store.

WITH MATT'S BIG FORD DIESEL TRACTOR providing all the power the hay-cutting machine needed, it could move swiftly through the clover, leaving a nine-foot swath of stubble and a loose windrow of conditioncd hay in its wake. Singlehandedly, Matt could lay down his four acres of thick clover hay in a few hours. The machine conditioned the hay as it mowed it down, crushing the stems and ridding them of their abundant moisture. Conditioning speeded up the curing process and allowed baling before the leaves were completely dry.

"Conditioned hay is *cured*, not dried out," he explained to Jim. "The old way of haymaking was to cut the hay and let it lie there until it was dry enough to bale. By the time the stems had dried enough, the leaves would shatter in your hand. Drying hay to that extent robbed it of a lot of its nutrients. If you baled with the moisture in the stems, the hay would get moldy. It could even catch on fire by spontaneous combustion—many a barn has burned down that way. And the time it took for hay to dry exposed it to more of a chance of rain.

"With the equipment we have, we can cut one day, let it cure the next, then bale the following morning after the dew is off."

Bradley's clover and Johnson grass hay regularly tested to 18 percent protein. He had several times reached 20 percent with the coastal bermuda. The testers at Texas A&M said they seldom saw protein contents in those ranges except for hay produced on A&M's own Pasture and Forage Department test fields. Matt was routinely producing hay that contained more protein than the best mixed livestock grain feed, which was twelve-percent protein.

He told Jim, "A cow could starve to death standing knee deep in six-percent hay; it won't even feed the rumen's organisms that digest food. Protein is what cows thrive on, the rest is fiber. So we want to store as much protein and as little fiber as possible. Filled with good hay, our barn holds about *fourteen tons* of protein. With poor hay we'd be lucky to have five tons.

"That's why Duffie can throw out fifteen bales of hay a day to seventy momma cows during the winter. With that, and the controlled green grazing that we *always* have, our cows winter just fine while some farmers' cows come out of winter looking awfully poor—I've wondered how some of them produce milk for their calves. And we've never even come close to using half our hay in any winter. That allows us to feed hay freely during summer dry spells to conserve green grazing. And we still have hay to sell when the price goes sky high."

Matt put his hands on his hips and gazed over the windrows. The first hay crop of the year always gave him a feeling of exhilaration. There was still a lot of little boy in him when it came to this farm, with so many opportunities for superior achievement. He turned toward the tractor. "Race you to the barn," he said with a grin that showed defeat before the race even started.

When Jim had climbed the rise enough to see the parking area in front of the barn, he was rewarded with the sight of his mother's car there. He leaned slightly forward and Old Black accelerated from a lope to a dead run.

From her perch on the corral fence Norma Bradley had seen

the little horseman and Matt together at the tractor. Now she saw his bandanna waving back and forth, heard his faint shouts, "Hi, Mom," as he came. She met him with a smile of absolute approval. His own was impossible to widen as he slowly turned Old Black around and around for her inspection. "Mom, this is Old Black. We found out he's the world's champion calf-roping horse."

"Beautiful!" she exclaimed. "Is he really the world champion? Oh, Jim, I'm so proud you have such a fine horse. And look at that saddle. Where did you get the saddle, the bridle—?" She held her palms out shoulder high, questioning.

"From Mr. Jones. He threw in everything. Even brushes, curry combs, a halter, a stable blanket for on the road in winter time, and some feed and protein supplement. Oh, and two bottles of Absorbine." Jim had dismounted and gave his mother a hug. "Thanks for the best birthday present I ever could get, Mom. Meet Old Black."

Norma Bradley was not a tall woman, but not petite, either. She was trim and carried herself straight, head high, which gave her a tinge of an elegant air and made her appear taller than she was. She had self-assurance to spare and fairly radiated it. Jim had inherited her pleasant personality and some of her features, but not her dark red hair or fair complexion—she was rarely outside without a big hat on her head.

Norma looked well-dressed in almost everything, prompting some acquaintances to believe she had a large and expensive wardrobe. She did not. In fact, she prided herself on how little she spent on clothing. Today she was wearing a denim skirt, and under a denim vest she wore a blouse made out of two blue cowboy bandannas. Her bandanna blouse never failed to draw nice comments. She had spiffed up the vest with colorful red, yellow, and blue embroidery. Around her waist was a sash fashioned by rolling up a red bandanna, which complimented the bandanna blouse while adding a sporty look and another splash of color. Her denim tennis shoes had been pepped up with some of the same threads used on the vest. It was an attractive ensemble that she had put together for less than forty dollars.

She was a happy person, friendly and outgoing. She almost never showed any anger; rarely did she speak of another with disapproval. In the rare instances that she became irritated, it was with good cause, and her cool, penetrating verbal sparring skills could be pure torture to her opponent.

Norma Bradley's husband and her boy were the keystones of her life. She was keenly protective of Jim and exercised her motherly responsibilities with careful deliberation. But she did so with such a delicate hand that her actions were not evident. To her, the tightly-knit Bradley family was protected by a moat against the perils that threatened every family in today's society, and she was the keeper of the drawbridge over the moat.

It was she who engineered the environment that presently surrounded Jim's life. He had friends and acquaintances at school, but they socialized little because he studied during the week and was at the farm almost every weekend and holiday. On occasion he had brought friends from Houston along, but not often because he discovered that they simply did not fit in here in the country where there was always work to be done. Even when his father said he could take the day off to show hospitality to his visitors, he insisted on working more than he should have. He had not invited any friends in a long time.

Alexandra Meridith, Oscar and Ruby Jackson's adorable thirteen-year-old granddaughter, was Jim's closest friend. Alexandra was stunningly pretty; she was intelligent and always cheerful. Norma claimed Alexandra's voice could only be described as musical, and in addition to the pleasing sound of her voice, she spoke with pure eloquence. It was evident how her speech had caused Jim to improve his own. He dearly enjoyed her company and because she lived close by, they visited each other frequently. Alexandra's father welcomed Jim, sometimes engaging him in long, leisurely conversations on many subjects as Jim watched spellbound as Mr. Meridith worked his magic in clay.

Norma had consciously sought to arrange his life so that Jim was more or less prevented from being close to other young people until he could identify worthy ones from the unworthy. To enable him to develop a discerning mind, his parents set examples and got him involved in activities that attracted good kids, like the 4-H club and the American Quarter Horse Association's youth group. His parents constantly demonstrated to Jim that those who live life by the highest standards and associate with others of the same caliber will be happy and realize big rewards throughout their lives.

She theorized that by the time Jim was of an age when he could no longer be kept on a tight rein—when her strategy would no longer be functional—he would have become discriminating. She was happy that he was attracted to Alexandra Meridith, pleased that he recognized her admirable character.

NORMA HAD BEEN TO MANY HORSE SHOWS and had studied Quarter Horse conformation right along with her son. After an examination of Old Black, she cried, "Oh, Jim. He's the prettiest horse! And I saw how easy you rode him. Look at that shoulder, and those forearms. His chest is so powerful! Won't Oscar and Ruby be surprised? And Alexandra! Do they know about him yet?"

"I rode over to the Jackson's and showed them Old Black. Mr. Jackson took my lariat and roped Mrs. Jackson's turkey-chopping stump from quite a ways off. Did you know he used to be a roper? He really liked Old Black, and his saddle; he could tell it was a real roping saddle. He wanted to know why the owner would sell his horse and saddle if he was rodeoing with him."

"Why *was* the man selling the horse, Jim?" she asked. A tiny wrinkle appeared on her forehead.

Jim's expression darkened and she was immediately aware that she had asked a sensitive question. She knew his tender heart, that he would anguish over someone else's misfortune. "I don't know why, Mom. Ask Dad." He brightened. "Come to the tack room—we used to call it the feed room, but it's really a tack room now." He led Old Black with his mother walking along on the other side. She talked to the horse and patted his neck briskly as they walked.

Jim removed the breast strap and released the cinches; then he positioned the horse outside the door and dragged the saddle and blanket off his back. He put the saddle on the rack and threw the blanket onto a feed box.

"Take the reins and move him so you can come in," he said to his mother. Then he added with some authority, "Then just drop the reins on the ground. That will ground hitch him."

When she was inside, he showed her the saddle, with its thick, hand-tooled leather skirts and fleece lining. He pointed out the big roping horn and its rawhide reinforcing. Caressing the saddle, he said, "See how it shines, Mom. Isn't it some saddle?"

"Jim, it's a much finer saddle than we could ever have afforded to buy. I've heard what some of these high-end saddles cost, prices that would scare wealthy people. Well . . . and you got a lariat too?" She fingered the rope still hanging from its strap on the saddle.

"Mr. Jones just gave it to me, right at the last minute. He picked it out special from several others. It's a thirty-five-foot heeling rope. He said I should never be without a lariat. Mr. Jackson is going to show me how to throw a loop, and then I have to practice, practice, practice." Thoughtfully, he ran his hand over the lariat. "I sure hope Mr. Jones isn't sick or anything," he said with grave sincerity.

He was still grim when he removed the saddle to expose the rack for her inspection. "Mom, I'm going to brush Old Black down. I'll be back in a minute. While I'm gone, look at this saddle rack. Dad said it looked like a piece of furniture. And look at those pegs. I know you'll recognize them." He grabbed a brush and jumped to the ground outside the tack room.

She was examining the pegs when he returned. He put the saddle on its rack and said, "Don't you think those pegs look just like the ones in the chifforobe? I told Dad I bet the same man made them."

She looked at them closely, felt the carved features. "There's no doubt about it. None whatever. I suppose he made the saddle racks too. What's this?"

"Blanket rack," he said, stepping up on a bucket and putting his saddle blanket on it. "See, it's made with slots, to air the blanket out. Isn't this a great tack room?"

"It is indeed, Jim. I've never really looked around in here."

"Mom, I have to put Old Black in the pasture. Be back in two minutes," he said, and he was gone.

She said again, aloud, "I've never really looked around in here." She looked now, touching, feeling the workmanship of the blanket racks, the unoccupied saddle rack, the feed bins. Her sharp eye fell on the long, carefully made shelf that held the brushes, curry combs, Absorbine, and other things. Her fingers ran along its carved edges, softened by the careful hand of some proud and skilled workman so many decades ago. "Imagine someone caring so much about what a shelf in a barn would look like!" She spoke softly, as if describing the details of the room to someone standing nearby.

She lifted the lid of a feed box. "They made things to work and to last. Just imagine, a wooden feed box lined with metal. These nice lids with the hinges set in so carefully. Yes, it is like furniture." She leaned way into the feed bin and picked up a feed scoop. "And these scoops, so well made. Today people use barrels for feed and coffee cans to dip with. This is all so much prettier, and it's lasted a hundred years."

She put her hands on her hips and turned around, taking in the room. "Yes, this is a beautiful tack room." Jim bounded into the room without using the step.

Norma held up a cautious finger and said, "Jim, you must call Alexandra. She knows by now you have a horse, because Ruby knows. But you should personally call her. She'll be so *happy*. She's been dying for you to have a horse . . ." She looked around the room. "It's getting dark in here."

About thirty yards west of the Bradley house was a deep wooded draw that spanned both the Bradley and Richter places. The sun had already slipped behind the tall trees along the draw when Jim and his mother walked to the house. Matt was standing on the porch barefoot, wearing jeans topped off with a white tee shirt decorated with a colorful logo for "Bradley's Ale House, Perth Australia." He had a towel in his hand and his hair was wet from the shower. "Hi, honey," he said. "What do you think of our new horse?"

She said without equivocation what she thought of wonderful, majestic, gorgeous Old Black. When she reached the porch he put his arms around her waist and lifted her off the floor, swinging her in a gentle circle. She lifted her feet up and clung tightly to him. He kissed her lightly and put her down. "Us farm workers are out of gas. *Hungry*. What does the chef have to report on menu possibilities?"

"The chef is out of the mood. Headache, that's it," she said, and threw Matt a significant, devilish smile. "Let's celebrate Old Black by splurging on a chicken-fried steak at Mrs. Schumann's Country Steakhouse. I'll buy—paying with your check of course, hee, hee."

"Boy oh boy!" Jim cried. His eyes rolled toward his mother. "Do you know what I like best on a chicken fried steak?"

"Of course I do," she said assuredly. "Cream gravy."

Jim was shaking his head before she finished speaking. "No, that's second. What I like best on a chicken-fried steak is *my teeth!*" His expression became serious. "Mom, can we invite Alexandra?"

"Of course we can," she replied. "Then, before Jim could react, she added, pointing a finger at him, "You go shower. I'll call

Alexandra. Matt, I think we should invite her parents, too. I'll tell them the late notice is due to this being a spur-of-the-moment thing to celebrate the coming of Old Black."

When Jim appeared, barefooted and struggling into a tee shirt, she said, "Andrew said Alexandra is visiting at her aunt's in La Grange until Sunday evening. He invited you over Monday morning, and he said he hopes you'll let him ride your new horse."

Jim said, "Shucks. I was going to ride Old Black over there tomorrow." He brightened. "Sure he can ride Old Black. Can I can go over Monday? Mom? Dad?"

His mother gave an indifferent shrug. "Fine with me." Everything reasonable was fine with Mom, he thought happily.

"We have to bale that clover hay Monday, Jim," Matt said. "But that won't take, ummmm, maybe four hours. Tell you what. Let's figure on starting the hay baling about eleven. You can ride over and visit Alexandra before we have to go to work. Okay?"

"Fine and dandy," Jim said as he trotted off to feed Old Black. When he returned they got in the car and headed for Mrs. Schumann's Country Steakhouse.

CHAPTER 8

Jim was up before the sun. Moving about silently, he slipped on a pair of jeans and a shirt. A hurried stop in the bathroom, some water splashed on his face, and a quick hair-combing held him up another thirty seconds before he slipped softly from the house carrying his boots and socks. Matt had once spoken to Norma about the efficiency of kids. "I recall when I could get up and be out of the house in less than a minute, like Jim. Why do us grownups spend so much time getting ready? Especially—" Intimidated by Norma's cocked and primed index finger, aimed straight at his heart, the word "women" remained unsaid.

Sam slept on the enclosed back porch. Today she roused on hearing, feeling, sensing Jim's movements, and with her head down and tail waving lazily she arrived at the front steps where he was pulling on his boots. She went into a prolonged stretch, ending it with a mighty contraction of her body that left claw marks in the turf. Then she luxuriated in a long yawn that displayed a formidable set of white teeth and a pink tongue that was long and lively, all the while voicing a weak, drawn-out "Eee-yoow-lll." Moving lethargically on stiff legs, she came to Jim for a pat.

"You gonna make it, Sam?" he asked in a voice pretending grave concern. He took her head between his hands and rubbed briskly. "I know what ails you, Sam. You feel like mashed potatoes when you get up sometimes, just like me on school days."

Sam's head cocked left, then right, brow rippling and furrowing. Her big brown eyes fixed on Jim's face, looking every bit like she was trying very hard to understand him. He scratched at her chin; up went her nose to expose her throat to his caressing fingers.

"You're a good girl, Sam," he said, giving her a few solid pats.

"Why don't you run down and bring Old Black up?" Sam promptly sat down. Jim grinned at her and walked to the gate, scanning the bottom pasture for Old Black. He climbed onto the top rail of the fence, steadying himself with an arm around the gatepost. Slivers of sunlight peeped through the trees on the ridge. Parked low in the eastern sky was a lonely gathering of bright yellow clouds with silvery linings. They bounced the sun's first rays down to earth, lighting up the delicate dusting of dew on the grass in the bottom, giving it the appearance of a dazzling blanket of frost.

Once on a miserably hot summer day, Jim had sat with elbows on the window sill, chin in hands, looking out of the kitchen window. His gaze fell on a field of Johnson grass standing parched brown by the drought that plagued the countryside that year. A gentle breeze began flowing up the hill, pushing, pushing, pushing the sea of grass in endless waves. Jim had let his mind recall the same scene often observed in the wintertime when the grass was always dead; then he imagined it *was* winter. Soon he found himself chilled by the cold vision he had summoned up.

That incident was a great discovery of mental power and he had built upon it often to play even more elaborate mind games. The sun struggling through a thin overcast on a summer day, scarcely able to cast more than the impression of a shadow, could easily be transformed into a weak winter sun, for a moment. It was no effort at all to mentally convert a scattering of puffy cumulus clouds, scooting briskly along in a cold and windy winter sky, to the clouds of a fine balmy summer day.

His most functional use of his imaginative powers was applied one day when he and his father were hauling hay in from the field. With a few dozen bales still to go, Jim was so tired that the muscles in his arms and shoulders were burning and refusing to lift another bale onto the hay wagon. Making an effort to conceal his weariness from his father, he had privately turned away with his arms hanging relaxed at his sides. Then he closed his eyes and concentrated for a long, long moment on the feeling that he was refreshed after a nice rest. The exercise had revitalized him just enough to carry him through to the completion of the job.

On this morning as he stood on the top rail of the fence looking for Old Black he imagined the shiny whiteness of the dew on the grass down in the bottom was frost. Concentrating on the sparkling field transformed the morning into a chilly winter day. A cold wave passed over him and he shivered; goosebumps came on his arms. He smiled with satisfaction over the achievement.

The morning sounds of the country, not piercing like the city racket, were always comforting to him. As his eyes searched for Old Black, he suspected that he too, being a city horse, appreciated the pleasant lowing of the cows, the bawling of their calves—who had nothing to bawl about—the far-off barking of a dog, Mrs. Jackson's rooster greeting the sunrise . . . . The distant howl of an eighteen-wheeler going through the gears up the grade on the Rip Ford Highway reached his ears intermittently. His eyes roamed across the broad flat of the pasture, from one side to the other, across the scattered grazing cows. Old Black was not among them.

He expanded his search, confident he would discover the horse standing near a tree or somewhere in the treeline gloom. With his free hand shielding his eyes from the rapidly brightening eastern sky, he began a more orderly search of the pasture, scrutinizing every nook from the far left of the tree line along the creek and peering into the deep shadows of the outermost trees. Slowly, methodically he searched every place where Old Black might be standing unnoticed. He examined the murkiness beneath the pecan trees, the scattered patches of the low bois d'arc trees. Then he looked once more among the cattle. Old Black wasn't there.

A feeling of dread was fast overcoming his belief that the horse was down there where he was supposed to be, in a pasture enclosed with sturdy barbed-wire fences. Anxiety began to tighten its grip on his throat. Could Old Black have become frightened of this unfamiliar place during the night and somehow gotten out?

His hands were trembling as he climbed down from the fence. Before asking his father for help, Jim decided to run far enough over the hill so he could see the one place not visible from where he stood: where the hillside met the bottom.

The trees along the top of the ridge had lost their grip on the sun and a broad, molten glob above the treetops warmed Jim as he scrambled to the ground. Just as he was breaking into a run, he heard a strong, deep neighing. He stopped in mid-stride, whirled around, and there was Old Black! All that time, he'd been standing only ten yards behind Jim. His head was extended far out over the rail and he seemed to be wondering why he was being ignored. Sam sat sedately outside the fence, her face a blank mask as she ignored Jim and looked straight ahead at nothing. To Jim, her behavior was nothing less than a crafty disguise, a cover-up of her role in a practical joke.

"Wh—why, Black, there you are!" Jim cried, scrambling back over the gate. "You had me scared. And you've been watching me the whole time, laughing I bet." He spoke in his sternest voice, but any sign of reproach was betrayed by an undisguised note of relief. Reaching the corral, he stroked Old Black's face, then scratched under his jaw.

"Just for being here waiting for me I'll give you a bite, a treat." Sam trotted along with him to the tack room. He looked down on Sam with a scowl. "You could have said something, Sam, instead of sitting there like a dummy while I looked for him," he scolded.

Old Black nickered soft and low and long as Jim reappeared with a scoop of Omolene. He crowded Jim from behind all the way to the feed trough. His nose was waiting greedily when the first grains landed, his big lips scooping the feed into his mouth. Chewing, he turned his head to look at Jim, his eyes expressing gratitude, grains of feed falling from his mouth to the ground. In a moment his head was back above the feed trough. "Attaboy, Black," Jim said approvingly. "If you're going to drop feed, let it fall where you can get it back."

He let out a deep breath and stroked the horse's neck. "If Dad doesn't have something for me to do, I'll saddle you up in little while and we'll go see if Buddy is here yet."

He leaned against a support post that held up the extension of the barn's roof, daydreaming of coming adventures. His eyes fell on a spider web twinkling silvery in the morning sun. "Wow, Charlotte, you really have a pretty web this morning," he said while walking over.

Charlotte's superb webs were things to marvel over; this one was a vast spectacle made more dazzling by thousands of liquid crystals, tiny drops of dew encrusting the delicate strands like shimmering diamonds. A third of the web was in shadow. Jim theorized that Charlotte's strategy was to draw a fly's attention to the obvious display, causing it to unwittingly detour into the strands that were lying in shadow. She had made a good catch, he noticed.

Even as he watched, a fly, an early riser, flew right into the camou-flaged area of the web and was snared. "Ha!" he exclaimed. "Drygulched him for sure, didn't you?"

He watched Charlotte's web billow with an unfelt movement of air, then promptly balloon in the other direction. Then came a light breeze that filled it like a taut sail until it seemed it had to break under the strain, but Jim had never known her web to fail, even in a strong wind. "Where are you, Charlotte?" he called. When he saw her creeping out from behind the wood brace that formed an anchor for one side of her web, he threw a look at Old Black, "Don't come over here and walk through Charlotte's web, boy. She's part of the family around here."

He heard his mother's "Yoo hoo, Ji-uumm" and went running to the house for breakfast. "Don't you run off," he shouted over his shoulder to Old Black.

He took two pancakes, two eggs and three pieces of bacon from the platter his mother held before him. Long ago he had noticed that they always had big country breakfasts at the farm and skimpy city breakfasts in town; his mother claimed they did enough work on the farm to use up the calories.

"Did you hear Mehitabel's maneuvers last night?" Jim asked. "Mehitabel's maneuvers" were the nighttime sessions during which the farm's cat trained her kittens to hunt live game.

Mehitabel was as untamed as any creature in the wild. Yellow with dark tiger stripes, she had appeared out of nowhere one day, taking up residence in the attic of the house, coming and going through a hole she created by tearing off a wood shingle. When Matt replaced one shingle, she'd just tear off another, so he had decided to leave her alone. One missing shingle couldn't let in much rain, and Mehitabel had demonstrated her worth in a short time by slaughtering the mice that had been eating holes in the bags of feed in the feed room.

Matt had named her after the cat in *Archie and Mehitabel*, a book Jim had read at his father's urging. The Bradley's Mehitabel was a romantic lady of the night, much as the fictional one, and therefore was rarely without a litter of kittens.

Where she found her mates was a mystery, as well as almost everything else about her. At some point very early in her kittens' lives, she began teaching them how to catch their own food. In her classes she used mice and birds she'd caught and then crippled before she placed them before her young for practice, so the inexperienced hunters would have a sporting chance. Their scrambling after the doomed mice and birds—the "maneuvers"— caused a commotion in the attic and always seemed to take place in the wee hours.

So many mouths to feed and teach to hunt kept Mehitabel constantly on the prowl for food and practice subjects. Within a year of her arrival she had so thoroughly rid the entire hilltop of mice that she could often be seen slinking down in the Johnson grass pasture, constantly expanding the demilitarized zone around the house.

Barney, the old king snake that had lived in a hole in the dirt floor of the hay barn for years, was so deprived of mice to eat that he had to pack up and find a new home. About six feet long, Barney had scared the daylights out of Jim before Duffie explained that he was good to have around. "He catches mice. And old Barney wouldn't hurt a body to save his life."

His mother had not heard the maneuvers last night, she said, probably because Mehitabel preferred to conduct them over Jim's end of the house.

Matt passed his napkin over his mouth. "With the hay baling coming up tomorrow, I don't think we need to set out any serious work schedule today. What are your plans, Jim?"

The boy looked at his plate, thinking fast. He had a lot in mind to do today. Little of it had been actually thought out, and all of it involved Old Black. He was going to see Buddy and take him horseback riding. Then he thought he might do some exploring down Hickory Creek. He reasoned that there should be some work in his schedule somewhere, though, and cleaning the tack room was in his plans. "First, I thought I would give the tack room a good cleaning. I didn't notice how dirty it was in there until yesterday. Then Buddy is coming to the Jackson's and I want to give him a ride on Old Black." He looked brightly from his father to his mother and then added cautiously, "Unless you have some plans for me."

Norma Bradley's chin was propped up by her hand, a serene smile on her face. Looking at Jim, she said, "When something needs cleaning around the house, nobody notices it but me. But now that Jim has put something valuable in the old feed room it has become an elegant *tack* room, and a tack room must be kept sparkling clean." Then she leaned forward and patted his hand approvingly. "Jim, I'm proud that you decided your tack room needs cleaning. I'll get you set up with some janitorial supplies. How's that for support from headquarters?"

Jim liked to watch his mother when she talked. He did not know another kid who had a mom near as pretty. Her voice was pleasant and she had a way of holding her head up and cocked slightly to the side when she was being frisky, which was often. He sometimes imagined he could see the perfect words fall gently from her lips.

He didn't answer, but just sat staring at her with a dreamy look on his face. After many seconds had gone by, she passed a palm before his eyes in a manner intended to break his spell. "Are you with us, Jimmy boy?"

He jerked to awareness. "Mom, you talk so pretty. I just like to watch you talk," he said.

Laughing, she took his chin in her hand and shook his head gently, playfully. "Do I talk so pretty that you can't listen at the same time? But I like being told I talk pretty—I just might like it more than being listened to. If you're about to ask for something, Jim, anything whatever, the answer is yes."

He grinned sheepishly and was silent.

Matt watched the exchange with a grin on his face. A moment of silence passed, and then he sat bolt upright. "Gosh," he said. "We haven't even made our inspection, but I guess I've lost my inspection partner. I have no plans for you at all today, Jim. I would say you deserve to spend the whole day with your horse affairs."

Jim's bright expression faded into a gray mask with the realization that he had thoughtlessly overlooked a ritual they had never missed. Even when his father was away on a flight Jim made the farm tours by himself, with his mother, or with Duffie, carefully noting every important condition in the book. Matt and Jim had even donned raincoats and boots and made their tours during glorious rains.

The tours never failed to reward them with discoveries that went beyond observing the state of the pasture grasses and the condition of the soil. During the springtime, they usually found a new calf, sometimes several—there was nothing more adorable to Jim than a brand-new calf, standing knock-kneed on unsteady legs, the white tip of its tail whipping nervously about as it cringed timidly in the sanctuary of its momma's flank. Wildflowers would be blossoming along the fence lines and in the woods; the unknowns they would try to identify from their *Texas Wildflowers* book when they got back to the house. When the signs pointed to an abundance of blackberries, there was rejoicing over the cobblers and pies in their future. They often saw deer and other wildlife, occasionally a fox or coyote, and once even a wolf. And one or the other always wrote all of this down in the book.

The realization that he had forgotten all about the tour caused a sad ache to sweep through his body.

"Oh, no, Dad," he said quickly. "I didn't mean before the tour. I intend to clean the tack room after—"

Norma stopped him with an upraised hand. She had seen the gray veil descend on Jim's face. She often cringed inside over the little pains he suffered thinking he had hurt the feelings of another.

She said, "Matt, I want to go in Jim's place today. I haven't been on a walking tour in quite a while. Can we go down to the creek?" She clapped her hands together and described what she hoped to see—dogwoods in blossom, the blackberry vines, baby calves; she wanted to sit on the bridge with her feet dangling in the spray of the rushing water, and she *had* to smell the new clover hay.

"I want to come," Jim said in a somber voice, his eyes on his plate. "We can all make the tour."

Norma was ready for his response and had prepared a little verbal ambush. "No, you can't come," she said emphatically, an impish smile playing on her lips and in her eyes. "Matt and I are going to play on the creek bank. We just might want to hold hands and whisper little secrets to each other without your big ears snooping from the bushes."

Jim's hand went to his mouth to contain an outburst of snickering. "Aaa-ummm," he teased, pointing an accusatory finger at one and then the other.

Norma Bradley had once again snatched a mantle of distress from the shoulders of her little boy.

CHAPTER 9

Cleaning house country-style was something Jim had learned from his mother. First, he flung handfuls of water from the pail onto the tack room floor to hold down the dust. After he swept a big pile of moist dirt and feed into an old metal dustpan, he walked several paces away from the barn to dump it.

With the big long-bristled paint brush, he dusted off the saddle and blanket racks, getting into every crevice. Standing on an upturned five-gallon bucket, he dusted everything as high as he could reach.

Then he wet the rag, wrung it out and wiped down the racks, the shelf, and the pegs. He restored the saddle and blanket to their racks, then wiped off the Absorbine bottles and the other supplies before lining it all up in a nice display on the shelf.

He sprinkled down the floor and swept again, collecting quite a bit of new dust. It was then that he smiled with the realization that he should have tackled the floor last, not first. However, the moist dust had served as a sweeping compound and the multiple sweepings had scoured the wood until it shone. He noticed the rich color of the wood and its grain now, beautifully sculptured by a hundred years of traffic.

Sweeping up and removing the remnants of feed in the feed bins was the most tedious job. He had to stand on the five-gallon bucket and hang from his waist upside down to reach the bottom.

Finished at last, he looked around, feeling a sweet satisfaction from what he saw. A narrow slash of the mid-morning sun angled through the doorway. It landed with dazzling brightness on the white bags of feed supplement stacked against the wall, flooding the room with light. Sunbeams floated lazily in the air. The unused saddle rack shone with a dark golden hue in the places with the most wear, and a deep warm amber elsewhere. His saddle, sitting on its rack, completed what could have been a beautiful picture from *Western Horseman* magazine.

The whole room, further dressed up by everything in it, was warm and inviting: the richness of the leather and the contrasting bright colors of the blankets, the shelf decorated with brushes and supplies, the articles of tack hanging from the pegs, and the sculptured boards of the floor.

He tried to imagine what the room had looked like in the days when people went everywhere on horseback or in wagons and buggies. The Bradleys had learned from local tales that the original Rosenbaum house was one large room. In 1896 it had been expanded to its present size and the barn was built soon after. Jim and his mother, wondering when automobile transportation might have become common, had learned from the encyclopedia that Henry Ford showed off his first car the same year: 1896.

Jim's father had speculated that country roads could not have been passable by cars or trucks in wet weather for decades after cars became common in the towns. "League Line Road is a gravel road even today," Matt reminded them. "Horses and mules could pull wagons along the muddy roads that no truck could travel.

"I suspect that transportation for the original Rosenbaums was horseback or horse-drawn as long as they lived. We'll have to ask Oscar about the history of transportation around here."

WHILE JIM WAS REGARDING THE SATISFYING RESULTS of his work, Matt and Norma sat on the limestone bridge over Hickory Creek, his arm around her waist, their bare feet swinging back and forth above the fast, cold water.

"Jim is so thrilled with Old Black," Norma said. "How did Mr. Bonner ever *find* such a horse? And why did the man sell him? When I asked Jim, he clammed up and said to ask you."

Matt stared at the flow of the creek below, watching the roiling surface against the bank as one might stare into a fire. "I'm pretty sure that Buck Jones, the man we bought Old Black from— you should've met him, Sweetheart, a genuine cowboy from out of the old west and a real decent guy. I hate to even think it, but I'm afraid Buck has cancer. He let it slip that he had been spending some time at M.D. Anderson hospital lately, and cancer is their only specialty, you know. And he said that he'd been looking forward to his first hundred-thousand-dollar year, but apparently he quit for good after competing in Houston in March."

Matt looked at her and said solemnly, "Sweetheart, he just oozed with love for Old Black. It would have broken your heart to see that man keep up a lighthearted outer shell knowing he would probably never see his old pal again. I watched him in the mirror as we drove away. He was leaning against a big tree by the road, watching us go, and he stood there as long as I could see him. He looked positively forlorn, and I'm sure he was. But now I know he was happy, too—I just *know* it."

Matt fell silent and squeezed her hand. "Anyway," he continued, in a voice that was back to normal now, "we were at the right place at the right time." He glanced at her and squinted his eyes. "Actually, it's only now that I can see that *everybody* was at the right place at the right time. Mr. Bonner had known Buck a long time, and Old Black too. I knew Buck had learned from Mr. Bonner some things about us, about Jim anyway, and that we had a farm. Buck brought that up on his own, had me tell him all about our place. He fairly fell for Jim right away . . . and Jim fairly fell for Buck Jones, too.

"You should have seen him show Jim the horse, like he was showing away to a halter judge. Believe me, Buck was seriously impressed with the way Jim looked the horse over." Matt's head bobbed sharply. "Seriously impressed. And he wasn't the only one.

"He put Jim on the horse and he could tell right away that Jim had a light hand, which was important to Buck. Then he just turned him loose on Old Black and hustled me into the house for a cup of coffee to let them get acquainted." Matt gave Norma a look of surprise. "I didn't know Jim could ride as well as he can. He and Old Black were practicing keyhole races before we left there."

Another period of silence passed. "I don't mind saying I liked the man then as much as Jim did. And yesterday afternoon something came up that just—well, I couldn't have more respect for a man today than I do for Buck Jones. He was going to take care of Old Black's future. That was his plan, and that's what he did."

Norma was patient. She noted that Matt was having to measure his words, that his emotions were very close to the surface. She felt it would be best if she kept staring into the creek, without speaking, without looking at him.

"I was reluctant to even go clear across town to see an eighteen-year-old horse. But Mr. Bonner had described Old Black as an ideal horse for Jim, spoke of Buck in the highest way, and he's not exactly lavish with praise about people. As I look back on it, Bonner kind of diplomatically nudged me into going to look at the horse."

Matt watched some floating twigs and leaves that were drifting slowly toward them. They gathered speed as the stream narrowed, going ever faster until the water swept them through the passage in the stone below. With that attraction gone, he placed both hands on the rock surface, as if to steady himself, and stared upstream. Silently, his wife watched the water coursing below, waiting patiently to learn the rest of it.

"Buck had me describe our place to him, the pastures, the lay of the land, the barn, the fact that we have cows, because Old Black likes cows. Then he told me about how Old Black never had a problem with barbed-wire fences the way so many horses do." He looked at Norma significantly. "See, he was pointing out qualities I might appreciate.

"I had already seen that the horse was a performer. And I'd been watching out of Buck's kitchen window as Jim rode him around. Boy, how they got along! I knew pretty quick that this was the horse for him. If the price wasn't too outlandish, Buck had a sale. I asked him what he wanted for Old Black.

"Honey, I almost fainted when he said, 'How about six hundred?' But how was I to know how much a retired roping horse is worth—"

"Six hundred dollars? Weren't you expecting to pay much more for a proper horse?"

"Good grief, Sweetheart, I was prepared to spend maybe two thousand, then add another six, eight hundred for a saddle and bridle and all the other things we'd need. I presumed at the time that Buck had priced him at the rock-bottom end of what he might bring—well, what he might get from somebody else, because Buck knew we would be a good home for Old Black. But I should have known that any horse ready to go for youth activities with Mr. Bonner's okay was worth a lot more than six hundred. It's clear to me now that Buck didn't set a price until after he got a good picture of our place out of me, and until after he'd become acquainted with Jim.

"Here's another clue. After the horse deal was done, when we were getting Old Black ready for travel, Buck said out of the clear blue that the saddle and everything else was included—Jim looks lost in that big roping saddle, doesn't he? But I bet you couldn't trade him out of it for the finest youth saddle made."

He looked at Norma with a painful expression. "Who is going to throw in a thousand dollars worth of extra gear—or whatever it might be worth—with a six-hundred-dollar horse? I don't know what the saddle's worth, but a rodeo cowboy would be riding a pretty good one. I bet it would sell to any feed store for five hundred cash."

Suddenly Matt broke the intensity of his discourse with a robust laugh. "You should have heard Buck after I said something about paying for the saddle and the other stuff. He nixed the idea, then laughed and said, 'A fine couple of horse traders we'd make, Matt. Me throwing in free extras and you trying to jack up the price!' I quit arguing about it, but I made the check out for a thousand—I didn't think he would look at it, and he didn't. And the extra four hundred is nothing compared to what the gear is worth."

Matt began in an unsteady voice, stopped and waited a moment. Then he said with a nervous little laugh, "As Paul Harvey would say, here's the rest of the story." The levity loosened him up and he spoke easier. "I just presumed that Old Black was too old to sell as a rodeo horse. That is, until I heard what Garner told me—he's the fella who hauled Old Black here from Buck's.

"When we got here, Garner began to fish around for what we'd had to pay for Old Black—not in an offensive way, though. He was an okay guy, congenial, but curious—all right, nosey, even. He said something that floored me."

Norma observed an expression bordering on anguish pass over Matt's face. "He told me—" he stopped for a moment—"He said a calf roper who wanted to buy Old Black in the worst way stopped by his place on his way over to Buck's. And he showed Garner a cashier's check for *twenty-five thousand dollars* made out to Buck Jones."

Matt chuckled in a way that was more cynical than humorous. "That gives you an idea how much I know about what horses are worth. Anyway, Garner and this cowboy both thought that sure ought to get the horse bought, seeing as Buck had just up and quit using him. But the guy came back by Garner's, all down at the mouth, and said Buck had turned him down flat."

Matt's head was cocked to one side, "Now, that happened only a week ago, which had to be just before Buck went to see Bonner about finding a home for Old Black as a youth horse.

"I'm just now waking up," Matt said with a note of reproof in his voice, his brow furrowed. "I'm finally waking up. When Garner told me Buck wouldn't sell Old Black for twenty-five thousand, I had a flash of disbelief. But Buck just wasn't going to let Old Black be ridden into the ground in rodeo arenas, not for any amount of money."

Matt became solemn again, his eyes fixed on a distant hawk gliding through easy circles, patrolling its hunting ground below. He bit his lip as his mind worked to find the words. Then, holding his hands cradled close before him, he looked at them as if they held a precious object. "See, Buck had carefully worked out a plan for Old Black's future, and he faithfully carried out that plan. He decided Old Black was going to be a kid's horse, but it had to be the right kid, and the kid had to have a nice home for the horse."

At last he looked into Norma's eyes. "It was a big order for Buck to put those pieces together, Sweetheart. Bonner was part of the plan, and we became part of it because we fit it so well, maybe better than he'd dared to hope. *Money* didn't figure into the plan at all. And at some point, after he found out what he needed to know, Buck decided that Old Black was going to be Jim Bradley's horse and live on the Bradley ranch. Period!" His voice finally trembled. "Six hundred dollars! He was *giving* us the horse, Honey, but he didn't want us to *know* it—you know how people get suspicious about something that's free. Then, after the deal was made, he started throwing in all the tack and supplies—"

Norma took his face in her hands, looked into his eyes and gave him a quick, strong kiss. Then she gently passed her thumbs over his damp eyes; her eyes scanned back and forth as she looked into them. She kissed him again lightly and said, "Darling, that's the most precious, tender story. That dear Mr. Jones, so very ill, but looking out for the horse he loved so much. Well, maybe someone bigger than all of us was looking out for everybody—for Mr. Jones, for Old Black, for our little Jim . . . and for you and me, too."

CHAPTER 10

With hands cupped around his eyes like binoculars, Jim stared down on the Jackson's house, his eyes squinted against the bright day outside. From the elevated doorway of the tack room he could see it clear: a dishtowel was hanging in the pear tree. He hurried back to the house with the cleaning gear and put it away. Then he ran to the corral. Old Black was standing there under the extension of the barn roof, quietly enjoying the shade.

Jim was still saddling him when he saw Mr. Jackson's pickup coming up the lane. He stood in the barn door and looked close. Suddenly Buddy's entire upper body shot out of the truck's window like a jack-in-the-box with a waving arm. Jim waved his hat.

"Hi, Buddy! Hi, Mr. Jackson," Jim called as the pickup came to a stop.

"Jim!" Buddy shouted in his high little voice as he leaped from the truck. "Grandpa said you have a horse and this is him, ain't it?"

Oscar interrupted, "You boys are on your own. Where's your daddy, Jim, down in the pasture?"

"Yes, sir. He and Mom are down by the creek, probably at the rock bridge." Mr. Jackson nodded and drove away. He rounded the barn and Jim could hear his truck stop at the pasture gate. Jim ran through the barn, scaled the corral fence and got there just as Mr. Jackson was getting out of his truck. He opened the gate and waved the truck through. Mr. Jackson threw Jim a big smile of thanks.

Buddy was looking at Old Black when Jim came dashing back into the tack room. His expression was sober, filled with awe.

"Gosh, Jim. Your own horse," he said breathlessly. "Your own horse. Do he kick or bite?"

"Heck no, Buddy. He's a Quarter Horse. He's used to being around people too. He *likes* people." As a demonstration of Old Black's benign nature, Jim crawled under his belly to the other side and beckoned Buddy to follow. The little boy hesitated, leaned way back with his arms stretched behind him, then closed his eyes and *flung* himself under the horse, popping up on the other side like a ferret. Old Black's skin quivered. His big neck curved rearward and he looked wide-eyed at the boy.

"It's best if you don't make real quick moves around a horse," Jim cautioned mildly. "Watch this." Jim walked toward the horse's rear, putting a hand on his rump as he walked by, then he picked up his tail and stood facing Old Black's hind feet.

"Wow!" Buddy exclaimed. "Junior, that's a boy I know, he got behind his grampa's horse. And that horse—wham! He sent him flying." Buddy waved his arm in a slow arc, his eyes focused far into space, recalling Junior's entry into orbit.

Buddy was eight, and his knowledge of the woods and wildlife impressed Jim so much that he saw the boy as a young Daniel Boone. He had spent much of his life with his grandparents on the Richter farm, and had made broad forays into the more interesting places within a couple of miles of it.

Buddy was thoroughly at home in the Baumberg woods and spoke of many fascinating sights and places in that mysterious forest. Strange things went on in there, he said. But his claims beyond the ordinary were listened to with only half an ear by Grandma and Grandpa Jackson. He had been talking for over a year about a criminal hideout in the Baumberg woods, providing a detailed description of a gang of dope smugglers armed with machine guns, a tale taken by everyone as one of his more imaginative flights of fantasy, everyone except Rufus.

Rufus, who had lived all of his sixty-some-odd years in the immediate neighborhood, supported Buddy's claim. He had, he said, traveled Buddy's "highway in the sky" to the place where the smugglers camped out. Even though he was a man of character and truth, nobody would take his story seriously because it had originated with Buddy.

Rufus only told the story to his small circle of friends—to Duffie and the handful of older black men in the immediate vicinity. He had not even told Matt; it was Duffie who had told Matt and Jim, related it in all earnestness because he respected Rufus. Furthermore, Rufus often fished the Brazos River at the mouth of Hickory Creek, near the abandoned village of Klanke's Mill, and he had told Duffie of recognizing one of the smugglers in a jetboat that had pulled up to the old cotton dock there.

Matt didn't know what to believe. He did mention the matter to Sheriff Martinez, who investigated every report of suspected criminal activity no matter how far-fetched. He'd sent his chief deputy to Klanke's Mill to investigate. The deputy reported that there was no sign of human presence about the entire place.

It was long ago that Buddy had described to Jim his "highway in the sky," which was, he said, a thick bed of vines snaking through the tops of the loftiest trees. Jim had been anxious to see it, and his yearning was not dampened by the possibility, the *probability*, that Buddy might have been exaggerating. Some of Buddy's claims had turned out to be flights of fancy, but Jim was tolerant of that harmless aspect of Buddy's nature.

During the entire time that Buddy had resided at his grandparents' house, Jim had had little time for exploring. He had work to do alongside his father. For the last year, however, Duffie had been assisted by Rufus, who was as willing a worker as Duffie.

It was the years of ceaseless work by the Bradley gang, often assisted by Oscar Jackson's voice of experience, that had made the property a functioning ranch. Most of the projects that had once been dreams were now realities. The large, rambling house that seemed to drape over the hilltop had been leveled "so we can finally fill a soup bowl over half full without it spilling," Norma said.

Norma had unequivocally set the priority for indoor plumbing at the top of the list, so Matt and Jim had built a bright new bathroom in part of the middle bedroom. The house had been rewired to Houston city code standards, "with plenty of outlets in the kitchen," as Norma had demanded. They had a deep well drilled, water piped to the house, and presto, there was running water in the bath and kitchen.

Jim proclaimed when they were done, "Even if our farmhouse is a hundred years old, now it's as up to date as any around here, or in Houston, either."

Fresh, cold well water was also piped to the cattle holding area, several hundred feet downhill from the house. It was a place where the cattle could be confined in comfort, where they could dine on hay and lick protein supplement, hide under dense trees from the hot summer sun and find protection from winter winds behind yaupon thickets. It was a place where they could hobnob without trampling or overgrazing the pasture grasses. Its location and arrangement, with gates to all five pastures, allowed controlled grazing when grass was not abundant due to drought. At night, the cattle were held in the dry holding area without access to water. Each morning they were let into a pasture to graze, but only for a couple of hours—enough to keep them well nourished, but no more. When Duffie opened the gate to the water lot, a call to the thirsty cattle brought them on the run. Then he hayed them and left them to roam and lie about in the holding area and water lot. In the evening they got another ration of hay and the water lot was closed off.

Nothing could have been simpler or more functional than that system, and it was not matched anywhere else in the county. All winter, the Bradley's cattle could get enough green grass every day to keep them fit, but they could not overgraze the valuable winter pasture. The system was also employed during summer dry spells. The design of the pastures and holding pens came from the same source as everything else Matt had learned about grass ranching: the County Agricultural Agent's free booklet rack.

Next to the water lot, they had built a wood-rail corral for working the cattle. It had a long chute into which the cattle could be channeled and immobilized to be given shots, have worm medicine squirted down their throats, be dusted with fly repellent . . . .

Jim had watched it all come to be, and not a single task would ever be forgotten by the little boy from the city; instead, they were magnified by the child's perception of the enormity of each accomplishment, and by the remarkable results they had produced over the ensuing six years.

By the time Jim's labors had abated, Buddy had rejoined his mother in Round Top and Jim saw little of him. This was why his enthusiasm could not have been greater when he learned that Buddy would be visiting today, when he had a *horse* to show off.

"WILL HE RIDE DOUBLE WITHOUT BUCKING US OFF?" asked Buddy. "Sure he will," said Jim confidently.

Jim mounted from the doorway of the tack room. Then he told Buddy to stand in the doorway, so he could get his foot in the stirrup. Jim extended his hand, but Buddy was reluctant to make such a death-defying commitment and stood fixed in the doorway. He made several false starts, only to jump back each time to the safety of the solid floor of the tack room. Old Black stood perfectly still during all this, and perhaps encouraged by his patience, Buddy finally was seated behind Jim. Clearly, Old Black did not mind Buddy's weight behind the saddle one bit, as both boys together weighed less than half as much as Buck Jones.

"Wow! This is something," Buddy said, his arms holding tight around Jim's waist, his whole being experiencing the lofty horseman's sensation of superiority. "Glory be! You can see *everything* from this high up. Look, Jim," he said pointing. "There's Grandma hoein' in the garden. Don't she look tiny like a bug?" Buddy was properly amazed that Old Black could be moved sideways to close the barn door. "Old Black can really do tricks. Can we ride over and see Grandma?"

"LOOKIE AT WHAT WE GOT HERE," said Ruby cheerfully. She had watched their approach and was leaning on her hoe. "Two desperadoes if ever I seen any. My, I wish I had a Kodak for a picture. Where you boys off to?"

"We're going to ride down in the bottom and maybe explore the creek some," said Jim. "I'll get Mom to take our picture."

As they were riding back up the Bradley lane, Buddy asked, "Do you think we could go exploring in the Baumberg woods?"

"On the horse?" Jim had ventured only into the edge of those woods and knew they were too thick for a horse and rider.

"Yeah, on Old Black."

"No, Buddy. It's way too thick to ride a horse in there. We'd get scraped off by vines and limbs. I sure would like to see that highway in the sky, though. Do you think it's still there?"

"Yeah," said Buddy with assurance. "It'll be there to the end of the world."

"Buddy," Jim asked earnestly, "could you show me the highway in the sky today? Dad said I could do most anything today, because we have to bale hay tomorrow. Could you show it to me today?"

Buddy was strangely silent. Jim stopped at the pasture gate by the barn and got off. After leading the horse through he fastened the gate, climbed atop it at the hinged end, where his weight would not be a strain on it, and got back on Old Black.

The possession of a horse by Jim had sent Buddy's estimation of him, which was already high, soaring. Now he was being asked to lead Jim to his greatest treasure in the whole world. Already swelled with pride, Buddy said confidentially, "Okay. But it's a secret, and you can't tell nobody about it. Nobody but Rufus and me know exactly where it is. See, you have to know where to get *on* the highway—I've only ever found one place, and it don't look like nothing but an old tree lyin' down with grapevines all over it."

"Buddy," Jim said, trying to keep his voice casual so as not to inspire Buddy to invent a tale, "Rufus says some criminals have a hideout in the woods. Do you think it's true?"

Buddy was silent for a long time and when Jim turned around to look at him, his expression was thoughtful. "Yeah, I seen it lots of times," he said at last. "Most times they's nobody there, but I seen people there sometimes. It's easy to spot their camp. They's a place like a hog shed made out of tin. And they's beer cans and wine bottles all over—they're litterbugs.

"You can tell if anybody's there from a ways off because you can smell the marijuana smoke. They's a little clearing they made that they get to with their four-wheelers and motorcycles. They was real smart not to take the same ways in and out every time, so they ain't no real trails from the road. The place where they camp is right under the highway in the sky."

A rabbit scampered out of some grass directly in front of them, causing Old Black to start. It was no more than a faint jolt to Jim, but to Buddy it was more. "He almost bucked us off! Wow! I can tell the kids at school I stayed on a buckin' horse!"

After a short silence, Buddy continued talking about the criminals' hideout. "I've laid right over 'em, peeping down and they didn't know I was lying right over them. I could hear them talking. They have guns, too, and they shoot them off into the woods sometimes, practicing. Real soft-sounding—like BB guns."

Jim turned again and stared at Buddy. "Could we see it now, Buddy?" He was reining Old Black around to head back for the barn before Buddy finished answering.

CHAPTER 11

"Here boys, let me spray both of you with this insect repellent." Jim closed his eyes and pressed his lips tightly together while his mother walked around him spraying. She turned to Buddy, who was standing with one bare foot on top of the other, and sprayed him. "Don't you think you should wear shoes, Buddy? And you, Jim. You should be in boots instead of tennis shoes. What about snakes?"

"Buddy says we have to climb some vines and you can't do it with boots on." His hand darted into a pocket and came out with a big green rubber capsule. "I have my Cutter snake-bite kit. And I know how to apply a tourniquet and everything. You have to undo them every five minutes so blood can feed the arm, or the leg. In school they showed us a video on how it works. Where's Dad?"

Norma Bradley shivered inwardly at the thought of Jim applying a tourniquet to himself after being snake-bit. But she stoically recognized that the woods were a magnet for boys and was comforted slightly by her belief that snakes usually avoided people. She considered, too, that a fair part of Buddy's life had been spent in the woods, and he had never been bitten by a snake.

"Take sticks along and beat the bushes ahead of you. Do you hear me? Your father went down to check the hay. Don't forget tomorrow is hay-making day." She raised his face and kissed him on the forehead. "You boys have a good adventure, a safe adventure." She gave Buddy a hug, and then a kiss on his forehead.

The boys waved goodbye and struck out across the pasture behind the barn.

Buddy said in a voice that was almost reverent, "Your momma sure is pretty, and nice, too. She always got that smile on, and she give us hugs and kisses."

Jim looked at Buddy with a warm feeling. "Yeah, I have the best mom in the—" Somehow he was aware that there was some strife in Buddy's home life and instinctively felt he should not be speaking about his own good fortune. "—I mean, I have the best horse." He laughed, and they began to talk about Old Black.

THEIR ROUTE TOOK THEM ALONG A NARROW STRIP OF PASTURE between a line of dense trees and underbrush and the Bradley's south fence line. It bordered a dark and forbidding swamp that began just across the fence on the Richter place.

Buddy said, "Don't ever go in that swamp, Jim. They's a jillion snakes in there. I seen whoppers shimmyin' along in there."

In response to the unseen peril, the boys crept along against the very edge of the tree line. The air was heavy, and they could smell rotting vegetation and mold rising from the swamp. But it was freshened with the fragrance of a profusion of small white flowers in the trees.

Buddy stopped short in front of Jim. "Lookie there!" he exclaimed, pointing. Jim was astonished to see the body of a snake crossing over a log just inside the tree line, not more than eight feet away. The snake was monstrous, as big around as Jim's thigh. Only three or four feet of it was visible at any time as it seemed to ooze effortlessly out of some high grass and over the log. Jim could see that its skin, moving with wavelike undulations as if the body were filled with Jello, was dark and mottled with gray. It shone like it was oiled.

"How much has already gone over?" asked Jim in a low voice.

Buddy stared, his head thrust forward. "I don't know, but see how he just keeps going? A serpent is what he is."

Still the huge snake moved smoothly, steadily over the log until finally its girth began to diminish. Then its blunt tail slithered up and over and disappeared in the brush beyond the log.

Jim was speechless. Buddy said, "Goshamighty! I seen some big snakes in this woods but I never seen any that big. I sure wish we could have seen him whole. I bet he was long as a gate post." Both boys whirled around at the sound of rustling leaves behind them. A few yards away an armadillo was rooting around. Jim's hand went to his beating heart. They laughed together. "You getting pretty jumpy, Jim. Me too. Even a *giant* would be scared of a snake that big! Grampa won't believe me when I tell him about that serpent. You'll have to back me up."

When they crossed the fence and entered the woods, Buddy turned and looked at Jim. "Once we get a little ways in, this brush will give out," he said.

It did. Then they were under high, high umbrellas of spring-fresh leaves. It became darker as they walked, and presently came the cry, "Whoo-ee-o, whooo, whooo, whooo." Jim had always thought of the owl's cry as mysterious and sinister, for they always seemed to come from afar, from dark, foreboding places. Jim had never once seen an owl. Buddy stopped and cupped his hands around his mouth, replying with the same sound, including the delicate warble on the end of the first cry and the long, slow beats of the ones that followed. "Whoo-ee-o, whooo, whooo, whooo," he called.

"Gosh, Buddy, you sounded just like him," Jim said, thrilled.

"Shhh," Buddy said, a finger to his lips. They waited. Then, much closer this time, came another call. Buddy waited for some seconds, then replied. Again he put a finger to his lips for quiet. The silence lasted so long that Jim doubted they would hear the owl again when, very close to them, the owl spoke. Buddy waited, waited, then replied. Almost immediately there came the sound of beating wings, and they watched a big brown owl glide gently through the trees. It swooped low to the ground, then made an elegant upsweep that took it to a tree limb directly in front of them. It settled for a moment with a fluffing of feathers and a peck or two at its fawn colored underbelly, then uttered a little cry and fled on noisy, beating wings.

"He seen us," said Buddy in a normal voice. "He seen us and know he been fooled."

Jim was astounded. "Where did you learn to do that?"

"You just listen to what he say, and you start trying to say it like he do and pretty soon you have it. Try it. Do it like this." Buddy demonstrated.

Jim did a poor imitation. He cleared his throat and tried again with some improvement.

"That's better. Make it longer, like this, Whooeeo, whoooo, whoo, whoooo. Do it again, Jim."

"One of your sounds was shorter this time, Buddy. And the others seemed longer."

"He do that sometime, old owl, make different sounds."

Jim held the cries longer on this attempt and Buddy was nodding approval before he finished.

"See, Jim, you just have to practice, practice, practice."

Everywhere Jim looked now he saw vines climbing into the trees.

Some of them were ancient and as big as Jim's leg, twisted and gnarled near the ground. Buddy put a hand on his arm and stopped. They heard a faint rustling ahead, off to their right. "A snake getting out of our way," Buddy said without concern.

"What kind, do you think?"

"Oh, it have to be big to make that sound. Not too many rattlers in these woods. Probably a cottonmouth. A copperhead don't make no noise, he just lay up in a bush and bite anybody that happen to come by. Copperheads is spiteful snakes, hateful as Old Man Skinner."

Jim shuddered. He knew what a cottonmouth was. His father had killed one down in the woods near the creek. It was about four feet long and thick, with jaws that opened straight away from each other. Its mouth was white inside. Long, wicked-looking fangs folded back from the front of its ridged upper jaw. Jim recalled those white fangs with a shiver. Oscar said a cottonmouth out of the water would run away from a person if it could. Beating the grass ahead of them with sticks, they walked on.

They had traveled a long way, all uphill. The dense foliage overhead obscured all but occasional patches of sky. The lowest limbs were now quite high, though, and they could see a long way through the gloom.

Buddy led Jim to an enormous cottonwood tree. He embraced the trunk with his arms extended as far as they would reach and walked halfway around the tree, spanning. "Lookie here, Jim. Three times is only half. It's six times as big around as I can reach."

Buddy motioned with a jerk of his head and led Jim around the tree to the other side. "How about that?" asked Buddy, standing back to observe Jim's surprise. The trunk was hollow; a wide opening extended from the ground to about a foot higher than Jim's head.

Buddy motioned for Jim to go in.

Warily, he stepped through the opening with Buddy close behind.

"Gosh," Jim exclaimed, looking around in the large chamber. Its inside surface was like black satin. "Look how big it is in here!"

"Lightning hit it and set it on fire," Buddy explained, leading him out of the hollow. He pointed up to a line in the bark that went straight up the tree trunk and out of sight.

They continued through the woods, still going uphill. Several rabbits scurried out of their way, a coon and a possum. Squirrel were abundant; the more indignant ones held tight to tree trunks, head down, and fearlessly scolded the intruders with their barking. The armadillos ignored them and went right on with their nosing around and digging in the forest floor. More than once Jim caught sight of a deer's white tail signaling its flight.

"No skeeters once you get out of that swamp," said Buddy.

Birds sang merrily. A redheaded woodpecker sounded like a far-away machine gun as it banged away at a tree trunk.

Buddy jerked his head to the right and Jim followed him to a giant fallen tree. Its roots still clung to a large circle of the forest floor. The tree had not fallen to the ground, however, because it was supported by a thick entanglement of vines among its branches. A vast number stretched away in many directions while others played their part in a latticework that vanished into the foliage above.

"Here's where we get on the highway in the sky," Buddy said, his face expressing the wonder of it. He began scampering up the entanglement, a natural ladder. Jim's eyes followed as up and up he went, becoming smaller and smaller until he disappeared into a mass of green. "Come on up, Jim," he shouted from on high.

As soon as he began climbing, Jim was surprised at the ease of ascent, aided by an abundance of strong handholds and footholds. Sure that he had climbed a great distance, he looked up but still could see only the thick green ceiling. When he looked down, he was startled at the great distance to the ground.

He climbed higher and entered the soft mass of leaves that Buddy had disappeared into. He called out, "Buddy?"

"Up here, Jim. I can see you now."

Jim searched the foliage above as he climbed through an opening in a mass of twisted vines that went ever upwards, as if it was never going to end. At last he caught sight of Buddy's red and black checked shirt, and there was Buddy, sitting cross-legged on a spacious mattress of vines. Jim crawled over the springy growth and sat beside him. "Wow," he said.

"This is the highway in the sky, Jim." Buddy's hand swept the scene, showing him how the surface they sat on swept away to the south.

Jim followed it with his eyes to where it went out of sight around a bend. He began walking cautiously around on its bouncy surface.

"Boy oh boy Buddy, this really *is* a highway in the sky. It has to be the only place like this anywhere."

Buddy jumped to his feet and fell backwards, laughing, to be gently absorbed in the greenery.

Jim followed his example and fell into the soft, springy mass.

Buddy stood up. "Watch me," he said and began springing up and down. On the third jump he sprang high and did a somersault, landing on his back. Soon they were both jumping and laughing as if they were on a trampoline. Now and then a foot would break through, but it would soon encounter stronger vines. There was no danger that either of them could break through the yards-deep mass. "Come on," said Buddy.

Jim looked about with awe as they trotted clumsily along on the bouncy, uneven growth. The width of the mass was irregular, sometimes as wide as fifteen feet and then narrowing in places to four or five.

They came to a place where they could see a broad patch of sky overhead. Buddy looked up and stopped, then kept his body as stiff as a board as he fell to the mat on his back; Jim imitated his dead-man's fall.

"Look up at the sky, Jim. Pick out a cloud and see how we drifts along under it."

Jim stared at a cloud and immediately had the sensation that the clouds were stationary, it was their highway that was carrying them along beneath the sky. The sound of wind in the trees came swooping up from the south and Jim listened as it came closer. At its loudest it was a breeze upon them, rocking their treetop and bathing them in its coolness. Just as it came, the breeze died away and he could hear it traveling off toward the north. He resumed his observation of the clouds. Buddy's highway in the sky was amazing.

"I told you, didn't I?" Buddy asked. "And I didn't lie. Would you tell Grandma I didn't lie, Jim?" He got up and Jim followed.

"I sure will," Jim said. "Where's the criminals' hideout?"

Buddy pointed ahead. "It's a ways, yet."

The two boys ran freely along, laughing occasionally as one or the other's foot plunged harmlessly through the floor of their carpet. Jim looked down on squirrel nests and bird nests.

They had traveled a very long way when Buddy held up a hand and stopped. He turned and put a finger to his lips—*shhh*. His head tilted back and he tapped a finger to his nose. The smells of foliage and the occasional whiff of blossoms were there. Jim moved up and when he was next to Buddy he inhaled deeply. Buddy watched his face for a sign. Smoke.

Buddy whispered in his ear, "Marijuana."

CHAPTER 12

Buddy moved expertly, silently, ahead, his body in a half crouch, hands paddling down and tapping the vines for balance as he went. Jim followed, but not silently. Try as he might, even though he carefully placed his feet, there was an occasional snap that seemed deafening.

They had gone about fifteen yards when they heard the low drone of a man talking. The smell of marijuana smoke was quite noticeable now, inspiring Buddy to act out a jerky pantomime of staggering about. It was evident to Jim that he was not frightened.

Closer they crept, more carefully, and the low tone was joined for a moment by a high-pitched voice, which was interrupted by a loud and angry "Dammit, Winnie, stop butting in." Buddy moved like an animal, slithering along steadily, soundlessly. Jim crawled with great care, but continued to make noises he feared were too loud. Once, when his arm plunged into the matting and made a loud thrashing sound, Buddy looked at him and made a face.

Buddy stopped, stretched out face down on the mattress and buried his face in the foliage. His head came up and he pointed at the scene below. Jim did the same and saw first a man sitting on the ground, then a maroon motorcycle with a man leaning against it.

The distance to the ground was surprising—at least thirty feet, Jim figured; they didn't have to worry about anyone getting up to where they were. Shifting his point of view he saw a small green pickup truck with two men in the back. One of them was sitting on the tailgate holding a can of beer and talking steadily.

The other man, in a tee shirt with a Marlboro cigarette pack on the front, lay on his back smoking a cigarette in the bed of the truck. A blue bandanna was tied around his head as a sweatband.

Tailgate extended an arm behind himself and The Marlboro Man passed him his cigarette.

Jim moved his position slightly and brought the motorcycle back into his field of view. A burly, redheaded man sat sideways on the seat. He constantly ran a hand through his heavy red beard as he looked at the ground and listened to Tailgate.

Another shift of angle revealed the fourth member of the group, sitting on the ground near the truck. He was slight, almost frail, with dark hair, and was younger than the others. He held a short military-looking rifle and was wiping it with a cloth. Attached to the end of the barrel was a curious tubular device, much larger than the barrel and about eight inches long. The rifle had a telescopic sight; a long, curved magazine could be seen extending underneath the rifle.

The Rifleman reached toward Tailgate and received the community cigarette, which by this time was quite short. He sucked on it in one long puff until Jim could see the fire glowing bright on the end. It was brighter still an instant before The Rifleman dropped his gun and sprang to his feet, coughing and spitting and grasping his throat. He grabbed his beer and choked as he tried to drink and cough at the same time.

Tailgate said to nobody in particular, "We got tons of that stuff and he stovepipes a roach."

Redbeard laughed and watched The Rifleman cough and beat himself on the chest between swigs of beer. He said, still chuckling, "People that think they have heartburn don't know what it is till they suck the fire out of a roach, do they Winnie?" Winnie wasn't talking.

"Look here, dammit," said Tailgate in a loud voice, looking around and glaring at each man angrily. "If Winnie kills hisself doing a fire-eating act, that's too damn bad. It wouldn't bother me none. But we got some things to get straight before tonight. The next guy that lights up a joint, I'm going to blow his head off." He drew a pistol from his belt and waved it in the air.

Jim saw smoke coming from the barrel and at the same time heard "Whoof, click." It was not much louder than a BB gun. He noticed that the pistol also had the same kind of tubular device at the end of the barrel, though not as large as the one on the rifle. While shifting his position to get a better angle of view, the weight of his supporting hand broke through some small vines. The noise it made was not loud, but it came at a time when the three men were apparently intimidated by Tailgate's pistol and no one was speaking.

"What was that?" Winnie gasped, his voice still only a squeak. He turned all around quickly, searching. He grabbed his rifle off the ground, then stood very still and listened intently, his head cocked to one side. "I heard something," he said.

"Aw, you're just spooky," said Tailgate.

Redbeard stood up by his motorcycle, looking up in the trees. "I heard something too, and don't try to tell me I didn't. It sounded like it come from somewhere up there." His eyes intently searched the foliage overhead.

"Well, for chrissake," said Tailgate in an irritated voice, "animals live in the woods, and animals move around. Let's get this plan down pat and we can all get the hell out of here."

"That wasn't no animal I heard," squawked The Rifleman, who was now looking up, searching, searching . . . His stare seemed to linger on Jim's eyes, giving him a frightful chill as the two seemed to look directly at each other. It was a long moment before The Rifleman's eyes moved on.

Then he heard it—"*Click-click-crack, click-click-crack* . . ." The "cracks" were not much louder than a cap pistol. He saw The Rifleman shooting rapidly, randomly into the trees. Bits of leaves erupted in several places close to where he and Buddy lay; shredded leaves drifted down about them.

Buddy was now looking at Jim with an expression of terror. He put his hands over his ears and buried his face in the vines.

Jim was so scared he felt like his throat was going to close up. When he somehow brought himself to look down through his viewing hole, he was relieved to see that now The Rifleman was shooting on a level into the woods. For the first time Jim noticed the brass cartridge cases flying out of the rifle and collecting on the ground. The pungent smell of gunsmoke overcame the odor of marijuana.

Tailgate said impatiently, "Okay, Win, *okay*. Cut it! If anything was out there you had to plug it by now. Let's go over it again. The plane comes in around midnight. The Brentwood airport is closed and the drive has a chain across it, so we cut the chain and fix it with a split link. Then if someone comes snooping by while we're in there they won't see the chain's down. That's your job, Al."

The Marlboro Man sat up. Tailgate continued, "Your tools: one large bolt cutter and split links of at least three sizes so we know one of them will fit the chain. You cut the chain near the end where it's fastened to the post. That way the substitution won't be so noticeable." He turned to face Redbeard.

"Red, you seen that chain. Is it galvanized or rusty?"

Redbeard ran both hands through his beard as if the action stimulated his brain. "I don't remember."

"I don't remember," Tailgate mimicked in an exaggerated tone. "You check out the place and don't see nothin'. You saw a chain, right? Okay. Was it shiny or dull?"

Redbeard stroked his beard harder. "I don't *remember*, Brad."

Tailgate looked at him shaking his head. "Pulling off serious jobs with jerks like you guys ain't no fun." He rubbed the stubble on his jaw in angry contemplation. "Al, bring along a can of brown spray paint, a color like rust. If the chain is galvanized, the new split link won't be so noticeable. If it's rusty, you can spray-paint the new link to look at least something like the rest of it. I just don't want a brand-new split link on a rusty chain shining in the headlights of some snoop.

"Red, you're driving the van. You let Al out at the end of the runway that the lighted wind tee is pointing to. If there is any wind at all it'll be south. So you set up at the south end. He prefers to land south. That way, if anybody comes up and he has to cut out, his takeoff run will be going away from them.

"Al, you have a charged car battery. Put it on the ground with the Q-Beam spotlight hooked up. When the plane approaches he's going to blink his landing lights three times. When you see that, point the light right at him and turn it on for three long dashes. About three seconds on, three seconds off, three seconds on—. One thousand, two thousand, three thousand—that tells him you're there and that you're not in handcuffs. If he don't see no light, he won't land. If he sees a light that ain't three long dashes, he won't land. So if you have any visitors, don't show no light. He's going to land as close to midnight as he can, so be standing out there and listening good at least a half hour before.

"Red, you stay parked until the plane comes over. Then you drive off the approach end of the runway about a hundred feet with only your parking lights on. When you get there, you turn your headlights on bright so the pilot can see them. When he's about a mile out, you turn the van around fast and point your headlights down the runway. Keep your foot on the brake pedal to light up your stop lights. You'll be easier to see. You sit there until he goes over you, then turn out your headlights and drive down the runway behind the plane.

"Al, your light should be pointed down on the white stripe of the runway. Keep it down out of the pilot's eyes. When he touches down, you turn off your light. He raised holy hell about Joey blinding him by zeroing in on the windshield right in his eyes even while he was on the ground. He'll park pointed back up the runway so he can cut out in case anybody comes charging up. Whether he's unloaded or not, if he says 'get clear,' then get out of the way because he's cutting out downwind.

"One thing to remember. He usually cuts the left engine, the side the door's on. But if he don't, you might try to keep from walking into the prop. It gets blood and guts all over the place. When you're unloaded, go to Garner's ferry landing by the back roads.

"One last thing, Red. If you have to abort and there's any heat on you, call me on the radio. And remember I'll be listening on one-thirty-five-ninety-five. It's at the high end of the aviation band. The scanners that tune in cop bands can't pick it up, and the aviation guys don't use it much. Then come straight here and hide out."

He looked from one face to another. "Any questions?"

"Yeah," said The Rifleman. "What do I do?"

"You and Joey are going to stay at Garner's ferry landing to guard the boat. When it's loaded, Al joins you for the run up to Klanke's. Joey drives the boat nice and quiet like. Tell him that. And slow, so you can see any trees coming down—after the rains lately there'll be some trees, I guarantee. If you guys sink that boat and what's in it—well, you might as well go down with the ship. You hear?"

Tailgate leaned back, took a beer from the chest, and then lazily got out of the truck bed. He was halfway in the door when The Rifleman asked, "What are *you* going to be doing all this time, Brad?"

Tailgate turned and looked at him for a long time. "I don't have to account for what I do to pipsqueaks like *you*, you little jerk. But just so you'll know, I'll be sleeping.

"Red, you follow me on your bike. Joey's out on the road watching for cars. If they ain't any coming or going, he'll step out on the road and then we come out of the woods. You get off the bike and help Joey straighten out the bent grass and weeds."

Redbeard started his motorcycle, creating enough noise that

Jim and Buddy could finally begin to move without being heard. Jim was stiff as he turned around and started crawling away. Buddy was in a low crouch, bounding squirrel-like over the matted vines. Jim moved as fast after him as he could, but he could not catch up.

It was difficult to run on the spongy surface of the vines. Jim was still a good fifty yards behind the nimble little boy when Buddy reached the ladder descending from the highway in the sky.

THE BRADLEY KITCHEN LOOKED LIKE A WORKSHOP. An old door supported by two sawhorses served as a work table. On it was a saber saw and some other tools. Sawdust covered the floor. Norma was standing by, handing Matt tools on demand. He was almost finished installing a vent over the range.

"This is wonderful, Matt," she said. "It will keep cooking odors out of the house, and the smoke alarm won't keep going off."

Matt was leaning over the stove backwards, setting some screws that secured the vent to the cabinet. Presently, he swung his upper body free of the hood and straightened up, holding his back.

"Mighty pleased to be of service to you, ma'am," he said with an exaggerated Southern drawl. "But I'd hate to do this for a living. I'll take the cockpit of a Learjet in the wild blue yonder any time."

He leaned against the wall and picked up his Coke, took a long swig and was quiet for a time. His expression became thoughtful and he said, "Did I tell you what Jim asked me the other morning, about what I wanted to be when I grew up?"

She gave him an inquiring look. "What did you want to be?"

Matt grinned. "I was glad he asked, because I hadn't thought about it in a long time. I wanted to be what I am, an airplane pilot. I told him how I used to watch planes flying overhead, especially little planes because you could sometimes see the pilots in them, and I remember how I envied them.

"I told him about the time when I was about ten, helping a neighbor fix fences on his land when a small plane landed right in his pasture. A Piper Clipper. We watched it approach, prop dead still, watched it make the smoothest landing you ever saw. Out climbed this cute little lady who calmly announced that she was out of gas. She said she'd sure appreciate it if somebody would go to a filling station and get her some Ethyl, our high-test in those days. The man that decided to go looked at me and asked if I wanted to go. Shoot, no! I wanted to look at that plane!

"The lady pilot let me sit in the cockpit and look at the instrument panel, cluttered with all of four or five instruments. I was fascinated by the small bucket seats, the safety belts, the control stick, the rudder pedals. She let me work the stick left and right and then pointed out how I was moving the ailerons out on the wings.

"The guys came back from the station with the gas too soon to suit me. After thanking everybody, she got in and buckled up, leaving the door open and hooked on the stop. She waved and started the engine, and after the first starting burst, it ticked away as quiet as a car engine. Then she taxied to the downwind end of the field and turned into the wind, what little there was. The door closed and the plane sat there a minute as she went through her mag check. Then she started her takeoff run."

Matt smiled and looked far off at his mental picture of that plane taking off. "I'll never forget that sight. She lifted off before reaching us, but kept that little tan Clipper about three feet off the ground, picking up speed. When she flew past she waved to us, then made a steep climbing turn and flew straight away. I got goose bumps watching that sight. That day was the closest I had ever been to an airplane. I *sat* in it. That was when I made up my mind: 'I'm going to do that. I'm going to learn to fly.' Funny, I haven't thought about that in years. But it was a big event in my life."

Norma stepped over and hugged him with her head on his chest. "I'm glad you got to do what you wanted, Darling. Most people don't. Most young people have no idea what they want to do, much less get to do it. I worry that many of them are just leaves in the wind. But our Jimmy isn't going to depend on fate, I pro—"

She abruptly stopped talking and cocked her head to one side. They both heard the boys shouting; their voices were urgent.

JIM AND BUDDY WERE SO OUT OF BREATH they couldn't talk when they staggered up to the house. Norma was terrified by the frightened looks on their faces. She asked if either had been snakebit or injured, all the while feeling their arms and legs through their clothes. Jim shook his head weakly.

"Lie down on the porch, both of you," said Matt, turning to Norma with a finger to his lips. He helped each of them to a position on their backs, pulling their legs up with knees bent. Quickly he unfastened their belts and the top buttons of their pants. "Don't try to talk. Breath deep and slow, not fast," he instructed. He saw that little Buddy was close to hyperventilating, and lifted with his hands under his upper body several times to help him regulate the timing of his respirations and increase the intake of air. He spoke soothingly to him, and with the flat of his hand on Buddy's chest helped him get control of his breathing rhythm. Buddy tried to speak and Matt put a finger on his lips and shook his head. Then he quickly moved to help Jim.

Buddy rolled over, crawled to the edge of the porch and vomited in the yard. Just then Norma rushed out of the house with a pail of water and a washcloth. She kneeled down and sponged Buddy's face with the cool, wet cloth; then she dipped it in the bucket and held it over his head and squeezed, sending cooling, refreshing water cascading over his head, down his back and chest. "Can you lie down now?" she asked. He nodded and she gently helped him. Matt lifted his knees again.

She squeezed another cloth of water over Buddy's chest, then administered the same treatment to Jim.

Both boys were gasping audibly. "Slow down, take long breaths. I know it isn't easy, but you have to force yourself to take longer breaths." Matt formed questions that only required head movements. "Don't try to talk, just move your head. Are either of you hurt? Good. Was someone chasing you?" Jim shook his head, but Matt instinctively looked searchingly over the field they had crossed.

"Whatever you boys ran into, it must have been scary. But you're safe now, so relax as much as you can and get your breath." Matt's eyes once again searched the area around the barn, and the pasture behind it. "You're sure nobody is following you?"

Jim nodded. "Dad, Buddy and I saw the criminal hideout—that Buddy found—that Rufus talked about—the criminals were there—I made a noise—one started shooting up in the trees—almost shot us."

He stopped and breathed deeply. He looked at his hand and saw that it was trembling.

Buddy had also regained the ability to talk. "They was tryin' to kill us! Shootin' up in the trees where we was hidin'—"

Norma was back with two glasses of water. "First, rinse your mouth out," she said. "Then swallow only a little bit."

Buddy took some water and swished his mouth out. He looked around. "Spit it right on the porch, Buddy," she said. He did, then took another gulp.

After their ability to breathe returned, the boys told what had happened.

Matt declared that he was going to call Sheriff Martinez. In a minute he came out of the house. "He's on his way," he said, and glanced toward the Jackson's house. "I'd better go get Ruby."

Norma continued bathing the boys' faces with cool water. "How many men were there?" she asked.

Buddy held up four fingers. Jim nodded.

"How did you get close enough to hear them?"

"We were right over them, in the trees," Jim said.

"You were directly above them? Goodness! You *boys*—"

Soon Matt returned with Ruby in the car with him.

Ruby revealed surprising control. She listened patiently as Buddy explained what Matt had already told her. Then Ruby said to Norma in a low voice, "He been telling us all along they was a gang hideout in those woods and we wouldn't believe him." Then she shook her finger at him. "If you didn't fib so much, Buddy . . . cryin' wolf."

THE SHERIFF'S CAR WAS NOT TEARING up the road, no lights were flashing or sirens blaring, but it was moving with some dispatch.

Sheriff Martinez was not over five feet ten, but he was built like a heavyweight boxer, big in the chest and with muscular shoulders and arms. He filled his uniform admirably, without a sign of fat. His expression was, as usual, serious.

Matt met him as he stepped out of his car; they shook hands warmly. "It sure is good to see you, Matt. I hope you got my thanks for your generosity, buying a whole book of barbecue tickets. I was hoping to see you there."

Matt explained that a flight had kept him away.

"Hello, Mrs. Bradley." He called out, sweeping off his hat and exposing black, wavy hair cut in a 1945 style. "Good to see you, ma'am. And dear Ruby Jackson, it's been too long since I saw you last. I hope Oscar's all right." He laid his hat on top of his car and stepped up on the porch.

MIKE MARTINEZ WAS A DEPUTY two years ago, when the former sheriff was caught up in a federal drug-running probe and abruptly resigned from office. Martinez had been on the force five years and had gained a reputation as a courageous and considerate lawman. He did not treat people as if they were presumed to be criminals, quietly working instead against the more offensive policies of the sheriff, to the extent that he could without getting fired.

Probably because he was simply a decent human being, he was sympathetic toward the law-abiding black people in Winchester County. He regularly overlooked harmless transgressions of the letter of the law, the kind of violations that were sometimes unavoidable in daily life, even though department policy demanded that deputies pounce at the sight or even the suspicion of the most trivial infractions. The practice of rigid enforcement had become so common over the years that the revenue from fines was an important component of the county budget.

"It's this way, Martinez," his corrupt former boss had vehemently reminded him, and not for the first time, "I don't care who it is—dirt-poor niggers or redneck Bubbas that claim they're broke because they just bought a new pickup. *Anybody* can cough up whatever it takes to keep their butt out of jail—or to get out once we throw 'em in. *Anybody!*"

He'd scowled significantly at his deputy. "*You* know what it takes to make this department tick, Martinez: *money!* And a lot of that money comes from fines, fines that the commissioner's court is generous enough to split with us. And we have a solid citizen here in the bonding business, a good supporter of this department that has a right to stay in business." What he really meant was that the bail bondsman's financial support went to the sheriff, personally.

The county political machine embraced neither the Democratic nor Republican parties, claiming instead to advance the best features of both as an independent organization. It's replacement for the deposed sheriff was the even more corrupt Chief Deputy, Dilbert Swagger, a man who had spent his adult life in servitude to people in influential places. They handed the nomination to him on a platter after receiving his solemn assurance that he would do what he was told and keep his mouth shut.

The machine's nominees were shoo-ins for election in Winchester County. With feet propped up on their porch railings, they could sit back and wait for the votes to roll in. It was the way elections worked as far back as anybody could remember. And no special election, for any office, ever drew many voters opposed to the hand-picked candidate. What was the use of going to a polling place just to waste a vote?

Deputy Mike Martinez had raised some eyebrows when he announced his candidacy for the job of sheriff, running as—what else?—another independent. The eyebrows went up because of the laughable hopelessness of his candidacy. By throwing his hat in the ring he did provide some sprinkles of merriment among the county big shots. "A Meskin running for sheriff?" was the question Old Man Skinner asked repeatedly, and with animated astonishment. "An *independent* independent running against the legitimate one?" asked others. "Well, at least he's rolled up two votes, his and his wife's!" declared County Commissioner Stockmeyer. In a downcast, resigned voice, County Judge Ovashefsky had confided to Doc Smith and Matt Bradley, "Fats Swagger will fire the most qualified deputy on the force the minute he's sworn in. That's all that will come of Mike's bid for sheriff."

Fats Swagger was indeed fat. His nickname was earned in the line of duty, sponging donuts, sandwiches and fried chicken while maintaining a "police presence" at places that served food. He was an eager yes-man to those who counted, or who he thought might someday count. He reserved his resentment for common people, those he could abuse with no comebacks.

Matt had learned a lot about Martinez and Swagger through the grapevine. His information was confirmed by his friend and country lawyer, Judge Ovashefsky. His confidant Ruby Jackson was even more emphatic in her contempt of Swagger and her admiration for Martinez. If further condemnation was needed, it was provided by Old Man Skinner, who was an enthusiastic supporter of Swagger.

While Matt felt strongly that Martinez *should* be the new sheriff, the practical side of his mind accepted Judge Ovashefsky's view of the inevitable, that Fats Swagger was unbeatable, that a decent member of the force would soon be looking for a job. The sheriff's department would become more corrupt than ever, but Swagger and his gang would be no personal threat to Matt. As only part-time members of the rural social structure, the Houston briefcase farmers enjoyed an elevated aura of affluence. Simply being able to buy farms that the locals couldn't afford gave them presumed financial power, and money is about the strongest political influence there is. They were treated with deference by local peace officers and mainly left alone.

A good example of that deference was in the handling of a speed trap set up about ten miles north of Brentwood. There the speed limit on the Brentwood-Rip Ford Highway inexplicably dropped from 55 to 40 for a mile, then went back to 55. The southbound 40 MPH sign was just over the top of a rise, so it came into view all of a sudden, and a convenient patch of small trees just beyond it was large enough to hide a police car. Motorists were seined in there in large numbers. Citizens whose appearance suggested they would not tolerate such flagrant treatment were either not stopped or waved on with a smile, but motorists with the look of vulnerability were a gold mine. Matt Bradley had sailed through that trap way over the speed limit a dozen times in his distinctive blue company car with the red and white oil company logo on the doors; not once had the hidden patrol car stirred.

Matt was keenly aware of the never-ending conflict between just and unjust in politics, and he was troubled by much of what he saw. But he was smart enough to know that he could consume himself fighting for justice without ever making a particle of difference. He had seen good people completely expend themselves in such crusades, all for absolutely nothing.

Matt had long believed that certain circumstances were ordained by fate, but it was a belief that was becoming frayed. His entire existence had been spent in a middle-class social cocoon in the city, so it was not surprising that when he'd first encountered the country blacks who would become his friends, he had already been influenced by the local perception that they were hard-working folks, but had little sense of direction or purpose. It had taken some time, living in the community and observing first-hand the more subtle aspects of the social fabric there, for Matt and Norma to discover that their black neighbors hung tenaciously to the very highest human principles, and under the harshest circumstances.

It became evident to the Bradleys, too, that blacks were condemned by ingrained influences to be insulted, abused, and sometimes flagrantly robbed by supposedly upstanding citizens. It was no secret, either, who the hawks were who preyed on the black people—most often peace officers, but also certain bankers, lawyers, tradesmen, and government officials. His conscious mind was completely in the dark, but the election of the Winchester County Sheriff was taking on a significance to Matt Bradley that went way beyond a desire to see good prevail over evil.

It was inevitable that the Bradleys would find dear friends in Ruby and Oscar Jackson, and they became much more than mere employers of Rufus and Duffie. Love and understanding created an empathy that ultimately allowed the Bradleys to see that these members of society deemed low class had refused to give up what those who disdained them had lost forever: a genuine faith in God, an acute appreciation of the line between right and wrong, a resourcefulness to somehow scrimp along honorably on almost nothing during the worst of times, and an inner strength to serenely endure injustices against them with stoic heroism. And through it all they had always retained their dignity.

When Mike Martinez became the longest-of-long-shots candidate for Winchester County Sheriff, it was these influences that eventually overwhelmed Matt with the conviction that Martinez simply *must* be elected to the job. He saw it as the only chance to end the plundering of these people. And once he discussed it with Norma, she saw it as an unavoidable obligation.

What was riding on this particular election was extraordinary. A victory by Martinez would provide, for once, full-fledged citizenship status to the most deserving people in the county. It would also end a reign of flagrant piracy.

Matt Bradley became driven by a burning obsession that Mike Martinez would be the next sheriff of Winchester County. He was determined that he would not, *could* not, leave a single strategy unused that might bring in votes. And so he began to explore election strategies. Matt's employer had excellent political connections, and owning a Learjet significantly strengthened them. Statewide and national political candidates have a lot of ground to cover, and nothing beats corporate airplanes for getting around nimbly. They are fast, not hampered by schedules, and, importantly, they do not consume precious campaign money.

Piloting political aspirants around and observing the operations of big-time campaigns from the inside had been a valuable education for Matt. He had seen firsthand the lamentable reality that the best candidate for an office can often be the least able to secure it through the so-called democratic process. It therefore did not surprise him that the personal attributes that would make Mike Martinez a splendid sheriff would be of no value whatever in the formidable struggle to get him elected. If he *was* going to get elected, Martinez needed top-notch strategists and skilled grass-roots organizers.

Although his employer owned the plane, Matt Bradley was the visible agent in charge of it. Consequently, he had a pile of IOUs available for redemption. Redeeming them would be made easier because it was an off-year, when the election specialists were sitting around waiting for another general election; then Matt's services would once more be sought after by those whose chits he was now calling in. Matt was able to present the Martinez-

Swagger campaign to some genuine campaign experts, masters at running big-time contests against gritty, professional opposition. From them he obtained valuable organizing advice, but he also learned that an off-year special election was winnable by an under-dog, *if* the campaign was conducted like an all-out war.

"You say the machine's candidate is the hare and your guy is the turtle, huh?" asked a veteran of some bloody campaigns. He rubbed his hands together and grinned wickedly. "Good. Outstanding. Because they'll be sitting on their hands and con-gratulating each other right up until they discover they've had the crap kicked out of 'em. Matt, if you really want to win this thing, here's what it'll take. First, a campaign takes money, and here's how you go about raising political contributions. . . ." Concluding that lengthy discussion, he held up two fingers. "Second, you need a seasoned campaign manager, a specialist at knocking off so-called unbeatable opponents. As it happens, I have the perfect team in mind for your campaign." He chuckled, a diabolical chortle that had sent a chill through Matt.

Matt went to work, with Norma serving as his capable lieu-tenant. Following the procedures described by the expert, Matt worked his field of potential contributors and Norma worked hers. The Houstonians who had farms in Winchester County—which was a much larger group than he had ever imagined—contributed almost without exception. And to the fundraisers' great pleasure, an impressive sum was contributed by people with no apparent inter-est in the outcome of the election except the chance to see a good candidate prevail over a corrupt one.

A strong group was assembled by Andrew Meridith, a big band of campaign workers and contributors of a lot of money. Meridith's many friends in both the Professional Rodeo Cowboys Association and the National Cutting Horse Association were enormous assets.

The war chest that was raised was huge by county standards. It allowed Matt to hire the professional man-and-wife team his expert had recommended, a duo renowned for creating victorious campaigns for long-shot underdogs. They had over the years been occasional beneficiaries of Matt's private airline, which may have enhanced their zeal for the Martinez campaign. They took up resi-dence in the county and worked quietly but feverishly at getting the small group of Martinez campaign irregulars—it was certainly no more at the time—hammered into a cohesive squad. Soon the squad was a platoon; ultimately it became a tough and disciplined guerrilla army.

The enthusiasm of the workers who could see it all coming together could not be contained. Soon the evidence of a major Martinez campaign was as plain as day to anyone with eyes. But the Swagger people steadfastly refused to believe the challenger had even a ghost of a chance. They were riding a high tide of optimism and no evidence to the contrary could dampen it; every single county commissioner and many city officials and employees had "Swagger with Sheriff Swagger" signs in their yards, prematurely bestowing the *title* of sheriff on Swagger even before the election. Swagger was a walk-in, they all told each other, and they believed what they heard from one another and what they, themselves, said. As election day approached, activity in the Martinez camp was becoming volcanic in intensity, yet Swagger's supporters couldn't—or *wouldn't*—see it. They complacently sat on their hands, content that their man would be swept into office.

Suddenly, during the last week before election day, large signs sprouted up in hundreds of front yards and on farmland fronting highways and roads across the county, including the yard of the county judge: "*For once in your life you can elect an <u>honest lawman</u>— MARTINEZ FOR SHERIFF*," they read. "Martinez-for-Sheriff" bumper stickers blossomed in astounding numbers. It seemed as if half the vehicles in the county suddenly sported the red, white, and blue triangular flags on their radio antennas that shouted, "Martinez for Sheriff." The Martinez campaign was in full afterburners.

On election day, five vehicles equipped with loudspeakers cruised every road in the county, playing patriotic marches and urging voters to "Go to the polls and vote for Mike Martinez for sheriff. Make the big shots behind Swagger throw their votes away."

Perhaps everyone in the Martinez camp except Matt Bradley was surprised to see first one little airplane and then another flying back and forth above Winchester County towing huge banners: "Martinez for Sheriff."

Matt gave Rufus and Duffie the day off to drive people to the polls. From the time the polls opened until they closed, hundreds of other citizens provided transportation for voters. People who had no intention of voting were roused out of their homes and from their jobs, and hauled to the polls to vote. Most of them would have voted for Ronald McDonald over Fats Swagger.

Despite flagrant "irregularities" in the voting procedure at some precincts, Martinez hammered Swagger by a margin of almost three to one. The election seriously bloodied the nose of the Winchester County political machine and demonstrated to the people who had long considered their votes to be worthless that collectively they had a mighty big say in county politics.

Now after two years on the job, Sheriff Martinez had turned the department upside down. Petty arrests and traffic citations had long ago ceased, and the bail bondsman who had prospered for so long started selling real estate and insurance to make ends meet. Official harassment of blacks was a thing of the past and black citizens in old vehicles discovered they did not have to drive ten miles under the speed limit to keep from getting a speeding ticket. When black people became victims of crime, the criminals were sought as diligently as those who committed crimes against whites. The sheriff and his deputies waved greetings to citizens as they passed on the roads, and their greetings were enthusiastically returned with waving arms, flashing headlights, and beeping horns. For the first time in anybody's memory, there was genuine harmony between the sheriff's department and the people, all the people.

Motorists who displayed the gaudy silver-star decals of the Sheriff's Club, identifying them as big donors to the deposed sheriff, discovered that they could no longer ignore traffic laws with immunity. They received real tickets instead of the good-old-boy winks they had become accustomed to. Those without Sheriff's Club decals on display learned that they were more likely than club members to be favored with a warning instead of a traffic ticket.

The Sheriff's Club died a swift death, but a few diehards still displayed their decals—Old Man Skinner for one. One day Skinner was stopped by Sheriff Martinez and given a written warning for having his rear window obstructed. "I'm not going to give you a ticket this time, Mr. Skinner. But for your own safety please remove those decals. No telling what might come up on you unseen. Good day, sir."

MATT INTRODUCED SHERIFF MARTINEZ to Jim and Buddy. He greeted them with friendly handshakes. Gently and skillfully he questioned the boys for a half-hour, prodding their memories and bringing out even minor details of the men, their clothing, speech, and mannerisms. He obtained good descriptions of the pickup and the motorcycle. He told the boys that the devices they saw on the rifle and pistol were suppressors. "They're often called silencers," he said, "but they don't really *silence*. The clicking sounds you heard were the actions of the guns. The cracks like a loud cap pistol were made by the bullets. You can't keep a supersonic bullet from making that crack. It's like a sonic boom made by a plane.

"Now, Buddy, Jim, you said they were going to take the cargo—it has to be marijuana or cocaine—to somewhere by boat. Something that sounded like Frankie, you thought they said. Hmmm. Doesn't ring a bell at all." He shook his head. "Did he say where the boat was going to be waiting?"

Jim thought and looked at Buddy. "I don't think he named a place. Buddy?"

"I didn't hear much after them bullets started flyin'. I shut my eyes and ears up tight."

Jim snapped his fingers. "Wait . . ." he said. "The main guy said they were supposed to go to a ferry." He frowned, trying to recollect more. "I can't think of the name of it. And he said to go there by the back roads."

Puzzlement showed on Sheriff Martinez's face. "Ferry? Hmmm." He ran his hand thoughtfully through his thick, wavy hair. "A ferry. Did they say the name of the body of water? A lake? Surely not the Gulf. A river?" Both boys were shaking their heads. "Did they mention anything about the boat trip that might be a clue?"

Buddy sat up straight. "The one with the bushy mustache said the guys in the boat better drive slow and keep a lookout for float-ing trees. The only place I know has trees floating down is the Brazos."

Sheriff Martinez brightened. "Good, Buddy. *Excellent.* That tells me a lot. But a ferry . . . ? Well, I thank you both, sincerely." He extended his hand to Jim, then to Buddy. "Now I want another favor. You absolutely must obey me or your lives could be in danger." He scanned the group. "Nobody here can say a word about this incident. If you do, the people involved will know you can identify them and they wouldn't think twice about killing you.

"I think I know the one you called Brad, the big guy with the bushy mustache. The others, Al, Red, Winnie—" He shook his head. "And there was one named Joey staked out on League Line

Road. All of it gives us a lot to go on. We'll be waiting for that plane tonight. Boys, you did good detective work. But you took a big chance. Too big a chance. Stay away from that particular place along your highway in the sky. Any time you hear voices or smell marijuana or even tobacco smoke, turn around and get away from there and call the department. Okay, do I have your secrecy pledge?"

"I won't tell nobody, not even the kids at school," said Buddy with extravagant zeal.

"Me either," said Jim. "I promise."

The adults engaged in genial conversation for a little while, the sheriff showing no inclination to go dashing off. Meanwhile, Old Black had wandered into the corral and stood with his head over the fence. A low neighing sound came from deep in his throat, causing everyone to turn and look at him.

Taking advantage of the break in the conversation, Jim said softly, "I got a horse yesterday, Sheriff."

"Well, you'll have to join my Sheriff's Mounted Posse. I'd like to have you as a member." He laid a big hand on Jim's shoulder and asked if he could take a look at his horse.

After walking slowly around Old Black, Martinez stood contemplating him. "Quarter Horse, of course," he said. "A good strong one, too. A bright eye. Plenty of sense. Old enough to know what's going on. Looks like you got a good 'un, Jim."

Jim's self-conscious grin was growing as the sheriff talked. "Yes, sir," he said and glanced at his father.

Matt nodded. "Tell Sheriff Martinez a little bit about Old Black, Jim. He's not just your ordinary great but undistinguished Quarter Horse, Sheriff."

Jim said, "He's the world's champion calf-roping horse. And he took second place in Houston just this year."

"I wasn't far off the mark, was I?" said Sheriff Martinez. "Even if I didn't realize he might be a world champ. Am I going to see you in our mounted posse?"

"Yes, sir—I mean, I sure hope so. Can I Dad, Mom?" Their faces told Jim the answer was yes.

CHAPTER 13

"Don't show up at the Meridith's even one minute before eight, Jim," his father had told him the night before. It was only seven-thirty and Jim had Old Black already saddled and ready to go. He had at least ten minutes to kill before he could start out, a long time when there was nothing to do with it.

He rode down the lane toward the gate with the hope that Mrs. Jackson might be outdoors. On crossing the wooden bridge, though, he decided to explore the deep draw that he and Buddy had spent so much time playing in—if he could find a bank that wasn't too steep for the horse. The deep gash across the Bradley property carried runoff from Richter's cotton field to Sandy Creek, which took the water to Hickory Creek. It was deepest, at least fifteen feet from the grassy bank to the sandy bottom, at a large, pear-shaped place just below the bridge. The water that coursed down the draw in wet weather stood in pools here and there for a few days following rains, and had nourished some fine woods along the banks.

Relishing his first lofty horseback view of this special place, he approached the draw on the south side and rode in and out of the trees along the bank. With no experience at all riding on steep terrain, he was reluctant to try anything daring. About half-way along the length of the draw, they came upon a cattle trail. If cows could negotiate that slope, he knew Old Black could. He gave Old Black his head and, sure enough, down he went. The going was easy along the barren floor of the draw; he turned Old Black back toward the bridge and rode between banks that gradually became higher and higher.

Thinking he might try climbing out on a steeper bank than he came down, he rode up to a place where the bank was about five feet high and fairly steep. Jim was still looking the incline over with the horse in a slow walk, undecided, when Old Black gathered himself up and in two leaps he was up and over the rim. He stood easy at the top, but Jim's heart was beating like a hammer! Still clutching the saddle horn and breathing heavily, he said audibly, "Whew!"

Could he descend as easily? Jim thought it better to let Old Black decide for himself. If he showed any hesitation, he'd turn him away and take the easy route down. He rode to the edge and stopped, then raised the reins and clucked softly. Old Black stepped right off the rim. He allowed his big feet to dig in just enough to keep his swift descent under control, like a skier skillfully using his edges, but to Jim it was such a free-fall that his insides rose up in his chest. It took both hands on the pommel to keep him from drifting out of the saddle.

This was *something!* Again he felt the rush of exhilaration. Now began a gradual escalation of the activity, taking higher and steeper climbs and descents. His strategy was to let the horse decide for himself what his limitations were. There seemed to be no daunting challenges so far. But as he rode closer to them, he saw that the walls around the damp bed of the deep bowl would be a different matter. A good look all around showed no place they could negotiate out of here. Wait! His eye fell on an angular cut in one slope—a diagonal traverse—that would allow an ascent at an angle. Even so, it was so steep and high that Jim wondered if any horse could climb that bank.

He rode slowly toward the place where the traverse began. With no notion at all to chance a climb, he leaned forward in the saddle to examine the place more closely. To Old Black, Jim's movement was the command to go, and with an explosive leap and one powerful jump after another he bounded up the face of the creekbank. Jim's head was alongside the horse's neck and both hands held on for dear life. In a final giant leap, Old Black cleared the rim of the draw. Jim's heart was drumming and his ears pounded with the resonating echoes of the hoofbeats, but Old Black was as calm as if he had been negotiating these climbs every day. With his knees shaking, Jim decided he should start for Alexandra's and pointed Old Black toward the gate.

Two minutes before Old Black came thundering out of the draw, Duffie had entered the gate. Disarmed by years of enjoying pure tranquility along this stretch of lane, he was serenely ambling across the bridge just as the horse thundered up the bank only sixty feet away. It was immaterial that the source of the commotion was screened from

Duffie's view, because he instinctively fled at top speed without so much as a glance in the direction of the terror behind him.

When he sensed that the main action had subsided, he threw a cautious look over his shoulder. Seeing a horse standing there, one that was not pursuing him, he slowly came to a stop and turned around. His expression changed from one of fright to astonishment to wonder to honest appreciation in a sequence that made Jim think of images flashing from a slide projector.

"Jim!" he cried. "Whooeee! I thought it was the devil's herd comin' out of that draw! Whew!" he panted, and began fanning himself with his hat as he wiped his forehead with his bandanna. "I mean—*that* was a thunderation!"

"Gee, Duffie. I'm sorry we came baling out of that draw just at the wrong time. I guess it would've scared anybody. I didn't know you were there," Jim said apologetically as he rode up to where Duffie stood fanning himself.

Duffie was more composed now; his shoulders relaxed as the tenseness left him. "Whew . . . Lordy," he said. He allowed himself a small laugh and took several deep breaths. "You got a horse?"

"Yeah, I do, Duffie," Jim said, nodding emphatically. "I just got him Saturday. He's the world's calf-roping champion. His name is Old Black. And the saddle came with him. His owner was quitting rodeoing. Aren't you amazed that I got a horse like Old Black?"

Duffie patted the horse on the neck. "Well, your daddy been threatenin' to get you a hoss. And I knowed he wouldn't get nothin' shabby. But a world's champion! And just look at that saddle. A fine one, it is, and not surprisin' since it was rode by a real cowboy."

Duffie stood back so he could admire the whole horse.

In a modest voice, Jim said, "Yeah, it's a good saddle. A little big for me now, but . . . I'm going over to Alexandra's, to show her Old Black. Dad cut the clover field, and we're baling at eleven."

WHAT COULD BE MORE EXASPERATING, JIM WONDERED, than to have such a story to tell and then be forbidden to tell it? Even without stumbling onto the gang, the highway in the sky would be an exciting thing to tell about. He had never heard of anything like that broad, cushiony, avenue of tightly-woven vines winding high in the trees for maybe a quarter of a mile. With the morning sun warm on his shoulder, Jim rode along with Old Black in a lively walk, reliving the whole experience.

Maybe he would have time to ride over to Richter's store on a roundabout way home. He was anxious to show Old Black off to Mr. Richter. He had been telling him he was going to get a horse, but he could see that the horse in Mr. Richter's mind was a kid's horse, maybe even a pony with a cheap, flashy saddle.

"Did you get to ride a pony at the Winchester County fair?" Mr. Richter had asked last year, as if Jim would ever want to sit on a scruffy Shetland pony that trudged around a twenty-foot circle. "You could have your picture taken on one," he had added in all sincerity.

Out of the bright sunshine, Jim rode, into the deep purple shadows beneath the pecan trees that lined the lane leading to Alexandra's house. Soon Alexandra's sorrel gelding, Applejack, came in sight, saddled and tied to the hitching post under the big live oak by the house. Applejack neighed loudly at their approach. Jim rode up to him, letting the horses smell each other's noses, getting acquainted. He was about to slide down from the saddle when Alexandra came bursting out of the house. "Jim! Hi, Jim," she cried, running up and reaching to take his hand in both of hers. She tugged at him playfully. Jim could not imagine a prettier face than the one before him; her eyes seemed to look into the very core of his being, and he felt a pleasant ache inside.

"And this is the famous Old Black!" she exclaimed in a voice filled with admiration, stepping back for a better view. Hands clasped beneath her chin and smiling broadly, she leaned back as she surveyed the wonders of him. "Uhh, ummm," she said as she walked around the horse. "Ummmm, yes. He's solid as a rock, isn't he, Jim? And what a bright eye! Oh, Jim, I'm so happy you have a horse. And what a horse you *have!* Daddy knows all about Old Black. He knows Buck Jones—"

"Hi, Mr. Meridith," Jim called out as Alexandra's father strode out of the house. "I hope I didn't get here too early, but I have to be home by eleven to start baling hay."

"Howdy, Jim," said Andrew Meridith. "You could have come an hour ago for this household. We get going early. You know what they say about being early and getting the worms. Trouble is, nobody around here likes worms." He laughed, stopping a few paces away from Old Black, looking him over. He stepped up and scratched him under the chin, then, using his knuckles, he vigorously rubbed the horse's face. Old Black leaned into the facial, showing how much he liked it. Jim tucked this away in his mind. It was another treat he could give Old Black sometime.

Meridith spoke to the horse in a low, private voice, "Hello, Black old boy. It sure is good to see you." Looking the horse in the eye, he said in a normal tone, "You did good, Jimmy. This is one heck of a horse. I've known Old Black longer than I've known my little girl, here." Alexandra was thirteen. "What a horse he is." He looked at Jim curiously. "Did Buck say why he sold him? That saddle—" He stepped up close and ran his hand over the pommel, then the rear skirt. "Let me see, here." He moved Jim's leg aside to reveal the saddle maker's mark on the stirrup leather. "I *knew* it! A Wehring!" he exclaimed, then said in an urgent voice, "This was Buck's saddle, wasn't it?"

Jim nodded.

"He sold his saddle," Mr. Meridith said, his voice grave.

He sold his saddle is an old-west expression cowboys used when speaking of a cowboy who had quit for good. Buck Jones was through rodeoing, Andrew knew that, for sure.

Meridith's sculpting career restricted him to the rodeos close to home: Houston, San Antonio, Austin, Fort Worth . . . He also made some of the other majors like Cheyenne and Calgary. And Buck Jones was always there, at every one. But here was Buck's famous horse, his Wehring saddle, bridle and other tack: his whole shooting match.

"What happened to Buck?" he asked in a concerned voice.

Once again Jim was being called on to speculate on why Buck Jones sold his horse. But what reason could he give? His father's guess was probably right.

"Mr. Meridith," he said at last, "Mr. Jones might be sick. When Dad and I saw him Saturday he was limping real bad. Dad thinks—"

"Limping?" said Mr. Meridith. "I never knew Buck to limp. And he was limping bad, eh?"

"Yes, sir, pretty bad. It got to looking like he was hurting awful before we left."

Meridith pursed his lips thoughtfully. An illness bad enough to cause Buck to sell Old Black and all of his gear would have to look like the end of the line, he figured. "I'll check up on him," he said. "I can tell you right now that you got a powerful good horse here.

Probably a better horse than you could possibly realize. What I can't figure, though, is why Buck didn't sell Old Black to a roper. He would have brought big bucks from a roper." He kept stroking Old Black gently and said, "Jim, do you mind if I ride him? I always like to get on a sure-enough horse every chance I get."

Jim readily agreed. Alexandra mounted Applejack and together they rode along behind Mr. Meridith as he walked toward the expansive barn that housed his training arena and art studio. They rode through the gate Meridith opened in the pipe fence. A few paces further on Jim stopped Old Black and slid down onto the earth floor. Meridith began to adjust Jim's stirrups to accommodate his six-feet-plus. He held the stirrup out toward Alexandra and said, "Look here, Alex. Jim needs an Easy-Up. Don't we have a spare?"

She went into her tack room and came back with an Easy-Up.

With the stirrups adjusted to his satisfaction, Mr. Meridith swung aboard in the graceful, effortless motion characteristic of experienced horsemen. He stretched the stirrups out with his legs. He wriggled around in the saddle seat. He leaned far right with his weight in the stirrup, then far left. Finally, with his left hand he picked the reins up off Old Black's neck and raised them a couple of inches. Old Black straightened up as he came untracked, ready for duty. Jim saw a slight smile cross Mr. Meridith's face.

Meridith leaned forward almost unnoticeably and Old Black stepped out smartly. They scribed a large circle to the right; then, responding to the slightest cue, Old Black began a circle to the left. Meridith leaned back a little and Old Black stopped. Meridith grinned openly, gave a signal that he wanted to back up and Old Black marched backward in a steady beat of quick steps. He asked for a more energetic backup and Old Black flew backward in a storm, raising a cloud of dust and bringing on another broad grin. Meridith laid a rein gently on Old Black's neck while giving leg cues and Old Black spun like a top three complete revolutions to the right, then to the left. His face now showed a huge smile as he loped away for a distance, spun into an easy reverse and loped up to Jim and Alexandra. "Is he an athlete or not, Alex?"

Alexandra was beaming. She hadn't expected Jim to come even close to the likes of Old Black. She'd asked her father if he could help find a good horse for Jim at a reasonable price, a thousand dollars, maybe a little more, she'd said. His pessimism had been obvious.

"Honey," he'd said, "any decent horse that comes through here is going to sell for several thousand dollars, at the low end—their owners know what they're worth. I'll keep my feelers out, though. But what Matt's gotta do is just spread the word he's looking and hope someone with a fairly good horse has to get rid of it for some reason."

Meridith turned Old Black away from them, stood him quietly for a moment, then in a burst of arena dirt they were off at a dead run. The horse began a hard slide and came tearing out of it in the opposite direction. Andrew asked him for a hard stop right in front of Jim and Alexandra, and he got it. He stepped off, slapped Old Black on the neck several times, then walked up to face the horse.

He rubbed both jaws vigorously. "You're something, Old Black," he said. "Jim's going to kick some tail with you. Ha!" He turned to his daughter. "You have some competition here, once Jim and Old Black get their feet wet. Competition that's going to be worse than that Ricky Hoffman, Sweetheart. We've got a class horse in our midst, here. Yes sir, when Old Black gets used to the drills, he's going to open some eyes, and make tears flow in some of them, too. But remember, Sweetie, it's always better to be beat by friends." He looked straight at Jim. "Lady Luck let old Buck Jones down, Jim. But she was sure enough smiling on you."

With her eyes going back and forth between Jim and her hands, Alexandra said, "I would stand second to Jim and Old Black any time and never once complain. I'll make no apology for getting beat by a world champion ridden by Jim."

Jim looked at her, his heart fairly bursting with the emotion that had enveloped him. He had taken it for granted that Old Black was a fine performer. He had taken Mr. Jackson's praise to heart, but here was an expert, a professional horseman praising Old Black to the heavens, and he thrilled to the expert's words.

Mr. Meridith began re-adjusting the stirrups for Jim. When he had finished, Alexandra handed him the Easy-Up. He attached it to the near stirrup and said, "Try this, Jimmy."

The stirrup was a good four inches lower now, low enough for Jim to reach it with his foot, even if just barely. He reached up and wound a pair of saddle strings around his right hand, took the stirrup leather in his left, and with a mighty spring he swung on board. It was the first time he had ever mounted Old Black without a platform of some kind. It was not a smooth performance, but he was in the saddle, and pleased as he could be with this new ability.

Mr. Meridith lifted Jim's boot toe. "Raise the stirrup with your boot." Jim did so and felt a click. He put his weight in the stirrup and it was as firm as before. "Before mounting, you just press here and pull the stirrup down," Mr. Meridith said, demonstrating.

Meridith stood caressing the deeply engraved saddle skirts. Then he grasped the big roping horn. He cocked his head. "Jim, do you have any idea what this saddle is worth?"

Jim mutely shook his head.

"Well, I'll tell you." He moved Jim's leg and pointed to the saddle maker's mark. "This is a Wehring roping saddle." He ran his fingertips over the mark as he talked, touching the stamping lightly, respectfully. Jim had studied the ornate oval design stamped into each stirrup leather; inside the scrollwork outline were the words *EZELL WEHRING, Maker*. In smaller letters on a second line was *Yoakum, Texas*. "There isn't a better saddle made anywhere. I can't afford to ride Wehrings because cutting wears saddles out too fast. I own just one Wehring— it's sort of my Sunday dress-up saddle.

"Old Ezell Wehring has two assistants, fine old Mexican leather craftsmen he's had for maybe thirty years, and maybe three or four helpers. It's just him and them, and there are certain things in the making of a saddle that he won't trust to anybody—he does those things personally, and keeps a keen eye on everything else going on. They can't make but so many saddles a year. I don't know how long his backlog is, and if you aren't somebody, you don't even get on the list.

"A big-time saddle company in Fort Worth tried to buy Wehring out. They wanted the name is all, and they were prepared to pay plenty to get it. No way could they ever make genuine Wehring saddles—I doubt if they'd even try. But the *name* would be worth a fortune to them, anyway. But Ezell wouldn't sell. He says when he dies the Wehring saddle line dies out too."

Meridith was still examining the saddle minutely. "I'm going to say that this saddle cost Buck Jones about twenty-five hundred," he watched Jim's eyebrows reflect his amazement. Alexandra inhaled audibly. "And because Buck's a long-time professional cowboy, he got a special deal. This saddle—used, just like it is—would easily bring three thousand, just like that," he said, snapping his fingers, "for the simple reason that they're so hard to get." He looked at Jim with a significant expression. "And guess what this saddle might be worth when you can't get a Wehring any more, for any price?

"Buck hasn't had this saddle more'n a year or two. It's just broke-in good—ropers don't wear saddles out like us cuttin' horse riders.

This saddle will last you the rest of your life and still be one your son or daughter would be proud to ride. And *their* kids." He chuckled. "You want to hear a good saddle story, Jim?" he asked.

Naturally, Jim said he would. Alexandra began to snicker at her recollection of the event and put her hand over her mouth. It didn't faze the merry dazzle in her eyes, though, and Jim knew he was going to hear something good.

"Mike Sanderford is a real rich guy—you've seen his Running-S Ranch on I-Ten, the one with a couple of miles of white pipe fences just before you get to the Brazos River? Yeah, I knew you had.

"Mike has some terrific horses, running Quarter Horses, mostly. But I've trained several of his horses at cutting—won the championship three years ago with Sandy Sue S. One day Mike comes by and takes a saddle out of the trunk of his car. It's a brand-new Wehring saddle." He tapped the maker's mark on Jim's stirrup leather.

"Mike's real. There's not a phony bone in his body. But he didn't want to be riding around on a brand new saddle, looking like a greenhorn. He thought maybe I could ride it some and take the new edge off of it, so he asked me about it. Sure, I tell him. Then I ask him how much he wants me to ride it. 'Andrew,' he says, and pokes me in the chest with a finger, 'you just ride it until I come back for it. If the seat's shiny by then, I'll be surprised.' I didn't say a word, just took the saddle." Meridith smiled.

"Well, Jim, the average guy would be dumfounded at how quick cutting horse trainers go through saddles. We're riding one horse after another all day long, and most of it's zigging and zagging. There's a lot of movement between the horse and the rider, and the saddle absorbs the brunt of that movement. Mike's kinda fond of claiming how easy us cutting horse trainers have it, charging a whole lot for a little bit of riding. When Mike dropped his saddle off, we were just getting ready for a futurity that was coming up; I was riding several horses regular, every day.

"I decided to rub his nose in that remark about him being surprised if I even got his saddle-seat shiny. Mike didn't show up again till over a month later. I was on a horse at the time. I dismounted and we began talking, mostly about his futurity prospect. Then he noticed the saddle I was riding. He couldn't *help* but notice because it was the raggediest-looking thing you ever saw. There were big holes worn plumb through the stirrup leathers, and holes through the skirts where they rubbed on the D-rings. The new front cinch strap stood out because it was plain new leather—light tan instead of brown like the saddle. The stirrups were worn plumb through the leather, right down into the wood. Powdered leather lay in every nook and cranny, like dust from termites at work. Brother, that saddle was ready for the scrap pile." He smiled again.

"Mike asked me why I was riding such a shabby old saddle. 'Old? It's not old,' I said. 'That's your saddle, Mike. I'm sure glad you showed up, because being a man of my word I had to ride that thing till you got back, but I was getting afraid it would fall all to pieces and dump me on the ground.' I unsaddled the horse right then and said, 'Here's your saddle, Mike.' And a Wehring, it was. I'll bet he paid five thousand for it, because Wehring sticks it to everybody but real cowboys. It was cowboys that put him on the map, and he likes to confine his output to them. He claims the prices he charges the rich guys help subsidize the cowboys.

"I've got to hand it to Mike. He was real good-natured about it. After he got over the shock, that is. He has that saddle on a rack in the big den at his ranch house, sort of like a trophy."

Now Meridith gently probed for some of the details about how Old Black had come to live on the Bradley ranch. Once Jim got to the asking price of six hundred dollars, the sculptor began to nod. "And what did Buck charge for his saddle, Jim?" Somehow, Meridith knew the answer that was coming.

"He didn't charge anything for the saddle. He told Dad he'd said six hundred, and to make sure there was no mistake, he said that included the saddle, too, and a lot of other tack and stuff. He went through his lariats and picked this one out special for me. He said it was a thirty-five-foot heeling rope."

Meridith was quiet. Jim noticed that he was biting his upper lip; his expression was grave.

At last he said, "I have it figured out, Jim. Buck wasn't looking to sell Old Black. He was trying his darndest to find him a swell home, with a swell boy or girl that would take good care of him. That's all. Money wasn't any part of it.

"It wasn't accidental that he went to George Bonner, either. One day—oh, it must have been a year or more ago—Buck and I happened to be sitting together in the stands among some other cowboys killing time at San Antone. Some kid events were going on and we were watching them, shooting the bull. Somebody said what good-looking horses the kids had.

"And Buck said, out of the clear blue, 'In my next life, I hope I come back as a horse, and fall into the hands of a kid like one of them down there. And it would make me happy if the kid's folks had a nice place in the country, so I wouldn't have to be shut up in a stall. The icing on the cake would be that my owner was a nice, considerate kid, and one with a light hand. And for my little master, I'd win everything in sight, too.'

"Guess who I would go to if I was looking for such a kid, Jim? George Bonner, that's who. And Buck knew who to go to, just as sure as I would." Meridith squeezed Jim's upper leg and looked at him with affection.

"Fate dealt Buck a bad hand, and I intend to find out what it was. Lady Luck knew that the closest thing to Buck's heart was Old Black, so she stepped in and gave him the big break he was looking for, and then some—delivered Old Black to the nicest, most considerate kid I know outside of my little girl here. And a lighter hand on bridle reins doesn't exist." He patted Jim smartly on the leg.

"I gotta go to work," he said, turned and strode off across the arena toward his studio.

Alexandra had been standing at Old Black's head as her father spoke, rubbing and scratching him. Jim watched Mr. Meridith go into his studio, a big room on one side of the barn. Alexandra looked up at Jim with an earnest expression. "If I was a horse, I would love to be your horse too, Jim," she said, her voice soft and warm.

Jim was overcome; he did not trust himself to say anything. He could only look at her.

She broke the tension by saying brightly, "Should we practice the keyhole race and then the flag race? Later, if you want to we can ride by Richter's store and get a soda. On the way back we can split up at the fork at Mr. Mabel's and you could still get home by eleven."

Still in a bit of a daze over what Mr. Meridith had said about Old Black, and about his Wehring saddle, he absently agreed. So Alexandra drew out the lines for the keyhole race, stepping off the distances with practiced precision. To lay down the white line of the circle, Jim anchored one end of a rope in the center and with her chalk-line marker tied to the other end, Alexandra walked the perimeter. With the same brisk movements she set up six poles in a straight line for the flag race, with Jim carrying the poles and stands for her to place in position. A flag was set in the recess at the top of each pole.

The keyhole race was nothing but natural moves for Old Black. The slot of the keyhole was entered at full speed; the horse was required to stop, reverse, and dash out of the keyhole without breaking a line. When an error was made, it was Jim who had erred, asking for the stop too late, causing Old Black to slide through the back of the keyhole. But soon Old Black began to understand the exercise and apply his own timing to the stop and reverse.

Alexandra was monitoring the timer. When the horse came out of the slot, she would ride up to the readout that showed the elapsed time between the horse's first crossing of the photocell's beam and then the second crossing, when the horse came out of the slot. They had been at it for some time when Alexandra announced, "Look, Jim, you came within six-tenths of beating me on that run." The feeling of genuine competition, even though it was between only two contestants, and friends, was exhilarating. A real clock and a real course!

Alexandra looked at her watch. "Do you think we should start running the flags now?"

Jim had seen the flag race run many times. He understood the course perfectly, but was not prepared for the difficulties he would encounter running it.

"Why don't you just make a run," Alexandra said. "Then we'll discuss strategies. We don't need to bother with setting up the clock, do we Jim?" He agreed they didn't.

Jim rushed Old Black to the first flag, overran it, and had to back up a step to make the exchange of flags. Then he stopped short of the second one. He dropped a flag, and knocked down a pole. The entire run of six poles was a ragged affair; the only decently performed part was the reverse at the end and the run for the finish.

Alexandra explained. "It's not as easy as it looks, is it Jim? Watch and you'll spot the places where you've got to do everything just right." She made a casual run, controlling her horse so he never went faster than a slow lope. She executed the stops smoothly, stopping at precisely the right spot, where she made a deft exchange of flags and then loped away to the next pole. At the last flag she made a reverse and only then did she show any speed, making a blazing dash for the finish, standing in the stirrups and leaning far over Applejack's neck.

She called Jim over to the rail, where they dismounted. "I can promise you that your next run will be much smoother. And even though you'll deliberately run the course slower, your *time* will be faster. Here's how my daddy got me started." To emphasize that this was the first of several points to be made, she bent her left little finger back with her right forefinger. "He had me run the course slowly, almost lazily, starting in a nice lope to the first flag."

Her forefinger took control of the next finger for the second point. "Stop without trying to drag your horse's tail in the dirt, but make sure the stop is right at the flag, and that your horse is very close to the flag so you don't have to lean over to make the exchange."

Her forefinger was now on her middle finger. "Third point. Hold the flag like this. Make the exchange by first taking the flag out like this," she demonstrated, "and replacing it with the new flag, like this. You won't miss if you do it like that every time. And when you stick the flag in the pole this way, bringing your hand on down and following through as you release it, you won't have to worry if it will stay put. But drop a flag on the ground and it's a lost cause. Now do it."

Jim ran the course slower, and with much, much more precision. He got mixed up on one exchange and didn't make the switch. "That's okay, Jim," she coached. "Now, if you thought that was slow, this time do it *twice* as slow."

She watched as Jim went through the course several times in a leisurely fashion. The last time was flawless.

"See, now don't you agree that the *strategy* of the flag race comes first, with speed a distant second? Now that you have the basics down, we'll gradually start speeding up in our next session." She dismounted, a signal that the session was over, and began taking down the poles.

As they were stacking the pole bases, Alexandra said, "In the variety of games we do, it's horse *and* rider. The horse has to know the drills, and the rider does too. And they have to be used to working together." She dusted her hands together, signifying the job was done. She looked at her watch. "That was a nice little practice session. Didn't we cover a lot of ground in a short time?"

Jim was enthusiastic in his agreement, but protested that the session seemed devoted primarily to him. "No it wasn't," said Alexandra. "You'll find that helping others understand the little strategies that shave time sharpens your own skills even more than practice does. Would you ride with me to Richter's store, Jim?"

An endearing feminine trait of Alexandra's was that she always made it appear that the other person was the ultimate decision maker. She had a way of establishing the course of action by asking a simple question that had only one plausible answer. Jim merely responded with that plausible answer: "Sure, I'd *like* to ride to Richter's. Mr.

Richter will be amazed about Old Black, don't you think?"

"Well, if he's not, we'll know he knows nothing about horses."

Alexandra's mother was a school teacher. She agonized about the use of "slanguage," as she called it, by the present generation of young blacks, and about the downright slovenly speech of white youths. Excellent verbal communication skills are critical for anyone who's going places in this society, she preached, and she insisted that Alexandra speak precisely, choosing her words carefully and putting them into sentences.

Jim had been present at more than one of her sessions with Alexandra. "Engage brain before opening mouth. *Think* about what you are going to say," Mrs. Meridith had instructed, tapping her head with a forefinger, "and concentrate on what you are talking about as you speak. *Punctuate* your speech, just as you do your writing. Pause where commas are called for, as I did right here, and indicate periods by lowering your verbal tones or expressing finality by some other means. We often hear speakers end all of their sentences with a rising verbal tone that *suggests* there's more to come in that sentence, when there is not.

"Strangers have limited yardsticks by which to measure us on first impression—our general appearance, how we present ourselves, and how we *speak*. If you are reasonably neat in your appearance, if you act like a person with good breeding, you'll make an outstanding first impression. Effective speech—and the critical ability to listen as well as talk—will set you apart from the great majority of people you're in competition with."

Jim liked Mrs. Meridith; he liked her lessons and he learned from them. He had often thought he would like to be in her class. He was influenced by Alexandra's precise manner of speaking and was conscious of working to improve his own speech, which had been subject to similar, if not nearly as strict, motherly demands. He often caught himself allowing lapses to creep into his speech, but Alexandra didn't.

Jim's mother strongly approved of his impromptu English lessons at the Meridiths. It was evident to her that the quality of his speech was good and growing. Norma just liked Alexandra, period! Unless there was some pressing reason that he could not be spared, all Jim had to do was even hint that he wanted to go to Alexandra's and his mother would have him in the car and on his way.

CHAPTER 14

They tied their horses to the ancient kerosene pump. It had a hand-operated pumping handle and glass tank with markers to show how many gallons it was ready to deliver. Off to the side as it was, their horses would be out of the way.

"Well if we don't have some fine horseback customers," said a beaming Mr. Richter, holding open both of the screen doors. His plump, rosy face reflected his jolly nature. "I'm so glad to see a genuine cowboy and cowgirl—drinks are on the house."

"That's very nice of you, Mr. Richter," beamed Alexandra with a slight bow. She took a Sprite from the box—a real ice box with crushed ice in it. Then she and Mr. Richter engaged in a happy conversation, with Mr. Richter laughing often. He dearly liked Alexandra, as did just about everyone.

Jim picked out a Coke. "Thanks, Mr. Richter," he said.

The storekeeper had been weighing and wrapping sausages. He wiped his hands on a towel, saying he wanted to take a look at the fine horses parked outside. "Is the one you're riding your own horse, Jim?"

"Yes, sir," Jim replied, his tone modest.

"Well, you've been threatening to get a horse, and I'd be the first to say you've earned one, with the work you do around the old Rosenbaum place."

The men who were gathered in the back of the store began to follow them outside. As Jim reached the horses with Mr. Richter, he saw that Mr. Skinner was striding along in front of the others.

Richter had never owned anything but plow mules, and his

knowledge of horses was scanty. He might notice hipbones that stuck out, ribs that showed, or feet splayed out, but such obvious defects were about the extent of his ability to judge horses. So he thought any horse that was plump and shiny and wearing horse-shoes had to be a good horse; a pretty saddle and bridle would make it even better.

Furthermore, Mr. Richter often looked for reasons to pay compliments to his younger customers, even if that took some head-scratching. Therefore, as he gazed upon two smooth, shiny horses wearing horseshoes and commendable leather, he offered up appropriate and enthusiastic words of praise. The customers assembled there were nodding in agreement. All but Mr. Skinner.

IN SELECT COMPANY, SKINNER REFERRED TO Andrew Meridith's fine home and training stable, along with his daughter's sophistica-tion, her always neat appearance and attractive clothing, as "nigger-rich showing off." Skinner held that Andrew Meridith's fame was bestowed on a mediocre talent because he was a *black* artist. He had said more than once—he said most disparaging remarks more than once—that a white artist no better than Meridith would be pump-ing gas at a filling station. He offered no explanation for the phe-nomenon that such mediocre work was sought by some of the most discriminating art connoisseurs across the globe, people who backed their judgment with large sums of money.

Andrew Meridith knew Old Man Skinner much, much better than Old Man Skinner knew himself. And so did Alexandra. She was not intimidated by his racism or hypocrisy, and had shown on more than one occasion that he was no match for her in a verbal sparring contest. Her frostily polite rebuttals to him in the past had caused Old Man Skinner to become red in the face with anger and lose some of his self-control. Consequently, although Skinner delighted in picking on almost every other black person that hap-pened to be in his presence, he studiously left Alexandra alone.

ALEXANDRA HAD ASSUMED A CASUAL STANCE leaning against the kerosene pump. Although Skinner did not look at her, he was aware that she was watching him, and her sweet-faced observation was making him nervous. Jim credited her cultured boldness to the fact that she was two years older than he was, more grown-up. As for her being black, he was so indifferent to that as to be unaware of it most of the time. When he looked at her, he saw as pretty a girl as he'd ever seen. She was polite and considerate—Jim couldn't think of a desirable quality that she did not possess.

When he thought of all the black people he knew—the Jacksons, the Meridiths, little Buddy, Duffie, Rufus, Mr. Burnell at the tire shop who'd showed him how he put new treads on worn tires—he reflected that they all had special likeable and ethical qualities. Furthermore, they were industrious and completely trustworthy. But he could bring to mind a few white people who he didn't think were very ethical, like Mr. Skinner, and the brazen young carpenter who'd openly bragged about how he was going to pick that city-slicker Bradley like a chicken when he built his new barn. Richter had reported the boast to Matt, who got another carpenter.

Old Man Skinner, though, was acutely aware that Alexandra was black. In select company, he called her a pickaninny whippersnapper. He knew that behind her sparkling smile and animated eyes was an ice-cold contempt of him. Even worse, she *knew* he was fully aware of her contempt of him. His blood boiled to have to tolerate a nigger pickaninny making game of him, a white man, and one of considerable political rank in Winchester County, Texas. In another day, and one not so long ago, either, her brazen conduct would have justified them to take her in the woods and the whole bunch have their way with her—she was about the right age for that, he thought.

When Alexandra's mother was her age, she was constantly in danger of white boys and even men "having their way with her." The danger had been so ever-present that Ruby Jackson carefully drilled her daughters on the diplomatic strategy of avoiding rape. "Don't ever tell a white boy he can't have it, or he'll take it," she warned. "If you get cornered, tell him he can have it *tomorrow*, always tomorrow. Thataway, you're not turning him down flat. Always tomorrow. Then, come tomorrow, he can have it *tomorrow*, and jes hope that tomorrow never comes."

But Alexandra's aunt, her mother's sister, did not grow up without being taken into the woods by a group of white men who had their way with her. One day when she was thirteen, she had stumbled home, bloody from her waist down to her shoes, and out of her mind with terror.

Although she identified several of the young men, the sheriff claimed he could not find any evidence to back up her accusations, and even suggested that in the unlikely event anything *had* happened, she must have enticed the boys.

Alexandra knew the story well, and she burned with hatred for people like Old Man Skinner, who, she decided, would have been the worst kind of hateful, arrogant teen. She was not the slightest bit fearful of him. As a black in Winchester County, she had been fortunate; the professional and social stature of her father had made his family untouchable as far as physical abuse was concerned.

MATT BRADLEY HAD ALWAYS BEEN CAREFUL to make it appear that his financial condition was somewhat tight, that every purchase had to be made with careful consideration. He drove a company car   that was periodically replaced with a new model, but he liked to boast that he had never personally owned a new car. He bought good used ones instead. This image as a person who had to watch his money very carefully was not only cultivated in the Bradley's country life, but at all times and to all of his acquaintances. Excepting, of course, his co-pilot and business associate, Vincent Tedesco. Fortunately, Tedesco was as tightlipped as Matt about their personal business activities. As for *his* image, he derived great pleasure from appearing almost indigent.

Matt's little Ford 8-N tractor had been bought used, *well* used, from Mr. Richter. Then Matt had it completely overhauled and painted just like the original red and gray color scheme. The big Ford 5000 tractor and all of the other farm equipment was purchased new—new equipment would last for the rest of his life. He had financed it at a local bank on long terms, knowing that the information would be public knowledge to anyone, like Skinner, who had the inclination to pry into his affairs.

A few months later, he had the equipment note purchased by a bank in Houston that handled some of his more imaginative financial activities. He made sure that the officer who dealt with the Brentwood bank described the transaction as a debt consolidation loan, which made his financial condition appear even tighter yet. Matt was actually maneuvering to pay the loan off with his own money. Rather than buying the equipment cash initially, he felt that the expense of a few months of interest at the Brentwood bank was worth the preservation of his image as a person in tight financial circumstances.

In truth, while every purchase of significance by Matt Bradley *was* made with careful consideration, simply as a matter of good sense, the financial condition of the Bradleys was extremely healthy. Old Man Skinner would himself have wished to have been as well off, if he had known. But he did not, and rather enjoyed his presumption that Matt Bradley was skating on thin financial ice.

Though Jim had known that his father had been dissatisfied with Skinner's haymaking on the Bradley place, a third of his young life had passed since then, and his knowledge of it had always been rather blurry. He was certainly not aware of Skinner's burning hatred of his father.

EMBARRASSED BY THE ATTENTION of so many men, Jim felt himself wearing a nervous little smile and a flush on his face. For want of something to focus his attention on, he made needless adjustments to the cinch on his saddle and checked the slack in the flank cinch.

Old Man Skinner's knowledge of horses was zero. It would have meant nothing to him that Applejack, whose registered name was Wimpy's Applejack, was a descendent of the legendary Wimpy—AQHA number P-1—and a horse of indigo bloodlines right up to his sire and dam. But with Andrew Meridith being wealthy and an expert horseman, Skinner assumed that his daughter would ride nothing less than a superior horse. It therefore wasn't knowledge that influenced his opinion of these two horses, but assumptions. Having no knowledge of a particular subject, however, had never deterred Skinner from speaking on it with presumed authority.

Consistent with his notion of Matt Bradley's snug financial circumstances, Skinner presumed that any horse purchased by him would have to be nothing more than a kid's horse, a nag, and one bought dirt cheap. Skinner even considered the possibility that the horse had been given to Bradley to get it off someone's place.

He ignored Alexandra's horse, and applied all his sharp-faced attention to Old Black, the horse belonging to Jim Bradley, son of the man that had welshed on a haymaking deal, son of the man behind the election of that "nigger-loving Meskin sheriff."

The other men stood around, observing Old Black with untainted goodwill, still unaware of Skinner's intentions.

Skinner's long, claw-like fingers entwined studiously behind his stooped, cadaverous frame as he sidled around Old Black. Jim stood well aside and nervously took little sips of his Coke. He was certainly aware of Mr. Skinner's hatefulness. Who wasn't? But he had never been a direct object of it and was in no way expecting what was coming.

At least Skinner *tried* to ignore Alexandra. He could not avoid an occasional quick glance at her, for her unwavering gaze fixed on his eyes was as soft and delicate as a tempered steel stiletto. Her concentration on him was undermining his observation of Old Black, inspiring a dangerous recklessness in his ultimate judgment. The pressure of her silent ridicule—unseen by all but Skinner—caused the veins on his temples to stand out prominently. He looked down his long, vulturine nose with his left eye closed, as if he had the horse in his rifle sights. He sighted in, looking for any features that he thought might identify Old Black as a cheap kid's horse.

With his inspection completed, Skinner turned away from Old Black, toward the men he knew were waiting for his evaluation. He held his hands before him, turned them over and studied them quietly for a time, his bushy eyebrows pulled down in a way calculated to project an appearance of contemplation, a reluctance to criticize. The dramatics were wholly ineffective; every man there, and Alexandra, knew a sharp criticism was forthcoming.

With his back to Jim, he announced to the assembly, "Giving a boy a horse today borders on committing a crime. It is a waste of money in the buying of it, and the horse is just another mouth to feed—in this case, one that can hardly be afforded. And a horse means there must be a saddle."

He glanced toward Old Black and considered the man-size saddle with its stirrups taken up all the way to the fenders, a sure sign to him that Bradley could not afford a proper saddle for the boy. To Old Man Skinner, who had never owned a saddle, one was about the same as another. The saddle he saw on Old Black looked to him just like the one he had seen hanging in Marvel's Swap Shop with a fifty-dollar price tag on it. Maybe, he thought, it was the very same one.

"And even if this cheap saddle cost only fifty dollars," he continued, "that would buy half a ton of fertilizer, which would produce hundreds of dollars worth of forage for Bradley's *productive* livestock.

"Furthermore, and perhaps more harmful, this horse will take the boy away from his work. There is no question that it will lead him to bad company." Skinner was not so bold as to dare a glance in Alexandra's direction, although his meaning was evident.

Alexandra did not stir from her relaxed position against the pump.

Skinner lifted his head, sighted down his beak at Old Black's head, and shook his own in a sadly negative way. He stepped back and stared disapprovingly at Old Black's slightly cresty neck. Then, as if seeing was not believing, he stepped up and grasped the horse's neck in several places along his mane, then looked down with an expression of revulsion and sighed. Running a hand over the knot on Old Black's left knee, he pronounced in a snappy, authoritative voice, "Obviously, the horse is unsound. He could perform no demanding task with such an unsoundness as this."

Standing back a pace with his hands on his hips, he looked sorrowfully at the horse before him. Speaking in a tired voice, he said, "In any case, I feel confident in saying that this . . ." he hesitated, "that this *horse* . . . is not registered, so there's no way of knowing if he carries an ounce of decent blood in his veins."

Throwing out his hands in a way that expressed resigned acceptance, he said, "But, shoot, any old nag is good enough for a kid to plod around the little Bradley place on. And, when his time comes, which will be soon, he'll make many a can of fine dog food."

He surveyed his audience, displaying an expression designed to wrest from them some notion of impartiality on his part. Then he turned to face a stunned, shattered Jim Bradley. The eyes he focused on Jim, unseen by any but the two young people, were cold and fierce, his expression hard, the corners of his mouth tucked down in wrinkles. Old Man Skinner was certain that this visual flogging would provoke a hasty outburst of angry jabber that would undermine the high esteem that he knew those present held for the boy. "Be sure to favor that bad knee, boy," he said, and continued his visual provocation.

Jim's face burned with anger and humiliation. His mind raced to find words, *any* words, but not a single sentence formed in his head. Then the serene image of Mr. Bonner appeared in his mind with the advice that one should never respond to another's provocation with angry words, that usually the best response to angry words was to thank the person with a smile and turn away.

With his mind cleared somewhat by these thoughts, Jim was able to recall the words of Mrs. Jackson during one of their gabfests on the stump: "If somebody deserve an ugly word from you and he don't get it, he's hurt worse, because you won't be lookin' the fool trying to tell him off while you're hot under the collar."

To smile was impossible, but Jim looked Mr. Skinner directly in the eye and said, "Yes, sir. I will." The briefest leer crossed Skinner's face, but it faded as fast as it came, for there was something about the boy's cold, expressionless look that implied danger; Old Man Skinner turned slowly away. Jim pulled his hat down to hide the anguish that he knew must show in his face and stepped up to his horse.

Alexandra thought Jim had taken the abuse admirably, although she feared at one point that he was going to retort. Now she had the opening, and the right, to mount an articulate counter-attack.

She had broken a stout, supple limb from a small willow tree growing nearby, and as if it was only something to occupy her hands, she had stripped the branch down awhile Skinner preached. Now she had a strong, limber whip. She arose from her languid position against the kerosene pump and soundly slapped the whip against the boot-top beneath the leg of her jeans. Its shrill hiss and the *whack* of its impact seized the attention of the men just as they were turning to go back into the store.

"I have something to say," said a smiling Alexandra.

The curious men stopped and turned around.

She pointed her willow whip at Old Black, off to her right. Her eyes, though, shone straight ahead, on Mr. Skinner. She bathed him in her brightest, sweetest smile. *Whack!* went the whip against her booted leg. Her head was high and she turned it slowly toward the farthest reaches of the loose group. Her eyes rolled in her head as they stayed locked on Skinner until he fidgeted uncomfortably. *Whack!*

Finally her gaze left Skinner and moved slowly across the group, searching the eyes of the other men. She was still smiling brightly when she began to speak and her voice rose and fell musically. "This horse is none other than Buck's Old Black. That's his name in the registry of the American Quarter Horse Association.

A famous horse." *Whack!* "Famous! I said. How famous? Old Black holds the calf-roping championship of the *world!*" *Whack!* "He won the title two years ago, many years after the injury that caused the knot on his knee." *Whack!* "He's as sound as can be.

"The next question is, is there an ounce of decent blood in this horse? Old Black's pedigree shows that he has Flying Bob's own blood flowing in his veins. And King's. And Peter McCue's." *Whack!* "How proud we should be to have a world-champion, blue-blood registered Quarter Horse in our friendly little neighborhood. Old Black rodeoed all his life under the famous calf roper Buck Jones. If Buck Jones hadn't retired, Jim and his daddy could have looked the rest of their lives and not found the equal of this horse. You'll be hearing more of Old Black as Jim competes on him." *Whack!*

Alexandra turned and mounted Applejack with an easy, fluid movement that ended as she picked up her offside stirrup with the toe of her boot. Then she touched a slender forefinger to the brim of her hat and turned an adorable smile on Mr. Richter, punctuated by a charming flutter of eyelids. She said, "Thank you *evah* so much for the soda, Mr. Richter."

The same smile was on her face as she turned to face Old Man Skinner, but only Skinner could see the venomous glare she poured down into his dispirited eyes, *down*, because she was now on horse-back and Skinner was at the physical disadvantage of having to look up to her. More importantly, Alexandra's moral advantage over her adversary was overpowering. Unable to stand up to her visual assault, Skinner's eyes darted left and right, and came to rest on the ground.

"And a very good day to *you*, Mr. Skinner," said Alexandra sweetly, forcing him to meet her eyes. "It is no disgrace for one to know nothing about horses when he appears to be so well informed on everything *else* under the sun. Why, your prediction that Jim's horse could lead him into bad company is proven—he's already hobnobbing with a 'nigra.'" *Whack!* Then, with a slow, deliberate motion, as if throwing a spear, she accurately sent her willow whip sailing in a fast, low arc toward Mr. Skinner. Before his mind could refuse it, her whip was in his hand. He looked at it for as long as it would have taken him to examine a rattlesnake, dropped it, took an impulsive step back, and stood looking down at it. Absently, the hand that had held the offensive article was wiped in a circular cleansing motion on his shirtfront.

Jim was happy that all eyes had been on Alexandra and not on his clumsy mounting style, a bit of nervous awkwardness brought on by Skinner's startling disparagement of Old Black. From his lofty seat, Jim saw that Mr. Richter was almost bursting with mirth, his beefy shoulders twitching rhythmically with silent chuckles, his eyes shining merrily. Jim noticed, too, that the eyes of most of the onlookers were now on Old Black, and they were looking upon him with expressions of admiration.

"Jim?" said Alexandra, looking at him with raised eyebrows.

Without a show of haste, Jim waved to the group, reined Old Black around in a splendid reverse and went swinging off down the road in a smooth jog trot. Alexandra dashed up and fell in close beside him. Stirrup to stirrup, they rode away.

CHAPTER 15

Alexandra adroitly kept the conversation light on the way to the fork in the road where they would part. She focused on their future practice sessions, eager to discourage Jim from dwelling on the cruelty of Old Man Skinner. By the time they reached the fork, Jim's spirits had returned to normal and he rode off toward home in a bright mood.

After closing the gate back at the ranch, he got another boost in spirits when the Easy-Up allowed him to mount like a horseman instead of crawling up like a kid.

As he rode up the lane he heard the big Ford tractor moving around up near the barn, probably being maneuvered around to hook up the hay baler. When he turned the corner of the barn he received a shock. Standing there proudly erect on its four wheels and jack stand, as if it just couldn't wait to take to the road, was Buck Jones's yellow two-horse trailer. Old Black showed recognition, sniffing at it in a cagey manner. Then he neighed mightily and began to give the trailer his unreserved attention, smelling here and there, and poking his head over a door to peer inside.

Jim dismounted and put the reins over Old Black's neck, giving him permission to move around. He noticed that the trailer sported four new tires. The light patches of rust on the outer edges of the fenders had been buffed out and some kind of treatment had given it a nice sheen.

Jim opened a door to look in and before he knew what was happening Old Black had shouldered him aside and was clambering in. Jim laughed out loud. His attention fell on his father, who had been watching him from nearby.

Jim looked at him inquiringly.

"Don't ask me, Jim. That fella Garner pulled it up here early today and left it. He wouldn't answer any questions, only said that Buck Jones told him to deliver it, and that his job was done when he got it here. He gave me this envelope. It's addressed to you."

Jim clucked to Old Black, who obediently backed out of the trailer. He took the envelope, turned it over in his hands, but found himself strangely reluctant to open it. He looked at his father, who nodded. "You may as well see what this is all about, Jim."

He took from the envelope a sheet of ruled tablet paper. The note was written in a large hand:

Dear Jim, This trailer belongs to Old Black so I had Garner clean it up and haul it over to him. The only thing that ever goes wrong with trailers is wheel bearings and tires. I had the bearings replaced and they were greased and the races adjusted by somebody that knows what hes doing. You should not have any trouble with them for years. I figured it out some time back that Old Black has rode in this trailer far enough to go around the world six times at least. He feels good in it and any horse would as soon be hauled in his own trailer. Jim - Garner told me all about Old Blacks fine new home. He said its fit for a king and you cant imagine how glad I was to hear that. There never was a better horse and to my way of thinking he could not have found a better cowboy to be with than Jim Bradley. Im counting on good luck being yalls sidekick along the trail.
Your friend - Buck Jones.

THE NOISY BALER HAD BEEN SHUT DOWN FOR AN ADJUSTMENT, allowing Jim and his father to talk with ease above the sound of the idling diesel tractor. Jim told of the great things Mr. Meridith had to say about Old Black and described Mr. Meridith's big approving smile as he rode him.

Jim said, "When he got off he said, 'You're going to kick some tail at the shows, Jimmy boy.' That's just what he said. And he told Alexandra she better look out, too." Jim laughed happily.

"But he's worried about Buck Jones, Dad. He wondered why he would sell his horse, and his saddle, too. Would you be surprised if Mr. Meridith told you that saddle is worth three thousand dollars, *used?* That's what he said. He said Buck probably paid about twenty-five hundred for it, but a good used one is worth more than it cost because it's so hard to get a Wehring saddle. He thinks it's strange that Buck's friends don't know anything about why he's quit rodeoing.

Mr. Meridith said he's going to check up on him."

Matt looked at Jim a moment with his brows low, thoughtful. Then his eyes went to his hands, which he was absently interlocking between the fingers and pushing together in a way that snugged up his gloves. "I sure want to hear the minute he learns anything, Jim. Yeah, I'm real worried about him. Wasn't that a swell thing for him to do, spruce that trailer up and bring it over?"

Jim thought it was the most wonderful thing. "And him making out like it was Old Black's trailer—and I guess it is. Old Black has his own trailer that he's rode in as far as six times around the world. How far is that?"

"Has ridden, Jim, not 'has rode.' The earth is roughly twenty-five thousand miles in diameter, so six times that is a hundred and fifty thousand miles. That sounds like a lot, but for a cowboy on the road all the time it wouldn't take too many years."

Matt paused. "I sure hope whatever it is with Buck turns out okay. I get to wondering if I have a right to be curious."

Jim had the feeling his father had more to say, and he did. "I wasn't going to mention this to you Jim, because I don't believe people should go around crowing about what things cost. You know how some people are always talking about what something cost—"

Jim grinned. They had a neighbor who bought a motorhome, who had told them many times that it cost thirty-two-thousand dollars. "Like Mr. Grubbs?"

"Exactly. I don't think you would ever go around bragging about what something cost—I hope you *never* tell anybody what that saddle is worth. A few people will know when they see that stamp on the stirrup leather, but the best thing would be to never mention it."

Matt frowned. "And Jim, Andrew Meridith is right about Buck wanting nothing more than a good home for his horse. Here's something that'll give you a little more insight into what a swell man Buck Jones is. While he was looking for a good home for Old Black, a rodeo roper made him an offer of twenty-five thousand dollars for him. Buck turned him down flat."

"Wow," said Jim, his eyes wide. "Wow!"

"See, that's what anyone would think if it got around that you have a twenty-five-thousand-dollar horse and a three-thousand-dollar saddle. 'Wow!' And people would get the idea we're rich, instead of far from it. A few of them might get the notion they need Old Black or his saddle more than you do. You wouldn't want people thinking that, would you?"

He thought a moment, then looked at his father, his head shaking briskly. "No, Dad, I wouldn't want people to think that."

"I'm glad to hear you say that," Matt said. "Here are the facts. Old Black cost six hundred dollars. I gave Buck a check for a thousand dollars—four hundred for the saddle, bridle, blankets and everything else. That's what we can truthfully tell people the horse and everything else cost—*if* it ever needs to come out. But the best policy is not to discuss what you paid for anything."

Jim was quiet as Matt finished the adjustment he was making. When his father straightened up and was ready to get back on the tractor, he said, "Dad, Mr. Jones sure wanted a good home for Old Black bad, didn't he?"

"Yes, Son, he did. He sure did. And he found the kind of place he wanted, too." He looked directly into Jim's eyes. "Son, I'm mighty proud to be able to say he found the right boy to have that horse he loves so much. That note he sent with the trailer says volumes about how he feels about you, and about Old Black's new home."

Jim had decided he would not talk about Mr. Skinner. "Alexandra and I rode by Richter's store," he said. "Mr. Richter gave us a free soda and said some nice things about both our horses."

Matt nodded, smiling. Then he looked at the little Ford tractor with the extra wagon hooked on behind and said, "We're going to go ahead and get started. After you get Old Black unsaddled and taken care of, drive that tractor down and meet us. And use low gear only, Jim." He watched for Jim's affirmative nod, then stepped up to the big tractor and got on. Duffie and Rufus were sitting on the wagon hooked on behind the baler, their hands braced out to their sides to absorb the motion as the rig trundled away.

DRIVING DOWN THE HILL ON THE LITTLE FORD 8-N, Jim grinned at the sight he likened to a train: the big Ford 5000 diesel tractor was the locomotive, the New Holland hay baling machine was the first car and the rubber-tired farm wagon made up the caboose. As each new bale was ejected from the baler, it pushed the ones made before it along a chute that delivered them back to the trailer. Duffie and Rufus took them as they came and stacked them on the trailer. Jim didn't have to wait long before the wagon was full. They switched wagons and Jim headed for the barn pulling the full trailer. Never on the Bradley farm did a bale of hay reach the ground, and never did any baled hay get rained on. Windrowed hay could take a little rain and not be damaged, but not baled hay; wet bales had to be broken up to dry out and then burned.

The first load was made up and Jim drove it to the barn. He was loading bales onto a conveyor that carried them up into the hayloft when Rufus walked up. "Duffie can handle that stacking," he said.

"Your daddy said for me to come help you. He don't want you running that conveyer by yourself, Jim. You might get caught up in it." Every so often, they stopped and went up into the hayloft to stack the hay dumped off the conveyor. The wagon attached to the baler would be full about the time they unloaded their wagon and got back to the field. Then they would exchange again. In only a few hours they had 370 bales of top-quality clover hay stored away in the barn.

After the baling was done, Jim saddled Old Black again and rode down into the bottom. Oscar was there in his pickup, talking to Rufus and Duffie. They were discussing moving the supplement feeder to another spot because the cattle had cut the ground up around it, and a mudhole would be created there when it rained. Duffie went to the little Ford tractor and began unhooking the fence-fixing trailer, intending to pull the feeder to a new spot.

While looking absently at the subject of their discussion, Jim's eye fell on the feeder's towing ring, fastened to a stout timber that tied the skids together. With his lariat in hand, he dismounted and tied the lariat to the towing ring. Mounted once more, he placed the loop over the saddle horn. After moving Old Black a few steps, the slack was out of the rope and the horse began to pull. The strain began to show on the breast strap and the saddle cinch.

Oscar was in a discussion with Rufus as Jim began to ask Old Black to pull in earnest; the lariat was as tight as a bow string.

The feeder made a groaning sound that attracted the attention of the men. When Oscar's mind comprehended what his eyes were seeing, he sprang from the tailgate of his truck and ran toward Jim, frantically waving his arms and shouting, "Stop! Stop, Jim," he yelled,

"You'll make him bust a gut!"

Jim pulled the horse up sharply. Oscar strode up panting and swinging his arms. "Good gosh, Jim, he'd bust a gut sure before he budged that dead weight. I'd have given you credit to just naturally know that a horse couldn't pull that thing. With the supplement in there, it's got to weigh over half a ton."

Seeing Jim's forlorn expression as he slowly removed the lariat from the saddle horn moved Oscar to show Jim an understanding smile; he stepped up and laid a hand on Jim's knee. His voice was gentle as he said, "You can't pull something like that with a horse, Jim. But he has so much faith in you that if you tie onto anything he'll just ordinarily think he should be able to pull it. A mule would stop pullin' before he hurt hisself, but a horse like Old Black will die tryin' to move the earth for you."

Jim got down and removed his lariat from the feeder. Oscar watched him, his mind studying how he could take Jim's mind off his mistake. "Come over and keep me company a minute, Jim."

Oscar looked off in the distance. "Somebody might have lost a cow," he said nodding at a flight of buzzards circling way off in the sky. In a detached tone he said, "I recall once when the water tanks was way down and Mr. Hodde's big bull got bogged down in the mud tryin' to reach the water. Mr. Hodde had that great big roan gelding then. A strong horse he was, for sure. He tied onto that bull with old Roan, and that horse got settled down for some real pullin'. He dug in and as the rope got tighter old Roan got lower down, until he was pullin' with all his might. I was afraid the saddle was about to come apart—he didn't have no breast strap like you got.

"Jimmy, that lariat broke with a crack like a thirty-thirty rifle. A loose end whipped around and broke Mr. Hodde's arm, just above the elbow. A hoss will pull till he busts a gut or something else breaks, or until he kills hisself." He arose and put his hand on the boy's shoulder. "It makes me remember that me and Mr. Hodde was as dumb as you about what a horse can pull and what he can't. I was a grown man then, too. You know about it already, at your age."

Jim and Oscar sat on the tailgate of the truck and watched as Rufus and Duffie pulled the feeder on the end of a chain tied to the drawbar of the 8-N. The little Ford crept along easily in low gear. Jim was thinking of all he had yet to learn, depressing him.

He said, "I'll be glad when I'm grown up, and know everything I need to know. Weren't you glad when you got grown up, Mr. Jackson?"

Oscar scraped the bowl of his pipe with a match stick. He was loading it with tobacco when he answered. "Jimmy, as old as I am, I'm surprised at the things I don't know even yet. Your daddy has showed me some ways of raisin' cows without hurtin' the land a'tall. I didn't know those things, and nobody else in this county did either, that I know of. But he got the directions from pamphlets he got free from the County Agent, and they been there all the time for everybody to read. So the information can be lyin' there, but it ain't gonna jump up and light on your brain. You gotta read that stuff, like your daddy did, if you're ever goin' to get it.

"The older I gets, the more things I discover I don't know. It's plumb discouraging, but I don't let it get me down. Nobody can know everything. As far as wishing you're grown, now that's a different matter, and awful serious."

Oscar looked at Jim with his head cocked. "You're living the best years of your life, boy. Oh, not just years, but months and even days. Live each one of 'em like it was your last, like there was some awful happening just around the corner. Here you are without a care in the world. You got a fine daddy and a wonderful momma. And y'all have this beautiful place, maybe the overall best place in the county. Now you got a world's champion calf roping horse that can't hardly go to sleep at night without cravin' to see you the next day." He squeezed Jim's shoulder and looked down at his face, Jim looked up and they smiled at each other.

"And you want to throw it all away and grow up, go off to college, go to work for some big company? And make a lot of money and forget about Old Black, poor old Oscar and Ruby and Alexandra and everybody else? You'll hardly ever see that beautiful creek, or catch a fish out of it once you grow up. And you sure enough won't ever have time to just sit on the bank and daydream, like I seen you do many a time." Oscar winked at Jim and let a period of silence pass.

"When I was little, Jim, I *knowed* what it was to be grown and work day and night, 'cause that's all anybody did that was grown. What kid would crave to do that? I was *afraid* of growin' up, because I didn't know if I had the timber for it."

Thoughtful, he cautiously stabbed a finger in his pipe bowl. "Well, things turned out all right. I growed up and married Ruby and both of us have worked like the dickens ever since. But we don't mind work. Me and Ruby have had the best life me or her could've ever imagined. We have some fine children, all growed up without losing ary a one. We got some money saved and don't have to worry about how the light bill's gonna get paid this month, or ever. We got some wonderful friends all over this end of the county, and most especially right here at the Bradley place," he looked down at Jim. "*Wonderful* friends, I mean.

"Ruby talks all the time about your mother, how she treats Ruby like a real friend. Shucks, like a sister, she does. Your daddy is so nice and thoughtful. And Jimmy, you're a boy that I'm mighty proud to know. And you're so sweet to my Ruby. I seen y'all sittin' on the turkey-choppin' stump having a big time. Yep, Ruby love you like her own baby. None of our kids ever fooled around and told stories with Ruby, and read history books together like you do. It's humblin', it is, to know such a fine boy." He put his hand out and they shook. Jim's face was flushed with pride and embarrassment at the same time.

"So I want you do me one powerful important favor. I want you to tell me you're content bein' a boy, and taking your sweet old time growin' up. In no time you'll be packing off to college, and that'll be the end of me and Ruby and Old Black as far as you're concerned."

Jim thought he heard a tiny quiver in the old man's voice, and he said quickly, "Oh, no, Mr. Jackson. I'll come see you and Mrs. Jackson and Old Black forever. I might even go to Texas A&M. That's so close maybe I could live right here all the time I'm in college!"

"Maybe you could at tha—What you boys got over there?" Oscar was looking at Duffie and Rufus now. They were under a big tree poking at something on the ground. It was a cottonmouth moccasin they'd killed, to Jim about the deadliest-looking creature on the place. Duffie had the dead snake's mouth pried open and his fangs extended with a stick, awful-looking fangs.

"That's why they calls 'em cottonmouths," said Rufus, using a twig to point out the white inside the snake's upper jaw. When he strikes at you all you see is a flash of cotton."

After the snake lost its allure, Oscar and Jim went back to the tailgate of Oscar's pickup.

"So hold off growing up as long as you can, Jim," Oscar said. "And for goodness sake don't do nothin' so foolish as wish away your boyhood. When you're my age you'll wonder where life went. You have to taste every little thing, mark it down in your memory, and you'll look back on it and see all the little happenings that made it up. Mostly nice happenings, unless you're like Old Man Skinner." Oscar shook his head with pity.

"Kids graduating from high school. Kids graduating from college. Jim, when Doreen, our first child, graduated from college, Ruby and I laid in bed and talked almost all night about how wonderful that was. That we could have a daughter that was a *college graduate*! Now *that* was something.

"I know you already seen it happen—the thing you was lookin' for to be so fine turned out to be mainly wishful hopin'. Not worth wasting even *that* day on, much less those leadin' up to it just to get 'em out of the way." He looked at Jim sharply and saw that he was smiling. "Ain't it so?" he asked. "Ain't it already happened like that?"

Jim nodded. He was thinking of more than one such time.

"So use every day, Jim—shucks, even every *part* of every day— like they was as valuable as diamonds. Look at every day before you use it up, then while you're usin' it, and then *after* you used it. Even usin' all that care, when you look back on them, you'll wonder where they all went. And you'll be glad you were such a tightwad with 'em. Promise me that you won't wish away a single day."

Jim promised. And he meant to really try.

Oscar cocked an ear. "What's that horn blowing for, do you suppose?"

Doc Smith, who had been the vet for the cows ever since they had any, was due to come by to see Old Black today, to start him on a regular routine of health care. They also had a sick heifer in the corral at the watering pen. Jim liked Doc Smith a lot.

"I bet it's Doc Smith," he said. "I'll ride on up."

Doc Smith stood off and looked Old Black over. Then his hands went over the horse with practiced skill. He felt of the knot on Old Black's knee and dismissed it without comment. He paused, sniffed the air and continued his examination. He sniffed again and said, "What's that I smell? Smells like fresh clover hay, but that can't hardly be, this early."

Jim explained their baling of the clover field and invited Doc Smith to come up in the loft and take a look at it.

Up they went. "Seeing is believing, Jim," said the vet. "I expect this is the first hay made in Winchester County this year. Good looking hay, too. Cured *just* right—your daddy sure has the recipe for hay-making. Can you imagine a better smell than a barn full of fresh clover hay?"

Back on the ground, he said, "You sure got yourself a good horse there, Jim. I was watching when you rode up, the way he moved. He's a real Quarter Horse. Old Black, huh? And holds the world's calf-roping record! By golly, when you did get a horse, you sure went all out.

"I'll take a sample of his stools and a blood sample and check for worms. But worms won't be a problem on this place, with him able to roam over all this territory and graze good pasture. I notice ya'll keep the flies away from your herd with those dusters they rub on. Flies are a source of worms. Throw a little Sevin dust on him once a week and after rains and the bot flies will stay away. We'll see, but I don't think we'll have worm problems. He's in excellent health. Where's that sick heifer your dad spoke about?"

DOC SMITH WAS DEPARTING WHEN SHERIFF Martinez drove up. They exchanged greetings at the gate and Jim ran into the house to tell his father the sheriff was coming up the lane.

"Hi, Mike," Matt said warmly.

Sheriff Martinez flashed a big smile, something rarely seen on his face. "How's it going, Matt, Jim? Doc Smith says you folks've made a cutting of hay already. Every time I hear one of the old-timers around here laughing about briefcase farmers I think of this place. Most productive farm in the county, and run by city slickers."

Sheriff Martinez became serious. "Jim, you and Buddy told me that the dope plane was coming in at midnight. And that's what I told my chief deputy, Dilbert Swagger." He sighed and threw out his hands. "We didn't catch them. He staked out the airport because I was covering something else with the Austin County Sheriff—I *had* to be there. Swagger claims he misunderstood, thought the plane was to arrive sometime after one a.m. They got there at one and nobody showed up. The dope plane probably had come and gone."

His eyes narrowed and he nodded his head slowly, deliberately, as if he had come to some kind of conclusion.

"Don't get the idea that the discovery you and Buddy made yesterday went for nothing. The information y'all provided started some wheels in motion. What you gave me and what I'm learning along the way might allow us to land a bigger fish than we would have if we had netted that plane. Remember that, and remember to keep this confidential."

LYING IN BED THAT NIGHT, OSCAR related to Ruby the story about Jim trying to pull the feeder with his horse, and his reaction to Oscar's reproach. "That boy tries so hard to do everything just right, it really bothers him when he messes up even the tiniest bit. That's why he learns so dern fast, because he's always trying to be perfect. And doin' a man's work, most of the time. That boy beats all, Ruby. I swear I never seen a boy like him."

CHAPTER 16

Norma Bradley eased the car off the asphalt road and drove slowly through the grassy entrance of the horse show grounds. As soon as the trailer was well clear of the road she allowed the car to come to a gentle stop and studied the place, looking for a suitable parking spot. The area was large and studded with oak trees. Matt had been giving her lessons on handling the car with the horse trailer hitched behind, but she was glad there was no shortage of parking places. She was not anxious to practice maneuvering the trailer in tight places.

"Let's pick out a good parking place, Jim," she said, "one that's easy to get in and out of. I don't want to have to back up."

"Don't worry, Mom, I'm used to backing up the hay wagon. I can always extricate you from any problem," Jim said airily.

His mother was studiously biting at her bottom lip, her eyes searching the grounds. She said absently, "You can 'extricate' me, huh? That's a big word for a such a little guy."

"Let's park out here on the outskirts like those people did," Jim said, the sweep of his hand taking in a few rigs that were parked away from the others. "There's a good place, Mom, by that tree." As she brought the car creeping alongside it, Jim watched their progress and coached. "Just a little further. Put the trailer in the shade so Black won't have to stand in the sun. Okay, right here."

Norma got out and looked around, massaging her tired shoulder muscles. Driving with the trailer behind was not difficult at all, she reasoned, but there was still a beginner's tenseness to it. She just needed a little practice, she reasoned.

They heard the clanking sounds of microphones being shuffled around. A woman's voice, speaking low and conversationally, began issuing instructions: "Joe, get that boy on the tractor to—he's going too fast, just givin' it a lick and a promise. Get him to go over the far end again." After a long pause, she said, "That's better—Hank, you might want to think twice about where you're putting that timing light. I guarantee somebody'll step right in front of it where it is, and if it happens during my daughter's run—" A murmur of laughter drifted across the grounds.

Norma was pleased that they'd arrived with so much time to spare. The drive had taken far less time than she had allowed, and as this was their first show, she wasn't sure how long the registration process would take.

Now they heard the shouts and laughter of people having a good time. Horses whinnied, inspiring responses from others, and still others. A dog barked and received a reply. Hoofbeats approached, and with the creaking of saddle leather a girl cantered by on a bay mare. She talked softly to the horse as she put her through a drill.

Old Black heard the sounds too. From the trailer came the clomp, clomp of shod hooves stamping impatiently on the wood floor. When Jim opened the trailer door Old Black moved backward, taking small steps until he found the edge of the floor. Then he felt for the ground with a careful toe and, finding it, marched decisively out of the trailer. Jim took the lead rope and laughed as Black tried to look in every direction at once, his head high, eyes wide and nostrils flared, his lips quivering excitedly. His ears flicked constantly to locate the direction of the horse sounds that reached them. He made a low, throaty sound, then neighed long and lustily. Jim beamed with enormous pride and grinned broadly, a little nervously. He pulled the brim of his hat down a bit and was glad that their spot here was private.

"C'mon, Black. Let's take a walk. You're sure excited. Anxious to be back in action, ain't you?"

The horse wanted more than a walk. He trotted sideways, still high-headed and wide-eyed, performing a little dance at the end of the halter lead. Feeling a bubbling delight, Jim trotted along with him, talking softly to him all the time.

Several young people rode by in a group with two dogs ambling along with them. Boys and girls practiced setting up their horses for halter judging, others were tuning up—walking, trotting, rocking along in a slow lope, turning, stopping, backing, standing very still.

Norma saw that Old Black had settled down and was in a smooth, going-nowhere trot alongside Jim, carrying his head just right, his nose about level with the point of his shoulder. Being a participant instead of a spectator was an entirely new experience for them. When they had decided he would enter this show, it was still a month away—the proverbial bridge they could cross when they came to it. Now they were there.

Well, they had made it here to the showgrounds at least. So far Jim had exhibited no more than just a trace of anxiety; he certainly seemed relaxed now. And true to his advertising, Old Black did indeed appear to be at home in these surroundings. She looked inside the brown envelope in her hand and checked that she had everything required to register for the events they were planning to enter. She checked for the presence of Old Black's AQHA registration certificate. Clipped to it was Jim's certificate of membership in the American Quarter Horse Youth Association. "Let's wander over and get registered," she said to him.

Jim led Old Black into the pool of shade and tied him to one of the steel loops on the trailer. "There you are, Black old boy. We'll be back when you see us coming," he said and stroked the horse's neck. Old Black watched him until he and Norma disappeared from sight.

Jim wondered if his nervousness showed. His mother seemed intent on the scenery ahead of them. He looked down at his clean, sharply-creased jeans. From his back pocket he took his bandanna and wiped first one palm and then the other. As they began encountering more people, he saw that a lot of the kids seemed to know one another. They looked so much at home that he felt lonely. He found himself wishing they had waited and come with Alexandra, but Norma had wanted to come early to their first show.

Some people lounged around in folding chairs and on blankets in the shade of their trailers—but that wouldn't last long, he thought, glancing at the sun climbing in the sky. Beach umbrellas were popping up here and there and awnings sprouted over the rear ends of pickups where tailgate parties were in the making.

"Gosh, Mom, look at the wheels some of these people come in!" He pointed with his head to a motorhome with a fancy four-horse trailer behind. They stopped and gaped. Both the motorhome and the trailer displayed lettering on a fancy scroll background: "Screech Owl Ranch~Dime Box, Texas." Next to the rig a white picket fence enclosed an area shaded by a bright striped awning that extended from the motorhome. White plastic chairs and tables had been placed about in informal groups under the awning; a big table in the center of things was covered with bowls of chips and dips, munching vegetables in bowls of ice water. Next to it was a red Igloo ice chest brimming with drinks packed in ice.

Norma said softly, "Now, *this* is the way to come to a horse show. We'll have to talk to your father about getting rich."

"Look," he said, pointing.

Lined up on stands alongside the motorhome were three beautiful hand-tooled saddles, their stirrup fenders tooled with the names of the shows that had awarded them.

Two outstanding Quarter Horses, a dapple gray mare and a sorrel gelding, were tied to the trailer. The gelding was saddled. A pair of leather chaps lay across the saddle seat, batwing chaps of medium blue suede decorated conservatively with small white leather flowers on the outer edges.

Norma felt a gentle hand on her arm. "Howdy, folks," a man said. Norma realized that they were blocking the lane into the Screech Owl Ranch's hospitality suite. The man was tall, his weathered face drawn into a pleasant smile. "Hugh Robertson, Ma'am," he said, taking the brim of his hat politely between his thumb and forefinger. Norma took a hasty step aside, bringing Jim with her.

"Hello, Mr. Robertson," she said, returning his smile. "I'm Norma Bradley and this is my son Jim. Sorry to be in the way—we just stopped to look."

The man extended his hand to Jim. "Jim," he said. His voice was coarse but had a congenial tone.

"Hello, Mr. Robertson," said Jim, touched by his easy friendliness.

"Well, Norma and Jim, y'all come on in and get acquainted," he said. An attractive red-haired woman came up to them. "This is my wife Helen," he said.

Introductions and greetings were exchanged. Before Norma could protest, Helen Robertson had deposited her in a chair among a small group of women and made more introductions. With an easy manner she offered coffee, and gave a signal to a girl of about twelve who brought it on a small tray with sugar and cream on the side. Mrs. Robertson pointed out the cooler of soft drinks and said, "Jim, help yourself to the soda box. This is our younger daughter, Elizabeth.

Libby this is Jim Bradley." A sunny Libby Robertson's smile displayed a small, one-wire arrangement of braces with little silver pads on each of her six front teeth.

"Hi, Elizabeth," he said, looking into her eyes.

"Hi, Jim. Are you showing?"

He nodded and said, "Yes." Jim could be called reserved, but he was not shy. He had been trained by his parents to meet people with positive eye contact and a friendly greeting, along with their name. Adults got a "Mr." or the all-purpose "Miz." Young people were to be called by their full names—Elizabeth in this case, not Liz, and not Libby, even if she was called that by others. "Yes, I am, Elizabeth. This is my first show, so I'm kinda nervous."

"You sure don't *look* nervous," she said. "I remember my first show, and I really *was* nervous. I couldn't sit down for more than a minute before the classes started." She laughed. "But once I got on my horse I forgot all about being nervous. Carol, my sister, shows too." She turned right and left as if expecting the sister to appear. "She wins all the big prizes in our family. She's seventeen, so I guess I'll have to play second fiddle to her till she goes off to college or gets married or something." She huffed theatrically and rolled her eyes in a congenial display of mock discouragement.

Elizabeth Robertson spoke softly, enunciating her words well. She smiled easily and gave enthusiastic emphasis to her speech with her tone of voice, her eyes, and her hands. Mrs. Meridith would have approved. She waved toward the horses tied by the trailer. "That gray gelding is my main horse—Jack. Polly is my barrel horse. And she halters real good."

"Mom and I were admiring your horses, and your trophy saddles—"

"They're Carol's saddles. She's won *three!* She's a tough competitor. The big shows that have saddles for trophies draw such competition! I'm just not good enough yet—I hope you don't have a knockout junior gelding, because Jack's my only chance for a red in this show. You can write off the blue; it belongs to Ricky Hoffman." She thought for three seconds and before Jim could answer she corrected herself. "I mean, I hope you *do* have a knockout junior gelding, if you have a junior gelding. But I hope you didn't bring him today. *That's* what I meant."

She assumed her theatrical manner again, wringing her hands in distress, and drew her forefinger knife-like across her throat. Jim laughed and laughed. He liked Libby Robertson. She was tall and willowy, red-haired like her mother. A few freckles paraded across her nose and cheeks. There was an honest warmth about her—and her father and mother, for that matter—that made Jim very comfortable.

"I don't have a junior gelding," said Jim, still laughing. "I only have one horse. He's a gelding but not a junior gelding by a long shot. But I'm not entering him in halter. Old Black, that's his name, Old Black won't halter. He's a good performance horse, but he's got no business in a halter arena." He told Libby that he was entering all of the performance classes, but that he didn't expect to win anything until he and Old Black got some show experience.

"You go out there to *win*, Jim," she said showing a determined fist. Considerately, she asked questions about Old Black. When she learned that he held the calf-roping championship, she said, "Well, I wouldn't feel too bad about being beat by a world champ—there's my sister Carol, now."

She waved to a girl who was just riding up and leading another horse on a halter rope. Jim noticed how easy she sat in the saddle, dismounting in a smooth and effortless motion, touching down like a feather. Her gracefulness reminded him of Alexandra. Like her sister's, Carol's chaps were suede batwings, a dusty rose color with nickel conchos. She wore a matching suede vest and a felt hat of the same color. A loose blonde bun was visible below her hat. She threw a smile toward her family and tied up her horses.

When Jim was introduced to Carol, Libby told her he had a Quarter Horse named Old Black who was the world champion calf-roping horse. She related that Jim said he was a little nervous about riding in his first show.

"Nervous?" asked Carol. She looked him over as if sizing him up and gave Libby a devilishly significant look. "Be careful, Lib. He might be sandbagging, trying to catch us off guard. You start hauling in the blues, Jim, and I'm going to talk to you about that *nervous* routine."

Jim shared in their laughter. Norma was glad to see him so at ease with the girls. She had begun the day with some tenseness herself, and was glad they'd happened by the Robertson's Screech Owl Ranch encampment.

"Ricky's the one we'll have to ground tie," Carol said. "Ricky's the one. Do you know him, Jim? Ricky Hoffman?" When he shook his head both girls began speaking at the same time. They left no doubts that Jim would know Ricky Hoffman before the day was done.

"He's a hot dog on a fifty-thousand-dollar horse," Libby said.

"And this one's a *real* fifty-thousand-dollar horse, not one of those ringers floating around," Carol said, her eyes twinkling. "He's by Nizhny! And he's a flyer. *Beautiful* horse. Wins blues and purples right and left. His name is Gorky."

Jim knew of Nizhny. He was the current "designer" horse—megabucks breeding fee, offspring tearing up the tracks, and a big name in cutting and halter arenas, AQHA Champions beginning to roll off the assembly lines. "What do you mean by ringer?" he asked.

"A breeder's ringer," said Carol. "Some breeders try to jack up their stallion fees and the value of his offspring, by arranging phony sales for big bucks. Say a horse that might really be worth five thousand sells in an auction for *twenty* thousand. It happens that the buyer and seller are in cahoots, and they had some phony bidders who had no intention of actually buying the horse for more than the last legitimate bid, but ran the price up. Say the genuine bidding stops at five thousand, and the phony bidders run it up to twenty and one of them supposedly buys the horse. Later they all settle up. But the horse *sold*," she held up two fingers of each hand as quotation marks, "for twenty thousand, supposedly. That's running a ringer."

Libby laughed. "Once a friend of my Dad's was telling us about his new twenty-thousand-dollar horse. Dad asked him how he could afford to spend that much for a horse, and he said, 'I just hit it lucky. The seller was looking for a couple of good cats, so I traded him two ten-thousand-dollar cats for the horse,' and he broke out laughing."

Norma saw them laughing and talking and gave up the last of her apprehensions. This was going to be a good time.

"You'll know Ricky the minute you lay eyes on him," said Carol. "*Super* dark chestnut gelding. One fine Quarter Horse. The real fifty-thousand-dollar horse. His dad is Hoffman's Furniture in Houston. The story we heard was that he got Ricky into horses to keep him out away from the dope scene. Dad says it looks like it worked, and the Hoffmans can afford it, so it was worth it."

"He rides a black saddle loaded with silver," said Libby. "Black chaps. Black hat. Black pickup. Black everything."

"He's stuck on himself," said Carol. "But he's okay. Tell you one thing, Ricky Hoffman's the boy to beat in just about any timed event. And he owns the halter arena. I can tell you without even seeing your horse, Jim. Almost. Don't show your gelding at halter unless you want no better than a red."

"I don't plan to show him at halter at all," Jim said. "He won't halter. And I don't expect to beat Ricky in performance, either."

The trio was still discussing him when Norma gathered herself and Jim and proceeded toward registration. "They seem to be such *wonderful* people," she said. "They know Alexandra! They're very good friends with her parents. Everyone agrees that Andrew doesn't seem to even be aware that he's so famous. He'd told them about us, Jim. As soon as Mrs. Robertson found out where our place was, and that we were from Houston, she asked me, 'Is it your husband who is the pilot, flying all over the world in his jet?' I told her the jet belongs to his company, and that he's flying around this minute while I'm learning how to trailer a horse!"

Jim thought of Libby Robertson and jumped a few steps. "People are friendly at horse shows, aren't they Mom?" When he saw the brown envelope in his mother's hand he said with some concern, "Mom, we gotta get registered! Then I have to get back and see how Black's doing. Maybe I could ride over and see Carol and Libby and show him to them."

"Mrs. Robertson said we have plenty of time, Jim. Halter is first, and they'll be taking performance registrations all through the halter classes. But let's get registered so we can look around. Then you and Old Black can visit the Robertson's. Maybe you can pick up some pointers before the classes start."

"Maybe," he said without conviction. "Alexandra has been drilling me on the events and I think I could run them blindfolded. Old Black knows them, too."

They continued making their way through the irregularly parked array of vehicles and trailers and tents and umbrellas and every other kind of festive outdoor arrangement imaginable.

They walked among a sea of horses. Many were tied to trailers, some were saddled, some were covered with light stable blankets—halter horses, thought Jim. Horses were being led here and there. Riders casually sat their mounts, chatting with other mounted kids. Others rode their horses in last-minute tuneup activities. Inevitably, there was a match race between two horses. The announcer denounced the racing and questioned the sense of anybody trying to show a horse after it had been run into the ground.

Any critic of the dress habits of modern youth would have been pleased at the sight of this throng of young riders. The boys' obvious favorite was jeans, almost all of them dark blue though with the blue-black newness washed out, starched and sharply creased. White western-tailored shirts were plentiful as well as every color under the sun. Tan was a popular hat color for the boys, as was brown, silver belly, black, forest green, and plenty of straws—fine straws.

Jim saw a lot of spurs and big silver-and-gold prize belt buckles, as well as leather chaps and breeches. Expensive saddles and show halters were in abundance though he saw more common and utilitarian tack, like his own. He doubted that anyone would recognize a Wehring saddle, which would be all right with him.

"There are plenty of people here like us, Mom," he said, seriously. "But a horse that cost fifty thousand dollars?" He tried to imagine something that could cost fifty thousand dollars.

"Oh, isn't she cute!" said Jim's mother. She stopped and watched a little blonde girl in a red and yellow western outfit who was no more than six or seven. She was beginning the process of mounting her big Quarter Horse. An extra stirrup hung from the saddle horn, much lower to the ground than her riding stirrups. The saddle strings on the skirt behind the cantle were very long, no doubt lengthened for the purpose they were being put to. With the saddle strings wrapped around her right hand and her tiny boot in the low mounting stirrup, she grasped the stirrup fender and began climbing aboard. It was a long, laborious procedure—no help wanted, thank you. When she finally settled into the saddle seat her body relaxed noticeably and she emitted an audible sigh.

Most of the girl riders were dressed in gaily colored western outfits, many with matching hats. There were plenty of reds, greens, yellows, blues, purples and fuchsias to perk up the palette.

Jim saw a girl dressed in a pale green blouse and matching hat, bright green pants and matching green snakeskin boots with silver caps on their pointed toes. Attached to the bridle of the horse she was riding was a green pom-pom, and a green saddle-pad showed around the saddle. He tapped his mother on the arm to get her attention and rolled his eyes. "Wow, Mom," he said softly. They watched as she trotted her horse up to a candy-apple-green trailer hitched to a candy-apple-green Caravan.

Norma smiled. "Old Black might be ashamed of his lot in life when he gets a look around here, Jim. Do you think we dare expose him to all this elegance?" She put an arm around her son and lovingly squeezed his shoulder. He looked up and smiled back at her wink.

Jim laughed. "Old Black will think we came to the wrong place when he gets a look at all this."

Jim was eager to see the packet of papers that his mother had received during registration, especially the descriptions of the courses and the rules for each event. "Let's leave them in the envelope until we get back to the car," she said.

He began to rise on tiptoes, searching for their car and the yellow trailer, and Old Black. "I hope Old Black's okay," he said.

"Jim, Old Black has been to enough rodeos to know how to stand tied to a trailer—he's all right. But let's move along just to be on the safe side."

They were walking along the arena fence when Jim saw the spectacle: the fanciest pickup truck and trailer he'd ever seen, parked next to a kind of roped-off corral. The sleek, black Dodge Ram pickup sported chrome spotlights on each side of the windshield, and three antennas gave it an air of communications central. Attached to the pickup was a black horse trailer trimmed in gleaming chrome. Cream custom striping with a fine red shadow line adorned the truck and trailer. Then his eyes fell on a glistening black saddle, deeply hand tooled and loaded with silver. On a rack beside it hung a matching bridle, breast strap, martingale, and show halter.

"Mom, look!" said Jim.

Seven saddle racks were lined up in a row, each displaying a prize saddle. Mounted on display boards nearby were groups of ribbons with legends printed below each one. Artfully positioned about the boards were photographs of a tall, smiling teen-age boy and a superb chestnut Quarter Horse. The photos were professionally matted and under each was a printed caption.

Jim pointed to the driver's door of the pickup, "Ricky Hoffman" was painted in fancy lettering outlined with elaborate scrollwork.

Three boys sat in folding chairs in the bed of the pickup. Several others lounged around in the roped-off corral. There was no sign of the fabled horse or his master. But Jim saw the name "Gorky" on the side of the trailer.

They were still talking about Ricky Hoffman's rig, his corral, and his displays when they arrived at their own rig. He patted Old Black on the rump. "Hi, Black old boy. Did you think we'd deserted you?"

Jim took two folding lawn chairs out of the trailer and placed them in the shade alongside Old Black. Sitting down, he took from the envelope his red-and-white checkered Purina contestant's number: twenty-seven. His mother pinned it on his back. He took out the course descriptions and began studying them. When he finished with the pole-bending pattern, he passed it to his mother.

"Have you seen anything that you weren't expecting?" she asked.

"No, it's pretty much what Alexandra and I have been practicing.

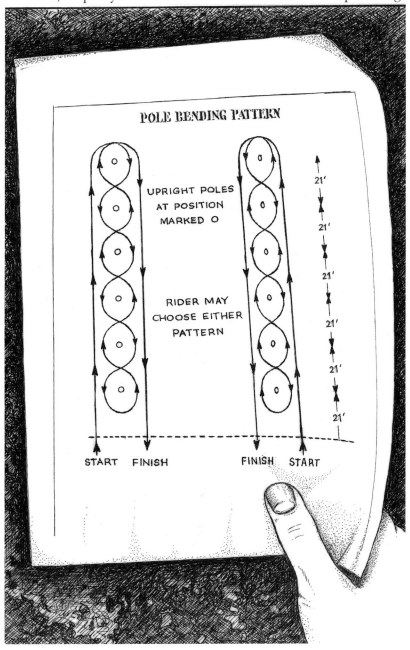

Just about what we've seen at all the 4-H shows."

He stared off into space, thinking.

"Mom," he said solemnly, "I'm not going to push too hard, because there isn't any chance of me winning anything today." He looked at her with such a somber little face that her stomach tightened. She silently agreed; winning could come later. She only wanted him to finish this show with a feeling of accomplishment. "I hope you won't be disappointed if I don't win anything."

She took his chin in her hand and shook it tenderly. "Everybody has to win their spurs, Jim. Not just in there," her head indicated the arena, "but in everything else you do in life. You don't have to apologize for anything, especially for not *winning*."

He looked at her with gratitude in his eyes. "I'm just going to try to run the courses right."

He looked at Old Black and was glad he was not going to be standing in a halter arena with the likes of what they had seen. Pole bending was the first class, and although he knew it by heart, he once more studied the course description. Butterflies were beginning to flutter in his stomach.

ALEXANDRA HAD ARRIVED IN THE NICK OF TIME to get Applejack registered. She was standing with him in the halter arena; the judge had examined his class and was making one last, quick examination before beginning his selection. All the exhibitors' eyes were on him when he started to point out horses. The ring steward was standing by the first one he pointed out, Gorky, and directed Ricky Hoffman to a place along the rail. After the judge had sent eight more horses to the rail, the rest of the class, about thirty horses, was excused from the arena—they got the gate, the "prize" for the losers. Applejack did not get the gate. Jim caught Alexandra's eye and struck out with a victorious fist.

The judge arranged his class. After a chin-scratching last-minute examination he switched two horses in a move that advanced Applejack from fourth to third. Oh, boy! thought Jim.

Alexandra was holding the yellow ribbon high as she led Applejack out of the arena. Her father gave her a hug.

"All *right!*" said Jim. "That was a tough class, Alexandra."

Her big smile said third was okay with her. "I'm glad that's over, so I can saddle up."

"Can I use the bed of your pickup to saddle Old Black from?" Jim asked.

"You don't need to go through that routine, Jim," Mr. Meridith said. "I'll put Old Black's saddle on him."

Once both horses were saddled, Jim and Alexandra rode away. Norma and Andrew strolled toward the Robertson's camp.

From there, Norma saw that they would not even have to move to the stands to watch the show; the pipe rail allowed an excellent view from ground level. She noticed, too, that Ricky Hoffman's corral was set up diagonally across the arena at a corner, near the end of the stands. The famous Gorky was indeed something to look at. The nickel silver on his saddle and other tack must weigh a lot, she considered. Ricky looked to be about seventeen. He sat on his horse, talking with some animation to a group of boys, most of whom seemed slightly younger than he.

The contestants began to make their way to the staging area where they would draw lots for the running order. She hoped Jim would not be so unlucky as to draw the starting number. The six poles were already standing in the arena, twenty-one feet apart, according to the course description they had studied.

The dead sound of a P.A. system about to say something came on. The announcer said, "Our first contestant in pole bending is entry number eleven, Josh Barlow, riding Smokey. Because we're using an electric timer, the rider can start at will. The timing light will start the timer, and when the horse crosses it at the end of his run it will stop the clock. Any time you're ready, Josh."

Josh rode Smokey at a walk to a position about twenty feet from the white line that marked the start and finish. He shoved his hat down tight; losing it during the run would cost him a five-second penalty. He leaned forward and Smokey was away. He thundered in a bee line the length of the course, about a hundred and fifty feet, and then started bending his way back down the poles, weaving in and out until he reached the last one, then rode back up the serpentine course. After rounding the last pole he flew straight for the chalk line he had crossed to start the run.

Josh stood up in the stirrups and let Smokey slow down easy. He trotted out the gate, and another horse walked in.

The announcer said in a voice of approval. "Well, Josh, I think it's safe to say you just took the lead." Josh smiled broadly. There was a murmur of laughter from the spectators, and exaggerated cheering arose from the boys gathered around Ricky Hoffman's rig.

Eleven riders had run the course when the woman announced, "Next contestant: entry number twenty-seven, Jim Bradley riding Old Black." Hearing his name over the speakers sent a wave of excitement through Norma.

Jim knew the course, and it helped that he had been able to watch it run repeatedly. He gave Old Black a suitable starting space and pushed his hat down tight. Then they exploded across the starting line. Old Black stretched out in his distinctive running style, his nose reaching far out and his feet tearing up the arena. To Norma, he did not look like he was as fast as the others, although he seemed to be putting more effort into running. A din of hooting arose from the boys at the Hoffman corral.

When Jim reached the Hoffman end of the arena, wild cheers and waving arms greeted his turn around the first pole. Old Black made the turn smoothly and began weaving in and out down the row of poles. His movements were swift and graceful. His lead changes were perfectly executed, allowing him to reach out as far as possible on his new lead. At the end of the row he made his turn around the last pole so tight that it looked as if he might hit it. He didn't, but he accelerated noticeably on his run back up the row of poles.

Andrew Meridith was smiling. He turned to Hugh Robertson and said, "Old Black figured out on his way down those poles that he didn't have to give them so much clearance, Hugh. See how he's crowding them on the way back? And see how he's getting a bit more reach as he comes out of those lead changes?"

Robertson nodded, smiling approvingly. He was watching the run intently.

Jim crossed the finish line. Letting Old Black slow down at his own pace, they trotted out of the gate. He was satisfied with his run, and relieved it had gone well. It had *felt* good. He knew the run wasn't good enough to earn a placing in the event, but he'd run the pattern according to the rules; he didn't knock a pole down or lose his hat.

Norma Bradley found herself applauding. She thought Jim had done better than some of the other riders. She sighed with relief, and then her attention was attracted to some activity in the Hoffman corner. The boys were running around, lined up one behind the other, leaning forward and craning their necks, their heads stuck out far ahead of their bodies and making motions with their hands, apparently simulating flying feet, and all of them crying "Whoo, whoo, whoo . . ."

She looked at Jim just as his attention went to the boys. A pleased expression had come onto his face, but just as quickly it dissolved into one of chagrin; he turned Old Black away from them. She heard Hugh Robertson say to Andrew, "Those boys that hang around Ricky Hoffman—" He shook his head. "That was a nice, smooth run, even if the horse isn't all that fast on the straightaways."

"Don't worry about Jim," Andrew said with an air of confidence. "He'll be rubbing their noses in it soon enough. He sure doesn't have to apologize for that run. There's two things in Jim's favor, Norma. He can ride, and he's aboard a genuine champion."

From the loudspeakers came the announcement of Jim's time. "A new fifth place. *Good* run, Jim," she said.

Before Jim ducked his head, Norma saw a smile spread across his face. The boys at the Hoffman corral quieted down.

Surprised, Hugh Robertson said to Andrew, "Gosh, Old Black makes better time than it looks like he's doing, doesn't he?"

Andrew laughed. "He's been fighting that clock all his life. He'll find ways to shave time off of these games, once he's settled down. He's new to this kind of rodeoing. You wait until he gets a few shows under his belt. If he was to re-run that course right now, he'd beat his first time by two seconds at least. In a few more shows, he's going to be setting these games on fire. Just wait."

Ricky Hoffman came in first and rode off with another beautiful gold and silver belt buckle to add to his collection. Alexandra placed third. Jim was edged out of tenth by one-fifth of a second.

The other events seemed to streak by. Jim had a chance to place in the reining class, but he made a mistake during the complex pattern: beginner's nervousness. He was rewarded by derisive hoots from the Hoffman corral. He ran the stake race in commendable time, ahead of twenty-two other contestants, but he didn't place. They made a decent run in the keyhole race, but not fast enough to get a ribbon.

Alexandra won the flag race. It looked as if Jim was going to place at last, but he was eased out by the very last contestant. He had no chance in the barrel race, which was a pure speed event.

He won fourth place in the western pleasure class. His hatbrim was not large enough to conceal his extravagant pride as he rode out of the arena with his very first ribbon. Alexandra was second, winning a pretty stable blanket along with her red ribbon. Ricky Hoffman was third. He already had three firsts—in pole bending, barrels, and the stake race—and was second in the flag race, behind Alexandra.

The last event in the show was western riding. The pattern was right out of the AQHA handbook, one that Jim and Alexandra had practiced many times. He'd explained it to his mother that morning, as they sat studying the course descriptions.

"In western pleasure both horse and rider are judged. But in western *riding*, the performance of the *horse* is judged. See what it says:

Western riding demonstrates a sensible, well-mannered horse with free and easy movements. The horse will be judged on quality of gaits, change of leads, response to the rider, manners, disposition, and intelligence."

He looked at her. "The rider is judged on faults, not how good he does anything. Here's what it says about faults.

The following are considered faults and should be judged accordingly: losing a stirrup or holding on; any unnecessary aid given by the rider such as verbal commands, spurring, quirting, or jerking of the reins.

"Old Black is sensible, Mom, and he's well-mannered. He has *free and easy movements*. And I don't have to do any of the things that are faults for him to do well on *this* course," he said, tappng the paper significantly with his finger. He wrinkled his brow and was thoughtful. "Mom, we have a chance in western riding."

He'd outlined the course for her with his finger. "You have to open this gate from horseback, then go through it and close it. I close the barn door all the time like that, and gates too."

His eyes left her face and returned to the course description. "Then we walk straight ahead and step over a log—nothing to that; Old Black steps over logs all the time. We break into a trot here, make a left turn at the end of the arena, then half-way across we go to a lope for the rest of the course. Let's see," he counted the markers shown, "there are eight cone markers. You weave in and out of these five, sort of like an easy pole bending course. Then you ride across the arena and begin a zig-zag pattern all the way back down. You have to jump the log at a lope here." He grinned, "That's a toothpick compared to some of the logs we jump sometimes. No fancy riding in any of that. Lope half way back up the arena and stop. Then we make two side-steps and back up at least ten feet.

"We're supposed to change leads halfway between each cone, where they have these marks." He pointed out the wide black boxes on the course diagram. "We'll see some busted leads along here, where the horse changes leads in front but not behind. You remember, don't you?—we've seen that lots of times."

His finger had traced the line back and forth down the page. "It's coming back down, where these four zig-zags have a straightaway all the way across the arena; this is where me and Old Black are liable to

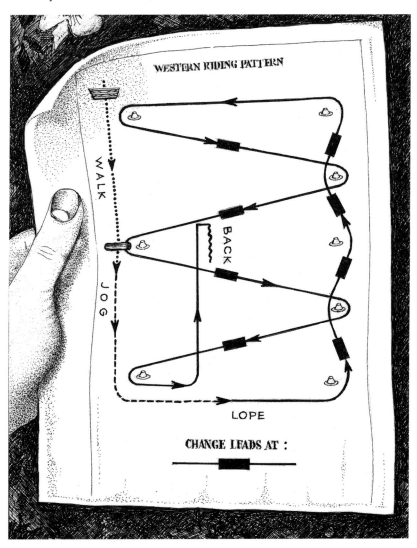

pick up points. See, the lead changes are supposed to be made in the middle, on the long straightaways. Here's where some horses will have trouble." He tapped each of the specified places where lead changes were required. "Some horses won't make those flying lead changes;

they won't change leads until they see a change in direction coming up."

He'd grinned knowingly at his mother. "And here's where some *riders* will get faults. You'll see them throwing their weight around trying to make their horse change leads—that comes under the 'unnecessary aid' fault. There's nine placings, Mom. We could—we have a chance to place in this class." A cautious little smile had played on his face.

"Me and Old Black change leads all the time down in the pasture, while we're loping along in a straight line—sometimes bareback and without even a bridle. If Old Black is on a right lead and I want a change, all I have to do is barely shift my balance to the left just as he's collecting his hind end, before beginning his reach with his forelegs. I can feel him making the lead change in midair, and when his forefeet come reaching out, the left one is leading. You can feel it in his shoulders—your right leg was just a little bit ahead on the right lead, and when he makes the change your left leg will move ahead with his shoulder. Old Black will change leads as smooth as you ever saw it done."

Athletic skill had never come naturally to Jim. Mr. Bonner had long ago observed that students who achieved goals only by persistent hard work would often trudge past their counterparts to whom the basics came naturally. Too often, alas, he'd encountered students whose easy natural ability had robbed them of persistence and determination. They would rise to a fair level of accomplishment and stagnate there. When further progress required actual *work* to stay ahead of the less gifted, many would drop out of the class.

Mr. Bonner had watched more than once as Jim had struggled to learn a difficult aspect of riding—leads, for example. He'd coached patiently as Jim grappled with the problem until finally, *finally*, click, like a light coming on, Jim would have it.

"Four-legged animals that gallop assume *leads* as they run," Mr. Bonner had told the class. "On the left lead, the left fore and hind legs reach noticeably out ahead on each stride. On the right lead, of course, both right legs are reaching far ahead, *leading*—thus the term *leads*." He'd had a skilled class member lope Jupiter down the arena—nice and easy so the action could be observed as if in slow motion. Three strides into a lope on a left lead, the rider gracefully arched her upper body to the right; Jupiter smoothly changed to a right lead in response to his rider's new center of balance. She continued to change leads every few strides. By watching these demonstrations and experiencing lead changes on their own, the students gradually acquired a basic understanding of those mysterious leads.

Mr. Bonner once seized an unexpected opportunity to discuss leads. He'd called attention to two dogs who were chasing each other playfully, running in first one direction and then another. "Concentrate on only one of the dogs," he had instructed. "Notice that your dog frequently changes leads. Sometimes it changes for no apparent reason, at least not apparent to us because we tend to associate leads only with changes in a horse's direction. But that dog changed leads for a reason. Maybe it was something to do with balance during his play, or perhaps he anticipated making a move that never came about because of a countering move by the other dog."

He spoke of the grace shown by horses and dogs and other *quadrupeds* as they changed leads on their own: "It won't hurt you to know that four-footed animals are quadrupeds, and isn't the word a nice, crisp replacement for 'four-footed-animals?' Without a rider, most horses will demonstrate the precise changes of leads we want to see in the performance arena. When an unskilled rider attempts to put a horse through a drill its leads often go all to pieces—fore feet on one lead and hind feet on another. Why? Because the rider is giving commands in ways that can't be properly executed. Busted leads, they're called, or split leads."

He'd used military drill instructions to make his point. Lining up some students in a column, he gave them a quick marching lesson as the rest of the class looked on. The basic element of the drill was the command "Company . . . halt!" After only a few attempts, the little drill team would halt nicely on the properly timed command, "Company-y-y, *halt!*"

"But look what happens when I give the command in such a way that the drill team cannot prepare to execute it." As they marched along he said lazily and with no pause between words, "Comp'ny-halt!" The marchers stopped with as much precision as a train wreck—stumbling and falling all over each other. He looked complacent and said, "I gave the command without the verbal cadence they had come to expect, and I caught them in mid-stride so they could not collect themselves for a proper halt.

"Timely warning and proper execution of commands are essential for man or beast being *commanded* to perform maneuvers. As we saw with the dogs, when they are allowed to move freely on their own, not handicapped by our clumsy commands, they make the most elegant changes of leads. Our horses will too, if given timely warning and commands they understand."

Mr. Bonner had kept Jim working on leads until he got it—one day, all of a sudden, he could *feel* Jupiter's movements beneath him. And once he got it, he wondered why it had seemed so hard.

JIM WAS NUMBER TWENTY-ONE IN LINE to run the western riding course, so he had some time to kill. He was sitting with his mother at the Robertson's encampment, observing his competition. Alexandra and the Robertson girls would be early riders and were on their horses.

Watching a particular entry, Andrew said, "You can tell that horse has been ridden through many a gate. Did you see how he marched right into it as they were closing it?"

As the horse progressed through the course, Helen Robertson remarked that he had busted a lead going up the easy markers. "Yeah," Andrew agreed. "He's been late on changing, too. He's not likely to do too well on the zig-zags coming back down."

He didn't. Attempting to make the horse change leads midway between markers, the boy finally resorted to throwing his weight left and right to force lead changes. His timing was taking the horse by surprise, making him cross leads.

It was not a good run, and a feeling of compassionate empathy welled up in Jim. He clapped and was pleased to hear a scattering of applause from other considerate observers, which no doubt consisted of the boy's family. "He sure backed up good," he said as the horse concluded his run.

Andrew agreed, then said in a negative tone, "But I don't see how anyone who doesn't understand leads and lead changes can expect to compete in these games, Jim. The only thing that saves them is that so much of their competition is in the same boat."

Hugh Robertson said in a friendly, chiding voice, "Not everybody has an equine drill sergeant for a daddy, Andrew. And a fine, indoor practice arena." He chuckled, just lightly, then added without humor, "That's where 4-H made the difference for Carol and Libby. They learned a lot in 4-H."

"That's where Jim got his training, didn't you Jim?" Andrew said. "At a 4-H club in Houston taught by George Bonner. You know him, Hugh?"

"Know *of* him, in cutting. A man with an outstanding reputation. I didn't know he taught 4-H."

Alexandra was entering the arena. She opened the gate, rode through and closed it smartly. Applejack stylishly picked up his feet as he crossed the log, then broke into a nice trot, made the turn, and at the precise spot called for broke into an easy lope. He wove through the first five markers with ease, loped across the arena, then swept around the first turn of the zig-zag. He responded gracefully when Alexandra adroitly asked for lead changes, exactly in mid-arena. He gracefully sailed across the log, and at the finish dropped down into a nice slide, stepped sideways three paces, stopped for a split second, and backed up smartly.

Jim was clapping before she finished. Norma took it up, then everyone else around the Robertson camp; from there the applause spread through the crowd. "I don't see how it could be done better," Jim said happily.

"She did a superb job—has this class won up to now," said Robertson. "Did y'all notice how she gave the marker by the log such a wide berth? That swing gave Applejack a straight approach where it has to be crossed at the lope. I noticed several riders approaching that marker by the log too close, putting their horse out of position to jump it."

A few minutes later, Andrew leaned close to Jim and said confidentially, "Jim, I hate to give you any ammunition for beating my little girl, but I know you can run this course as well as Alexandra just did. Here's an extra little enhancement. On those long runs between markers back down the zig-zag, move out with some speed between them, and then bring your speed down approaching the markers so it doesn't look like you think you're running barrels. I'm not talking about a lot of speed—not even *near* so much that the judge will consider it sacrificing safety. Just shift gears and accelerate to a good clip on those four crossings, and then again on the final leg to the finish." He looked at Jim significantly. "It's a variety in the pace that can set you apart—a little polish, Jim."

Jim grinned sheepishly. "I'll try. But I don't see how I can even come close to that run of Alexandra's."

Carol Robertson's run was almost as good as Alexandra's, Jim thought. The judge may even have even considered it better. Libby's was all right, but not in the money.

Ricky Hoffman wasn't a threat in this class, or in any of the judged performance events where precision and control were factors. As Ricky was coming down the zig-zag part of the course, Robertson said, "If that boy could sit still for some riding lessons, he'd be the dickens to beat with that horse. But look how heavy-handed he is." Sure enough, Gorky began throwing his head and mouthing the bit. Ricky snatched the reins a time or two and spurred him repeatedly.

Alexandra joined them now, smiling jubilantly. She was always satisfied with a good performance, whether it won or not. "You had a *super* run," said Jim with evident feeling. "There was not one fault by you or Applejack. It was pretty to watch and I bet you win." Wanting to give himself plenty of time, Jim went to his horse.

"Was I really as good as Jim said, Daddy?" she asked.

"Yes you were, sweetheart. The only threat to you is Jim himself. Let's see how he does. If he doesn't beat you, I don't see how anyone else can. There's just too much finesse needed to turn in a top-notch run in western riding, and you and Jim are the two best horse-and-rider combinations at this show. Old George Bonner really put his stamp on Jim. That boy can ride, and he's got the *perfect* horse for his gentle way of doing things."

Andrew looked at his daughter with affection. "And you've helped him a lot. You've been real generous to him, and it's showing up today. I'm real proud of you for that, Honey." He winked at her and she beamed up at him.

"I like the way Jim's handled his first show, Norma," Andrew said. "He took a little razzing off those boys over there, and did it like a little man. He'll be mopping up in no time, and those boys with Ricky Hoffman who were making fun of the way Old Black runs will be singing a different tune." He laughed with anticipation of the welcome event.

"Well," said Alexandra, "I certainly wouldn't have to hang my head if I got beat by a world champion, would I?"

Norma noticed with admiration that Alexandra's expression was not light and gay, for once. It was pleasant, but earnest.

Hugh Robertson leaned close to Andrew and said in a low tone, "When Jim had his horse over here a while ago, I got a glimpse of the maker's mark on his saddle. Could have sworn it was a Wehring. Can that be?"

Andrew nodded.

Robertson's eyebrows went up thoughtfully. "I've been trying to buy a Wehring for three years and I'm still on the waiting list. Can his daddy afford that kind of a tab for a saddle?"

Andrew laughed and made a negative motion with a hand. "Even if Matt Bradley inherited from a rich uncle, he'd never buy a Wehring saddle. It came with the horse, standard equipment."

IT WAS TIME. JIM APPROACHED THE GATE and touched his hat to the judge. He went through the gate with commendable dispatch and Old Black moved out at an energetic walk. He stepped over the log, looking at it as he did so, which pleased the judge. Old Black's gait changed to a jog and then at the prescribed place in the course he made a quick move into a slow lope. Andrew Meridith liked the tiny explosion between the trot and lope—it expressed energy.

Entry number twenty-seven loped up the arena, weaving in and out of the four markers and making lead changes easily, smoothly between them. Old Black always worked with his lips clamped resolutely shut, and he did so now. There would be no fault for an "excessively open mouth."

On passing the fifth marker along the easy side of the course, Old Black was sweeping around the left turn, just beginning his lope across the arena, when Meridith saw Jim's balance move delicately forward. It amounted to no more than an inch at his shoulders, but Old Black accelerated noticeably. In only three strides, Jim's balance moved back imperceptibly and Old Black eased off the pace as he approached the marker that he would round to begin the zig-zag. "That was real pretty," Andrew said softly. Alexandra, who had heard, smiled up at him, her head bobbing emphatically.

Once around the marker, Old Black again accelerated, this time with a touch more power. Only two strides at the new pace and just as he was collecting his hindquarters, Old Black felt a few pounds of his rider's weight shift easily to the right, and precisely in mid-arena he performed an elegant, fluid flying change to a right lead. Two strides later he began smoothly decelerating so as to round the marker at the safe, comfortable lope that the rules called for.

Though the judging was slanted toward the *horse's* performance, one could not watch the horse without being influenced by the plain grace of the small boy in the big roping saddle. He seemed on one hand to be a living extension of the horse, a horse that was running the course with perfection entirely on his own. But there were delicate contradictions of that perception as the rider adroitly gave his horse cues that were so subtle as to be unseen by most onlookers, but which provided a stirring intensity to the performance in the eyes of those capable of observing them; they made up the minority of the audience. To the majority of spectators, it was an elegant exhibition to watch, if for reasons they were unable to describe in so many words.

Andrew Meridith was a talented and experienced artist, and he was therefore a talented and skilled observer. He focused his artistic talents almost entirely on horses and their riders, which required that his observations penetrate to the bones, sinews, and even the spirits of his subjects. His eye for observing horses had been further sharpened by his many years of riding and training them. There was no other witness to this performance, the judge included, who observed the western riding demonstration by entry number twenty-seven with a more discerning eye than Andrew Meridith. And there was no other spectator to the performance, Norma Bradley included, who looked on with greater appreciation. The artistic expression being exhibited called to the edges of his mind the elegant dancing of Fred Astaire and Ginger Rogers. He glowed with the feeling that saturates the senses of an enlightened spectator witnessing a purely exquisite performance. He realized he had been unconsciously holding his breath, and now he exhaled audibly.

Recalling Mr. Robertson's comment during Alexandra's ride, Jim took Old Black wide of the marker at the log, and Old Black sailed over it in a long, graceful leap that subtly suggested a momentary state of weightlessness.

As Jim and Old Black continued through their flawless performance, Meridith felt a wonderful flush of admiration for the boy out there, and for the horse that had been derided at the beginning of the show. The dynamic bursts of speed Jim was introducing were made even more dramatic by their short duration. The graceful deceleration only two strides after Old Black's smooth and effortless lead changes was another sweet note in a stirring visual orchestration. The whole was a more stirring rhythmic diversity than Meridith had envisioned in his mind's eye when he described the strategy to Jim, and it was incredibly beautiful to witness.

After making the final turn for the run to the finish, Jim let Old Black out and he fairly flew up the arena. That is, he fairly flew in his own unique style, one as unknown to Jim as it had been to Buck Jones, since neither of them had ever observed it. The sight of so capable a horse striving courageously to deliver the one ability he no longer possessed never failed to arouse a surge of encouragement from a rodeo crowd, and it did not fail to arouse one here.

Just when it looked as if he would overrun the chalk line, Jim leaned back in the saddle slightly and Old Black's tail went into the dirt in a demonstration of his spectacular stop. The arena dirt flowed up and over his haunches and left a boiling ocher wake, his front feet barely off the ground, head tucked, eyes afire and lips pressed tightly together. Then, there he stood: parked dead still.

A smattering of applause rippled about, then died away as pressure from Jim's left heel sent Old Black three quick steps to the right. He was motionless for a heartbeat, then backed up at a brisk pace, stopping a yard beyond the ten-foot minimum called for. Now a real surge of applause broke out as the crowd expressed approval of the new kid and the old gelding with the funny way of running.

Having felt so often that he was behind and struggling, Jim would never fully realize what tremendous ground he had covered under Mr. Bonner's hand. But George Bonner knew, and he had known how the boy and this horse would come together. If Bonner had been observing Jim and Old Black during this performance of western riding, he would have smiled with gratified approval. But he would not have been a bit surprised.

Andrew felt a tightness in his throat as he sat there, quietly enjoying a warm and satisfying glow.

Alexandra stood on tiptoes with her hands held high, applauding vigorously, her smile never more radiant as Jim rode from the arena amid the continuing applause. He tugged at his hatbrim to hide his reddening, smiling face.

Perhaps momentarily overlooking that there were still horses to run the course, or perhaps considering that there was so little possibility that any horse yet to perform could display more precision and style than that he had just witnessed, the judge stepped forward a few feet from his box and joined in the applause.

The gang in the Hoffman corral stood silent, stupefied.

"Sorry, honey," said Andrew, turning to Alexandra with a huge smile on his face, "but you just got beat."

"Oh, Daddy, I'm *sure* of that," she cried, her face radiating happiness. "And isn't that the sweetest thing that could happen?" She turned to Norma. "He has it won, Mrs. Bradley. Jim has first place in his pocket. Isn't that the *nicest* thing that could happen at this show? A *perfect* ending. Perfect!"

Norma sat very still, smiling nervously, unable to say a word. She watched the remaining contestants quietly, unseeing, afraid to accept the predictions of Andrew and Alexandra.

None of the horses that followed Jim even came close, leaving Old Black and Jim in first place in the western riding event. The prize was a blue ribbon and a big, handsome belt buckle inlaid with silver and gold, inscribed with the name of the show, the event won, and the year. Alexandra won second place and was awarded a red ribbon and a fine leather show halter.

As they drove back to the Bradley ranch with Old Black, there was little room for more happiness in either Jim or Norma this day. Lost in delightful thought, Jim was fidgety and his fingers constantly caressed the engraved surface of the heavy prize belt buckle, examining it as closely as an archeologist might scrutinize an ancient artifact. Its box and the cotton packing lay on the seat beside him. A nervous smile kept coming and going on his face.

Norma was glad she had a steering wheel to keep her hands occupied and a highway ahead to command her attention.

"Mom," Jim said, speaking very softly, "wasn't that a great first show for us, for all of us? For you, for me, and for Old Black, too? And won't Dad be amazed?"

Despite the fact that her face was positively glowing with happiness, Norma's chin quivered slightly as she turned to speak. Not daring to chance a verbal response, she looked at him with intense pride.

Then she composed herself and said gaily, "Yes, Darling Jim, Dad will indeed be amazed."

CHAPTER 17

The night sky was taking on a softening tinge of pink in the east when Jim eased his bedroom door to and stepped quietly out onto the porch. He moved across the porch and dropped onto the grass—to descend the steps would have been a few feet out of his way.

Sam's head lifted alertly from her bed on the enclosed back porch, but only to satisfy herself that the sounds were Jim's. Sam and Norma Bradley were of the same mind when it came to remaining snuggled deep in their cozy nests for as long as that could be decently prolonged.

Sam had never shown much interest in accompanying Jim on his ramblings off the place. Even before Old Black's arrival, when Jim and Buddy had forayed into the Baumberg woods, Sam had always turned back at the fence line and headed home. Now, after an exquisite stretching, she nestled deep down in her bed, squirmed luxuriously, and then uttered a long, sweet sigh of contentment.

Jim closed the gate in the picket fence that enclosed the little yard—slowly, to keep the old iron gear that served as a gate-closer from clanking—and walked across the graveled parking area to the corral. As he opened the gate he looked at the pinkish tint in the eastern sky. His eyes focused on a dazzling white star, alone and about thirty degrees above the horizon and so brilliant that he watched it for a minute to make sure it wasn't an airplane showing a landing light.

He thoroughly brushed Old Black down and combed his mane and tail. By the time he had him saddled, the coming sun had painted the eastern sky pale yellow and the star was now barely visible. When they jogged away from the barn, shafts of sunlight splattered through the trees atop the Baumberg woods and the star was gone.

Jim had permission to depart early this Saturday morning on one of his explorations down Hickory Creek. "But be back by ten," his father had instructed, "so you can help Duffie and Rufus on that fence that washed out. Remember, their workday ends at noon and I don't want them held up."

Jim's help was needed to properly engineer the fence braces. The strain of four strands of wire strung tight was what the end post had to stand up against, so the brace must be designed to resist that strain. The geometry was puzzling to Jim at first, but a simple explanation by his father, with a description of the opposing forces, made it clear as could be.

"The wire pulls hard from the left, but the way the end post is braced provides more than enough resistance for all the strain four strands of barbed wire can put to it. See, the very end post is braced against the second post by two wood braces. The slanting brace would have to push the second post sideways through the ground for it to give an inch. The horizontal brace pushes against the top of the second post. It can't give because it's held fast to the bottom of the end post by several strands of wire twisted tight. Built like this," he said, a sweep of his hand taking in the finished project, "you could stretch the wire to breaking and it wouldn't move the end post an inch."

Some fence builders never could figure it out, though. Jim and his father sometimes saw along county roads brand-new fences that had end-posts built exactly backward, already leaning with the strain and the taughtness gone from the wire strands.

The last heavy rains had brought debris down Sandy Creek that wiped out a short section of fence—an old section that crossed the little creek—between the Bradley place and the Baumberg woods. Today a temporary repair would be replaced with a proper fence.

Jim inventoried his equipment as he jogged along. His lariat hung from the saddle. He patted a breast pocket of his jean jacket and felt the capsule-shaped Cutter snakebite kit, then passed a hand over the familiar bulge of his pocket knife in a pants pocket. He tugged at the big blue bandanna hanging loosely around his neck; a glance over his shoulder confirmed that the canteen of drinking water was tied to the saddle underneath his jean jacket.

The cattle gap through which he'd passed on leaving the Bradley place was about a half-mile behind him when he put Old Black into a gentle lope. He liked to jump the big fallen tree that lay just around the next bend, and he could tell Old Black enjoyed it too. They approached the big trunk at a gallop, with Jim holding the reins in both hands.

Not too many jumps ago he would have been holding onto the saddle horn with one hand. When he felt Old Black collecting himself for the takeoff, he dropped the stirrups, which were too long for jumping, and gripped with both knees, bareback style. Old Black sailed smoothly over, and the whole of Jim's upper body yielded to absorb the shock of the landing.

They were now passing the south boundary of the Baumberg woods. He rode along some distance from the creek bank, following close to the tree line where the woods began their rise out of the lowland to the high ridge that was the horizon for the Bradley's every sunrise.

When he reached the highest point of open ground, Jim stopped Old Black, slung a leg over the pommel, and sat looking at the scenery along the creek below. His eyes followed the gentle incline on the creek's far side, and away in the distance he saw the high rise of pasture land studded with patches of woods. The slanting rays of the sun fell dazzling on the eastern slopes and hilltops, while the land in shadow was still clad in a dull purple. The scene had never suffered a single change in Jim's memory and the thought brought him comforting reflections on the stability of the countryside.

"Richter's store was old when you were born," his father had once remarked.

Duffie and Rufus marched into his consciousness; both had been born within walking distance of the old Rosenbaum place, they said. Alexandra's grandparents, Ruby and Oscar, and *their* parents, were born in the general neighborhood—generation after generation staying put. That was changing, though. Many of the young adults were deserting the country for jobs in the cities, and you couldn't blame them.

His mind drifted from the scene before him to Houston. Although he had lived in the same house all his life, only the family across the street went as far back as he could remember; new families had come and gone on both sides. Only a few of his classmates had been there since the first grade.

The freeway in Jim's own neighborhood had been changed so

dramatically that their familiar and vibrant neighborhood shopping center was left cowering in the shadow of an elevated highway, inaccessible and deserted. Friendly business people the Bradleys had known for years had disappeared overnight.

But in Jim's young mind, the country had a single, permanent face; it changed only with the seasons.

He thought of their farmhouse and barn sitting right there for over a century. He saw a mental picture of young Oscar Jackson taking a shortcut across the old Rosenbaum place when he was courting Ruby, and he smiled at the story he told about being screamed at by a screech owl sitting in the very same pecan tree that stood there today.

Although Houston's landscape and population seemed to be in a constant state of change, Jim's country universe had stayed the same, and he felt it probably always had and always would. He sighed and patted Old Black's neck affectionately, regained his stirrup, and angled off down toward the creek at a brisk lope.

THE SUN WAS HIGH ENOUGH TO TELL HIM it was time to turn around when he spotted a highway ahead. Its bridge spanned the creek on tall concrete supports; the roadway was raised above the terrain on either side by high embankments. Wondering what highway it could be, he rode up the near embankment, then sat and watched the cars go by as he studied it. It was the Brentwood-Rip Ford Highway, he decided, thinking how different it looked from horseback by the roadside than from a car. He turned Old Black toward the creek, let him descend slowly, then headed back toward home.

Jim had just fastened the cattle gap when his attention was attracted to Duffie, waving his red bandanna from far off. Jim rode over and dismounted near the men, Rufus standing with his hands tucked in the bib of his overalls, Duffie busy re-tying the bandanna around his head, making a sweatband.

Duffie leaned forward, as he often did when he had something important to say. "Jimmy, your momma showed me and Rufus all them pretty trophies and ribbons you been winnin' at the shows. You and Old Black must be the talk of the town."

Rufus arched his lanky frame backward for the same reason Duffie leaned forward. "I bet Joe Lewis didn't win no more trophies than you got already. I ran into Mr. Meridith and his little girl at Brentwood Produce the other day. She said you been beatin' the tar out of some smart aleck in them horse shows, a rich man's boy that was whippin' up on everybody till you come along on Old Black."

Rufus looked at the horse with real respect.

Jim felt his face getting warm. "Well, we've had a lot of luck so far," he allowed. "But you can't start crowing or fate might hear you and teach you a lesson."

"Maybe so," said Rufus with a chuckle. "But little Alex ain't worried about you losing your lucky rabbit's foot. She says you and Old Black is the best team in these parts for slick ridin'. Better'n her by a long shot, she says . . . She's not whinin' about that, though," he added quickly. "Mighty proud of both of y'all, Alex is."

Jim was as happy as he could be over the success he and Old Black had been enjoying, and indeed they were winning their share of performance classes, especially those events that didn't require blazing speed. He had quit running barrels because he didn't stand a chance of winning, and he thought all that wide-open running might be taxing on Old Black. That was Ricky Hoffman's domain, and when Ricky had bragged that Jim quit running barrels because he was tired of getting beat, Jim smiled and admitted that he was right about that.

"Been out explorin'?" Duffie asked.

"Yep. Went all the way to Brentwood-Rip Ford Highway. It looks a lot different from down along the creek bed—not like seeing it from a car on the highway. I had to ride up and look at it from the side of the road to tell what highway it was. There isn't a single fence between here and there."

"They can't be no fences across Hickory Creek, the way it gets up like a roarin' river ever so often," Rufus said. "It's been tried, but every fence that's ever been built across it has washed away. Was they any water in the creek at the highway?"

"A little," said Jim. "Only a stream about a yard wide."

"Well, it's got plenty of water in it where it dumps into the Brazos. I caught the biggest catfish anybody ever caught out of there that I heard of, and I caught it at the mouth of this here Hickory Creek. It's like a little river down at the Brazos. Never does dry up. Those big cats like to hang around there and snap up the fish that comes down." He laughed heartily, "I gave that old graybeard something to snap up that had a hook in it."

"Yep!" Duffie said with pride. "I seen that fish with my own eyes. We weighed it on a beam scale at Brentwood Produce: seventy-two pounds, just over."

Rufus was famous for catching big catfish out of the Brazos. Jim asked him what he used for bait and tackle.

"Ummm. If you gonna go after *big* cats, you'll need a *b-i-i-g* bait.

A hog liver is what I caught that big 'un on. I've used big perches, even a whole chicken picked and made all bloody. As for *tackle*, well I don't exactly use tackle. As for hooks, I traded a day's work to Mr. Blacksmith Werner to make me some *big* treble hooks, and I keep the points real sharp, store 'em an oily rag, too, so they won't rust. And for line I use stout trotline cord. I don't use no fishin' pole. Ain't ary one I know of would hold a big cat over fifty pounds. I use a hand line and just fight it out with him. If he gets too much for me, I let him have the line, because it's about fifty feet long and has a five-gallon can tied to the end, like a big cork. Then I just row along, following that can when it comes up, until he wears hisself out and I can handle him. I was almost afraid to pull that big 'un in the boat with me."

Rufus's eyes went to the ground and an expression bordering on shame came across his face. "That place where I fish, you know, where this here Hickory Creek runs into the river, that's where Klanke's Mill is. Went there with a wagon load of cotton many a time, before it closed down when cotton went out. On this day, though—"

"Me too," said Duffie, interrupting. "Been there many a time my own self. Klanke's Mill was hummin' in them days, wasn't it Rufus? Funny, I didn't know you then, and if I ever seen you there, I don't remember it."

"I don't remember you, neither. Yes, suh, it was as busy as a town, they was so much goin' on, with the cotton gin, the corn mill—Mist' Klanke ran that sto' that had about everything you could want. Mist' Rosenbaum bought a thirty-thirty rifle there once when we took a load of cotton in. They had a stock sale every Saturday where you could sell or buy anything on four feet—well, two feet, even, what with the chickens, ducks, turkeys. But when cotton went out, that was the end for Klanke's Mill."

Now Rufus was pensive. When he spoke again, his voice was subdued.

"I didn't even tell you about *this*, Duffie. I was so shamed the way the law done me. It was a little over two years ago, just befo' Sheriff Rosenstock was run out of office by them gumment agents. That day I'd been fishin' in my hole for the longest, and I ain't had even a nibble. I decide to tie up and take a look around. The old mill is about two hundred yards from where I was, so I amble through the woods, not figuring to do anything but take a look around for old times' sake.

"But after I was there awhile, rememberin' back about all the fine times I had there on Saturdays—everybody millin' around talkin' and jokin', and the gin runnin' wide open with bales comin' out every so often, and the sto' buzzin' with people, something drew me into the big old tin building with the gin and mill in it. It was spooky in there, dim with what little windows they was, and them all dirty, so quiet every little sound you made just clanged out. And all that machinery still just sittin', cotton lint everywhere just like it was yesterday.

"I go up to the loft over the east end. You know, Duffie, where the sacks of corn meal was stacked after they ground it? We always had to go up there ourselves and put the sacks on that balance elevator so they would ride to the ground. So I go up there, and it's kinda dark, but it's mornin' and sun is beamin' in the dirty old windows on the east wall. I notice somethin' shiny behind a pile of old sacks lyin' there—funny, because nothin' else there was shiny. I step over and see it's a *badge*, pinned on the shirt of a law man. I—"

Duffie leaned back with a snap and tucked his chin. "You mean they was a po-lice in there?"

"I mean a *dead* po-lice. I near about fainted, and I'm meanin' to get out of there fast! But before I took off, I leaned over so I could see his face—his head was throwed back. They was a bullet hole right by his nose. Shot, he is, and they's a big pool of blood on the floor, maybe a yard acrost. A trooper, because his hat was lyin' there, and no law man I ever seen wears a hat like a trooper's. I struck out of there like a deer and took off rowin' down the river to where I put in. I mean to tell you, it's all still as plain in my mind as if I had took a picture with a Kodak.

"It must've just happened, I figure, because there wasn't no smell of a dead man. And then it come to mind that the blood was red—you know how hog blood gets black in only a few hours? This blood was still red.

"I get my skiff loaded in the back of my pickup and I speed down to the sheriff's office in Brentwood. The first person I see when I go bustin' in there is that Deputy Swagger. I tell him I seen a dead law man at Klanke's Mill. He took me in a little room and closed the door. Real polite-like he asks me all about it. Then he says, real confidential, 'Go home, Rufus, and stay there until I come out to see you. Don't tell a soul, or your life could be in danger. I'm going up there and investigate.'

"I went home and waited. I was even afraid to tell you, Duffie. This is on a Saturday, about noon. I wait and wait, and no deputy. He don't come till Sunday, and I had to miss church and can't tell nobody why."

Rufus wrung his hands at the memory. "I'm sittin' at home, my pickup's in the yard—people can tell I'm home, and I'm supposed to be doin' my job as a deacon in the church. People start comin' by after church to find out if I keeled over or somethin'. I'm lookin' fine but can't tell them why I didn't go to church. Then along comes Deputy Swagger, and when he sees I have company he turns on his red light and siren and stops in a cloud of dust. Then he runs everybody off and puts me in handcuffs and takes me off in his car.

"We go a few miles and he drives into this place and parks in some trees. He takes his gun out and points it right in my face and says they wasn't nobody at Klanke's Mill like I said they was. He said I musta been on dope and had a vision. He said, 'Everybody knows you smoke dope, Rufus.' I say I never had a whiff of dope in my life, I'm a Christian and a deacon in my church. And he say if I go around tellin' that story about a dead law man, everybody will know I'm on dope. He talked rough to me for the longest. Then he took me home.

"I like to of never got through making up stories about why the police took me off that day, lyin' through my teeth all day and beggin' the Lord to forgive me at night."

Rufus looked Jim in the eye, then Duffie. "But I seen a dead trooper, and then the news had it on all week that a trooper was missing that had been on a dope investigation. He never did turn up. I *knowed* it had to be him, but I was afraid to tell anybody else. Pretty soon after that, them gumment agents nabbed Sheriff Rosenstock for dealing in dope, so I get mighty suspicious about this chief deputy.

"There ain't no tellin' what happened to the body of that shot trooper. Maybe somebody took his body away before Deputy Swagger got there. But they was a lot of blood lyin' there, and to clean that up they would've had to leave a mighty big clean spot on that dirty old floor. After the way he come on to me, I sort of knew in my heart that Swagger had a hand in it. But if they'd kill a *trooper*, what would they do to me?" Rufus threw his hands out in a furious gesture of rejection. "I pushed the whole thing right out of my mind."

He held up his hand as if being sworn. "So when little Buddy showed me that gang's hideout in the Baumberg woods, I wasn't about to back him up, and have them come down on me again. So they thought he was lyin'. I felt awful about that. But look what happened last time."

Jim's heart was beating fast. Imagine, he thought, real mysteries right in this part of Winchester County. Rufus had a legendary reputation for honesty; his word was gospel, and Jim believed every word.

"Gosh! Rufus," he exclaimed. "After Sheriff Martinez got to be sheriff, did you tell him?"

Rufus looked positively forlorn. "No, and I ain't ever goin' to mention it to another soul. I should've kept my mouth shut today. I don't know what come over me to start talkin' about it. They ain't no good can come of tellin' it, nohow."

Jim felt sorry for Rufus; he saw how his spirits had fallen as he recalled the incident, how reluctant he had been to talk about it. They abandoned talk and concentrated on building the fence.

Except for the few words needed to further the work, nobody spoke while they went about their fence-building. After a while, Jim broke the silence. "There's another place about two miles from here where the springs come out again."

"Yassuh, Jim. I've knowed about that maybe fifty years. Good perch fishin' in the deep pools, like here in your creek. But it don't run along very far, do it?"

No, Jim agreed. The stream traveled no more than two hundred yards before it disappeared back underground. The banks of Hickory Creek there were lush and lined with big trees, like here. "Rufus, why does the water come *out* of the ground, and then go back *under-ground*?"

"Old Mr. Lester from Brentwood Lumber Company said one time that maybe an earthquake busted up the rock layers, allowing the water to rise out where it does, and then a crack downstream sucks it back in. How long ago it might've happened, well, the shape of the woods on the banks over there says that water's been running like that for at least two hundred years—just *look* at some of them trees! But maybe a *thousand* years, because you can't tell how old woods is over a certain span, because the old trees die and new ones come along."

Rufus looked up toward the house. "Mr. Lester said the boards on the sides of your barn come out of longleaf pine trees off this place. They was growin' on the south and east sides of the hill, a big patch of 'em, maybe thirty acres, when the Rosenbaums came here, about eighteen-eighty. Old Mr. Rosenbaum told it that somebody had to've planted that stand of pines, 'cause they wasn't no other longleafs anywhere close to here. Mr. Lester said it come down that somebody counted the rings, and those trees was *every one* about ninety when they was lumbered in . . . oh, they got started around eighteen ninety and kept at it for several years, I hear tell. That tells you right there they was planted, don't it? But who would've been planting trees back then, when Texas belonged to Mexico? Indians? It just don't figure. Mr. Lester says Indians ain't never lumbered. Who would plant acres and acres of a crop that would take longer to come to harvest than they would live? And Indians wasn't known to stay put." Rufus looked puzzled. He shook his head.

"Anyway, you look at them boards on the floor of your feed room, where you can see the ends of 'em when you open the door. The growth rings ain't hardly that far apart." He held a hand before his eye with the thumb and forefinger about an eighth of an inch apart. "You look at 'em, Jimmy. That wood growed so slow they ain't hardly any sapwood in it. That's why it's so hard and stout—pine so hard you'd think it was bo-d'arc if you tried to drive a nail through it. The boards on your barn ain't had no paint on 'em as far back as I can remember—before you and your daddy painted it, I mean. They's still as sound as can be with only a little rotted wood around the bottom ends, where dirt laid against it. Imagine pine lasting a hundred years and still sound as all get out, like it was cypress."

Jim was thrilled that Rufus was in this reflective mood. He loved to hear the history of the old Rosenbaum place. He grinned and unconsciously examined the thumb and forefinger of his left hand. "You're right about it being hard," he said meekly. "I really whopped my finger with a hammer when me and Dad were re-nailing those boards, before we painted the barn."

Rufus was nodding his head before Jim finished. He laughed, his eyes on Jim's hand. "Shoot, Jim, I hardly ever seen you without a black fingernail. Until lately."

He was quiet for a minute, standing in a meditative pose with his hands stuck inside the bib of his overalls. "Up at ya'll's new corral, that's where old Mr. Rosenbaum made charcoal. That's what he did with a lot of the oaks and other trees on this place. It was solid woods, this place was." His eyes roamed the Baumberg woods. "Like Baumberg's is now. Old Mist' Rosenbaum made charcoal and sold it to the blacksmith shops, to people for cooking, to Brentwood Coal and Coke Company—we had to tend those fires day and night, to keep the fire from breaking out and just burning the wood up."

Rufus described how they dug a big round pit and stacked wood on end in high, cone-shaped heaps, then covered the whole stack with turf scraped from the grassy bottom with a fresno. Mr. Rosenbaum made holes in the bottom and a flue in the top for just a little bit of draft. "After he set it on fire just so, the pile inside that mound would burn for the longest, little more'n smolderin'. Once in awhile some of the dirt covering would cave in, and we had to get it sealed back up right away. Mist' Rosenbaum said if we didn't, in no time the whole pile would just burn up instead of turning into charcoal. Always two men standing guard day and night while two others were asleep on pallets. And when the burnin' was over we left it to cool for three, four days. When we uncovered it, there it was: a big pile of charcoal under the dirt, and we dug it out. He made a lot of charcoal, Mr. Rosenbaum did."

Rufus rubbed his chin. "He made it for maybe fifteen years that I know of—from when I was about ten, and I don't know how long before then. He run out of trees about the time they graveled League Line Road. He kept the five-acre wood lot over there so the place wouldn't never run out of firewood for the cookstove and the heat-stove. He said it would produce plenty of firewood for a thousand years and more, with trees growin' back to replace them that was cut.

"And he wouldn't touch a tree along that creek," he said, pointing toward Hickory Creek. "Or this one, or even along any draw he wouldn't cut no trees. That's why y'all got so much woods. He only cleared land that was going to crops or pasture. The land where those woods is behind the new corral y'all built wasn't in the place then. That was bought by Mr. Eric Rosenbaum sometime after the old man died. It's good cover for the cattle in winter.

"The house and barn, and the corral up there was all made out of that longleaf pine. They set up a sawmill right up there on the hill. A bi-i-ig sawblade was set to spinnin' by a belt drove by a steam engine. They say they was only a one-room house there for a while, the room that's your kitchen today—and then they added onto it and built the barn and corral. Then they commenced sellin' lumber. They sold a lot of it, too, the old-timers said. As they cleared the land it went into cotton. I can remember when I was a little boy, watching old Mr. Rosenbaum makin' terraces with a fresno pulled by a mule."

Jim smiled. "We still have the fresno. Dad found it in the back of the barn under some old, old hay. We didn't even know what it was until Mr. Richter told us."

The fence got finished. Rufus produced his pocket watch. "Time to spare," he said with pride. "Quarter to."

"Can I see your watch?"

"Sho, Jimmy." said Rufus, handing it over.

It was a Westclox Pocket Ben. "Bought that in fifty-two. At Mr. Richter's," Rufus explained. "I remember because that's the year they built the new church that sits there just up from Richter's store." He laughed. "I'd been lookin' at those watches in the case and wishin' I could afford one. Then I got hired on to that church job and was able to buy it. I won't say the Lord provided, 'cause he don't listen to nobody wishin' for things like watches. But it was—fortunate, that's what it was. Cost four-thirty-five. Would've been a dollar less without the luminous dial, but I wanted to be able to see it in the dark. Got a second hand, too. See?"

Rufus accepted the watch back from Jim and looked at it for a long time. "That watch was a good 'un. Never has stopped, not even once—except for a time or two I forgot to wind it. Only have to set it about once a week, and then just a minute or two. But it set me back four dollars and thirty-five cents. A lot of money in fifty-two. I still have the case it come in. But it don't shine in the dark no more."

AT THIS STAGE OF HER LIFE, nothing was as grand for Ruby Jackson as an evening at the Bradleys. She and Oscar were there on this Saturday evening, sitting in the living room. Ruby was telling tales of the past and Norma, Matt and Jim were listening spellbound. Ruby was wearing what had been her favorite party dress for the past twenty years. Except for Sunday church, she seldom had an excuse to dress up anymore. Norma came in with a tray that held some glasses and a frosted pitcher. "I made some margueritas for us to unwind with before dinner." She looked at Ruby, whom she doubted had ever had a marguerita. "They're very weak, Ruby. Jim, here's a frosted lemonade for you." She had decorated it with red and green cherries.

Ruby turned toward Jim. "Jimmy, I read that book about Ben Franklin. I would've brought it over but I have a few pages to go. It's a *fine* book. He was a smart man, Ben Franklin. He figured out the lightning rod," she turned to Norma, "and did you know he invented the mile posts that we have on the freeways, where they say 'mile seven hundred and something?'" She looked at Matt and then at Norma. Both were shaking their heads and Ruby was obviously proud that she was able to add the fact to their knowledge. "Well, he did. And he voted to do away with slavery almost a hundred years before it happened. And he put the post office to rights—he sure did."

Then her eyes fell on Jim again, her expression soft and warm with adoration. "I look for Jimmy to do big things too, awesome big things. Yes I do."

Norma smiled with great sentiment on the lovely old lady. Yes, she thought, Jimmy was destined to do some swell things.

Oscar rarely had much to say during evenings at the Bradleys. He preferred to sit and smoke his pipe and listen. He laughed easily, and he spoke up to confirm a point of Ruby's now and then, or to lend some emphasis to her words. A deep affection for Ruby was evident in his every attention to her. Ruby loved to talk, to relate little vignettes of life, and she made them come alive.

Now she leaned back in her chair and said, "For some reason my turkeys don't like little Buddy. Jimmy can walk amongst 'em, and you too, Miss Norma, you walked right into the flock. But they just tear into Buddy, beatin' him with their wings and scratchin' and peckin' him. About a week ago he figured he would fool them turkeys.

"He put on my bonnet, my rubber boots, he put my purse over his arm and he strolled out amongst those turkeys, talkin' like me, he thought." She laughed and tossed her head. "Those turkeys wasn't fooled one bit. They tore into him and when I heard the racket I had to come out and rescue him. Poor little fella."

She was silent for a time, and with no other voice rising to take the floor, she went on. "This Sheriff Martinez is the first one we ever had in Winchester County that black people don't need to be scared of. When my boy was a teen, they used to look for whiskey stills in the Baumberg woods—they was full of stills in them days. Because Junior played in them woods, the sheriff figured he knew where the stills was. They would come and haul him off. And there I'd be, running down the road after that pó-lice car like a cow following a calf.

"We got a sheriff now that don't bother nobody unless they need botherin'. Everybody knows what you done, Mist' Matt, gettin' Sheriff Mike elected. At last, black people can be at peace drivin' down the road. Lordy, used to we could be drivin' down the road as meek as a lamb and 'Whooeee,'" she said, making a sound like a siren.

Oscar nodded. "I remember that time I had to sell our best hog to pay a fine for driving too slow and having a broke headlight in the daytime. I knowed it was broke, but I didn't go nowheres at night, so I wasn't in no hurry to fix it. We didn't have inspections back then, and you only need to have lights at night. They didn't have no grounds for finin' me for that; they jes made up a law and added over a hundred dollars to the ticket. And I found out that drivin' slow wasn't against no law, either. Besides, if you drove anywhere even close to the speed limit they fined you for speedin'—your word against theirs."

He puffed on his pipe, sadly shaking his gray head. "And that big, fine hog was going to make our Christmas—we didn't have much of a

Christmas that year. I've paid over a thousand dollars in fines in my life—oh, yeah, easy a thousand—and ary a one for speeding."

Jim sat clutching his hands together and hoping that nobody would interrupt Oscar, that he could continue with his stories of the old days. "Shoot," said Oscar finally, jerking with a silent harrumph of contempt. "I got off easy, compared to some people. My daddy had a team of fine mules confiscated one time. *Fine* mules—won best team at the Winchester County Fair three years in a row. Daddy and me was in town pickin' up some seed corn and cotton seed," he turned to Jim. "We traveled by wagon in them days, Jimmy.

"Some white boys was tormentin' them mules while they was tied to the hitchin' rail at Brentwood Produce and one of 'em got kicked. His whole injuries was a bruise on a leg. The sheriff came up real huffy and took Daddy off to jail in handcuffs. He fined Daddy the seeds we had bought and danged if he didn't take them mules, sayin' they was a menace, like mad dogs. Those mules lived their lives out workin' the sheriff's land. I don't see how we made it that year, with no seed to plant and no money to buy any more, and no mules to work the land with, but we made it somehow."

Jim stole a look at his father. Matt sat with his hands on the arms of his chair, his expression had first been one of outrage, then gradually it changed to one of pleased, undisguised accomplishment. Jim was immensely proud of his father's role in putting an end to what Matt said were generations of legalized robbery committed by gun-toting outlaws with badges.

The lack of emotion in Oscar's voice as he spoke of losing his Christmas hog caused Norma to swallow hard to keep her own feelings from showing. She felt an inner shiver of pride in her husband, and was pleased at the devotion she saw in her son's expression as he looked at his father.

Suddenly, Oscar waved his pipe in the air impatiently and looked down, shaking his head vigorously. "Wait a minute! I told a white lie. We had a fine Christmas, even without our hog money. I just wasn't able to get Ruby a main present and give her the money she always needed for presents for the kids and all. But we had a *fine* Christmas, didn't we Ruby?"

"Yes, we did, Oscar," she said with soft emphasis, smiling at him tenderly. "You always provided for a wonderful Christmas. Presents ain't all Christmas is about. They's just the icin' on the cake."

Oscar turned to Jim. "Jimmy, with this cool spell coming through tonight, I plan to kill a hog tomorrow. And Jessie Wilkins wants to kill two. You're welcome to come over. It'll be after church, of course. We'll have plenty of blood sausage and cracklin's and other stuff I know you like."

While observing their first hog-killing, Matt and Jim were offered small pieces of Oscar's blood sausage and glanced at each other as they cautiously tasted it. Matt was surprised to discover that it was very tasty and had gladly taken more when it was offered. To his surprise, Jim had eagerly taken seconds as well.

"Oh boy Mr. Jackson!" said Jim excitedly.

Norma didn't share their enthusiasm for the delicacy, probably turned off by the name "blood sausage," Jim suspected. "We should have told her it was called something else, Dad," he'd said later.

JIM HAD WATCHED ANXIOUSLY AS THE BLUE-GRAY smoke from the Jackson's hog-killing fire rose straight up from their little valley until it encountered the northerly flow aloft. Then it tore off to the south in a troubled line. From the top rail of the corral fence he saw Duffie's pickup and six or eight other cars and trucks, proof that the event was under way.

His father was doing some fixup work around the house and he'd felt obligated to help. Now the work was done and he approached the Jackson's place on Old Black, the horse's head bobbing as he stepped out in a lively walk. From the Bradley gate, Jim could see three hogs hanging by their hind legs from singletrees in the tallow tree. About thirty yards from the tree Old Black shied with such violence that Jim almost fell off. He hung on, sharply rebuked the horse, and soon Old Black stood still, his nostrils flared and his breath coming in terrified gasps.

When Jim was sure he had the horse under control, he urged him on. He took tentative steps, cautious and fearful steps, until he would go no further. For each step forward he took one step back or sideways. Finally, Jim was sufficiently exasperated to tie him to the fence and continue the last ten yards on foot. When he arrived there was only one hog left hanging in the tree. One was being cut up and another one with the hair still on it was being cut in two right down the backbone from snout to tail.

Speaking low so the other men couldn't hear, Oscar said mildly, "Old Black smelled blood, Jimmy. Some horses gets mighty fearful at the smell of blood. You have to introduce 'em to it easy. Bein' a rodeo horse, he probably never was around no ranch work like butcherin'."

He let the matter drop and then said in a normal voice. "Won't be long till the first batch of cracklin's is due to come out. They's off of Jessie's hog, and he was a fat 'un. I know how you likes your cracklin's good and fat, like I do." He laughed and patted Jim on the leg.

Jim watched for a while as several men worked on the hog carcasses like butchers. Duffie was pouring boiling water over half lying hair-up on an old barn door on sawhorses. He explained that the boiling water loosened the hair so it could be scraped off. He poured slowly and kept moving his arm so as to keep the carcass drenched. A cloud of steam engulfed him. He refilled his pan from a big black pot of water at a rolling boil and concentrated his stream on the head and ears, then the legs.

"Watch this, Jimmy," he said. Holding a large butcher knife with both hands and using the blade as a scraper, he ran it down the hog's hairy side. The hair came off in a swath. He continued to scrape and the hair fell to the ground in clumps. After the main part of the body was clean he worked around the legs, head, ears and every place there was hair. Occasionally he poured more boiling water in places where the hair was not giving itself up.

They had already skinned one hog, and another even larger black pot was sitting high on flat stones over a hot fire, bubbling away with lard. A lady was ladling liquid lard from the pot into big tin cans that had handles on two sides; the can being filled was sitting firmly on a big board flat on the ground.

Ruby came out of the house carrying a huge white porcelain pan. She went around to the men and collected certain hog parts. "Come inside, Jimmy, and keep us women company," she invited. "We already got some blood puddin' done, but we're tearing into it like wild animals. You better get some while the gittin's good." A hog killing was a bountiful time, and because during her long life Ruby had endured times that were bleak and lean, even her usual good nature was elevated by a big, bountiful hog killing.

Jim followed her into the house and she cut him a generous piece from the irregularly shaped gray link of sausage—the blood pudding. He savored its pleasant smell as the steam rose from the cut piece— even better than last year, he concluded after a taste.

The door opened and a man entered sideways, carrying in his free hand a foil-wrapped dish that was obviously a pie.

Ruby smiled broadly at the sight of him. She put down the things in her hands and wiped her hands on her apron. "Willie Dawson, come in this house," she said in a pleasantly commanding voice. She looked around the room. "Y'all all know Willie Dawson—

Jim, this is Willie Dawson, moved here from Bryan this year. Willie stays in the old Gregerson house just past Duffie's. Welcome, Willie. What you carryin'?"

Willie Dawson smiled shyly. He was in his mid-fifties, about Duffie's age, and small in stature. He worked for the railroad and had been transferred to Brentwood early in the year when the maintenance section at Rip Ford was merged into the one at Brentwood. "I brought you an apple pie, Miss Ruby. Baked it myself—storebought pie crust, though." He showed a trace of bashfulness as he surveyed the room, his head still tilted down a bit. "Yes, ma'am. This apple pie was made from the apples growed right on my place. Jes picked this year."

Ruby looked at him curiously. "What apple trees are you talking about?" The question was asked with good humor, but her voice was skeptical. "They's no apple trees on the Gregerson place."

Dawson's chin tucked. "Oh yes they is, Miss Ruby. Got two apple trees right in the front yard. They put out those green apples—green even when they's ripe."

Ruby laughed loud and long. "Those ain't apple trees, Willie. They's *pear* trees. Been there I don't know how long. Lordy, what made you think they was apple trees?"

Willie stood speechless as Ruby took the pie from him. She opened the foil and was sniffing the vapors approvingly when Willie said in an authoritative voice, so commanding that it was at odds with his prior appearance and demeanor. "They's *apple* trees, Miss Ruby. How do I know they's apples? Cause I made you an apple pie out of 'em. *That's* how I know."

Ever the diplomat, Ruby patted him affectionately on the arm and showed him a chair. "If you say they's apples, then as far as I'm concerned they's *apples*. It's a good-smelling pie, and you can't hardly tell a pear pie from apple, anyways. Tess, cut Willie a nice piece of that blood sausage."

Ruby picked up a huge white enameled pot and announced that she was going to get some cracklings out of the cooking kettle.

Jim jumped to his feet, anxious to be of some use. "I'll go do it, Mrs. Jackson," he said eagerly.

"You can come along, but you better let me dip those things out. If you got into that hot lard, Jim, or even got splashed—ummm, uh, it would be awful. Plumb awful."

He watched as Ruby ladled the cracklings out of the bubbling, steaming lard with a huge dipper that had holes in it. She swept the caldron for the last crackling and then began adding raw hogskin cubes to the kettle from a tub. They sizzled, popped and steamed furiously as they sank into the bubbling lard. When she was satisfied with the amount she had put in, she stirred the big pot with a wood boat oar. Jim took one handle of the pan of cracklings and with Ruby on the other they carried the big steaming pan into the house, filling the room with an aroma that got the attention of all present. Each person got a big crackling from the pan and bounced it from hand to hand, blowing on it to cool it off. Jim watched as Ruby filled to half-way a doubled paper sack, which quickly took on the stains of the hot lard from the cracklings.

"Jimmy," she said, "I know your folks would love some hot cracklin's. You run these along home. And *this*," she momentarily displayed a foil-wrapped package before placing it in the sack "is for you and your daddy. Blood sausage. A whole one. Then you come on back whenever you please."

Jim smiled gratefully and licked his lips in an exaggerated demonstration of expected pleasures. He said, "I'll be back in a little while. Mom wants to buy some pork, she told me to tell you. And she said her and Dad will be over to see you about it."

"Well, your momma can just name her cuts." She handed him another sack of cracklings and said, "Give these to Oscar as you go by. I'd hate for the men to go on a strike for not getting cracklin's."

Jim departed, carrying the two sacks. He stopped at the killing table where both halves of a skinned hog were being butchered. A man was carefully preparing the two halves of the hog's head, which were side-by-side on the table, grotesque eyes staring straight up. He knew the heads would go into boiling water and ultimately be made into hog-head cheese, another delicacy to him and his father. Even Norma was beginning to like hog-head cheese.

Oscar was alone, sitting in front of a tub of water cleaning hog guts that would become sausage casings. A large bowl of cleaned intestines was sitting on a small wood table beside him and next to the cleaning water sat a bucket of intestines yet to be cleaned.

Jim placed the offering from Ruby on the table. "Here's some cracklin's Mrs. Jackson sent," he said.

"Sit down for a minute, Jimmy," Oscar said, indicating an empty chair. "By gosh, you can't disguise a bag of cracklin's," he laughed. "I know you're supposed to be taking that other bag to your momma and daddy while they's hot, but sit just a minute and have yourself a few. This is an *occasion*, a hog killin'." He wiped his hands on the towel he kept in his lap for that purpose and got out his pipe. "And it's comfortin' to me and Ruby to have you around on such a nice occasion. With our kids all gone, it's not as exciting as it used to be when they was kids everywhere, happy and laughin' because they knew we was goin' to eat that winter. Heh, heh—" he chuckled softly. "But it's still a good time, collecting up some good old friends as it does, and it brings back mighty fine memories, too."

He filled the pipe and tamped the tobacco to just the right density with the tip of a forefinger. Then he scratched a match on the sole of his boot and when it flared to life he held the small inferno just above his pipe. "You know—" he puffed and set the tobacco aglow. "Hog killin' was always one of the best times I can remember. Almost as exciting as comin' home from the gin with the cotton check for the year.

"A hog killin' brings friends together in a way such that the work of it ain't a chore but a joyful time. And all the while you can eat your fill of the best things. A hog killin' is a *celebration*." He ate a couple of cracklings and then called the other men's attention to the sack. They began to come over and get handfuls of their own, nodding their thanks to Jim for bringing them out.

Oscar appeared to be overflowing with pleasure and contentedness. Jim munched happily on cracklings and watched him as he puffed on his pipe, lost in the memories that stirred him so.

"When you get down to it, Jimmy, the good life is the memories you got stored away," he said. "Memories that come out of a lifetime of steady hard work and some nice times in between. In the end, you got a bushel of good memories and the satisfaction of knowin' you ain't never done anybody no harm. *That's* the good life.

"God blessed me by giving me the love of the only woman I ever laid eyes on that I wanted, and he gave me the sense to conduct my own self so as to never bring no hurt on her or torment on her mind." His expression became soft and worshipful as he continued. "My, my, Ruby was pretty. I used to choke up jes lookin' at her," he dabbed at an eye with the towel, "and I still do to this day."

Jim felt a glow of simple greatness radiating from the old man whom he held in such reverential esteem. He had a crackling in his hand but did not want the sound of his eating it to intrude on Mr. Jackson's mood.

"Sometime me and Ruby are ashamed of this old tumbledown Richter farmhouse, but it's tolerably comfortable and we is at home in it. The main thing is that after we're gone, it don't matter if we lived our mortal life in this old house or in the Clemson mansion. Rich as they is, the Clemsons are poor while me and Ruby is rich." He shook his head sadly at the irony of this.

"The three Clemson children turned out awful—one killed in some mysterious way that was hushed up, one in the pen, and the other, the girl, has been in drug rehab for no tellin' how long. I'm sad for them old folks, rich as all get-out with money, but poor as church mice in their tormented old years.

"So in spite of some awful hard times, *some* times when we all went to bed with grumblin' bellies we was so hungry, the Lord gave us the important things: health and happiness, the willingness to work, and He made us amiable. Without bein' amiable, you can't be truly happy, Jim. I'm glad He didn't give us a sack of money to go crazy over.

"And all of our kids has done themselves honorable and made us proud. Me and Ruby won't ever have to worry about money no more, so you might say we's wealthy in the money line, as well as bein' rich every other way. We never gypped anybody out a red cent or failed to help a friend in need." He looked straight at Jim. "All I needed when I felt a little tug of temptation was to see my momma and daddy looking over one shoulder and Ruby looking over the other, and it wasn't no trouble decidin' the right thing to do."

He was quiet for a long time, his expression serene. "When we lay our heads down for the last time, me and Ruby, we can smile and say we left this world at least as good as we found it, and we was happy every day of our lives doin' it—*most* every day, anyway."

He looked into Jim's eyes, right into his mind. "Just imagine that your momma and daddy and old Oscar and Ruby are watching what you do every minute of the day and night, just *bustin'* out with pride." He punctuated his words with a strong jerk of his chin and an emphatic winking of both eyes.

"Yes, sir, Jim. You're the brightest boy I ever did know, and they ain't no close second place for bein' the *nicest* boy, either. You got it in your heart and bones to always do right, Jimmy. Natural. I'm of a mind that you'll never lose a wink of sleep when you lay your head down on your pillow—not over anything *you* done."

CHAPTER 18

On his outing today, Jim passed under the Brentwood-Rip Ford Highway in what seemed like no time. Old Black's rhythmic walk, the serenity of the patch of earth he and Jim patrolled and the morning sun's tranquilizing warmth had lulled Jim into a procession of daydreams.

After passing this landmark of their deepest previous penetration of the frontier along Hickory Creek, he stood higher in the stirrups as he searched for the cattle feeder that had been washed away. He would sure like to tell his dad that he'd found it, because it was built too stout to have been damaged much. They'd built it from some plans his father had found in *Farm Journal* magazine, out of a whole pickup load of lumber and steel corrugated roofing that cost over a hundred dollars. The construction project had taken up the better part of a weekend. Oscar said it was the best feeder he'd ever seen, as well as the easiest to fill, with its hinged roof; it held a whole half-ton of protein supplement and protected it from the weather. It was ingenious the way the mix trickled into the lickbox, as Oscar called it, making the cows stretch their necks with their heads sideways to get their licks.

"Makes 'em work to get at it," Oscar had explained. "That, and the salt mixed in keeps 'em from getting hoggish."

The thought of the feeder reminded Jim of the time he'd tied Old Black to it, to pull it to a new place, and how Oscar had made him understand that a horse could kill himself trying to exceed his physical capability.

He was wondering if they ever got old man Zimmerman's big bull out of the bog when suddenly Old Black gave a stiff-legged and sideways skip that jolted him back to the present. The horse stood dead still with his neck craned and his head extended toward the base of an oak tree two or three yards away. His ears were perked hard on the object of his attention. When Jim gently urged him to move forward for a closer look, he only took a few tiny steps in place and snorted. Jim had to keep letting the reins slip through his hands as Old Black extended his nose even farther, like he was pointing at something; he trembled slightly.

Jim scanned the tree and the ground around it and saw nothing. He pushed his hatbrim up an inch and leaned over Old Black's head to get a better view, but could see nothing but scattered leaves and the trunk of the tree.

"Boy, if you see something there, Black, it's sure invisible to me," he said.

The horse answered with a flick of an ear and a few quick, audi-

ble breaths. His nostrils were now flared so wide that they were sharp on the edges and quivering slightly.

Then Jim saw it! He reacted with such shock that he backed Old Black a half-dozen steps without realizing he'd even moved. It was a big, fat cottonmouth moccasin, coiled in the sun next to the tree, its dark mottled markings a perfect camouflage against the leaves. Now that he had made it out, the snake was as plain as it could be.

He looked about and spied a long, skinny branch under a nearby tree, dismounted and tied his red bandanna to the end of it. Then he approached the snake warily. It stood its ground in a coil with its head high, as still as a stone image, its eyes fixed dispassionately on him. Extending the branch with both hands so as to keep all possible distance between the snake and himself, he began poking at it, trying to torment it into doing something. Inspired by the snake's inaction, he took a step closer and shoved the bandanna right in it's face. Jim saw the flash of a big white mouth, wide open, and felt a twitch at the end of the stick as the snake struck.

The explosive violence of the strike sent him in full flight. When he glanced over his shoulder to see if it was pursuing him he saw that it was slithering lazily off in the other direction. He retrieved the bandanna from the stick and, holding it out by two corners, examined it carefully. Half expecting it to be in shreds, he was surprised to find no mark of any kind. Just in case there was some venom on it somewhere, he gingerly put it in his back pocket instead of tying it back around his neck.

When he put a foot in the stirrup and saw that his raised knee was trembling, he smiled sheepishly. "Boy, Black!" he said as he mounted, "His mouth was so big a rat could have jumped in it." He was half right: a number of rats had gone into that mouth, whole. But he was half wrong, too: they hadn't jumped in.

How could Old Black see that snake so quick? He considered the possibility that animals might see things somehow differently than humans. Maybe to a horse the snake's colors didn't blend in with the background of leaves and sticks and ground. Some people said horses were color blind. He wondered if snakes might only be invisible to humans. Then again, maybe Old Black smelled the cottonmouth.

He reflected again on that big, white mouth, open so wide that he'd seen the grooves across the inside from ten feet away. He should be looking out better for the feeder, he thought, and began to pay more attention. The creek banks were much higher here, and the creek itself was too wide to cross anywhere. What had been patches of woods had gradually become a mature forest on both sides of the creek.

They came to a place on the bank where cattle had worn a wide cut, going down to water. Old Black took the trail almost on his own and descended to the water's edge. The bank was steep, and when Old Black put his head down to drink Jim had to hold on to the cantle to keep his seat. Thinking back on the cottonmouth, he searched the water's surface, concluding that if Old Black could see or smell or sense a snake from ten feet away, he sure wouldn't stick his nose right in one's face. The horse thrust his nose completely under and drank deeply.

The water was calm on this side, but it swept a course of leaves and twigs swiftly along the far bank and even made a small imitation of roaring rapids out of sight somewhere downstream. Old Black played, tossing his nose about until the water made his lips flap. When his head came up he was mouthing and smacking his lips. Water cascaded from his mouth. He breathed in deeply, satisfyingly, making the saddle creak with the expansion of his body. Then he drank again. Jim reached behind him, untied his canteen, and took a drink himself.

Back on high ground with Old Black standing still, Jim glanced at the sun and figured that it could not yet be much past noon. He had at the very least another two hours to explore before turning back to get home before five, and that without even hurrying. A second later he found himself looking squarely into the eyes of a big whitetail doe. Head held high, she stood for a moment before turning and bounding away. For the first time, he saw the two spotted fawns that were now racing along behind her.

He turned the horse up the trail. It wasn't much of a trail anymore, and soon there was no trail at all. It was easy traveling in the woods, though. The trees were so big that their shade had discouraged the growth of brush underneath. The darkness in which they rode now was a sharp contrast to the bright sunshine of the open ground, and the pleasant coolness reminded Jim that the day had grown warm. Old Black was glistening with a light sweat.

Just as he began to feel a bit uneasy about the gloom there seemed to be a gradual brightening up ahead, and then he began to see splotches of bright sunshine. Soon they emerged into a clearing that wound its way out of sight in both directions. Here it was fairly wide, but it pinched down to only a dozen or so yards to his right, where it quickly disappeared around a bend. There was more clear expanse to the left, and he could see farther than the length of a football field. The forest began again on the far side.

Except for the interlude with the cottonmouth, Jim had been in the saddle over two hours. He decided this would be a good place to stretch his legs. After dismounting, he left Old Black free to sample the foot-tall grass.

The sun was too hot now for his jean jacket, so he slipped it off and tied it on the back of his saddle. Old Black was enjoying big mouthfuls of the lush, green prairie grass that grew in a bowl about a hundred feet in diameter at the edge of the trees. The bowl no doubt collected water because the grass was much greener and more luxuriant there. Jim had learned in 4-H that the native prairie grasses were often tastier and more nutritious than many of the cultivated varieties. One drawback was that they grew slowly, producing less forage per acre.

"That grass sure has your seal of approval, don't it Old Black?" he asked, taking long, exaggerated steps and bending deep at the knees to flex his legs. He wandered further out into the clearing. Tire tracks!

The lay of the grass in the tracks said that the vehicle had come from his left. The tracks could be faintly seen going around the bend to the right. Intrigued by this practical application of his Cub Scout tracking skills, he sank to his knees and bent low until his nose was touching the grass in the tracks. He sniffed. The odor of crushed grass was strong. Then he moved and smelled of some undisturbed grass. The odor was faint by comparison. He grasped a handful of grass, ripped it off and brought it to his nose. Its odor was stronger than the grass in the tracks, but not by very much.

"These tracks are fresh, real fresh," he said to himself. He selected a clean white stem and put it in his mouth. It tasted sweet. He understood Old Black's enthusiasm for the even lusher grass in the bowl where he was grazing greedily. "I'll give you a few more bites, Black," he said to himself, and stretched out on the soft carpet. It wasn't long before the powerful sun brought him to his feet.

He had taken a few steps toward Old Black when a thought that had been nagging at the back of his mind surfaced. "One way tracks," he thought. "Someone went that way but didn't come back out. What could be at the end of that trail?" He put the reins over Old Black's head, mounted, and rode into the woods on the other side of the clearing. The mystery of the tracks was soon forgotten.

They encountered more brush under the trees on this side, making for slow going as they wound around through it. He had almost decided to double back when it thinned enough to allow easy traveling. "Not too long, Old Black, and we're going to have to think about heading home." The horse blew through his lips, sending a spray of saliva flying. It was green from his mid-day snack. Jim smiled at the sure knowledge that Old Black understood some of what he was saying, and patted him affectionately on the neck. "You're a good pal, Black. We'll come back to this place for a treat every chance we get."

It wasn't long before the deep shadows gave way to streaks of sunshine, and then the trees opened to a vast, bright emptiness, as if there was nothing ahead but sky. Jim stood up in the stirrups to improve his view, but he could not make anything out of the scene ahead. As they approached the last of the trees it was as if they were approaching the top of a ridge with the sky for a backdrop. But how could that be? They were on completely level ground. He heard a rushing sound, like wind in the trees, but when he looked up, the tree-tops were still and silent.

Then they emerged from the trees into the open, and Jim saw

that the land ended, just ceased to exist, less than ten yards ahead. The base of an enormous, uprooted tree seemed to be looking at them, its roots reaching out in every direction. And there, meandering in a hushed noisiness way below, was the Brazos River.

"Wow, Black, we've come all the way to the river!"

The broad river gave the illusion of being placid until Jim saw a log moving steadily downstream at a good pace; in only a few minutes the current took it out of sight beyond the bluff on their right. Looking at a place where the bluff swung into sight on his left, he saw that the red wall looked as high as a tall building.

From his viewpoint on its high bank, the Brazos was the biggest river Jim had ever seen up close. In contrast to the high cliffs on this side, across the way the terrain rose gently from the water and quickly became farmland. He could even hear the distant, intermittent sound of a farm tractor, and finally made it out in a far-away field.

Below, more flotsam drifted by. He was surprised at the swiftness of the current. He looked again at the uprooted tree and saw two others hanging over the cliff-like bank, dangling by their last roots until further erosion would eat the soil from beneath them. Then they, too, would plunge top-first into the river and begin the long voyage to the Gulf of Mexico.

How much time had passed since they had arrived at this discovery Jim didn't know, but he suddenly realized that the sun had inched farther over in the sky and that they had to head home. Recalling the underbrush that they had worked their way through after crossing the long, winding clearing, he decided to avoid it by heading directly for the trail, which he theorized would be a shorter ride through the woods. He picked a heading and pointed Old Black in that direction.

CHAPTER 19

Once Old Black had carried him two dozen steps into the deep woods the going was easy. Here too, underbrush could not live in the low light under the dense canopy of the immense trees. Jim allowed Old Black to step along in a brisk walk.

They had traveled only about half a mile when the gloom was broken by brilliant shafts of sunlight up ahead; they pierced the canopy like high-intensity stage lights and danced like pools of yellow fire on the forest floor.

As the forest became less dense it harbored a few dogwood trees, their snow-white blossoms dazzling in the shadowy contrast. He got a glimpse of a clearing ahead, and after traveling another hundred yards he could see that instead of the broad green trail he had crossed on his way into the woods, the clearing ahead was mostly bare hardpan, broken by occasional patches of weeds.

"None of that lush and tasty range grass here, Black old boy," he said; they had no time for snacks, anyway. As he approached the edge of the clearing he began to make out an old wooden structure. Then he saw another, made of corrugated metal.

When he rode out into the open, he found that he was behind a barn with the remains of a corral sagging away from one side. Way off to his left was a big, tall building with strange extensions jutting above the roof. A smaller building had the familiar false front and porch of a country store. A faded sign said, "F. Klanke, Prop."

He was at Klanke's Mill! The large building on the left must have been the cotton gin and corn mill. "Wait till I tell Rufus!" he said out loud. Across a wide span of bare ground was a house with three gables. It sat in a weedy yard with a spindly dead tree, enclosed by the remains of a picket fence.

The place seemed totally deserted except for a few items of clothing hung from a clothesline on the long front porch of the house. There was an eeriness about the place that made Jim uneasy, but he gave Black a little squeeze and reined him toward the open courtyard. Black moved out smartly, but Jim noticed that his ears were busy and he carried his nose a bit higher than usual. Was he alerted by something?

The stories about the old days at Klanke's Mill by Oscar, Duffie and Rufus had planted in his mind a picture of the place in full swing, and now it came to life in his imagination. In his mind's eye was a courtyard full of high-sided wagons loaded with cotton to be ginned, the wagons headed by teams of mules. The platform in front of the gin was crowded with bales of cotton standing on end in neat rows; others moved out of the wide door on an overhead rail and traveled slowly along the platform. Two men at the end of the growing rows wrestled bales into position, their cotton hooks flashing in the sun.

His eyes glanced back at the corral, now full of imaginary livestock for sale or trade. He recalled Oscar's description of the bustling store that carried just about everything from sacks of flour to bolts of fabrics, from seeds and farm implements to rifles and ammunition. People afoot and on horseback moved casually between the buggies and wagons, and among groups of people engaged in gossiping, horse trading and socializing.

A sudden loud creaking sound behind him brought him quickly around in the saddle. He was relieved to see that it was only a small door of the barn swinging slowly on rusty hinges, pushed by a miniature dust devil. Its cone was clearly defined by whirling leaves, dust, and debris; the door became still as the miniature storm moved on and dissipated. He grinned sheepishly to himself over how it had unnerved him, but when he scanned the windows in the big gin, he had the sensation that someone was peering out at him.

Old Black drew in a deep breath, causing the saddle leathers to creak. The sound was loud in the heavy silence of the place. The only movement of any kind now was a shadow cast by a passing cloud, providing welcome relief from the warm sun.

He rode closer to the old general store. On the front porch was a long, weathered bench against the wall. He saw gray phantom men perched on the bench, having a Saturday beer and talking as he rode along the near side of the store. On a platform behind the store were some old wooden casks, hoops askew and their staves falling in.

A glance at the sun reminded him that he had to get along toward home, a decision made easier by the unsettling air about the eerie place. The courtyard was left behind at a fast trot and within a few strides Old Black broke into an easy lope on his own. He seemed to have had enough of the spooky old place, too.

About fifty yards ahead Jim saw a low, circular stone structure of some kind—the remains of a water well? As they neared it he saw that some of its stones were scattered about. It was the last relic he would see of the legendary old Klanke's Mill, so he headed straight for it to take a quick look as he rode past.

Thirty feet before reaching it, Old Black stopped abruptly. It was not his smooth, tail-dragging stop, but a stiff-legged, bone-jarring halt that almost caused Jim to tumble over the horse's shoulder; he lost both stirrups and found himself grabbing mane and leather to stay on. Even after he'd stopped, Old Black stood bouncing on his forefeet, first one way and then another, throwing his head and snorting with fright.

Jim regained his seat in the saddle and shouted, "Whoa, Black! Whoa!" It was only when he slapped the horse smartly on the neck with the reins and spoke another sharp "Whoa!" that Black calmed down some. But he still stood there stamping his feet and craning his neck and throwing his nose about. His ears were laid back, his eyes glared with fright, and he inhaled in short, nervous gasps—just the way he'd acted at Mr. Jackson's hog killing.

Jim stroked his neck. "Calm down, Black," he said soothingly. "Boy, I've never seen you so skittish. You almost threw me. Calm down, boy, and let's take a closer look at what you're so scared of."

A horse can have the wildest imagination, he thought, recalling the time he'd walked out in the pasture carrying a closed umbrella. When it began to rain he'd popped it open and Old Black had jumped five feet, staring scared and bug-eyed. Seeing new things was an important part of a horse's education, Jim theorized.

He urged Old Black forward. The horse moved reluctantly, taking one step sideways for each tiny step ahead. About ten feet from the well, Black stopped and started throwing his head and sniffing and snorting again.

Jim knew that in Black's current state, the appearance of so much as a rabbit out of those stones would cause him to jump, so he kept a good seat in the saddle, a grip on the horn, and both feet planted firmly in the stirrups. Black was still acting positively terrified.

Jim decided that he wasn't going to let Black get away with a balk like he did at Mr. Jackson's hog killing. There couldn't be any blood in this well, and it would be setting a mighty poor pattern in his training to let him get away with something like that again. After all, he'd won trail classes where everything you could think of that might scare a horse was put in his way or thrown at him.

In one motion, he set the bit firmly, reined to the side, and gave the horse a smart kick in the flank, putting him into a spin. Then with him pointed once more at the well, Jim smacked him sharply on both sides of the neck with the reins. "Walk, Black. Walk!" he demanded, almost shouting, and gave the horse his head. Black obeyed reluctantly. Taking short, hesitant steps, tapping the ground as if he expected it to cave in, trembling with fear, he slowly walked to the stone rim of the opening.

"Good boy!" Jim said with feeling and patted him vigorously on the neck. "Good boy." He leaned over for a better view, but not so far that he might be left sitting on thin air if Black suddenly decided to be somewhere else. He could see only a short distance into the stone-lined shaft.

"See, boy?" he said, surprised at the unsteadiness of his own voice. "A whole lot of nothing. What did you expect?"

He reined the horse around and wiped his sweaty palms on the legs of his jeans. Just as he picked the reins up from Old Black's neck and raised them to move out, a man's voice sounded from the depths. Then it came again. "Hello up there! Hello, hellooo."

CHAPTER 20

Coaxing his trembling horse the two steps closer to the well opening was not easy. But move him Jim did, and he peered as far as he could into the well. He could see only a few feet into the shadows before everything became coal black. Laying a hand on his knee, he noticed that Old Black was not the only one who was trembling. But the voice didn't seem to be threatening, and it came from so far down the hole that it didn't seem to present a danger they couldn't run away from.

He looked anxiously all around. Seeing nobody, he leaned toward the well and put his hands to his mouth. "Hello down there! Is someone in there?" he called, his own voice hollow and loud. Once again, he looked cautiously all around to make sure someone wasn't sneaking up behind him. The hair on the back of his neck was tingling, and he could tell he had goose bumps on his arms.

A deep voice boomed "Hello! I need help. Did I hear a horse up there?"

Old Black was still fidgety, but he had steadied down. So had Jim. "Yes, sir. I have a horse. Do you need help?"

"Yes. I'm Sheriff Mike Martinez. Who are you?"

"Sheriff!" Jim exclaimed. In one motion he slid down from his horse and threw the reins on the ground. He pointed sharply at the reins and barked, "Stand!" He turned and dropped to the ground, bracing his hands on stones at the mouth of the hole. He thrust his head down into it as far as he could, letting his eyes adjust to the darkness. "Sheriff!" he called, "I'm Jim Bradley. How did you get down there?"

"Howdy, Jim." Sheriff Martinez's voice sounded very tired, but there was definite relief in it. "I'm mighty glad to see a friend. We'll talk later. First, let's see if we can get me out. Do you happen to have a lariat?"

Jim looked over his shoulder at the lariat tied to his saddle.

"Yes, sir. I have a lariat, and Old Black can pull you out."

Jim barely heard the response, spoken softly because it wasn't meant for him, "Thank you, God."

Speaking louder, Sheriff Martinez said, "Now listen carefully, Jim. I've got a busted leg, but I also have a good one to work with. Maybe if we work together real close you can pull me out. But it's going to be a chore. Are you and your horse up to it, or would you rather ride for help?" His words echoed slightly as they bounced off the stone walls, but Jim had no trouble understanding him.

I don't know where I'd ride to, Jim was thinking. It's miles to the closest road. I could flag down a car there, but what if a car doesn't come along? I could ride to the Brentland-Rip Ford Highway in an hour, maybe. He tried to imagine getting somebody to stop, and then to believe explanations coming from a kid on a horse, the time it would take to get a rescue party together and back out here if somebody did stop. "I think I could have you out before I could get any help. Are you further down than those boards?" He could barely make out the images of timbers in the darkness.

"Yeah."

"But how did you get—"

"Jim, we can't get into a discussion just now," Sheriff Martinez said with a sharp edge of authority in his voice. "I want you to do as I say. This is going to be a big job, so you must strictly follow orders. Do you understand?"

"Yes, sir."

"Now take a good look all around. Do you see anybody, or hear anything?"

Jim raised himself and looked in every direction. Old Black was now standing obediently, watching him intently. He no longer appeared frightened. Jim was pleased to see that his ears were flicking back and forth, showing interest, not fear.

"No, sir. I don't see or hear anything. And my horse don't hear anything, either."

"How long you been on the place?"

"Not too long. I rode around over there where the buildings are. I didn't see anybody, or hear anybody either."

"Okay. Now if you see anything I ought to know about, or hear anything, say so. Understand?" Without waiting for an answer, he continued, "Jim, if I tell you to break off, I want you to obey the order. Let me down as easy as you can, but in a hurry. Then you ride like hell to the first house you can find, phone the department and tell them who you are, and the fix I'm in. Tell them I said to send me a lot of help as fast as possible. If you see a car, try to get it to stop and tell them to call the department from the first phone they can find. Understand?"

Jim felt a prickling on the back of his neck; fingers went to the goosebumps on his arm. "Yes, sir," he said, looking over his shoulder for a quick scan of the old place. Old Black's attention was riveted on his master. "Keep a sharp lookout, Black," he said softly.

"Fine, Jim," Sheriff Martinez said. "I got a hunch we'll both find out how tough we are today. And your horse, too. This won't be easy. Are you sure you want to try?"

"Yes, sir. I'm pretty sure we can do it." It was clear in his mind that Sheriff Martinez was in serious trouble—and with a broken leg, he'd said. Jim could see how easy it would be for him to be pessimistic about Old Black pulling him out, so he disregarded the words of doubt. Grown-ups usually told kids this job or that one would be a lot more work than it would turn out to be. He felt confident Old Black could have Sheriff Martinez out of the well in no time.

"That's sure good to hear, boy. When I get out of here I'm going to want to know how you happened along. Now, get your lasso, tie it off on the saddle, and throw the loop end down to me. Whatever you do, don't lose your end or we're sunk. I hope it's long enough."

"It's a thirty-five footer," Jim said before he darted from the hole.

Down in the well, another prayer of thanks went through Martinez's mind. How did this kid happen to be carrying a lariat so long that only a strong cowboy could take advantage of it? The extra length might just make the difference. Martinez knew his situation was desperate. His right leg was smashed just below the knee. Bone splinters stuck out through the skin and had cut a vein or artery. There was no telling how much blood he'd lost while he was unconscious. He had controlled it with only by grasping his leg above the knee with his hands. The bleeding was stopped, for now.

A blow to the head, which accounted for his being down here in the first place, had put a deep gash in his scalp. His free hand went to the wound and found it matted with a hard crust of dried blood. It seemed to have stopped bleeding on its own. He knew he was weak, and couldn't be much help to the operation.

Shootouts are many times more bearable than something like this, he reflected. Things are moving ahead fast and furious in a gunfight, leaving you no time to worry about the outcome. Suddenly it's over and you're still in one piece, able to see the sky and smell the lingering gunsmoke, able to hear the sirens announcing the arrival of Johnny-Come-Lately and friends.

He was afraid it might take more than a rope-wise horse to do this job. More like a team of horses. He rejoiced that his prospects had improved one thousand percent with this kid's miraculous appearance, but he became dismally pessimistic as he looked up at the disk of daylight high above.

Strung out on dope as they were, those punks could still take a notion to come back. They'd need to come back for a second boatload, one had said.

He cursed himself for coming out here without telling anyone in the department, but it was on just the faintest hunch that had struck him on the spur of the moment. He was driving back from Rip Ford and thinking again of the furtive look in Swagger's eyes when the deputy had described his search of Klanke's Mill, claiming he found nothing.

Martinez had certainly seen plenty of signs of habitation. Once inside the house he could tell that they'd been camped out here for a long time. In the five minutes before they'd bashed his head in, he'd seen clothes and other stuff scattered everywhere; there were even clothes on a clothesline in plain sight. He couldn't wait to get his hands on that larcenous deputy. But would he live to do it? He'd lost an awful lot of blood, and the bleeding was beginning again.

He was shaking his head over his own stupidity when a shadow appeared overhead. "Here comes the rope, Sheriff," the boy called out. He looked up to see a rope uncoiling in slow motion as it floated down from above. It fell onto some old timbers jammed up in the shaft and the boy spent a minute fishing it down through them. The rope dropped on down and he caught it. Martinez took the loop in his hands and spread it to about double the size he thought he'd need for a proper harness.

"How much do you have on your end, Jim?"

Jim disappeared from the mouth of the hole. The slack was taken up, and after some activity on the surface he reappeared.

"Enough, Sheriff. I was able to move Old Black about ten feet away from this edge. I think that's enough pulling room. He's ready to pull you out."

Mike Martinez smiled with relief at the realization that at least this boy wasn't going to need a recipe for every move. There was enough rope left at Martinez's end to encircle his body and allow him to build a stop knot to keep the rope from passing through the eye. He was thankful for this blessing, because an ordinary loop without such a stop would tighten on his body until it near about cut him in two.

He wondered at the unbelievable good fortune of a kid on a good horse wandering by, packing around a thirty-five-foot lariat—and a darned good one, too, he noticed as he worked with it. He placed the loop over his head, past his arms and around his chest, and fashioned the stop-knot loosely. Then he tried the harness out for size, made an adjustment in the position of it to give the horse another foot to work with, and pulled the harness up tight. He was ready.

Sheriff Martinez looked up through the boards above him at the silhouette of the boy. "Jim, those planks are about a third of the way between you and me. You'll have to stop there and give me time to work my way around them. I'm ready if you are."

"We're ready, Sheriff," Jim said. "I can make out the boards fairly good, so I should be able to see you when you get up that high."

"But you'll be on your horse, son. Will he stand there when you have to come back here to check on things?"

"I don't have to be on Black, Sheriff. He'll do what I tell him. I'm going to stay here. Should I start now?"

"Let's go."

Jim jumped up and trotted off toward his horse. The weariness in Sheriff Martinez's voice was more evident now, and he felt a deep sense of compassion for this lawman who had seemed so invincible. He was just becoming fully conscious of the responsibility that had fallen upon him. He might be a little late getting home, but he would just stand quietly while his mother lectured him, and when she asked why he was late—which was always asked last, when he thought it ought to be asked first—he would answer nonchalantly, "Oh, I was held up by having to save Sheriff Martinez's life." He would also have to answer a thousand questions from the other kids at the horse shows. Fame had already become a burden on his mind.

He tightened the cinch on the saddle and he moved to the horse's head. "Okay, Black. Let's show Sheriff Martinez how tough we are." He picked the reins off the ground and threw them over the horse's head. "Walk," he said sharply, moving slowly beside the horse and carefully watching the slack come out of the rope.

In a few steps Black had pulled all the slack and the lariat became a dead pull on the saddle horn; the saddle creaked as the leather took the strain; the breast strap tightened. "Whoa." Jim was pleased to see that they had gained another yard of rope, which would give it a better angle. "Stand!" Jim ran back to the hole.

As he dropped down, Sheriff Martinez's voice came from below. "Just right, Jim. I'm ready if you are. Let's go."

"Walk, Black," Jim shouted. The horse felt the strain coming on to the saddle cinch, and the tightening of the breast strap against his chest. He leaned into the work and began to trudge mightily. The muscles bulged on his hind legs as he took small, powerful steps. Slowly, he began to move ahead. Jim felt a thrill as he watched his mighty horse begin the rescue. "This won't take any time," he thought, as he watched the tension in the rope increase until it was as rigid as a bar of steel.

"Walk, Black," he said again as he turned back to the hole. He watched as it moved slowly over the rock's edge, the hard-twisted strands making a low, raspy, singing sound as they ground against the soft stone.

From the hole came a slightly more relieved voice. "Just like an elevator, Jim—making good time—I hope your horse holds out. We've got about four feet to go before you'll have to hold up and give me time to clear the way through those boards."

"How did you get past them when you fell in, Sheriff?"

"They must have thrown them in behind me. I'm glad they got wedged, though. Else they would have hit me."

Jim's brows went up in wonder. *They?*

CHAPTER 21

"Walk, Black," Jim called out, more for encouragement than out of need, for the horse was tramping deliberately, steadily ahead.

Jim strained to see down into the dark depths. "I believe I can see you, Sheriff," he shouted excitedly. He let himself down on his stomach to get his head down deeper, shielding his eyes with both hands. "Did you wave your hand just now?"

"Yeah."

"I saw it. Now I can almost see you good." With the sheriff's khaki shirt as a lighter backdrop, the boards that blocked the way were more distinct now.

"Be prepared to hold up in another foot, son. . . . Hold up right here!"

"Whoa, Black," Jim shouted. The horse stopped dead still and stood leaning against the strain.

"Some horse you got. Just right—you have me just right," the sheriff said, breathing heavily. Scraping and bumping sounds came up from the hole; Jim heard a clattering and then the sound of a board hitting bottom.

"There went the first one. Son, this'll take a few minutes. If you want to check on your horse, go ahead. And don't forget to keep your eyes open, you hear?"

"Yes, sir."

Jim carefully surveyed the whole place as he trotted to Old Black, who was now easily over twenty feet from where the lariat disappeared over the rim of the hole. Jim was elated. Old Black had hauled the sheriff over half the way up in one smooth go at it. Once the sheriff was past the obstructions he was working to clear, they had scarcely ten feet to go. "Yes, this is going to be easy!" he said to himself.

But even before he reached the horse, he could plainly see that Old Black had already put in some grueling labor. A white lather had formed between his haunches. He was in a hard sweat, with steady streams running down his rump and sides, dripping off his belly, neck, and chest. His shoulders were sopping.

"Golly, Black," he exclaimed when he saw the horse's condition. "This is a bigger job than I thought." He began stroking the horse's neck and raking the sweat off with the heel of his hand. He took off his hat, intending to use it to block the sun from Old Black's face. That slight movement of the hat, though, bathed his own face with such a refreshing swirl of air that he took the hat in both hands and began vigorously fanning the horse's face with it. The big, dark eyes half closed with relief. Jim fanned harder. He scanned the sky, hoping to see a providential cloud. None promised any shade.

Jim heard the sheriff's voice and ran back to the hole.

"Jim, if you could lift me about two feet—" Jim could hear him breathing hard. "Got 'em all but one, but—"

Jim looked over his shoulder without waiting for the explanation. "Walk, Black," he shouted sharply. With his hand on the rope he felt the tension increase until it seemed it would snap.

Finally, the rope moved, just an inch at first, but then it began to slide over the stone. Jim noticed that the lariat was wearing a groove in the face of the stone. Again he tested the rope's tension above the stone; then with the heel of his hand he pushed on the rope below it. The difference was startling! It was plain that the friction between the rope and the stone was making it much harder for Old Black to lift the burden on the end of the rope. Impatiently, Jim threw off his mental picture of a pulley—where would he get a pulley? Even as he watched, the small cone of dust cut from the stone by the rope grew larger, the slot in the stone grew deeper and longer, making the problem worse with every foot of rope that went through it.

"Hold it right there, son," said the sheriff.

"Whoa, Black," he said, his hand on the rope. Instantly he felt the brittle tightness go out of the lariat. His mind raced as he imagined various forms of lubrication. Mud? He glanced about, realizing immediately that there was no water anywhere nearby. He wished he could urinate, but he was soaking wet with the perspiration that was consuming the water in his body. Maybe Old Black had urinated somewhere. He looked over his shoulder and was frightened by what he saw. The horse was hunched lower, and his hind legs were trembling.

"Sheriff," he called down the hole, "can I go see about Old Black?"

"Sure, sure. I'll be a minute or so here."

He ran to the horse and with his hat in both hands began fanning the big, tired face. A blanket of shade suddenly arrived, sliding across the ground beneath a cloud. He gave a big sigh at the blessed relief from the blazing sun.

One of Old Black's hind legs was in a constant spasm now. The horse's lips, white with thick foam, were quivering, and he was mouthing the bit. Jim moved around him, fanning and talking in soothing tones and wishing with all his might that he could provide some water for him.

His canteen! Quickly he untied the canteen from the saddle, spun off the top and poured water into a hand held under the horse's mouth. As Old Black sucked the water up greedily, Jim kept pouring slowly into his hand. They didn't waste a drop. He wished for some himself, but kept dosing it out to the horse until—suddenly, a *maddening* thought came to his mind: "The water I needed for mud was here all the time!" He shook his head at the bitter mistake. A shake of the canteen told him there was not enough water left now to make even a small bit of mud, so he gave the rest of it to Old Black. Jim shook his head sadly and said, "I know you were thirsty, Black, but we would have been a lot better off with some mud to grease that rope than the little good that bit of water did you."

They had a long way to go, and the drag on the rope was going to get worse. Only when he heard himself utter a tiny whimper did his conscious mind face the terrible fear that Old Black just could not go much further, that he might not be able to finish this job. He went back to fanning the horse, feeling a chill deep inside and a tightness in his throat.

A mule would just quit working, balk, when he had done all he could. But a horse, especially one like Old Black, would work himself to death if you asked him to; he could bust a gut, Jim thought, just like Oscar had warned him the time he'd tried to pull the heavy cattle feeder. Jim looked up and silently begged the cloud—a nice, big cloud—to keep them covered with its shade.

He was rubbing the horse's legs when he realized that Old Black was trembling all over. Terror gripped Jim's mind, making it hard for him to think things out. Maybe he should go look for help after all. But go where? How would he get the rope off the horse with Sheriff Martinez hanging from it? And what would he tie off to, if he could get it off? He saw the weariness in his horse's eyes and fanned harder, spurred by the terrifying thought that Old Black might die if they kept trying. He put his arms around the horse's head and held him close.

"I'm sorry, Black. Please know I'm sorry. What are we going to do?" Tears filled his eyes and he gave in to fear, to the seeming hopelessness of the situation. Then a shout from the hole sent him running.

When Jim's shadow darkened the hole, Sheriff Martinez said weakly, "How's your horse holding up, Jim?"

"He's—he's real tired, Sheriff. He's, well, he's about gave out. I was just trying to figure a way to give him a rest. But there's not a thing to tie off to. And if there was—" Jim knew he *had* to do something. Old Black couldn't continue holding the strain much longer.

"I have an idea, Jim," said Sheriff Martinez. "If you can pull me up another yard, just past this board—" He was pulling at the board to determine how secure it was. "I believe it's wedged in tight enough to hold my weight—I can lie on it so your horse can have a blow. I don't know how long we've been at it, but he's got to be just about spent."

"Yes, sir, he is." Tears were running down his face and he was glad the sheriff could not see him. Could Old Black manage even one more yard? He stared at the grooved rock that was making the pull so much harder and thought of how dumb he was not to have remembered the canteen full of water. With the mud it would have made they might be done by now. He *had* to grease that rope somehow. If they could just get that extra yard so Old Black could rest, maybe he could think of a way. He whipped off his shirt and began wringing it out. He could see some water collecting in the lower section. It would never make any mud, but dropped right onto the rope it might make it a bit slicker.

"I'm ready," Sheriff Martinez called.

"Okay," Jim called down, his voice trembling. Quickly he wrung the shirt hard and a few drops of sweat fell, most of them where he wanted them, but it was a pitifully small amount of moisture. He hurried to Old Black, putting his shirt back on as he went.

His mind flashed back to the time he and his dad were hauling

hay; they were almost finished and Jim was bone tired. He was struggling to climb onto the hay wagon for the umpteenth time. His father
noticed his weariness, put a hand under his rear and lifted gently. That
little boost seemed like all the help in the world. Maybe if he pushed
on Old Black. . .

Jim walked up behind the horse and put a hand on each of his
thighs. He turned his feet sideways so he could dig in with his boot
heels while pushing. "Walk, Black," he said through gritted teeth and
pushed with all his might. His face was awash with tears. The big old
gelding gave the pull everything he had and Jim pushed as hard as he
possibly could, but it seemed that the rope was frozen to the stone.
Suddenly the friction lock between the stone and the rope was broken
and they moved ahead more than a yard in one second. Jim heard
shouts from the well. He called, "Whoa," and ran back to the hole,
desperate to learn when he could let Old Black back off of the strain.

Staring down the hole, he could see Sheriff Martinez plainly,
now. He was maneuvering himself onto the board he was going to use
as a resting bench.

"Be just—just a second here." He was panting with fatigue. He
wriggled some more. "I'm hurrying—your horse must be all in. Okay,
back off—just a little. See if this'll hold me up."

Jim was still for a moment, then said, "Sheriff, I'm going to be at
the horse. If it's going to hold, could you give out a holler? If you don't
holler I'll put the strain back on. I'm afraid that if I'm not there to
handle Black and you fell, it might take him by surprise and pull him
down."

He turned and ran as fast as his weary legs could carry him. Old
Black was trembling so that he looked like he might go down any
second. Jim took the reins at the bit and said softly, "Back, Black—
easy, easy." The horse relaxed his strain on the rope ever so slowly. On
stiff hind legs he took the smallest step backward, then another, until
finally the rope hung with just a bit of slack. Jim stroked Black's sop-
ping-wet neck as he listened for the signal. To make sure he could
hear the call when it came, he stopped rubbing and waited.

Just as he was despairing of ever hearing the shout he longed for,
a sharp "Okay!" came from the well, and he immediately backed the
horse another step to put slack in the rope. He released the lariat from
the saddle horn and threw it on the ground.

Old Black stood in his tracks, head down and breathing hard.
Jim dropped to his knees and began vigorously rubbing down a fore-

leg. After a half-minute he rose and loosened the cinch. Quickly, he moved under the horse's belly to the other foreleg and rubbed hard. Then he massaged Black's hind legs. He was conscious all the time that he should check on the sheriff but was resigned to the reality that he couldn't be in two places at once.

When he tried to lead the horse around, Old Black could hardly take a step; his legs were as stiff as if they were in casts; his hind legs seemed to be almost gone, they trembled so. Jim wished he knew more about treating a horse as exhausted as this, but he knew that light exercise helped get the stiffness out of himself.

"Come on, Black," he coaxed, hoping with all of his might the horse *could* walk. When he looked into Old Black's tired, half-closed eyes, tears welled up in his own and his lower lip trembled. He was glad he couldn't see well enough to make out his reflected image in Black's eyes, because he didn't want to see himself as Black did—the person who was responsible for this terrible situation they were in. Recalling the impossibility of pulling that feeder, and now putting Old Black to yet another hopeless task, he thought that he should never have been allowed to have a horse. And he was tormented over how he had tempted fate, boasting to himself that Old Black would have the sheriff out of the well in no time.

He sank to the ground, on his knees and with his arms around the horse's forelegs he laid his head against Old Black's legs and cried, the sobs racking his body.

He was startled by something warm and soft pressing on his shoulder, like a big, gentle hand, and he looked up with a start. Old Black's nose was pressing reassuringly against him, as if telling him not to worry. Jim rose to his feet and embraced the horse around the neck. "Come on, Black," he said, wiping his face with his sopping sleeve. "You have to walk around." And with weary resignation, he added, "Then we have to go back to pulling the sheriff out."

After Old Black had taken a few unsteady, hesitant steps, he said with mournful dejection, "But I don't see how we can ever do it."

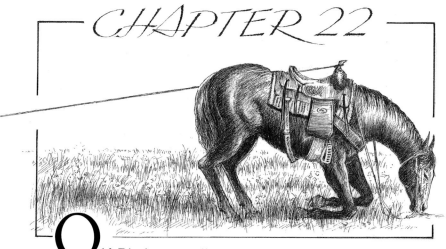

CHAPTER 22

Old Black was walking stiffly, but walking. Jim led him around in a big circles, troubled all the time that he should be checking on the sheriff.

He looked up at the sky. He had lost all concept of time. The sun was easily low enough for it to be five, or even later. He knew his parents would be frantic. No sooner had that anxiety gone through his mind than he returned to worrying about how he might reduce the friction between the lariat and the rock. In his mind's eye, he clearly saw a small can of bearing grease. He could see it sitting in the pump house on a shelf by the door. It was a can small enough to fit in his pocket. He wished he had that can of grease right now. How that lariat with a thick coat of bearing grease would sail over that stone!

Jim put the reins over the horse's neck so he wouldn't stand ground tied. "Walk, Black," he said, and he and the horse walked wearily, clumsily off toward the well. When he got into position he stared into the blackness for a minute until his eyes adjusted. Sheriff Martinez was sitting on the plank and tying something around his broken leg, a leg that was a bloody mess. One whole side of his head was caked with blood, and so was his shirt. Jim was beginning to feel overwhelmed. Everything seemed so impossible now.

After sitting down wearily, he realized he hadn't even once looked around the place for intruders. His heart was pounding as he jumped to his feet, but he saw nobody and he heard no sound. Old Black was moving around, still slow but seemingly with greater ease. Maybe he was more stiff than exhausted, he told himself; at least that was his hope.

For the first time, he realized that he was dead tired himself. He went to the horse, took the reins and clucked, leading him around as briskly as he could. The horse's movements were much improved now but Jim did not like the sound of his breathing. It was short and fast.

After making a wide circle, he led the horse to the hole. Getting down on his stomach again, Jim saw Sheriff Martinez leaning back on the broad plank, which provided an inclined surface to rest on. His broken right leg lay on the board. His left was propped stiffly against the opposite wall of the well.

When he sensed Jim was looking down on him, he looked up and said, "Jim, I bet if you'd known what was in store today you might not have got up this morning. How's your horse feeling, son?"

"He was real tired, Sheriff, and stiff as he could be. But I've been walking him around and he's better." Sheriff Martinez's eyes closed, but Jim could tell that he wasn't sleeping.

The declining sun was no longer so hot, but its angle bathed Jim from head to toe, so the effect was just as bad. He led his horse in a large circle again, stepping up the pace as much as he could on his own tired legs. He looked around carefully as he walked. The place could not have been more deserted. How did the criminals come and go without leaving tracks? He was sure the car tracks he had seen earlier were the sheriff's, but where was his car? *They* probably took the sheriff's car. But the tracks he had seen only went toward the place, not out. How many hours ago was all that? He could not even think.

This period of inactivity was giving Jim time to think, to worry. He glanced at Old Black and said sadly, "Black, I guess we better get back to work. I'll do my share, this time. We'll be through, after this, Black. I promise. We'll be done. You can rest as long as you want after this time. I won't even ride you home. I promise, Black." He patted the horse's soaking wet neck, turned, and went to the well.

The sheriff was lying so still Jim was afraid he'd passed out. "Sheriff," he called in a soft voice.

Sheriff Martinez was alert in an instant. "Someone coming?"

"No, sir. But we'd better start pulling again, don't you think?"

"Yeah, Jim. I wanted to give your horse all the rest we could. He must be some horse, Son, to hang on all this time. I'm sure sorry to be abusing him like this. Yeah, I'm ready. Let's go." His voice was softer and less resonant. The words were spoken slowly, carefully paced. Jim was worried that he was losing strength.

With Black once more in position, he tightened the cinch and tied the lariat around the saddle horn. He felt an inner dread for asking the horse to pull any more. "Black, I'll be pushing as hard as I can," he said with a tremble in his voice. He was relieved that there would be no waiting this time, no agonizing waiting with Old Black having to stand against that steady strain.

If he only had some *mud!* It was futile, but he looked around again for anything that would lubricate the rope and that stone. He thought of sap in weeds, vines, even Old Black's sweat . . . .

Back at the hole he found the sheriff was ready and waiting. "I'll be at the horse, Sheriff," he said. Sheriff Martinez noticed that fatigue was causing Jim to slur his words. "I have to help him by pushing. If something happens just call out, but we have to try to make it to the top in one pull. I don't know if Old Black could get started again if we stopped." The sheriff nodded.

Jim got up from his prone position and turned around just in time to see Old Black dropping a big pile of manure. It was collecting beneath him, wet and green from the grass he had gorged on earlier in the day. Jim ran to him as fast as his weary legs would allow.

He scooped up a double handful of the wet, smooth, slippery manure and ran back to where the lariat descended into the hole. He placed the manure in a pile on the rock and ran back to get more, this time being careful not to let any of the precious lubricant drop through his hands. When he had carried all of it to the rock, he packed the groove in the stone and applied a coating to the rope, leaning as far down as he dared.

Sheriff Martinez looked up and watched Jim intently; then he inhaled deeply to identify the odor. "I'll be—" he said to himself.

"I'm going to the horse now, Sheriff. We're going to start."

Sheriff Martinez noticed that Jim's voice, which had plainly reflected deeper and deeper discouragement, was livelier now.

Jim led Old Black forward until all the slack was gone and the saddle showed the strain of the rope. Then he got behind him in pushing position.

"Walk, Black," he barked, and pushed with all his might. He felt the horse's body tremble with the strain, and he seemed to pick up his feet as if they were so much lead. Jim could sense the tightness of the lariat, but knew from the total lack of sound from it that it hadn't moved even an inch over the rock. "*Walk*, Black," he said again and pushed with every ounce of strength he could muster. Suddenly they moved so far Jim almost fell down, and just as quickly he realized that the rope had bound up again when it reached the extent of its lubrication. "Stand, Black."

He rushed back to the hole, applied manure to the rope as far as he could reach, then to the stone, and ran back to the horse. Old Black's legs were trembling again. "Walk, Black," he commanded, and resumed pushing, digging in with his boot heels so hard his legs began shaking. After moving about the same distance, the now familiar sign of the tightening rope sent him back to the hole.

On his third trip he was thrilled to see that he could almost touch the sheriff's head. One more good pull would do it. Holding onto the corner of a rock, he stretched as far as he possibly could to coat the rope with the lubricating manure. As he approached the horse he gasped to see Black stagger and almost go down on his forelegs. He rushed to the horse's head and said urgently, "One more pull, Black. Just one more pull, I promise, Black."

He was crying openly, unashamed, and hating himself for what he was asking the horse to do. This time he started pushing before he gave the command. "Walk," he said, crying, and the horse made a hopping action with his forefeet and threw himself against the lariat, moving with such speed that Jim fell flat on his face. Even before he could scramble to his feet he heard Sheriff Martinez calling. He turned and saw the sheriff's head above the rim of the hole. He was struggling to pull himself over the edge when Jim reached him, but he did not have the strength to raise himself more than chest high.

"Wait, Sheriff," he said with a note of authority that surprised even himself. He took a position that allowed him to lift under one of the sheriff's arms. "Sheriff, I'm going to count to three. Push on the rim with that arm when I tell Old Black to walk. "One... two... " and on the third beat he shouted, "Walk, Black!" He lifted with all the strength he had left, the sheriff pushed as hard as he could, and the horse gave a mighty pull.

Sheriff Martinez came out of the hole so suddenly that both he and Jim went sprawling. His drawn lips bared his teeth and he groaned with the pain. He held his shattered leg with both hands. Now Jim saw that Sheriff Martinez had ripped a long tear in his pants leg to administer aid to himself, and the leg lay completely exposed, bleeding heavily.

Jim stared at the white spears of bone that stuck out of the blood-soaked wound. He felt weak and dizzy and sick at his stomach. His eyes fell on the taut lariat and in a daze they followed it to his horse. Old Black was down on his knees, still straining on the rope.

Sheriff Martinez saw the horse at the same time. His face contorted with pity for the horse and agonizing compassion for the grief-stricken boy.

"Black!" Jim cried, stumbling, falling, crawling toward his horse. "Oh, Black."

CHAPTER 23

"I'm coming, Black," he called out, his voice trembling. When he reached the horse he fought with the lariat, trying to release it from the saddle horn, but the strain on the rope held it fast. Jerking the straps desperately, he released the flank cinch and breast collar. Then he undid the cinch strap and helped it flow through its D-ring as the saddle fell away. The exhausted horse rolled over on his side, his legs twitching spasmodically. Jim fanned his face with his hat and cried, "Black, oh Black. It's over, Black. It's over! This time its really over, Black." With his hand he wiped a mass of cotton-like foam from the horse's mouth.

Still fanning furiously, his mind totally absorbed by the thought that Old Black was dying, he glanced back at the injured sheriff. He was trying to sit up and tend to his leg. He fell back to the ground.

With mortal agony everywhere around him and feeling his own exhaustion, Jim fell to his hands and knees, crying. He vomited, and when there was nothing more to come up, he retched.

Short, choppy breaths came as he gasped for air. "Please, can't somebody help us?" he cried softly between breaths. When he had caught his breath, he dragged himself to his feet, trying to control the sobs that came with every intake.

Once more Jim was over the horse, fanning. He moved around the horse twice before reluctantly leaving him. On unsteady legs he jogged haltingly to where the sheriff sat working on his broken leg. There was a growing pool of blood in the dirt and he was feebly attempting to stem the flow with a rag wrapped around his thigh. Jim looked at the man, then at his horse. His chest contracted spasmodically with silent sobs.

Jim knew what tourniquets were, and what they did. "Let me do it, Sheriff," he said. Sheriff Martinez lay back on the ground. Jim took the handkerchief, looked at it and threw it aside. He pulled his big bandanna from his back pocket and using his teeth tore it into three wide strips and tied them together with tight square knots. After twisting it he had a crude but strong rope about five feet long; he wound it around the leg as tightly as he could, making two wraps and crossing one over the other. He tied the first half of a square knot. "Put your finger here, Sheriff," he said, taking the man's hand and placing his index finger on the knot.

Just as he finished tying the square knot, Old Black clambered noisily to his feet. Jim shivered with numb relief at the sight of the horse standing up. Turning his attention back to the mangled leg, he tried to think of something to cover the wound with. He saw that Old Black was moving, moving woodenly, but moving. "Walk, Black," he said over his shoulder, and the horse began trudging slowly along. Jim staggered to where his saddle lay on the ground and untied the saddle strings that held the jean jacket.

"Sheriff, I'm going to—to wrap your leg." Working on the wound forced him to look at it closely, a sight that sent aching waves through his body. The slightest movement caused the leg to bend at the break, and the bones moved visibly. A splint came into Jim's mind, but he had nothing to make a splint with. When he had the leg bundled he tied the sleeves together. He stood up, then he noticed that the sheriff's holster was empty.

Sheriff Martinez had been lying still, his breath coming out in low groans. Now he brought himself to a half-sitting position, braced on arms spread out behind him. He looked all around. "Jim, if we can get me to my car I can radio for help," he said.

"Where is it?" Jim asked.

Martinez turned his head and threw a glance across the clearing. "Over there, in the trees."

It was plain that the man could not even crawl. He could hardly sit up, let alone move the fifty yards to the woods.

"Could I call for help on your radio?" Jim asked.

"I thought of that a long time ago. No. We have the ignitions tricked out for security. You'd never figure it out, even with directions."

He rolled over and brought himself up on his hands and his good knee. "If you could be a crutch I might make it," he said, motioning with his head for Jim to come over. Jim knew it would be impossible. He could hardly stand up himself, much less provide support for so big a man, but he went to the sheriff's side. He and Jim both went sprawling before he was halfway to his feet. He lay on the ground, holding his leg and moaning softly. "Damn," he said through clenched teeth. "Damn!"

"Wait," Jim said, gasping for breath. "Over by the barn—some tin—for a sled."

Glancing guiltily at Old Black and wishing he could go to him, he went to his saddle and returned with the lariat, on the way untying the stop knot the sheriff had made. Although Old Black looked exhausted through and through, he had been moving around, exercising himself. Now he was standing still, his head hanging down almost to the ground.

Jim was not going to ask Black for another solitary thing. Urging his own body to move, he started toward the barn and in a few steps he was in a weary trot. Soon he was back, dragging a rusty sheet of roofing metal. Near one corner of the metal sheet was a nail hole that had rusted into a hole large enough for the lariat to pass through. He sorted through the broken rocks, found one with a pointed end and pounded a hole in the other corner. Then he passed the rope through the holes and fastened the ends with knots, leaving the long center length as his halter. He pulled the makeshift sled up beside the sheriff and motioned for him to get on.

Without comment, Sheriff Martinez wriggled onto it. Jim had envisioned himself dragging it across to the trees but was shocked when he found he could not even budge it. Like Old Black had done on his final effort, Jim dug in his heels and flung all of his eighty pounds against the rope halter. It did not move an inch.

He did not think once of using his poor, exhausted horse, but stood in dismay, staring across the clearing at the woods where the sheriff's car was hidden. His mind raced through a string of unworkable ideas. He could drive a car in an emergency. But he could not get the car started because of the security switch. Even if he could, he did not want to leave Old Black out here alone. If it were not for the security switch he could get power to the radio and call for help.

Suddenly the sheriff rose on an elbow. He asked urgently, "Did you hear that, Jim? A boat?"

From far downriver came the sound of a powerful speedboat. The high-pitched scream died away for a moment as the boat passed some feature on the land that blocked its sound. When the sound returned it was louder. "Yes, sir. I hear a boat."

"Its them." Sheriff Martinez dropped back with despair. "It's them. They're coming back here." He cocked his head, listening.

"Who?"

"The gang that tried to kill me. They're a good ways off yet, but it won't take them long to get here." He turned to look at the compound of buildings, then to the woods that hid his car. "There's only one thing to do, Jim." The excitement of the boat had stimulated him, but it was evident from his voice and from his ashen face that he was now very weak.

He lay back. "I'd say we don't have much more than a half hour before they get here. You're going to have to get out of here, son. You've got time to do me one more favor." He pulled a set of keys from his pocket and held them out. "This round key fits a lock on the gun rack in my car. If you would bring me my shotgun, maybe I can hold them off." He stopped talking, breathing hard. Jim turned away.

"Wait, Jim—box of shells—rear floorboard. Bring 'em. Then clear out. Get to a phone—send help."

Jim stood in his tracks, stunned. "You mean you want me to leave you here?" He looked around for some means of protection. Even if he could move the sheriff to a position behind the well stones so he could use them as a barricade, there was no reason that the murderers—they *were* murderers, weren't they?—couldn't circle around to his exposed side. Sheriff Martinez might even pass out. Jim saw himself wandering aimlessly, looking for houses. Even from horseback he'd seen no houses after passing under the last road, and that was at least two miles up Hickory Creek. He had not seen a single car go over the bridge. And even if he knew where a nearby house was, Jim was not sure he could walk very far. Besides, leaving here would mean leaving Old Black behind. Sheriff Martinez would be dead before anyone could get here, and Old Black too.

He looked at the yoke he'd fashioned, and his eyes went to his horse. Old Black was walking very slowly with his head low. Without another thought, Jim went to him.

"I know I promised, Black, but we've got to pull some more. I'm going to do most of the work." He choked back sobs as he led the horse to a position in front of the sled. Working mechanically, with clumsy hands, he reworked his rope arrangement so that the two loose ends were laid out.

Jim looked at the heavy saddle lying on the ground and discarded the thought of lifting it. He made a large loop and placed it over the horse's head so that the eye of the loop was at his chest. Next, he tied a stop-knot in the lariat to keep the loop from closing. The other end he fashioned into a big knot for a handhold.

The scream of the power boat was closer now. He looked at Sheriff Martinez, lying on the sled with an arm over his eyes to block the sun. He looked at Old Black, then quickly dropped his eyes to the ground.

Even before his eyes closed, Jim was imagining that it was a balmy spring day. He saw himself rested, fresh and raring to go in a pulling contest with Old Black. In his imaginary scene he forged to the front, laughing and teasing Old Black as they sped across the clearing in the direction of the woods with the sheriff bumping along behind.

JIM BROUGHT THE ROPE OVER HIS SHOULDER and took the knot in both hands. He had closed his eyes again, and leaned far forward, putting all of his weight against the rope. A little smile broke out on his face. Then he opened his eyes and said brightly, "Walk, Black."

The horse began a dreadfully weary trudge, mechanically, his head hanging low. Digging in his boot heels, Jim heaved on the rope with all his might, and the sled began to move. In a few steps they were moving along at a good pace, Jim a few paces ahead of Old Black.

"Good boy Black!" he called. "Attaboy." He glanced up to measure the distance to go. I'm beating you—but that's okay. We'll be there in just a minute." Tears were streaming unrestrained down his face. His head was down and he pulled mightily on the rope until his thigh muscles burned like fire.

Never changing from the same slow pace, Old Black plodded resolutely along, planting each foot deliberately, moving one trembling leg at a time, looking like he would just go until he could not take another step.

Sheriff Martinez was barely conscious but he sensed he was being pulled rapidly across the ground. He agonized over both the boy and his horse amidst the steadily intensifying sound of the speedboat. He knew that the boy was in mortal danger. They'll kill him as quick as they'll kill me, he thought. The gentle bumping over the ground had a tranquilizing effect, and soon the sheriff thought of nothing that made any sense.

Jim saw the brown and tan patrol car immediately on entering the woods. He and Old Black trudged toward it, past it, and when the sled was beside the car he said, "Whoa, Black." It came out in a weak croak. Old Black stopped. His breath was coming in irregular gasps and he stood with all four legs trembling uncontrollably. It seemed to Jim like he was watching in slow motion as Old Black began to weave. Then he dropped heavily to his knees.

Jim threw off his loop and staggered to Old Black's side. He grabbed the rope strung tight from the horse's neck to the tin sled and pulled hard, dragging the lariat through the metal enough to get some slack. Old Black struggled weakly to rise but Jim dropped to his knees, put an arm around his neck and gently forced him to stay down. Old Black's drooping eyelids closed and he sank to the ground. He rolled over on his side and lay with his legs jerking spasmodically, his mouth and nostrils white with froth. His breath came in horrible, rasping gasps.

Jim fell forward on his hands, gasping for breath. He was desperate to clear Old Black's mouth and nose but was overcome by convulsive gulps and could do nothing. Finally he turned to Old Black and with shaking hands wiped the froth from his mouth and nostrils, wiping his hands on his shirt and pants.

If he only had one pint of water to wet Old Black's mouth with, he thought. The car! Maybe there was water in the car. He crawled over and opened the door. There was the gun rack, a leather-covered memo book with a snap fastener lying on the seat, a microphone resting in its clamp.

If he could only get that radio working. He remembered that he still had the sheriff's keys. He found the one that was most likely an ignition key and tried it. It worked. But his elation faded when he realized that nothing came on. He turned it to start position. No response. The security switch.

If he looked under the dash, he might be able to find the hidden switch, he thought, and crawled into the car. From the floorboard his eyes fell on a large vacuum bottle resting in a bracket on the hump in the floor. He wrenched it out of the bracket and could tell from its weight that it had something in it. Coffee, probably, he thought. Lukewarm coffee it was. He took a mouthful, swished it around and swallowed it. Coffee, yes, but it was deliciously wet. His eyes narrowed as he considered how he would get the coffee into the horse. He looked for a rag of some kind. Nothing. He backed out of the car and holding onto it for support, went to the trunk. It was half full of radio gear. No rag.

He went to Old Black's side with the jug of coffee and tried to slosh some in his mouth, but it only ran out. He needed a rag. He looked at his shirtsleeves and frowned. He pulled his shirt tail out of his pants and found it to be clean. Using his pocket knife he cut off all of the tail on the right side below where it was soiled with manure, dirt, blood, and dried slobber.

After sopping it with coffee, he put it in Old Black's mouth. The horse closed his mouth on the rag and noisily sucked the coffee out of it, the first sign of life he'd shown since he went down. His lips reached greedily for the cloth as Jim took it from him. Jim realized that the eager horse could swallow the rag; after wetting the cloth again, he held tight to a corner and put the rest of the cloth in Old Black's mouth. He watched the horse suck up the coffee again, realizing for the first time how thirsty he was. When all the coffee was gone, he used the damp cloth to wipe Old Black's mouth and nostrils. Now he thought of watching that driving flow of the Brazos River when he didn't need any water. It could not be more than a quarter of a mile from this baked hardpan, but it might as well have been a hundred miles away, he thought, and ran his dry tongue over his dry lips. He tried to imagine another source of water, but the bountiful Brazos flooded his thoughts.

The clear, unbroken howl of the speedboat was closer still. Their only hope lay in getting the sheriff to the radio. He should have already done that! And the tourniquet should have been loosened by now! He unwrapped the leg and loosened the tourniquet. Blood began flowing immediately. Ten seconds later he tightened the bandanna and wrapped the man's leg.

WHEN SHERIFF MARTINEZ CAME TO HIS senses it was deep evening and Jim Bradley was pulling on his arm. He stopped long enough to wipe tears and sweat from his face with as dirty a sleeve as Martinez had ever seen. Martinez was surprised to see that above him was the open patrol car.

Jim said, "The radio, Sheriff." He continued pulling on Martinez's arm.

Martinez shook his head to clear it. He must get into the car far enough to manipulate the battery cut-out switch so they could use the radio. He realized that Jim was helping him get to a sitting position. Jim reached in the car, and from inside the door post found the seat belt and pulled it out as far as it would come.

"Here, Sheriff," he said, holding the belt out to him. The sheriff extended his right hand and Jim put the belt in it, then put a wrap around his hand. The wrap gave him something to hold on to and it took up the slack.

Using what help the exhausted boy could provide, Martinez hauled on the car door and the seat belt until he was kneeling on his good leg, the other straight behind him. The seat belt provided no help for getting him into the car. Jim stood almost straddling him and lifted under his right arm. It gave the man enough support to allow him to drop the belt and, with enormous exertion, grasp the steering wheel. His right arm was shaking when he slumped onto the car seat.

"Keys," he said through gritted teeth. "Keys."

"They're in the ignition, sheriff."

"Jim—other side."

The sheriff manipulated something under the dash, then nodded to Jim as he entered the other side. When Jim turned the key this time some lights came on.

He took the microphone from its clamp and handed it to Sheriff Martinez.

"Flip that switch—the shiny one. No, this side."

Jim flipped the switch and a hushed rushing sound came over the speaker. Martinez pressed the microphone button and released it. "Click . . . click," came over the speaker. Martinez pressed the button again and said, "One to base."

A woman's voice answered, "Base. Go ahead one. Where you *been*, Sheriff?" she asked lightly.

"Millie, listen carefully—" said Sheriff Martinez, stopping for breath as he talked. "I'm in a bad fix at Klanke's Mill, busted up some—The Bradley boy, Jim, rescued me from a well and is with me now—There's an armed band of dope smugglers on their way upriver—almost here—We need help fast—Send help by car now." He stopped, panting, still pressing the mike button. "Get Miller Flying Service to bring some men in his chopper—Millie, tell 'em to hurry."

"Copy, Sheriff," said the efficient voice on the radio.

"And, Millie. See if Doc Smith, the vet, can come in the Miller chopper—Jim's horse is mortally played out."

"Copy that, Sheriff. Whereabouts are you on the place?"

In a moment the woman's voice came on again, "Do you read, Sheriff?"

Jim had been staring at the radio, their link to the outside world. Now he turned to see Sheriff Martinez thrusting the microphone at him. His eyes were almost closed. When Jim took the mike, the sheriff sagged to the ground.

Jim's hands were shaking. He held the microphone close to his mouth and pressed the button. "Ma'am, this is Jim," he shouted. "Can you hear me?"

"Yes, Jim. I hear you. Now just talk normally, Jim. You don't have to talk very loud. What happened to Sheriff Martinez?"

"I think he passed out."

The woman read the distress in the boy's voice and spoke soothingly but with a note of urgency, and with none of the detached unconcern that she knew drove desperate callers crazy. "Jim, I want you to know that people are already working very hard on this thing while we talk. So don't think our conversation is holding anything up. Where are the people Mike is concerned about? Are they close to you?"

"Yes, ma'am. They're coming in a boat. It sounds real close."

"Jim, if the sound of the boat stops, you tell me, okay? Can you tell me how bad Sheriff Mike is hurt? Has he been shot?" The woman's voice was still strong and authoritative, but Jim detected a tremble in it.

"No, ma'am. He wasn't shot. He has a broken leg and the bone is sticking out and he has bled a lot. And he was hit on the head, too."

"Okay," she said. "Jim, what did Mike mean when he said your horse was sick? And are you all right?"

Jim began to cry. "Yes, ma'am, I'm all right." He tried vainly to control his sobs, but the attempt to stifle them only made them louder. "Old Black, my horse, had to pull Sheriff Martinez out of a well—" The woman heard a sharp, sobbing intake of breath and waited patiently for him to resume. "The criminals threw him in it. And Old Black broke down after pulling him out. I believe he busted a gut." Again Jim tried to choke back his sobs. "He's—he might be dying." He let his hands drop and slumped in the seat, crying convulsively.

Her voice was tender and soothing, "I understand, Jim. Someone's on the phone to Doc Smith now. Now Jim, can you tell me where you are on the Klanke place?"

Jim took a deep breath. "We're in some woods on the right of the clearing, a good way from the barn."

"Okay, Jim. Now would you know if the right side is on the north or south, east or west?"

"Yes, ma'am. It's on the south side of the clearing."

"Fine, Jim. How far are you from the barn?"

Jim envisioned a football field and said, "About a hundred yards, I guess. The trees where we are kind of bulge out into the clearing."

"Okay. Jim, do you know what a tourniquet is?"

"Yes, ma'am. I made one out of my bandanna and it's on him."

"Oh, Jim, that's excellent. Is the break on the lower leg?"

"Yes, ma'am."

"Where is the tourniquet?"

"Just above his knee."

"Good, Jim, very good," she said with definite approval. "Now, you have to tend to a tourniquet every three to five minutes. Take it off for about fifteen seconds, then put it back on, tightening just until

251

the bleeding stops. If you can't get it tight enough to stop the bleeding, put a stout twig through the knot and twist it until it's tight enough. Every three to five minutes you have to let some blood flow to the leg below the wound."

Even as she talked to him, Jim could hear the woman quietly issuing crisp orders to people near her. He was reassured by her efficiency and her composure. "Okay," he said.

On the other end of the radio link, Millie Thatcher sat with tears streaming down her face. She rapidly turned pages in the Brentwood telephone directory, nodded to a man who had spoken a few words to her. When she spoke again, it was in a calm and reassuring voice.

"Jim, I have some good news. We have reached Doc Smith; he'll be on the Miller copter. Can I do anything for you, Jim? I'd like to call your parents." She quickly turned the pages, stopped, went back a page. "Here it is. It's M.J. Bradley, isn't it? On League Line Road?"

"Yes, ma'am." There was a pause and Jim heard a man's voice talking in the background. She said, "Do you still hear the boat?"

Jim had forgotten about the boat. He listened for two seconds and said, "Yes, ma'am, I hear it. It's real close." The pitch of the engine dropped, then dropped more. "I think it's here."

"We're coming, Jim. Now turn the radio off and stay as quiet as you can." The woman's voice was tight and forced, now, but Jim didn't notice. He was reluctant to break this connection to safety, but he flipped the switch down and all the little lights went out.

SHERIFF MARTINEZ WAS LYING ON THE sled unconscious, his breath coming quick and weak. Jim had taken the jean jacket off his leg. He loosened the tourniquet, and watched without emotion as the blood soaked the sheriff's leg. Counting out loud he said, "One thousand, two thousand, three thousand . . ." until fifteen seconds had elapsed, then reapplied the tourniquet, just tight enough that the blood stopped flowing. Gently he re-wrapped the leg. Finished, he put his hands on the ground and crawled to his horse.

Old Black's breathing was a terrible sound to hear, hoarse and loud and raspy. Jim rubbed his neck with long strokes.

He couldn't think clearly at all now, except that Old Black was here, and the sheriff was here, and they both might be dying. He looked up through the treetops, black silhouettes against a deepening blue sky decorated with the pink scraps of dying clouds. His parents wouldn't worry so much now, knowing he was with Sheriff Martinez.

CHAPTER 24

Mike Martinez opened his eyes and saw Jim on one knee, hovering over his horse. He could hear the horse's labored breathing. With a scrap of cloth, Jim was wiping the froth from his mouth and the snot from his nose. He could hear Jim talking to the horse. He watched as the boy gathered a big handful of grass and began rubbing Old Black down. He recalled talking to his dispatcher, and the sound of the boat. He had no idea how long ago that was, but he could see that it would soon be dark. Other than the sounds from Jim and his horse, there was silence.

A nauseating wave of pain radiated from his smashed leg, brutally bringing the desperate situation into focus and driving the haze from his mind. Propping himself up with an an elbow, he raised up enough to allow a hand to reach the broken leg, wrapped in the jean jacket that was stiff with dried blood.

He said quietly, "Jim, come over here, son." The boy crawled over.

"You've sure put in a day's work, and I'm grateful as I can be. You and your horse performed a miracle, and I know he suffered something awful doing it. How is he, son?"

Jim turned and looked at Old Black. When he turned back his eyes were fixed on the ground. "I—I don't know." His chin started to quiver and he said, "He's bad off, Sheriff. Real bad off—"

Sheriff Martinez slowly raised a hand to the boy's shoulder and grasped as firmly as he could. He waited for an aching tightness in his throat to pass, then he said, "Jim, we're in the hands of someone bigger than all of us, now. If my prayers are answered, real soon you and me and Old Black will be sitting around perfectly all right talking about that awful day we had at Klanke's Mill. Let's just look at it in the light that even though things look dark right now, we're going to make it through this, to a beautiful day just ahead." He grasped Jim's small chin tenderly and lifted his head until their eyes met.

The sincerity Jim saw was compelling. He tried to believe that somehow things would be all right.

"Did the boat get here? Have you heard anything?" Martinez asked.

"Yes, sir, it came. But I haven't heard anything since it got here."

"It actually stopped, here?" Jim nodded. "I was hoping—" Martinez did not say what he was hoping, but Jim could guess. "How long ago?"

Jim couldn't tell if time was flying or standing still. He had looked at the sheriff's watch, but it was smashed, and it was too dark to read the clock in the car. He had worked the tourniquet right after he turned off the radio and at least five more times, guessing about what might be four or five minutes each time. It was almost time to work it again.

"It seems like, uh, thirty minutes ago when I heard the engine quit, maybe a little more. Right after talking on the radio."

An urgency came into Martinez's voice. "Over a half-hour and our people aren't here yet? Get the keys from the ignition and get my shotgun. Do you remember the little round key?"

Jim nodded. Soon he emerged from the patrol car with the shotgun. He placed the butt on the ground near the sheriff's outstretched hand. Martinez's thumb went to the ejector lever. He turned the gun so he could see the ejection port in the waning light, opened the chamber far enough to tell that it was loaded and let the lever slide closed. Grasping the stock, he turned the gun so he could see the glint on the head of a shell in the magazine.

The boy's face was dry now, Martinez noticed, his movements mechanical, like a robot. The kid was totally done in, no doubt suffering from shock. And no wonder. Grinning for the first time that day, he said, "Jim, you're a mess. More blood on you than on me. You're a good man, Jim. And you have a mighty horse. I recall you said he's a champion? He sure proved that today." He smacked his dry lips. "Jim, in the car is some coffee—"

"No, sir. I gave it to Black."

"Good," Martinez said. "That was a good thing to do." He closed his eyes.

Jim worked the tourniquet and then crawled back to his horse. He cleaned Old Black's mouth and nose and then picked up the wad of grass and resumed rubbing him down. He wished with all of his might that they would really see that day in the future when they would laugh and talk about this. He tried to see the three of them and his parents laughing and remembering, but the image refused to form in his mind. The wad of grass dropped from his hand and when he picked it up and tried to rub, it fell from his grasp again. He was lonely; he felt total despair.

Jim sank down and let his head lie on Old Black's flank. When he awoke he realized he had dozed and the day had faded away; it was dark now in the trees, and only the last light lingered as a pink tinge to the dark sky. He could see some stars. The tourniquet, he thought. Then he heard voices from out in the clearing.

"He's gone from the hole! I told you to shoot him, Red. You are the absolute *worst* for doing things half-assed. *Dammit!* If he's got away there'll be cops all over this place, and nothing Fatso can do will stop 'em, neither. You're going to pay for this, Red!"

A second voice replied—Red's, Jim knew from that day in the highway in the sky—"But how could anybody live through the whack I gave him, Brad? I busted his head wide open. And how could he get out of that well?"

Pinpoints of light twinkled through the trees. Flashlights, Jim knew.

A new and high-pitched voice cried out, "Look—" a pause, and a light moved fast. "Look here, Brad. Look what I found. Here's a saddle. Hey, Brad, someone's been here."

"That explains how he got out of the hole, Red. Now, Winnie, why would somebody leave a saddle behind?" Brad asked. "Just why would somebody dump a saddle right here in the wide open?"

Jim heard without listening as he mechanically went through the routine of tending the tourniquet. He had no way of knowing it, but he was in deep shock, and he was further numbed by overwhelming fatigue. He felt no fear and very little curiosity; he could only comprehend the misery that was all about him. With the sheriff's leg re-wrapped, he went to Old Black, sat down by his head. He began stroking the horse's face. The voices of the men rose and fell, but he made no effort to listen to them.

And he did not worry that the men out there would want to enter his bloody nightmare.

Old Black stirred. Encouraged by his movement, Jim spoke softly to him. "Hey, Black. We're going to be all right. Doc Smith is coming. Everything is going to be all right, Black. We'll be home pretty soon."

He hoped they would think to bring water. How long would it take for help to come? Plenty of time had passed for someone to get here, even by car. Has it been another four minutes? Jim crawled to the injured man, who was either asleep or unconscious. He groaned as Jim removed the jean jacket and the boy was glad it was too dark to see the ghastly wound. He knew the procedure was done to prevent gangrene, but so much blood came out that he wondered if any was going where it was supposed to go when he let it bleed. To see if the blood was flowing, he felt of the place gingerly; thick, warm blood was heavy on his hand before he realized it. He wiped his hand on his shirt, then on his pants.

He reapplied the tourniquet and he gently wrapped the leg in the jean jacket. For the first time, the thought of the snake striking at the bandanna crossed his mind. Well, Oscar had told him that snake venom had to be injected into the bloodstream to do its work. You could drink it without harm, he said. Who would want to drink snake venom? He wondered who had drunk it to prove it wasn't harmful. Anyway, the only blood that the bandanna could get venom on was already out of the sheriff's body.

The sheriff had come back to consciousness while Jim worked on his leg. Sheriff Mike Martinez had never had to depend on anyone during his adult life. Now he lay completely helpless in the care of a small boy. But a strange, comforting sensation enveloped him as he watched the boy work. Once he had come to realize that he was totally dependent on this little man, he felt a warm security, knowing that everything possible was being done.

He recalled snapshots of the tremendous effort that it had taken to get him from the well to where he lay beside his patrol car. As his senses returned, he gritted his teeth at the terrible pain in his leg. He felt of his head, bristling with blood-coated hair, and thought with grim humor that if it were not for the overwhelming agony of his leg, his head would be killing him. The boy had finished and was now sitting very still.

Jim was startled by the sound of the sheriff's voice. "We sure found out how tough you are, Jim," he said. His voice was very weak now, barely above a whisper. "Any sign of life out there? Heard anything?"

"Yes, sir. There were some men out there. Walking around. I heard one cussing about you getting away."

The sheriff became more alert. "When? When did you hear them?"

The procedure with the tourniquet gave him a good perception of the passage of time. "Maybe six minutes ago. They must have left by now."

Sheriff Martinez felt for the shotgun and pulled it higher across his chest. He extended a hand to Jim. "See if you can help me sit up, son. If they find us we're dead."

Jim got behind the man on his knees and grasped him under an arm. With the sheriff pushing with his elbows, then his arms, they got him to a sitting position. But his head began to reel with dizziness and he sank back down.

"Dammit!" he said through clenched teeth. "Where in hell are our guys?" He lay there, breathing heavily.

The lights blinking from beyond the edge of the trees were much closer now. "Somebody's coming, Sheriff," Jim said quietly. His body weaved as he moved to keep the lights in sight through the trees. "They're coming this way. I can hear them talking."

Sheriff Martinez made a growling sound. He knew he was too weak to sit up and defend them; he knew, too, that the direction from which the men were coming would be behind him even if he could sit up. He would have to turn completely around to shoot at them. He pulled the shotgun across his chest, toward Jim. "Use this. Ever shoot a gun?"

"Yes, sir. My dad lets me shoot a four-ten."

"Same thing. This is just bigger and kicks a whole lot more. But it does more damage on the other end. Kneel—shoot kneeling on your right knee; with you left elbow on your left knee, lean forward so you'll be pushing against the recoil. If they get even close, press this button." He put Jim's finger on the button. "Push it, so you'll know." It clicked softly when Jim pushed it, and it clicked when Martinez pushed it back. "That's the safety—push it when you are ready—then lean forward into the gun—and hold the butt as tight as you can against your shoulder." He dropped his arm and caught his breath. "Point the muzzle right at a light—pull the trigger."

Jim's voice was filled with worry as he said, "Maybe it's Doc Smith! What if it's Doc Smith, Sheriff—it's so dark—"

Sheriff Martinez cut him off. "If it was him he'd be talking to us—and he'd have plenty of noisy company. Kneel down. If *anybody* gets close, point the gun in their direction—safety off, lean forward—and start pulling the trigger."

Jim took the big shotgun, being careful to keep his finger away from the trigger. Kneeling, he watched the light as it blinked and grew brighter. It was entering the edge of the trees. Sheriff Martinez, whose field of view was opposite from the source of the lights, saw flecks of light splattering on the car, twinkles striking Jim's face.

He spoke in a hoarse whisper, "Safety off. Shoot right at the light. But you better shoot!" He heard the quiet snap of the safety when Jim moved it. "Those guys want to kill us, Jim." He noticed that Jim had the shotgun trained on something. "Dammit!" said the sheriff in a tone of extreme agitation. "How come our guys don't come?"

The sounds of the approaching men were clear, now. "You better shoot, son. They're gonna be on us. Shoot right at the light."

Suddenly Jim was on his feet screaming, "Go away! Go away or I'll shoot. Please! Go away."

"It's a kid," a voice said, lightly, contemptuously. "Shoot? What with, kid?" The voice was strong and mean. Jim was certain it was the voice in the woods under the highway in the sky long ago. He heard sounds of men crashing through brush now, and the light was coming closer, and fast. Tears of terror filled Jim's eyes. The light was now a bright blur. "Shoot, huh?" the voice said. "*Here's* how you shoot!" A loud explosion and a bright flash came from the direction of the intruders, jarring Jim's ears and almost causing him to drop the shotgun. A sprinkling of shredded leaves fell from the foliage above.

"Shoot, Jim, shoot! Now!" growled Sheriff Martinez.

Jim pointed the shotgun at the light and pulled the trigger. The muzzle flash from the twelve-gauge magnum shell was as bright as a strike of lightning, accompanied by a tremendous explosion that rolled about in the woods. Jim landed on the seat of his pants from the recoil. A man's scream penetrated the reverberating echoes of the blast. Blinded by the flash and the sound still crushing his ears, Jim raised the shotgun, leaned forward as the sheriff had instructed and held it as tight against his shoulder as he could. Then he fired and fired and fired until the firing pin fell on an empty chamber.

The deafening blasts cascaded around in the trees, echoing, rumbling through Jim's head and pounding on his ears. Then a man's terrified voice penetrated his hearing, very close, "Christamighty—I'm shot—Jesus Christ. Red! Winnie! I'm bad shot."

"Let's get out of here, Brad." It was Red's voice, the sound retreating rapidly even as he spoke.

"Help me, Red! Winnie, say something! Don't leave us, Red. *Please!* Oh, God, Red. Winnie looks like he's been killed! I'm bad shot Red! I need help." Then Brad screamed, "Red! Blood's coming from everywhere. You gotta help me. I'm bleedin' to death, Red!"

Red's voice was distant now and laced with fear. "I'll help you, Brad—but you gotta come outta there. Get over here where I can help you."

Jim's eyes were useless for seeing anything but exploding roman candles of light. He sat on the ground staring wide-eyed but seeing nothing but the flashes. They burst brighter and brighter with an incendiary brilliance that now was lighting up the trees. It was illuminating the sheriff, who was smiling feebly at Jim, and suddenly the sky directly above them glowed with a brightness that seemed to light up the sky.

Jim wondered frantically if the blasts from the shotgun could have set the woods on fire. He jumped to his feet and ran to where Old Black lay. The horse's eyes were open wide, reflecting the white light. Jim dropped to his knees and began speaking to the horse. Could he get Old Black to his feet to escape the fire? How could he get the sheriff out of the woods? But he couldn't leave Old Black. He was trying to get Old Black to get up, but the horse was not responding with any more than a blink of an eye. The fiery light intensified, freezing Jim with still a new terror.

Then a new sound, a high-pitched scream, became so loud that Jim put his hands over the horse's ears. He felt a strange rhythmic pounding and a blast of wind struck the trees. Intense white light, brighter than day, seemed to be everywhere, lighting everything. Why was the sheriff smiling? Through the trees Jim could see people running across the open ground, brightly lighted now.

Horrified that some final catastrophe had come upon them, he buried his face in Black's neck and began sobbing. Then he put his hands over his ears and pressed his face hard into the horse, waiting for the new disaster.

JIM FELT A GENTLE HAND ON HIS SHOULDER. Someone pulled his hands away from his ears. "Jim—Jimbo, look at me, Jim, it's Doc Smith." Kneeling close beside Jim, the vet took the boy by both shoulders and Jim looked into the most welcome eyes he had ever seen. An expression of relief came over the boy's face that the vet would never forget. Jim seemed to be speechless.

Two men in white coats hurried past carrying Sheriff Martinez on a stretcher toward a helicopter in the clearing. Its slowly turning rotor blades broke the brightly lighted scene with shadows that swooped, swooped, swooped by in a rhythmic procession. The high-pitched whine of its jet engine was loud, steady.

Jim's ears were still ringing, but he thought he could hear other helicopters, long bursts of machinegun fire, explosions. The pungent smells of burning gunpowder and pyrotechnics wafted through the trees. Red smoke poured downwind in an illuminated plume from a flare lying in the clearing.

Doc Smith's eyes were now examining Jim's shirt and jeans, smeared thick with blood, slobber, manure, dirt. The only clean place on his face was around the eyes, where he had wiped away tears. "Hey, Jim," Doc Smith said softly, and bit his lower lip hard, "let's look at you, boy." His hands went quickly down Jim's arms, feeling. Fingers gently probed the boy's chest, ran over his back. "Where are you hurt, Jim?"

Jim shook his head. "Nowhere. It's Black that's hurt, Doc Smith. I think he's got a busted gut." His voice was flat with despair.

Doc Smith leaned down and patted the horse on the neck, then stroked his shoulder. "I'll get some things I'll need, then see what we can do for him." He sprinted toward the helicopter.

The two men returned with the stretcher. They had him sitting on the stretcher before Jim realized that they intended to take him away on it. He bolted away from them, dropping to his knees behind his horse. His frightened but hostile eyes darted warily from one man to the other.

"Come on, son," one said impatiently. "We have to take you to the hospital."

"I'm not *hurt*," he cried. "I have to stay with my horse."

The man who seemed to be in charge began talking in an artificially soothing voice, a voice that was contrived and sinister. "It's you we're concerned about, young fella, not that old nag. You gotta come with us." They approached from either side of him. Like a wild, cornered animal, Jim turned to face one man, then he spun around on his knees toward the other. He leaped to his feet and turned to run, but he was too late. They pounced and he was encircled in a mass of arms.

A wrist appeared in front of his face and Jim struck with the explosive violence of a cottonmouth moccasin, biting with all the strength of his jaws. The man's scream rose and fell in a continuing wail. Jim bolted away from him and again sought protection behind Old Black.

Just then Doc Smith came through the trees, loaded down and in a fast trot. His eyes immediately grasped what was happening. "Stop this!" he barked. "The boy's not injured and he's not going to leave his horse."

The bitten man, a hand grasping his arm, snarled, "He's our responsibility, Mr. Horse Doctor. Look at him, he's gotta be shot or something, with blood and corruption all over him." The man was finishing a hasty wrapping of his wrist. "Anyway, its policy. He's gotta go in for an examination. Damn!" he said, looking down at the bandage that was already bloodsoaked. He poured a furious look on Jim, then growled to his partner. "Okay, Joe, let's take him."

"Don't you move!" Doc Smith ordered in a stunning tone of authority. He dropped the things brought from the helicopter and was over the horse in one big leap. He assumed a fighting stance in front of Jim, knees bent for action, his long, heavy Maglight held menacingly in both hands, like a power hitter waiting for a fastball to knock over the fence. "By golly, I said let him alone. Make a move on him and you're the ones who'll be going to the hospital."

He threw a significant glance in the direction of the helicopter. "You gonna let the sheriff die while you're fiddling around here, trying to kidnap a little boy that's not even hurt?"

THE WHINE OF THE HELICOPTER ROSE to a scream. For a few seconds it seemed to be straining to free itself of the tenacious grip of the earth. Then it soared away, leaving the area below buffeted by its tempest and smelling of burned jet fuel. Jim turned away from its wild wind and suddenly the machine, along with its fury, its screaming noise, and its brutal attendants, was gone and the trees were still once more.

The night was lighted now not by flares but by burning, crackling buildings and a helicopter that circled constantly overhead with a brilliant light beneath it.

Doc Smith's hands were shaking and he was breathing rapidly as he opened his bag. His furious expression had softened and he looked at Jim with a nervous grin.

Kneeling by Old Black's head, he shined a tiny light into an eye and peered into it. He opened the horse's mouth and with a cloth he wiped away an accumulation of thick saliva. He pointed to a plastic jug next to his bag. "Hand me that water, Jim," he said. After sloshing some water into the horse's mouth, he wiped away some of the remaining matter with a cloth. The horse licked his wet mouth, weakly but eagerly. Doc Smith wrung out the cloth, wet it thoroughly, and put it in Old Black's mouth. The horse closed his mouth and sucked on the water. "I don't want him to choke on a big slug of water, Jim; I know he finds that refreshing. We're getting some good signs," he said.

He removed the cloth and dampened it, ran it over Old Black's caked lips, and cleaned his nostrils. Then he rinsed it and wet it to sopping. "Jim," he said, "hang on to this corner so he can't swallow it. As he sucks the water out give him some more." He moved to the horse's chest with his stethoscope. "I have Willie and some boys on the way with the large animal ambulance. They'll be here any minute." He listened to the horse's heartbeat. He listened to the sounds of his breathing, moving the stethoscope from one place to another.

After a full minute of this, he began grasping, massaging the horse's leg muscles, feeling for tightness and for trembling evident in the muscle tissue. His hands quickly, expertly examined each of Old Black's legs for strains, swellings, or broken bones. He moved to the horse's rear and inserted a thermometer in his rectum. He looked up at the boy standing over him. "He drank all the water," said Jim. Doc Smith nodded. "He's a pretty sick horse, Jim, but he'll make it. He'll need the best care we both can give him, but it's for sure he'll get that. Old Black will be all right."

Jim sank to his knees and put his cheek on the horse's great jaw. Raising a hand to shield his face from Doc Smith's view, he began to sob. In a minute he came to his knees and looked up. Still sobbing openly he said, "Please save him, Doc Smith. If he dies—" The boy thrust a pitiful, bloody, dirty, tear streaked face up towards the veterinarian, pleading for understanding. His hands were little fists clutched tightly against his chest.

"If he dies, it's because I *killed* him, Doc Smith. I gave him my promise that if he would pull one more time there wouldn't be any more pulling. But I broke my promise and made him pull some more." Jim collapsed, his head cradled in his arms. Doc Smith dropped to his knees, took him in his arms and held him close. "Jim, you have to let me worry about Old Black now," he said. "He's not going to die. He's going to *live*. I promise I won't leave him for a minute until he's out of trouble."

A Ford Bronco with a yellow flashing light on top bounced to a stop, illuminating the scene in its headlights. Two occupants came dashing up, one carrying a television camera on his shoulder. The man in the lead turned back and said, "Aw, hell—come on, Roger. It's just somebody fooling with a dead horse. Let's get back to the fire."

They backed out with tires spinning, made a tight arc and sped away across the clearing in the direction of the burning buildings.

Doc Smith approached Old Black's head, carrying a bottle of clear fluid with a tube connected to it. He was working quickly, efficiently. Jim sat down beside the horse's neck and began combing his mane with his fingers. Doc Smith shoved the rod of a bottle stand into the ground and hung the bottle from it. His fingers squeezed a clamp and allowed a short jet of fluid to escape through the needle. He examined the entire length of the transparent tube with his flashlight, then inserted the needle in the horse's neck. As he stroked the horse's neck toward the needle, blood swirled into the clear liquid in the tube. He removed the clamp from the tube. The beam of his flashlight played on the bottle and he watched the fluid drip for a minute.

Then his eyes went back to Jim. The exhausted boy was lying curled up with his knees and hands brought close to his chest, his head on the horse's flank, sound asleep.

Doc Smith wet a cloth and kneeled at his side. He began to wash his face. "I'll save him, Jim. I promise," he said to the sleeping boy. To himself he said, "God, I *hope* he pulls through."

Headlights swept the scene again and a big truck came lurching to a stop. The large-animal ambulance had arrived.

CHAPTER 25

The big double windows of Jim's bedroom that were situated at the east end of the farmhouse beckoned to the first light of every day. Ever so gently, the morning intruded, nudging him from the depths of sleep into the exquisite solitude of being half-awake in a house where not a living soul was stirring.

In the Bradley's Houston home, the morning routine was an eruption that began with *Rise and shine! Get ready for school!* Breakfast was a leisurely interlude, but then it was *Hustle off to school!* And since both of Jim's parents worked, it was hustle-off-to-work for them. His protracted awakening at the farm was a luxurious beginning of the day.

His parents occupied the back bedroom. The middle bedroom, Norma insisted, was to be converted to an indoor bathroom, and pronto. The old outdoor privy—leaning picturesquely, cradled charmingly in a remarkably luxuriant bed of wildflowers and draped in lacy, delicate ivy, its door decorated with the traditional quarter-moon cutout and the path to it still sharply defined—might serve as a quaint conversation piece, but Norma Bradley was never going near it, she declared, dusting her hands together in a gesture of finality. She suspected that the doors leading outside from so many of the bedrooms in these old houses might be associated with the "outdoor plumbing." "Whoever coined that phrase was a comedian," she said.

An exceedingly happy coincidence arising from the bedroom arrangements was reserved for Jim's mother. Norma felt that she was due some lying-in time on weekend mornings; she did not share Jim's eagerness to jump-start days that she knew full well would *never* be long enough, no matter what. So having bedroom windows facing north, the darkest of the four points of the compass, did not distress her in the least, nor did the presence of the large cedar tree that screened the double windows, a dense evergreen which, year-round, further postponed the coming of day to the master bedroom.

It was no small thing, either, that on some nights Jim could lie in bed on his stomach, his head in his cupped hands, and watch the moon float up from behind the Baumberg woods. Full moons were much bigger in the country than in the city—there was no question in his mind about that. He could even read a book by the light of the country moon.

His father had described to him each *face* of the moon—the part of the moon's surface that was reflecting light from the sun as seen from our viewpoint standing on earth. To illustrate, Matt had stuck a pencil in a tennis ball and in a darkened room had Jim hold the pencil at arm's length so the suspended ball was directly in front of him. Then Matt had shined a tightly focused penlight—the "sun"— on the ball from various positions around Jim. In the demonstration, Jim was to imagine that he was standing on earth and seeing the moon as represented by the tennis ball. When Matt was in front of Jim and shining the light on the side of the ball away from him, Jim saw a "new" or dark moon, lighted only on the fringes. With the light shining straight down, the ball was lighted as a half-moon, the phase called the first quarter.

When the tennis-ball's face was fully lighted, the flashlight "sun" was shining from over Jim's shoulder onto the full surface of the moon, and would do so all night, Matt said, because the moon and sun were moving somewhat together. The position of the sun directly behind earth—behind Jim—had been most graphically illustrated as Matt and Jim watched an eclipse of the moon. His father had explained how earth got in the way and cast a shadow on the moon's face. "Our head is in the way, blocking the sun's light from shining on the moon. If we could look at the moon from the sun, it would always be full, *except* during an eclipse. Then we would see earth sitting right in the way."

DURING JIM'S BLISSFUL, PROTRACTED AWAKENINGS, he often found himself lying deep in his soft mattress, his eyes dreamily contemplating the features of a water stain in the ceiling wallpaper. It so resembled a cloud that he fancied he was gazing at the sky. It was a sizeable stain, and had developed much as an artist might have painted a cloud with water colors, creating a variety of fluffy hues with darker, well-defined edges. He saw it as his friendly cloud, one he pretended would encourage real clouds to rain during droughts and others to come along and provide shade when they were baling and hauling hay. The shade from a cloud on a burning hot day was the most blessed thing he could think of—*instant* relief, and much more welcome even than a good breeze.

WHEN JIM WOKE UP ON THE SUNDAY MORNING following the incident at Klanke's Mill, he saw not his airy room and friendly cloud, but dark old planking laid on heavy timbers. As if the sight was not depressing enough to a person coming out of the nearest thing to anesthesia, its melancholy was intensified by dust-laden cobwebs and dirt-dauber nests, old plow points and other devices hanging from large nails and rusty hooks. His first impression was that he was in some kind of prison, or stockade.

What made him come to realize that he was looking at the floor of the barn loft—which he had never before examined with such close scrutiny—were other images that seeped into his mind from the corners of his eyes. The barn doors that he knew so well were directly beyond his feet, with the sturdy locking bars that he had helped his father make. He was aware that to his right was the familiar door opening to the corral, now glaring with the morning light. He attempted to raise his head and felt a searing pain in the muscles of his neck. He rolled his eyes downward and saw that he was lying in his sleeping bag.

Turning his head just a little allowed him to see Doc Smith quietly rolling up a sleeping bag. He could see the strong bands of muscles in the lanky veterinarian's forearms. Then he allowed his eyes to turn to Old Black, lying there helpless with tubes in his neck and a foreleg, carrying fluids from two bottles hanging from the structure above him.

He moved tentatively and found that he hurt from the balls of his feet all the way up through his thighs. His arms and shoulders fairly burned as he brought his elbows back and underneath him, first just one, then the other, to prop himself up. Trying to sit up sent more pains across his chest and abdomen.

Doc Smith stepped over and held out his hand. "Good morning, Jim. Let me give you a boost. Sore, huh? I'm not a bit surprised. Let's take off your shirt." He picked up a bottle of Absorbine.

"Do you recall your bath last night?" he asked.

267

Jim shook his head lethargically.

"I didn't think you would. You were out on your feet. The only thing you said was, 'I want to sleep in the barn with Old Black.' Your mom gave you a warm bath and then rubbed you down with Absorbine. I don't know if I'm right or not, but I believe it helps the blood carry away the debris from overworked muscles. You had as tough a workout yesterday as a body could possibly have, and you're going to be sore as a body can be for some time before it begins to let up."

The vet frowned as he examined Jim's right shoulder, badly bruised by the sledgehammer recoil of six powerful shotgun blasts. The bruises ranged from blue to purple to black tinged with a greenish cast, and had spread over the entire right side of his chest and down his arm to his elbow. "I believe we'd better have a doctor look at this. I'll speak to your mother," he said. He splashed Absorbine on his hands and gently massaged Jim's shoulders, back, neck, and chest. After fanning him dry with his shirt—the icy coolness was the only pleasant sensation Jim could immediately recall—Doc Smith helped him get back into it.

"Now if you were Old Black there, we wouldn't need any Absorbine. We're going to flush the bad stuff from his muscles with special fluids." He looked up at the floor of the hay loft, at the massive timber joists, noting with satisfaction that a stout rod ran through two joists. From the rod hung a clevis, a ready-made hanger for his five-gallon bottle. "The fluids he lost yesterday are being replaced through those tubes. We're going to try to get him up this afternoon, and if we do, we might get him to eat a little bit."

Jim stretched his arms and slowly rotated his hands, grimacing as he did so. Doc Smith smiled grimly. "Sore everywhere. I know, Jim. One time a guy told me about being so sore and bruised and swollen that there wasn't enough slack skin left on his body to allow him to close his eyes."

Jim grinned. He blinked his eyes and squeezed them tightly shut. At least his eyelids worked. Doc Smith applied Absorbine to his legs and massaged them ever so gently, watching his expression for clues to how he was tolerating it.

"It's going to hurt like blazes to move, but you have to work those sore muscles. Exercise pumps extra blood through them and flushes out the worn-out stuff. But don't overdo it. Get gentle exercise for very short periods." Doc Smith extended his hand. Jim took it and allowed himself to be pulled to his feet. For a short time he stood stooped like an old man, holding onto the hay bales for support, then he took a few steps, moving with great difficulty. He gave out a low whistle, revealing his astonishment at his condition.

"You put in your day of days, yesterday Jim," Doc Smith said.

The events of yesterday were still a tangle of submerged thoughts in the back of his mind, and he kept them there. Doc Smith had said Old Black would live, so he *would* live. That had to mean he would become strong again, and gaze merrily at Jim with his big dark eyes, and push Jim with his head when he felt playful, and eat grain heartily, and run wide open down the hill to the bottom when he wanted to, and graze the very best grass, and drink from the cold sweet water of the creek any time he was thirsty. He looked at the pitiful horse with all the longing a little boy could ever muster.

Doc Smith handed him a juice jug.

"Water and lemon juice, with some minerals added," he said. "You lost a lot of fluids yesterday, like Old Black did, and you have to replace them. Drink often, and a lot. Your mother will make some more of that when it's gone."

He drank. Then he said, still somewhat hoarse, "Doc Smith, I sure thank you for coming out yesterday and taking care of Old Black. I know he would've died if it wasn't for you. Now do you think he'll get all right?"

"Yes," said the veterinarian. "Yes, I do. But I'm taking no chances. I'm going to call A&M and talk to one of their doctors who's had more experience with this kind of thing than I have—just to make sure I'm doing everything that can be done."

At the sound of a vehicle driving up, Doc Smith walked outside. Jim moved about slowly, trying to get his body to operate. His eyes fell on Sam, lying almost camouflaged on the hay near Old Black's head. Her chin was flat on the hay, forelegs extended ahead and hind legs held out behind. Her eyes were sad and fixed on Jim, her brow wrinkled in a display of concern. Jim breathed deeply—which was itself painful—and worked his arms slowly across his body, extending them resolutely as far as he could against the pain. He could not believe that his body could be so totally sore, so tired in every muscle and joint.

He went to Old Black and kneeled by his side. He stroked him on the jaw and on the neck, being careful to avoid the IV needle. Old Black is breathing easier, much easier, he thought with relief. His eyes were open and clear, and he seemed to be watching Jim.

For the first time, Jim wondered what the outcome of yesterday was. Had Sheriff Martinez survived the ordeal? He *had* to—he just

had to. Jim thought of how concerned he'd been about Old Black's condition in spite of his own awful wounds. He massaged the horse's exposed ear with the heel of his hand for a long time. He wanted to believe Doc Smith's words of encouragement, but he still had an awful feeling in the pit of his stomach.

He sat down on a bale of hay and gazed at Old Black. Sam got up and came to him. She sidled up with her head low, moving slowly, humbly, somehow sensing that some grave thing was happening and seeming to know that Jim was very sad about it. She rolled her big brown eyes up until they looked into his. The worry wrinkles in her forehead undulated slightly. He patted her head. Then he leaned down, took her face in his hands, and held her nose against his cheek. In a voice that revealed his crushing sadness, he said, "Old Black is real sick, Sam, and it looks like you've figured that out. Thanks for feeling so sorry for him. He'll appreciate it too when he finds out."

He stood up and slowly eased out of the barn into the corral, feeling great pain at every step, supporting himself on hay bales, the doorway, posts and anything else handy. He wondered how he could ever move enough to work away the soreness.

His eye fell on the sculptured bottom of the feed trough that Old Black had eaten a small treat from only yesterday morning before they'd left for their ride. The day at Klanke's Mill seemed like it was ages ago. How could yesterday seem so far back in the past?

He stood in the shadow of the barn's roof and squinted at the sunlit brightness of the day. To a boy steeped in misery, a bright sunny day was somehow out of the order of things, against the grain. This kind of day seemed to flippantly dismiss the scene in the barn: the horse lying quiet and still, the bottles, the tubes draping to connect with the shiny needles protruding from his veins.

He moved slowly, deliberately, stretching his sore muscles with care. He arrived at Charlotte's web and saw that it was a glistening spectacle of elaborately woven silk, decorated with thousands of tiny beads of crystal dew. Its opulence struck him as an arrogant flaunting of Charlotte's own well-being in the face of Old Black's grave misery. He lashed out with an arm and wiped the web away. Instantly, his heart was flooded with keen remorse. Adding to his distress, he spied Charlotte glaring at him from behind the roof support brace that had anchored one side of her web before he'd torn it down.

He turned away from the indignant spider, dropped down on the feed trough and sat staring at the ground. He wished he could become unconscious and come back to life when Old Black was his old self again.

Sam laid her head on his leg. Jim scratched the base of her ears. He thought that if he could read Charlotte's mind, like he could read Sam's mind through her sad expressions and comforting actions, he would probably discover that *she* was sorry about Old Black, too. She couldn't stop building webs just because he was sick, or she would starve. He resolved that he would catch some flies for her—especially while she was building a new web—to make up for his vandalism.

"It near about made me sick to watch that mangy cur dog crow on TV about how he saved Sheriff Martinez," said Ruby with uncharacteristic vehemence. Her eyes were burning with anger. She had come early to the Bradley's house with a casserole of scrambled eggs, potatoes and ham. It was in the oven. "They wasn't a word said about brave little Jim and his brave horse. It near about made me cry—well, I lie, it *did* make me cry," she said under her breath. "It gives me the shivers just to think about it. And that cur dog almost was sheriff hisself." She stopped dead still a moment, her face an expression of fear. "And if Sheriff Mike dies, that fat snake will *be* sheriff sure enough. Merciful Lord, please, oh please, get our sheriff well," she pleaded.

Oscar's face displayed the pained expression he got when he wished Ruby would refrain from criticizing white people in the presence of whites.

Ruby saw it. "He would be a mangy cur dog if he was black," she snapped. "Or green or any other color."

Norma was making no attempt at concealing her anguish from these dearest friends; her lined and haggard face was one that Ruby had never seen before. The waiting for Jim to be delivered home last night had been a period of torture without equal in her life. The relief that came with the word that he was alive, and the assurances that he wasn't hurt, wore thin as the hours passed with her Jim still out there somewhere, and his beloved horse down and unable to get up.

Then the sight of him—my God, she thought, never had she seen anybody so covered with blood and gore, and carrying a burden of despair that would overwhelm a strong man, much less a small boy. And they'd said he wasn't *hurt*?

She knew at once that he *was* hurt, badly wounded in his tender little heart, where he was most vulnerable. Her sorrow was all the deeper because she could not let him see the extent of the consuming anguish that she felt.

How glad she was that Ruby and Oscar were there, rocks of strength, of *sensible* compassion. And, oh, what a release it was to be able to go into her bedroom, close the door and cry her heart out and come out not caring if they saw her red swollen eyes. She knew that Ruby and Oscar had suffered through grievous physical injuries and insults to their own children. So there was nobody Norma needed more urgently now than Ruby Jackson.

"What did the news say, Ruby?" she asked.

"Channel Six had the most of it. They showed the whole place burning up, everything that would burn anyways. And helicopters buzzin' around and around. And in every picture they showed, there was that Swagger waddlin' around with a seegar in his mouth and acting important. He lied—oh, how that white man told one bald-faced lie after another, telling how he did it all by hisself."

Ruby moved about the kitchen with a towel in her hand. She looked for even the smallest clean-up jobs to occupy herself, shaking her head at the memory of the news program.

"After Mrs. Thatcher from the Sheriff's office talked to you, Mrs. Bradley, she thought I might ought to know what was happening, in case you needed some support—a shoulder, so to speak. That was even before a living soul got out there to help poor little Jim. Mrs. Thatcher told me Jim rescued the sheriff and had him safe and sound in some woods, lyin' by the police car. So we knowed it was Jim that done the life-saving way before Swagger even got there.

"But there he is with that Rambo stuff going on in the background, telling them TV people *he* pulled the sheriff from out of the well, and when they asked him how he done it, he swelled up and said, 'Well, I commandeered a horse.'" She sniffed indignantly. "Mrs. Thatcher knowed it was Old Black that pulled Sheriff Martinez from the well. She told me so, and I know she told everybody else that would listen. She said Old Black was plumb tuckered out, maybe even wind-broke, and that Doc Smith was going out to see about him. Oscar said if that Swagger done the rescue, why would he use a horse when they got all them helicopters that could've plucked him out without a how-de-do? And he's right."

Matt, sitting quietly as he tended to do in times of crisis, reflected with approval on Oscar's acute reasoning. He also considered the ignorance of news people, so many of them complacent idiots without as much common sense as Oscar had under the nail of his little finger; Oscar had grown up curious; reporters seemed to have no curiosity. A primary job requirement for news people, he thought—and not for the first time by a long shot—was that applicants must be able to demonstrate that their minds were black holes from which no intelligence, however innocently acquired, could escape.

Ruby was still talking softly. "Then the national news had the same story and the same pictures. I was sick to my stomach. You wait until Sheriff Mike gets well, he'll fix that Swagger."

JIM HAD GONE BACK INTO THE BARN AND WAS SITTING on a hay bale beside Old Black when Oscar joined him. Swinging a bale to a convenient place where he could see Jim's face and still be out of the way, he sat down on it. They watched silently as Doc Smith and his assistant, Lonnie, hung a large plastic bottle from the clevis overhead. Doc Smith attached a needle to the end of the tube and deftly inserted the needle into a vein in Old Black's neck. With his free hand he stroked the vein hard in the direction of the needle, and when he saw blood coloring the clear liquid in the tube he released the clamp on the tube.

After completing this work, he took his rolled-up sleeping bag and put it aside on the hay. Jim felt good about his doing this because it was like a sign that he would be coming back tonight.

"I'm real encouraged by Old Black's improvement during the night, Jim," the vet said. "His breathing is a lot more regular, and I'm very pleased with the sounds in his chest. He's watching what's going on with alert eyes. He still won't be moving much, because he's resting. He was about as tired as a horse can get. But he's resting easy, I think. The bottles need to be replaced about two, so I'll be back before then. If anything changes in his condition that you think needs my attention, call me. My office will be able to get me on a minute's notice.

"Those fluids we're giving him will purge his muscles. So when he starts moving around he'll have to be watched close to make sure the tube doesn't get hung up on anything. But I don't expect him to move much in the next couple of days unless we ask him to. If a needle does get pulled out, don't worry about it. Just move it out of his way and shut off the fluid flow. You do it like this," he said, demonstrating in pantomime. "Call me, and I'll put in a new needle when I come. And if a needle gets in a bind and the tube is pulling on it, just pull the needle out of the vein and put the tube out of his way. And cut off the fluid flow."

He patted Jim on the shoulder. "You going to be okay?"

"Yes, sir," Jim said, getting to his feet. "And thanks, Doc Smith. Thanks for everything. For coming out there, for staying here all night, for everything."

The vet nodded. "Jim, you and Old Black performed with battlefield heroism yesterday. I'm glad you asked for me when you talked to Millie Thatcher, so I could maybe ease Old Black's suffering for what he did. I think he's going to be just fine. He'll just have to have some time to recuperate, but I know you'll give him all the time he needs."

Lonnie, who evidently had brought the carboy that was now dripping flushing medicine into Old Black's neck vein, had spoken only when he and Doc Smith discussed the procedures they were doing. Now Doc Smith said, "Lonnie here tells me he called the hospital this morning and learned that Sheriff Martinez underwent surgery on his leg last night. He's in intensive care and we don't know whether he's conscious or not, but the doctors are confident he'll make a good recovery."

Relief flooded Jim's face, and Oscar's. "Praise the Lord," Oscar said in a barely audible voice. Jim's voice was stronger now. "Boy, Doc Smith, I hope Old Black understood what you just said. But if he don't get it now, he will when he sees the sheriff. Boy! Sheriff Martinez is gonna make it too. Now *everybody's* going to be all right."

Doc Smith emerged from the barn just as Matt came up. Doc Smith repeated his prediction that Old Black would be back on his feet soon, maybe for a few minutes as early as that very afternoon. He looked at Matt, paused in thought for a moment. "Matt," he said, "did you get any word on Jim's saddle? I know how he cherished that saddle, because it was Buck Jones's, and no doubt an expensive professional roping saddle."

Matt looked puzzled. "No," he began. "with everything that happened, it never occurred to me that we didn't have it. It didn't come in the truck with Old Black?"

Doc Smith shook his head. He took Matt by the arm and leaned close to him. "Lonnie just told me—" he began in a confidential tone as they walked slowly toward his car. Matt had a grim expression on his face as he gave the veterinarian a pat on the back before he entered his car, told him to leave the gate open, and waved goodbye. Then he strode to the barn and went to Old Black. He listened to his breathing, nodded approval and sat down with Jim. After expressing his confidence about Old Black's recovery, he said, "I have to go to Brentwood, Jim, to the sheriff's office. I may be a while. Will you be around, Oscar? Good. And thanks. See you both when I get back."

Matt walked swiftly from the barn and broke into a jog as he headed for the house. He ignored the steps and sprang to the porch. Oscar and Jim were watching as he came out within seconds and loped to his car with Sam dashing beside him.

"Not this time, Sam," he said. Then he changed his mind, opened the door and stood back, letting her leap inside to ride with him, as she often did. He slammed the door hard. Tires spun as he departed.

Oscar raised his eyebrows and he and Jim exchanged curious glances.

After the sounds of Matt's urgent departure had died away, Oscar, in his meticulous, thoughtful way, began stuffing his pipe. "Jimmy, me'n you talked one time when you was wishing you was grown up. And you promised me you would think, and think regular, about how important it is to *know* it's wonderful bein' a kid while you *are* one. And not waitin' till you're grown and lookin' back and sayin' to yourself 'I wish I'd of known how wonderful life was back then, during the good old days.' Remember us talking about that?"

Jim nodded solemnly. "I remember. And I've been thinking about it, Mr. Jackson, just like I promised I would. I really have thought about it, and many a time, too."

"I didn't think for a minute you wasn't a man of your word, Jimmy," Oscar said. "Your momma don't ordinarily have worries, like a lot of mommas have, because of you bein' the fine boy you are. So she was sort of behind on worryin' practice—until yesterday evenin', that is. But she ain't behind no more. She got caught up quick, and now she's way ahead. I never *seen* such a tormented momma."

He examined his pipe. "Yeah. She was plenty worried. She didn't go to bawlin' and fall all to pieces, but I could see that awful dread in her eyes, dreadin' that her world done come all apart, she love her little boy so. And Ruby saw it too, the very same thing. She told me on the side, 'I ain't about to leave Mrs. Bradley here without she has a mother's hand to hold.'

"This morning your momma looks like she aged ten years overnight. She has a new worry, now—Old Black. Because of what Old Black means to you, and to her, too. But she's worried mostly over how his bein' sick has got you tore up. And she can't stand it. Your poor momma has took a beating, and she's still taking it. You're the only person on this good earth that can fix your momma's broke heart, and I'm gonna tell you how. That is, if you want to hear it."

He looked at Jim, who was looking directly, curiously, into his eyes. "I knew you would," Oscar said with a complacent smile. "You're a special boy, Jim. I heard Mr. Richter tellin' it in the store one time that you're as good a hand on a farm as a grown man, and I said he's sure right about that. And you're a darned *kind* boy, too."

Jim grinned weakly and his face reddened at hearing such a compliment. Oscar patted his shoulder and looked at him with open admiration.

"Jimmy, when Mr. Richter talked about how you worked like a man, he really meant it, but he didn't know the half of it—none of us did. There wasn't no way we could've knowed until the *big* test come along. I doubt there's one grown man in Winchester County that would've got the job done, and saved Sheriff Martinez like you did.

"The shape you was in when you come home—shoot, I never seen a boy so fagged out and beat up. And Old Black here, a horse as stout as him, done plumb in."

Oscar was figuring out how to deliver his real message. "Look how easy Old Black is breathin' and how he looks at you with a bright eye. He's gettin' better, Jimmy. Doc Smith wouldn't of said he's on his way back if he wasn't. So you should be trustin' that the Lord has been bringing Old Black back to health nice and easy, and that should be a cause for you bein' happy and full of joy."

Oscar paused and gazed at the horse with a sympathetic expression, but a confident one.

"And we just found out that your heroic work wasn't for nothin'! The sheriff's gonna live. Even without thinking about his wife and kids, who deserve our thoughts, or the sheriff hisself, think what his staying alive means to this county. And specially to me and Ruby, your little friend Alexandra and all her cousins and aunts and uncles, Duffie and Rufus, and hundreds—even *thousands* of others. We can hold our heads up and go down the road and not worry about bein' picked on, or worse.

"So you got a lot of cause for being proud today, Jimmy, proud and happy and full of joy in your heart."

Oscar looked over his shoulder, through the open double doors to the farmhouse. "Ruby brought breakfast over, and you need to go eat. Whether you feel like eatin' or not, you have to eat.

"Your momma's in there as sad as she could be unless you was in a pine box in the living room, laid out in your Sunday best. What would she give, you suppose, to see a smile on her little boy's face? A king's ransom couldn't buy what she needs. How high do you think your momma's heart would fly if you went running in there and gave her a tight hug and the biggest smile you can scrape up, and told her that Old Black's on the mend, that any minute now he's liable to get to his feet? How high, do you suppose?"

Oscar waved a hand toward the east, in the direction of Klanke's Mill. "And you got a story to tell, Jimmy. But you haven't said a word about what happened. And the sheriff is still out of touch. So nobody knows nothin' about the biggest thing that's ever happened in Winchester County. Oh, some of us know a little *piece* of the story, and them that listened to the news on TV knows a phony story. But just think, only two people in the world know what really happened. One's still out of his wits, and the other one's sitting on that bale of hay right there." The stem of his pipe was pointed at Jim. "So get yourself in the house and put your momma's mind to rest; then have some of Ruby's good breakfast, and start telling your story."

"MOM," JIM CALLED, TROTTING STIFFLY UP the steps. "Mo-omm." The screen door slammed behind him. He ran to his mother, grabbed her around the waist with both arms and hugged her tight, his face upturned and his eyes, his happy eyes, looking into hers. "Old Black's going to be okay, Mom. He's breathing good and looking at me straight, like he's about to get up."

Her eyes, which Jim noted with pain were red and surrounded by dark circles, were swimming with tears. But they were bright with happiness now, and a smile broke out on her face. "Oh Jim, I'm so happy. So very, very happy." She hugged him and lifted him an inch off the floor.

She stooped down and took his face in her hands, their eyes inches apart. Jim felt the sweetest pang of joy pass through his whole body as his mother's face reflected the relief that was still lifting her spirits.

"Mom," he said softly. "Would you like for me to tell you what happened?"

Ruby, unnoticed in the glory of the moment, stood relaxed and quiet with her hands clasped in front of her. Her face was beaming with an enormous smile, and her head was tilted slightly back and cocked to one side, projecting a total contentment of body and soul.

"Yes, I sure would like to hear the story. You can tell it while you eat this wonderful breakfast Mrs. Jackson brought us this morning."

Jim hadn't even noticed Ruby. "Hi, Mrs. Jackson," he said softly.

"Let me call Oscar in," Norma said. "He'd like to hear it, too."

THAT AFTERNOON, DOC SMITH RETURNED with a sling which, when placed around Old Black and suspended from overhead, would allow them to help him get to his feet. With him was a woman he introduced as Dr. Diana Coleman, a veterinarian with the Department of Large Animal Medicine and Surgery at Texas A&M University.

"Dr. Coleman," Doc Smith explained to the Bradleys, "has had much more experience with horses that have undergone abnormal physical stress than I have, and I've asked her to assist me, to make sure I'm not overlooking anything. I've also asked her to explain to all of us just what to expect during Old Black's recovery."

In a pleasant and compellingly professional voice, Dr. Coleman explained that Dr. Smith had done everything that could possibly have been done up to this point, and that she didn't believe he needed her assistance. But she was glad to respond, she said, to help in any way she could.

She gestured to the plastic carboy hanging from the loft joists. "Each carboy will last about fifteen to twenty hours. He'll have to keep getting the fluid for about three days. Dr. Smith said Old Black will lick at whatever is put into his mouth, so we can give him some anti-inflammatory medicine by mouth. It's a paste. That will be your job, Jim, and when you can't be here, it can be done by another responsible person."

Oscar raised his hand, expressing his wish to volunteer.

"The fluid will wash the breakdown products from the muscles through his kidneys, so his urine will be reddish brown during this time—about three days. The discoloration is caused by the normal elimination of products sluffed off by overworked muscles. Some other medication will be added to the fluid bags, so you'll notice a funny odor to Old Black's breath. Don't let that worry you." She turned to Jim.

"Are you going to be here with him? Fine, fine. His lower legs should be wrapped to keep them from swelling up. We'll show you just how, Jim. And we'll show you how to massage the hard, tight muscles. I might even have you spray them with water a couple of times a day."

She took a few steps around with a hand to her chin, the other on her hip, thinking. "Not all veterinarians would do this, but Dr. Smith and I have agreed that since the horse is a gelding we'll give him a sedative and blood vessel dilator to increase the flow of blood to the muscles and feet."

She had been looking at Old Black. Now she turned to face the

Bradleys, looking from one to the other. "Here's what I believe we can expect. After two or three days of fluid therapy, the urine should no longer be discolored and Old Black should show some perkiness, moving about here in the barn. Then we can discontinue all IVs. I see there's a pasture behind the barn. Can he get to it from the corral? Good. You could let him have free access to the pasture. If he wants to stay in the barn, let him. If he wants to stroll about and graze, let him do that. I would put him up here in the barn every night, mainly because this is where he has received some intensive, loving care. He'll sense that, and feel secure here.

"The paste—we'll continue that for another, oh, maybe five days. Seven days from now, he should be hand-walked for fifteen minutes at a time, every day until Dr. Smith says he's moving enough on his own about the place. He'll lose some weight, but that will be regained in a month or so. After, ummm, maybe five weeks, if he's coming along fine, you could begin some light riding, Jim, a little at a time."

She smiled. "Dr. Smith told me about what a success the two of you have been in the horse shows. It's entirely possible that he could return to showing in about three or four months."

Jim looked almost gleeful. In a small voice, his eyes on Old Black, he said, "I don't care, even if it takes six months, as long as he gets all right." He gave Dr. Coleman a look of gratitude and smiled at Doc Smith. "Duffie can walk him when I'm not here, can't he?" he asked his father.

Oscar was the first to answer. "Shoot, *I* can sure walk him, and I'll make it my responsibility. Do *me* as much good as Old Black."

THE VERY NEXT DAY, OLD BLACK GOT TO HIS FEET all on his own. By midweek he was making astonishing improvement. On Friday, Jim pitched in helping Duffie and Rufus rebuild a stretch of fence down by the Richter swamp. He showed them where he and Buddy had seen the big snake, and described it again. Duffie, who was standing in a way that gave him a view of the barn, looked up and pointed out a man walking down the hill in their direction. When he got close Jim could see a camera hanging from a strap around his neck.

The man came up to Jim and introduced himself: Paul Hardesty, a reporter for the *Brentwood Banner*. He produced a small notebook from one of the many pockets in the vest he wore and asked if Jim would provide some information on the incident last Saturday at Klanke's Mill. Jim nodded weakly, and Hardesty propped a foot on the bed of the old fence-fixing trailer and started right in.

"Jim, was Chief Deputy Swagger on the scene at any time that you were there—I mean before the rescue force arrived?"

"No sir."

"Swagger *says* he commandeered a horse. Do you know whose horse Swagger might have used, if he did indeed commandeer a horse? It wasn't your horse, I take it."

"No sir. I mean yes, sir, it was Old Black that pulled the sheriff out, but it was just him and me and the sheriff."

Hardesty nodded while he wrote. "I went out there, and it's quite a drive into the place. You have to know where you're going, the way it's grown up. How did you and, uh," he looked at his notebook, "how did you and Old Black happen to be out there, and how did you discover the sheriff was in the well?"

Jim explained his adventure route, how he'd stumbled onto Klanke's Mill by accident, and how he'd insisted that Old Black approach the well after he smelled blood. "But I didn't know he smelled blood yet. I just thought he was being skittish."

"Do you know what time you first found Sheriff Martinez?"

"Not for sure, but I figure it was about two."

"And you never saw Deputy Swagger."

"No, sir. He wasn't there to see," Jim said with finality.

"Jim, Swagger claims he shot two of the men as they were closing in on you and Sheriff Martinez, thereby saving both of your lives. After he'd already rescued the sheriff from the well, that is. Is that so?"

"No, sir. I shot at the criminals with the sheriff's shotgun, and I hit the one named Brad, and the one named Winnie. I knew that because after I finished shooting, Brad hollered to the one named Red, and Red answered back, calling him Brad. Brad said he was hit, and was bleeding all over. And he said Winnie looked like he was dying, so I guess I shot him too. But you could tell Red was running away and wasn't going to help anybody. Some more shooting went on around the gin and the house, but that was later, after the helicopters came. And it wasn't even close to where me and Sheriff Martinez and Black were."

Hardesty said, "I'll bet the sheriff's shotgun kicked a lot, didn't it Jim?"

Jim grimaced sheepishly and his left hand went instinctively to his right shoulder, pressing the area gingerly. "Yes, sir."

Hardesty laughed. "I remember once when I was your age, maybe a couple of years older, my grandpa let me shoot his twelve-gauge and it knocked me flat. Put a *big* bruise on my shoulder." His eyebrows went up. "And my grandpa's gun wasn't loaded with those powerful new shotgun shells like the sheriff's was." He took an empty shell from his pocket and turned it to read on the tube, glancing at Jim. "I found six of these on the ground in the woods where you were holed up. It says, 'Winchester three-inch Double XX Magnum triple ought buck.' They kick too hard for a lot of grown men. Did you get any bruises from that shotgun?"

"Yes, sir."

"Could I see?"

Jim hesitated, then unbuttoned his shirt and drew his right arm from the sleeve. From the middle of his chest, over his shoulder, and down to his elbow was the color of a purple plum, with streaks going on down his forearm. In places, the color gave way to a ghastly greenish black with pale yellow streaks. His mother had worried about blood poisoning but a doctor said it would be all right.

Rufus and Duffie looked on, shocked at the sight of Jim's bruises. They exchanged disturbed expressions.

Hardesty had his camera in his hands, making adjustments. "Do you mind if I take a picture of your arm, Jim?"

Jim hurriedly slipped his shirt back on and buttoned it. "My mom would have to say about that. I don't think I want a picture."

Hardesty did not push the issue. Fastening the cover back onto the camera, he said almost casually, "There was something about a saddle. Doc Smith told me here Saturday night right after they got your horse bedded down that they'd stopped near the well to get your saddle, but a man picked it up and walked off with it. Being in such a hurry to get your horse home, Doc Smith didn't pursue it, expecting it would be returned to you. I asked Deputy Swagger about it on Sunday morning, and he said he was holding a saddle as evidence." Hardesty put an emphasis on the word *evidence* and paused momentarily. "But it wasn't your saddle, he said. I asked whose it was but he didn't answer. Did you ever get your saddle back?"

A steely smile crept across Jim's face. "There wasn't any other saddle. Mine was the only one." He glanced toward the barn. "My dad heard Deputy Swagger had it, and he was suspicious that he planned to keep it. That was Sunday. Dad got in his car and took off, and when he came back he had my saddle. It's in the tack room." His smile broadened. "I saw blood on his shirt and his fists were skint up. Doc Smith had already brought my lariat home, so now I have my saddle and my lariat back."

Hardesty flashed an expression of honest surprise. "Did your father say what happened?" he asked.

"No, sir."

After a wait—the kind of tactical period of silence used by police and other interrogators to create discomfort which usually inspires the subject to talk—Hardesty saw that he would have to break the silence himself. "Well, what do you think happened?"

Jim shook his head and showed a blank expression. "I don't know," he said.

The reporter cackled with unrestrained amusement. "Deputy Swagger's face shows some definite signs of a serious physical encounter, his left arm is in a sling. And he's refused to answer questions about the cause of his injuries. I'm not implying that your father—but if I was, I would offer my most sincere gratitude. One last question. Did you see any of the TV news about the event at Klanke's Mill?"

"No, sir."

"Hmmm. There seems to be some large discrepancies between the news accounts and what you tell me, and even between what could have been at all possible. Deputy Swagger, talking to the television cameras, gave himself credit for killing every one of the criminals, said he crept up on Brad Lewis and another member of the gang as they were stalking the sheriff with a knife, so he shot them. And, he produced an old, rusty machete."

Jim did not respond.

"Jim, could Deputy Swagger have been out there and you didn't recognize him?"

Jim thought a few seconds. "If he had been there, and had come up before I shot at the criminals and used up all the shells, I would have shot him." Hardesty stiffened at the flat tone, the finality in the boy's voice. Jim looked up at him with no expression whatever and said simply, "Yes, sir, if he had come in where we were I would have shot him. Sheriff Martinez said for me to shoot anybody that came in those woods and wasn't calling out to us so we'd know who they were."

Hardesty was writing non-stop. Jim thought of something important. "Why don't you ask Sheriff Martinez? He was unconscious some, but it was him that told me to shoot them. And that's what I did. I was just about to shoot before they shot at us first."

Hardesty looked up with surprise. "They shot at you?"

"Yes, sir. A boom like a shotgun, and leaves came down out of the trees over us. That's when Sheriff Martinez said I better shoot or it would be too late."

"No kidding. Jim, Sheriff Martinez hasn't been able to see any-body, so we can't ask him anything quite yet. They operated on his leg and on his head, too. He was unconscious until Tuesday and has been out of it ever since—so up to now, the only story we have is Swagger's. Doc Smith says he arrived with the medics and of course he couldn't know what went on before he got there. But he insisted that your horse had to be the only one there. He said your horse had darn near killed himself pulling the sheriff out of that well by himself."

"And dragging the sled to the woods," said Jim. "That's where Old Black really got hurt, pulling the sled after he was all done in."

Hardesty cocked his head and raised his eyebrows in a gesture of fresh understanding. "That piece of corrugated roofing metal lying in the woods, with all the blood on it. Was that your sled? That's how you got the sheriff from the well to the woods?"

Jim nodded.

"Funny, Jim. You said the criminals fired a shot. Swagger said no guns were recovered. Five criminals were out there, supposedly so dangerous they all had to be killed, and no guns were found—*reported* found, anyway. And Swagger says the sheriff's shotgun wasn't on the scene, either. He says the sheriff evidently didn't have it with him. Yet you know you shot it, and I have the empty shells from it."

Jim's only expression was a gradual squinting of his eyes, an expression of disbelief to a discerning examiner, and Hardesty was a discerning examiner.

Hardesty stood chewing on his pen, squinting up at the trees, deep in thought. Then he looked down. "How's he doing? Is Old Black recovering all right?"

Jim smiled, and his body seemed to relax. "Yes, sir. He's coming along okay. Ain't that amazing?"

Hardesty displayed a pleased smile. "Yes, it truly is amazing. Jim, is there anything notable that I could write about your horse?" He laughed, then reprimanded himself. "As if rescuing the sheriff from certain death wasn't notable enough. What I *meant* was, has he done anything *else* that was notable? You ride him in the youth shows?"

"Oh, sure, he's plenty notable. Old Black's the world's champion calf-roping horse. He has the record time of eight-point-six seconds. We bought him from Mr. Buck Jones, a famous rodeo cowboy. Old Black is a registered Quarter Horse and he has some Flying Bob in him. We win our share of the competition events, and Old Black's the devil to beat in reining and western riding classes."

Hardesty was smiling hugely long before Jim had finished, his pencil flying. "Well, he certainly *is* notable, isn't he. Flying Bob, eh? I guess Flying Bob would be proud that one of his offspring became the world-champion calf roping horse and then went on to become a life-saving hero. Yes, he would. Thanks, Jim, for the interview. And a personal thanks for saving our sheriff. He's a good man, and it would have been a tragedy for the county if we had lost him." He held out his hand and they shook. Hardesty walked away briskly.

Jim went to the little fence-fixing trailer and sat down on its low bed. Rufus and Duffie, who had hung on every word of the interview, stood almost at attention beside it.

Finally, Duffie said reverently, "Good-gosh-a-mighty, Jimmy. Me and Rufus didn't know your shoulder was so awful beat up. Might-near petrified, it looked to me like. I heard those big hot-loaded twelve-gauge shells will fair stomp on a grown man. Like gettin' kicked by a mule, I heard."

Jim's hand went unconsciously to his injured shoulder. "It didn't seem like it hurt when I shot the gun. And I didn't ever notice it hurting much afterward." He grinned wryly. "No more than I hurt everywhere else."

With a grave expression on his face, Duffie walked up to Jim and extended his right hand. Jim got up from the trailer with a look of wonder and shook Duffie's hand.

"We didn't know much, Jimmy. Only what they told Miss Ruby from the sheriff office. So we didn't know you done the whole thing single-handed, and killed two cold-blooded murdering outlaws, to boot. You're the only genuine hero I ever knowed, and I'm right proud to be able to say I know you, even more than I was already."

Rufus stepped up; he shook hands with Jim silently.

Jim's face was red with embarrassment, but he was touched. "Well, *thanks*," he said. "But Old Black is the one that did it. He'll appreciate a pat." He looked around for some means of changing the subject. "We better get this fence built," he said.

CHAPTER 26

Alate morning sun shone on Sheriff Mike Martinez as he walked briskly up the sidewalk to the sheriff's office. Responding to shouted greetings, he smiled and waved to several people before he went in. He was back to his old physical fitness routine of workouts, competing in weekly practical pistol matches—a sport with athletic obstacles that put much younger men to the test—horseback riding, and playing in impromptu volley ball games in the city park. He claimed that he was in better physical shape now than he was before that day at Klanke's Mill three months ago.

When he breezed into the building he was not surprised to find the entire force assembled—he had called for a meeting of all hands. It was his first since Klanke's Mill, and every member of the department knew that the rescue force had so badly bungled its mission that the sheriff was lucky to be alive. An accounting had been expected, and there was little doubt in anyone's mind that this was going to be it. Martinez was usually pleasant enough, even if his general demeanor was serious and no-nonsense. But today he was surprising those in his presence with a rare air of joviality. He greeted each person individually, instead of his usual collective wave and a "Hi, everyone." Most curious of all was a light and sportive exchange that he indulged in with deputies Swagger and Grimshaw. It was evident from their awkward responses that they were as surprised as anyone; they were not prepared for conversation on such an amiable level with Sheriff Martinez.

The other deputies and the three administrative employees looked on with curiosity. It was generally believed that Swagger had delayed the task force to Old Klanke to allow him to have a television crew along to record himself in action. Martinez was certain in his mind that Swagger delayed the operation, hoping that he might die from loss of blood or be murdered by the men in the boat that was returning, which would have opened the door to Swagger's ascendancy to the office of Sheriff. It was widely known that Martinez loathed Swagger, and many wondered why he kept him on.

Martinez looked over the assembled group. Some were standing at ease while others perched on desktops. Only Millie Thatcher sat in a chair, in front of her battery of telephones, radio gear, computer monitors, and television screens. "Will you folks excuse me for a moment while I tend to a matter involving law and order, and life and liberty in Winchester County?" He said to Swagger, "Dilbert, come in here, please."

He turned on his heel and strode into his office with Swagger slowly following. When the deputy finally entered the room, Martinez was standing with his hands in his pockets, looking out of the window. Without turning around, he said firmly, "Close the door."

Swagger did so and stood with exaggerated casualness in front of Martinez's desk. The sheriff walked around it and in one quick move grabbed Swagger's shirt collar and slammed him backward onto the desk. As if by magic, Martinez's cocked Colt forty-five was in his hand and jammed so far into Swagger's mouth that the ejection port was barely visible. Swagger's eyes crossed as he attempted to focus on the pistol.

The sheriff's left hand reached across Swagger's chest and ripped the badge off his shirt. "You are no longer with us, Mr. Swagger," he said. Even without the pistol, Martinez's cold, expressionless face and the total absence of any emotion in his voice would have been terrorizing to Swagger. "In fact, you no longer reside in Winchester County. This is Saturday. After the stroke of midnight tomorrow night, every member of this force will have orders to bring you in to me if your face is seen inside the county line."

His eyes went from Swagger's eyes to his pistol. When Martinez thumbed the safety off, Swagger heard the metallic sound through his jawbones, as clear as if it was a hammer striking an anvil. He knew from the amount of force Martinez was applying that the grip safety was compressed.

He knew, too, that Martinez regularly competed in organized practical shooting with several clubs under the banner of the U.S. Practical Shooting Association. Swagger had once accompanied Martinez to a U.S.P.S.A.-sponsored shooting match, but he was astonished to discover that all but the rankest beginners among these civilian shooters were expert gunslingers. Swagger had been humiliated to have his own lack of gun-handling skills so conspicuously exposed and he'd never gone back. Martinez, he knew, had earned Master classification in the tactical category, second only to Grand Master on the scale of excellence. Eddie J., his gunsmith, had worked on Martinez's pistol until its action was as smooth as silk and deadly accurate, until the gun fit his hand perfectly. And the trigger was no factory seven-pounder.

"I have a two-pound trigger on this gun," Martinez said conversationally. "I wonder how much of that I've prepped off."

Swagger was not resisting. He was hardly even breathing, hoping to avoid getting shot accidentally, or even on purpose. He began emitting a series of whining cries. Martinez slowly withdrew his pistol, wiped it on Swagger's shirtfront, then wiped it more carefully with his own handkerchief. He threw the handkerchief at the wastebasket and holstered the gun. Then he violently yanked Swagger off his desk onto the floor. The ex-deputy lay there, whining like an injured animal, tears streaming down his face.

Martinez drew his sound left leg back and slammed a resounding kick into Swagger's ribs, smiling grimly at the cracking sounds he heard. "Get up, you miserable slob!" He barked. "The personal effects in your desk will be delivered to your house this afternoon. If you're ever caught inside this county after midnight tomorrow night, I'm going to personally take you to Klanke's Mill and stuff your dismembered body in that well—and get a thrill out of doing it. Leave the keys to your squad car with Millie. *Scram!*"

All eyes were on the door of the sheriff's office when it opened. Even those who suspected that there might be a firing in the offing were astonished at the tearful, terrorized look on Swagger's face, and at his pitiful, slumped figure. He crept along as if he might go to his hands and knees at any moment, his eyes darting about as if expecting a new attack from any quarter. He took the key ring from his pocket and selected from it. After placing the keys soundlessly on Millie's desk, he almost ran from the building, his arm clamped tight against his injured rib-cage. When he disappeared from view all eyes went to Sheriff Martinez, who had followed Swagger into the room.

"Folks, we have a pretty decent little force here." His eyes focused on a deputy who stood off behind the main group, seeming to be seeking invisibility. "At least we'll have regained decency when you're gone, Grimshaw," he barked at the man. "Leave your badge and car keys with Millie on your way out. Scram." Grimshaw had been suspecting that Swagger's demise meant his own as well and he was ready. In ten seconds and without a word said he was gone. A satisfied little smile played on Millie Thatcher's serene face.

"I want this department to be the finest in the state, and I can't imagine why every member of it wouldn't want the same thing. I want every citizen to know us, to *respect* us, as true public servants. We work for the citizens of Winchester County; they don't work for us. Our employers don't have to have connections or kiss our behinds to get courteous, professional, and absolutely fair treatment from their own employees." He struck out vigorously with an arm, pointing in the direction of the department's parking lot. "*To protect and to serve*, it says on those cars out there." He grimaced, looked down at the floor, and shuddered visibly. "That's been nothing but a mockery for the last hundred years, but that era is history.

"Another thing. I want criminals treated so rough they'll go ply their trade elsewhere. But by george they better be criminals—nobody is ever again going to get rough treatment from this department on suspicion.

"We are going to work very hard on these things as long as I'm sheriff. We'll never get perfect, but we are going to become as near perfect as we can be. Thank all of you who weren't on duty for taking personal time out for this little meeting."

He nodded pleasantly to them and left the building in a brisk walk. The robust applause and cheering that had broken out in the building behind him pushed his anger aside and filled him with a warm, satisfying glow.

CHAPTER 27

The door flew open and in swept Jim with an armload of books. He hooked the door with a foot and it banged shut. "Hi, Mom," he said airily. "I got my books from the bookmobile—all but one, anyway."

There was a time when she would have said, "Don't slam the door, Jim." Now, however, she *relished* the sound of the door announcing his arrival, and the more emphatic the better. She watched him as he laid the books on a table, looking at each one with admiration. She was glad he treasured books. She felt a shiver of delight at the sight of him.

When Jim and Old Black were overdue at the farm that horrible evening, when her thoughts of what might have happened to him became more terrifying with the passing of every hour, she thought of the times she had told him not to let the screen door slam. Oh, how she had longed then that she could hear that door slam behind him once more, a thousand times forever more. Since that unforgettable time, there had been no sound more beautiful to her ears than the door slamming behind him.

"Look, Mom," he said excitedly, holding out an old volume of *Treasure Island*. The cloth of its faded cover was worn through on the corners. Threads hung from the top of the spine where innumerable fingers had tugged it from bookshelves.

"And look *here*," he said, eager to point out additional wonders. He opened the front cover with the care due a priceless object, exposing endpapers brittle and cracked at the hinge, and pointed out a series of inscriptions. The first was, "From Carl McPherson to Billy Shore." Beneath it a similarly youthful hand had written, "From Billy

Shore to Charles Shore." Debbie Shore's name was the last to show ownership. Written under Billy Shore's name was a telephone number and address: *CA 5-2111, 942 South Pine Street, Lima, Ohio.*

Jim thumbed through the fragile, yellowed pages of his treasured old *Treasure Island*, stopping briefly at illustrations.

"Isn't this something, Mom? I bought this book off the sale table for ten cents. I wonder how it got here from Ohio? That had to be a long time ago. Mom . . . do you remember when phone numbers had letters like CA? And they must not have had ZIP codes then. I bet all those people are grown by now. But it shows that they read it and then gave it to someone they liked. This book has really been around. I'll just read *Treasure Island* again. It's a good story, and it was a long time ago that I read it. Long John Silver: he wasn't too bad a guy, for a pirate . . ."

He gathered up the books to take them to his room. Just as he was leaving the kitchen, he said, "I'm going to write my name in this book too, in case someone else gets it."

When he returned, he said, "Mom, when will Aunt Hazel and Uncle Harry get here? I can't wait to show them the sculpture, and all the ribbons and trophies me and Old Black has won, and—"

"Old Black and I *have* won, Jim"

"Yeah, Old Black and I *have* won. The trophies we *have* won. But when will Aunt Hazel and Uncle Harry get here?"

"They should get here sometime Thursday. Oh, that's tomorrow, isn't it? Well, we can expect them anytime tomorrow—since they got that motor home they're like leaves in the wind. We'll go to the farm early Saturday morning, as early as we can get everybody pointed in that direction."

Jim loved Aunt Hazel and Uncle Harry. They usually visited once a year. Uncle Harry had owned a machine shop, and sold it when he decided to retire. He had explained many things to Jim about machining parts out of metal, how machinery worked, and why.

"See the engine on your lawnmower?" he'd asked Jim once. "A fair amount of machining went into that little engine, all automated, done on computerized machines. Let me show you." They'd sat down at the table with a pad of paper and Uncle Harry began drawing. With a few deft lines he had drawn a sketch of the engine block, a good sketch showing the cylinder, the recesses in the bottom for the crankshaft, a glimpse of a hole for a valve, and the fitting that would receive the carburetor.

As he drew the crankshaft he described how it fit in the half-moon places drawn into the engine block, and where the connecting rod would fit around the crankshaft. Then came quick sketches of the piston and rod, shown apart but with lines showing where they went. He described how they would be machined in his shop, "usually from forgings—"

"What's a forging, Uncle Harry?"

"A blacksmith is *forging* iron when he hammers a horseshoe into shape after getting it red hot," Uncle Harry said. "In industry, we use big, machine-powered hammers, but the principle is the same. Forgings are stronger than castings, and they're more impact-resistant.

"Many metal parts begin life as forgings before being machined or milled to the final shape. During forging, the grains of metal are refined, making the metal stronger in the direction of the grain. This allows us to forge a part so it will be strongest in the direction strength is needed most. Bring me a piece of toilet paper," he ordered, holding his arms apart to indicate a length.

He took the yard-long piece of paper Jim brought him, and pointing out the dotted lines between sheets, said, "Toilet paper is famous for its stubborn refusal to tear on the dotted lines. There's a good reason, and everybody in the business of making toilet paper knows what the reason is: the grain of the paper is wrong. The grain runs *down* the length of the roll instead of across, the way it should."

Harry handed the paper back to Jim. "Try tearing the paper long-ways," he instructed.

Jim started the tear. It traveled down the length fairly straight. As it continued, the tear gradually wandered off to one side until it reached an edge about a foot from the end.

"See, that tear traveled two feet before it drifted off to the side. Two feet, and the width of the roll is about four inches. Now, take the piece that's still whole, that short piece right there, and try tearing it crossways, on a dotted line."

The tear began on the dotted line, but it had not even gone half way across before it left the line to travel a ragged path that turned down and went two sheets before the piece was torn in two.

Harry smiled knowingly. "Look at that. Even with a dotted line that's supposed to *make* the paper tear across, it tore further down over two widths of the piece. It's because the grain of the paper runs long-ways, and that's the way it wants to tear. So it veers off the dotted line and takes the easy path along the grain. If the grain went across the roll, the paper would tear straight across every time even without a dotted line. I've never talked to anyone in the toilet paper business, but

I can tell you what every engineer would say if I suggested they make toilet paper with the grain going across, so it would tear easy."

"What would they say?"

"Why, they'd say that keeping the grain longways makes it easy to roll it up during manufacturing. See, their interest is confined to *making* it, not with *usefulness*. Makes you wonder if the people that make toilet paper even use it—if they did, they'd see it needs improvement. In the metals business," he said with sudden pride, "we're not that stubborn. We figure out the direction that a certain part needs to be the strongest. Then by controlling the arrangement of the grain of the metal, we make it strong in that direction. Take that connecting rod right there."

He pointed to it in the drawing, and drew many short lines up and down its long dimension. "It has to be strong lengthwise, to keep it from snapping in the middle. So we set up the forging process to *force* the grain of the metal to run lengthwise, along those lines there.

"If a toilet-paper engineer ever had to design a rod, he'd probably set up the forging dies so the grain ran crossways. For sure, when they began to get reports of rods snapping in the middle, he'd be ready with a long list of reasons why making connecting rods that break is more efficient and cheaper than making rods that did the job!"

Jim laughed, but immediately became serious, his brow furrowed with curiosity. "But, if one engineer won't do it, why doesn't another—one with a different company—design toilet paper the right way?"

Uncle Harry had stopped drawing. He held up his pencil as an orchestra leader might hold a baton at the ready. "Ha!" he said, significantly, and jabbed Jim lightly in the chest with the eraser end. "Because they're all too close to the problem—they *know* it can't be done, so why try to do the impossible? Example: Eli Whitney invented the cotton gin, right?"

Jim nodded.

"Isn't it interesting that when he first started working on a machine that would separate the cotton from the seeds, he had never *seen* a boll of raw cotton? It's interesting, because that gave him the big advantage of not knowing it couldn't be done. He was on a gentlemen's hunting trip on a Georgia cotton plantation when he heard about an *insurmountable* problem that drastically limited cotton production: the workers had to painstakingly separate the cotton fibers from the seeds by hand—each worker only cleaning a few double handfuls a day! England was crying for cotton, but hand-cleaning it had American cotton production stuck at a couple of shiploads a year.

That was a few years before 1800.

"Well, hearing his host whining about the problem stimulated Eli's natural curiosity, so he asked to see a cotton boll. He examined it, pulled at the fibers that stuck to the seeds. He saw immediately that some kind of combing process would do the job, using combs with big teeth to hold the seeds and combs with fine teeth to grab the lint. In a few days—not years, or even months, but *days*—he had a rough working model of a cotton-cleaning machine. Presto, the insurmountable problem was surmounted. Within a year of that hunting trip he had a cotton gin in operation.

"That invention brought prosperity to the whole southern part of the U.S.A. For every shipload of cotton that went to England in the year that Whitney went on that lucky hunting trip, *twenty-five* shiploads were going overseas eight years later. England couldn't get enough of it and the plantation owners were getting rich."

Jim exclaimed, "It sure was lucky for them Eli Whitney went on that hunting trip, wasn't it?"

"*Double* lucky!" Uncle Harry snapped in a contemptuous voice. "The cotton growers began making gins on their own, infringing on Whitney's patent without paying him. He spent most of what the invention brought him on lawyers, fighting patent infringers. I can tell you, Jim, that the world hasn't changed much since then, either."

"Boy, Mom," Jim had said to her after that session, holding the pad for her to see. "Uncle Harry sure can draw, can't he? That's the engine on our lawn mower. All apart."

As he walked away, she heard him say, "If Uncle Harry ever starts making toilet paper, he's going to put everybody else out of business."

Hands on hips, she turned toward his disappearing back, her face wearing a perplexed expression. "Toilet paper?" she asked herself.

"Uncle Harry said to expect them when we see them; it's not so easy to get Aunt Hazel ready for travel. They're going to spend most of next week at the ranch. They want to tour the countryside, and Brentwood is a good location for their home base. You'll have all weekend to visit with them until we come home Sunday evening."

"Does Aunt Hazel still forget things, Mom?"

"Oh, yes. Uncle Harry says she's getting worse. Sometimes she doesn't even recognize him. So don't let it hurt your feelings if she can't remember who you are. She can barely recall what happens from one minute to the next, and gets things all mixed up in her mind. But

Harry says she's as healthy, physically, as can be. She gets frustrated, and has a tendency to argue. So if she takes issue with something you say, just take it in stride."

THERE WAS GOING TO BE A LOT to take in stride, and keep a straight face about it. Norma had not said the half of it. Aunt Hazel walked from the motorhome with Norma along the sidewalk, moving slowly toward the front door in her familiar rolling gait, eyes on the ground at her feet. She shuffled along in tiny steps, her ever-present purse over one arm, while Harry was still snuggling the big motorhome up against the curb. Jim thought she walked like a sailor.

Norma had her arm over Aunt Hazel's round shoulders. From where Jim stood at the front door he heard his mother speaking in low, pleasant tones, saying, "Since you and Harry got that motor home and spend so much time traveling, we don't see you often enough. We miss you very much, Aunt Hazel."

Still looking at the ground as she rolled along with a serious, thoughtful expression on her face, Aunt Hazel said, "That's sweet, Norma. I even miss myself."

Jim's smile doubled. "Hi, Aunt Hazel," he said.

"Well, hello to you," she responded cheerfully. She looked him up and down, stepped into the entry way, took two tiny paces, and turned back to face him. He was standing in the open door, waiting for her to move far enough into the vestibule so he could close the door, but Aunt Hazel was not going anywhere. She opened her purse and picked at the few things in it, wondering. She closed her purse and looked at him again with close scrutiny. "You're a nice-looking boy. Who are you, little fella?"

Jim looked at his mother, then back at Aunt Hazel. "I'm Jim," he said.

Aunt Hazel stepped up and put her hand on his shoulder in a stern, maternal way. "Oh, no," she said with authority. "You're not Norma's Jim. He joined the navy. Do you live around here, little boy?"

Jim smiled weakly and a nervous little laugh escaped his lips. "Yes, ma'am. I live here with Mom and Dad. I'm their boy Jim." He looked toward Norma for help.

"You can't kid me, sonny," said Aunt Hazel, turning to Norma. "You didn't have a baby, did you, Norma?" Looking back at Jim, she said, "Bobby, how do you like it here?"

At that moment Uncle Harry came to the door lugging two very large and obviously heavy suitcases. He stopped in the doorway because further progress was not possible.

"Hi, Jimmy," he boomed, flashing a big smile.

"Hi, Uncle Harry. I sure was glad when I heard you were coming. I have something keen to show you."

"Great—hey," he said, looking past Jim into the vestibule. "What's the holdup, ladies?"

Aunt Hazel began talking casually to Jim about his mother, who was gently tugging Aunt Hazel's hand to get her into the living room. Occasionally her words trailed off as she renewed her search inside her purse, then she would close her purse deliberately and begin talking anew, on a different subject, but she steadfastly blocked the entry way like a broad-based rock, immovable.

Harry looked down at the suitcases and said, "These are both hers, Norma. Here's mine." He pointed his chin at a small knapsack over his shoulder. "She has an evening gown in here. She hasn't worn an evening gown in twenty years. There's bathing suits from when we used to live in Maryland back in the sixties. She carries dress suits, dresses, a half dozen pairs of shoes, piles of slips and undies, even family pictures, old newspaper clippings, and—"

"Now don't go telling all that. I need those things because we might want to go out, and you never know where you'll want to go. And I want to be able to dress properly. Norma knows that."

Harry said in a glum voice, "I could go out to the motorhome and get anything you need. Usually we have things scattered all over the room and still can't find nothing. If it was in the closets or drawers in the motorhome, I could find it in an instant."

Norma looked at the heavy suitcases Harry still held and said, "Come in, Uncle Harry, just put those suitcases anywhere. With a hand on Hazel's shoulder, Norma gently urged her to move on into the room. But Hazel was not moving. Norma winked at Harry, who made an expression of exasperation, looked down and wagged his head. Jim took one of the suitcases from Uncle Harry. It was so heavy he had to hold it with both hands and lean backward for balance.

Harry took half a step, then his face flushed. "*Move*, Hazel. You heard Norma say come in and you haven't even budged. You're right in the way. Can't you move out of the way?"

"All you have to do is ask in a polite way. You don't have to get so huffy." Hazel made a face at Harry and turned a serene gaze on Norma. "How are you, Norma? And where's your little Jim?"

Harry's shoulders slumped and he studied the floor, his jaw muscles working. In a weak, tired voice he said, "Come on, Hazel. You can talk all you want to when we get inside. But you have to *move* if I'm ever going to get in this house. And the air condition is getting out the door. We're running up Norma's light bill."

"Why didn't you say so? And why don't you close the door so you don't run up Norma's light bill?" She smiled at Norma prettily and then stepped into the living room. Norma moved across the room to encourage further movement. Harry entered, followed by Jim.

"Where did you come from today?" Norma asked.

Aunt Hazel seemed to reflect on her journey and said, "Oh, we came from Boston. Tell her about our trip from Boston—" She had turned toward Harry, and when her eyes fell on him she stopped, her head jerked backward on her shoulders and her chin tucked in an expression of non-recognition. She said indignantly, "Who are you?"

He rolled his eyes upward, then to the side. He took a deep breath and exhaled audibly. "I'm your ill-fated husband, Harry. Harry P. Beams. And we didn't come from Boston. You've never been to Boston, that I know of." He looked at Norma. "We came from New Orleans, Norma. The French Quarter is really going to the dogs. I couldn't wait to see New Orleans in the rear-view mirror."

Aunt Hazel caught the last words. "New Orleans? That's a good idea. We ought to go to New Orleans."

"Hazel, we just *came* from New Orleans, and both of us said we didn't want to go back."

"Me? New Orleans? You're crazy. You must have been with somebody else."

Norma winked at Uncle Harry. "You'll have to take Aunt Hazel to New Orleans sometime." She put an arm around his waist and steered him to the family room. "Come on in and find a comfortable chair. I want to hear all about New Orleans—and Boston."

Uncle Harry eased his bulky body down and melted into a big chair. After looking all around the room, he said, "Where's the TV, Jim? I want to catch the news."

"I'll get it," said Jim, and he scurried away.

"Where's your paper, Norma? I want to keep up with what's happening on that airplane crash. You can't listen to the radio on the road with Hazel sitting up front and jabbering all the time. They think Iranian terrorists put a bomb on the plane. If I was president I would make 'em think twice about even looking in the direction of America. You haven't heard a peep out of that Khadafy since Reagan sent a strike force in there and whacked him good, and that's been I don't know how long ago. Man! Did he ever clam up. Not one little bitty peep outta him since that happy day."

Norma brought him the day's *Houston Sun*.

Jim rolled a small table bearing a twelve-inch Sony television set in front of Uncle Harry. He adjusted the volume so Uncle Harry could hear it, yet the others could talk.

"Maybe somebody else wants to watch something. Jim?" He looked at Jim inquiringly. "Do you have a favorite program? I don't want to hog the TV."

"Oh, no, Uncle Harry. You can watch the news or anything else. I don't watch TV much. I use it mainly to watch videos."

Harry laughed. "I never knew a kid that didn't watch TV. Man, that's a new one. Why not, I'd like to know?"

"The ticket price is too high," Jim said with a little laugh. "That's what Dad says, and I think so too."

Harry laughed. "There ain't no ticket price, Jim. TV is free unless you're on cable. Do you have cable?"

"No, sir, we don't. But the ticket is the commercials."

Uncle Harry looked puzzled. "You don't pay for 'em, and you don't have to watch 'em. Anyway, what's wrong with watching commercials? You learn about new pro—" He held up a hand. "Wait, here's something about that plane crash."

Jim's eyebrows knitted in thought. He avoided debating with grownups, especially people he liked, like Uncle Harry. He preferred to listen with an expression of agreement and evade the discomfort of explaining an opposing point of view. Now he had gotten in too deep. Uncle Harry had asked a question and he was obligated to answer it. The thoughts that came to his mind pulled the rug from under every answer, from Uncle Harry's point of view, anyway.

Uncle Harry had taken retirement seriously; he would have little use for the time he would save by not watching television. But Jim knew how valuable time was. His father had shown him with examples how time grabbed from here and there, otherwise gone forever, could be converted into immensely valuable knowledge, skills and completed projects. Matt Bradley focused on learning from books.

"There is hardly anything you can't learn from a book," he'd told Jim. "If more than a handful of people do it, *somebody* has written a book on it. But too many people, and I'm talking about people who are holding down good jobs, can't comprehend written explanations. They can't convert written words to complete thoughts; anything but the most basic directions are over their heads. So we're becoming a nation of people who must be personally tutored. Our company has teachers come in and tutor employees on the simplest jobs.

"Years ago I met a janitor for a company I was working for then, a Mexican who probably had trouble reading English. He was taking a correspondence course in radio and television repair. Not an easy thing for somebody to tackle, electronics. He was having a time slugging his way through those course manuals, but by golly he did it. Naturally, he wanted sets to work on, so I had him fix a radio of mine, and then I began sending friends to him, and they sent their friends. Soon he had all the work he could do. He *fixed* what he worked on, and his customers were happy. The last I saw of him he was still a janitor, but he was earning more from his home workshop than from his real job. And he learned it all from reading, and reading in his second language at that! How did he ever do it? He was *motivated*.

"That's why your mother and I have motivated you, encouraged you to read, and to read material you often thought was over your head. I would say that now, at eleven, you can read and comprehend almost anything that doesn't require a technical background. Look what you've gained from learning Microsoft Word upside down, learning from books that even the computer operators in our company can't understand—or *won't*. So they have to be tutored."

The news of the plane crash dominated Uncle Harry's news. It was the same non-information that had been reported from the first day, artlessly repackaged daily, introducing "eyewitnesses" who had seen nothing, but he sat boring in intently on every word.

"For news from down under," said the announcer, we go to Darwin, Australia and reporter Barry Davidson. Barry—"

"Thank you, Chuck," said Davidson. "Euthanasia is on the minds of many Australians these days. In Australia's Northern Territory, a stormy debate has raged since the passage of a law that legalizes voluntary euthanasia. . ."

"I'm undecided about this euthanasia," Harry said. "Sombody might figure I oughta be euthanized before—"

Aunt Hazel broke off her conversation with Norma and sat bolt upright facing him. "See, Harry," she said indignantly. "This isn't the only place where the kids are going crazy. What was it he said about the youth in Asia?"

"He wasn't talking about the youth in Asia, Hazel. He said *euthanasia*. Explain it to her, Norma."

Next came sports. He didn't miss a word and interacted freely and with spirit throughout the segment. When the weather came on he turned the set off.

"They ought to cut out the weather when it's the same every day. Just have a weather report when something's going to happen," he said.

"Dad says the same thing," Jim said charitably.

"You oughtn't to get worked up over them commercials, Jim. That's what pays for the news, so you don't have to pay for it."

"Nothing's wrong with commercials, I guess," Jim said, his face pensive, "except the time wasted. We started to watch *Lonesome Dove*, and after the first night Dad figured out that it was going to take, uh, well, I forget, but hours and hours of commercials. That was the price of admission, and we wouldn't pay it. We just waited a year or so for it to come out on video—then we watched it in two nights, and it only cost four dollars."

Jim felt that he could now make an important point to Uncle Harry. He said, "For only four dollars we saved hours and hours."

Harry sat up and pointed a finger at him. "Okay, I think I gotcha now, Jim. Just what did you do with that time? What did you do that brought in the four bucks to cover the video rental? I been a business-man all my life, and one of the first things I learned was that a man's time ain't worth a plugged nickel if nobody'll buy it."

Jim smiled and looked at his hands, lying idle in his lap. "Could I show you, Uncle Harry? I could show you better than tell you."

"Sure. I'd like to see what you have to show for that time you saved."

Jim stood up.

Harry rose from his chair, then he turned to Aunt Hazel. "Why are you looking at me like that, Hazel?" he asked. "Talk to Norma. She's talking to you and you're paying her no attention."

She pointed a finger at him. "Who are you, Harry?"

His eyes narrowed. "What do you mean, who am I? I am Harry P. Beams, retired machinist and not a candidate for President of the U.S. That's who."

"No. I mean, who are you? Are you my father?"

"I'm your *husband*, Hazel," he said with exasperation.

"Oh, nooo, you're not *my* husband." She laughed derisively and shook her head. "Are you my father?"

Harry looked at Norma for help. "Norma, will you tell her I'm her husband, and not her father?"

Hazel turned quickly to face Norma, still shaking her head. "He's not my husband." She glanced at him, then turned back to Norma. "I wouldn't marry an old geezer like him. He must be my father."

As Uncle Harry followed Jim to his room, he said, "How's that horse of yours? Your mother said you were winning everything in sight before you and him almost killed yourselves saving that sheriff. I'm sure glad Norma sent me those papers from Brentwood. I had trouble getting people to believe my own nephew was the hero in that caper. They all thought that deputy they saw on TV was the man of the hour. I was real proud of you, Jim—you should've seen how I swelled up when I stuck those articles under their nose. What's his name—yaaaaa, Old Black, I remember. World champeen. How's he doing?"

Jim's expression, always exuberant around Uncle Harry, softened to a look of serenity. "I think he's as good as new—maybe even *better* than new. We're back in training. I don't know how to describe it. He seems like a younger horse. You'll get to see him Saturday."

"I'm looking forward to it. Outside of Jack Dempsey, Old Black'll be the only world champ I ever personally laid eyes on, in the flesh. Yaaaaa, I'm anxious to see him—What's this?"

Uncle Harry's eyes fell upon a large plaster sculpture, well over a foot tall. Its irregularly-shaped base was about two feet at its longest dimension. The subject was a saddled horse standing near a large tree. A boy was sitting on the ground and leaning against the tree-trunk. His face was turned toward the horse, and something about his expression suggested that he was talking to the horse. That impression was reinforced by the way the horse stood with his head squarely, intently focused on the boy. Above the boy, the sculptor had painstakingly created a generous spray of the tree's foliage.

"Gee, this is *beautiful*, Jim. Where did you come across such a piece as this?"

"Well, it's Old Black and me under the pecan trees in the bottom pasture. Our closest neighbors at the farm—real, real good friends of Dad and Mom and me—one of their daughters is married to an artist. He did that sculpture of me and Old Black."

Jim pointed to the name inscribed in the base of the sculpture. "That's him, Andrew Meridith, and he's famous all over the world. Have you heard of him, Uncle Harry? Andrew Meridith?"

Uncle Harry had not. "Maybe he's just famous to people who like western art," Jim rationalized.

He pointed to a cork bulletin board on the wall where there were several color photographs of bronzes created by Andrew Meridith.

Jim pointed out one of a magnificent racehorse at full extension. His left forefoot was his only contact with the ground; the jockey was gripping his shoulders with bent knees, his body low on the horse's neck. His right arm, holding the crop, was extended but relaxed, motionless. Immediately beyond the horse was a section of the rail at the finish pole.

"See this one, Uncle Harry? It's the Thoroughbred horse Southampton, winner of the Triple Crown. Out of all the artists in the world that wanted to do this sculpture, Mr. Meridith got the job. *Sports Illustrated* had a big article about the horse, and about Mr. Meridith's sculpture of him. And he's right in Brentwood, somebody we know real well. And he talks to me just like I was somebody." Jim produced the issue of *Sports Illustrated* and handed it, opened, to Uncle Harry.

"Yaaaaa. It sure is something. He must've been at this kind of work a long time, and putting everything he had in it. In a machine shop you might have one man that can get everything there is out of the machines, one sure-enough artist out of a dozen machinists."

Uncle Harry seemed fascinated with the sculpture and moved around it, examining it closely from different angles. "Most craftsmen who've been on the job, say, ten years, are about as good as they're ever gonna get. They've quit progressing in their skills. But that one super-machinist might be sixty and still trying to get better. That goes for every trade—airplane pilots, doctors, auto mechanics, welders, teachers—it ain't one out of a hundred that's a craftsman. But this guy—yaaaaa, you got it right, this guy is something."

Uncle Harry looked at the *Sports Illustrated* article for a short but decent enough time, closed the magazine and handed it back to Jim.

He had hoped that Uncle Harry would turn the page and see the photograph of Andrew Meridith that he had autographed "To my good buddy Jim Bradley, a man among men, and a guy I'd ride the river with any day. With my every best wishes, Andrew Meridith."

Uncle Harry had turned back to the sculpture of the boy and his horse. He studied it from a new angle, then stepped around for the opposing view. "Hot dern if I don't think that's the prettiest thing I ever saw in the art line," he said. "And darn if he didn't catch you, Jim. Something about the way your body lays there, the way your leg hangs over the other one. I've seen you chewing on a piece of grass like that, too. Sorry to say, one horse looks like another to me, but does this favor Old Black?"

"Yes, sir, that's him. The spittin' image," said Jim. "Even the saddle is my saddle. You can tell if you look at my saddle and then at this one. 'Course Mr. Meridith knows Old Black real good. Me and his daughter are good friends; we go to the horse shows together. Maybe we can go over and see them while you're at the farm. You would like Mr. Meridith, and Alexandra, and her mom, too. You'll never meet nicer people than them, not ever."

Uncle Harry looked at Jim inquiringly, holding a plump hand palm up toward the sculpture. "How'd you get him to do this? It *had* to take a lot of time. Did your dad have him do it? It must have cost a mint." He looked at Jim with squinted eyes. "Or is he buttering you up for his daughter?" He laughed with zest. "Any father would do a lot of groundwork to cultivate a lad like you for his daughter. Maybe that's it, hey Jimmy?"

Jim blushed and said, "No, sir. Mr. Meridith just did it. I didn't even know he was doing it. But a funny thing was that a good while back he had me lay down against a big pecan tree in his yard, like I am right there. And he took a lot of pictures. I was wondering what it was for. Then last Saturday the Meridiths invited us to their house for a cookout. Sheriff Martinez and his family were there, too. And Doc Smith—he's our vet. It was him that saved Old Black's life—Doc Smith was there with his wife and little girl.

"After we were there a little while, Mr. Meridith called everybody into the living room and Alexandra went to stand by a table holding something covered with a red cloth. She was smiling real big and holding her hand over her mouth to keep herself from giggling. Then she lifted off the cloth."

He reached up and let his finger run gently over Old Black's rump, neck, and head. "I didn't know what it was at first—I don't know what I thought, but I sure didn't dream that it was me and Old Black. Nobody said anything for the longest. Then Alexandra took me close to it and it began to sink in that the horse looked just like Old Black. The saddle looked like my saddle, with my jean jacket tied behind the cantle."

His serious expression gave way to a smile. "I began to think it might be me and Old Black, but then I still couldn't hardly believe it could really be us until Alexandra told me it was."

Jim got very close to the sculpture and pointed to the horse's left knee. "If you look hard, you can see a knot. He really has one there. I looked at Mr. Meridith, and—" he swallowed hard—"he was smiling so nice. I was amazed. I'm still amazed. I'll always be amazed."

"He must think a lot of you, Jim. That don't surprise me, though," Uncle Harry said with feeling. "Did he just come up with the idea of doing it? A thing like this, coming from a famous artist—from *any* artist—you'd have to think it represented something mighty special to him, just to take the job on."

Jim didn't want to risk trying to explain why he thought Mr. Meridith had done the sculpture. "He just decided to do it, I guess."

"Well, something besides your courtin' his daughter made him take on a job such as this. Just look at the leaves of that tree hanging out over you. Boy, that's—that's *delicate*, like fine lace, ain't it?"

He stooped way down and looked up, so he could see beneath the foliage. "Ah, ha! I see how he did that. It looks like those leaves are floating in air, hanging from some branch that's out of the picture, so to speak. But he built a buttress—that's what we would call it in the machine shop—he built a buttress, hidden by the leaves, that tied the leaves in with the trunk. Ain't that something?" He turned to Jim. "You must be mighty proud of that, Jim. You and your horse, immortalized in a sculpture. I'll be."

Harry looked around the room. There were pictures on the walls. Some were of Jim's father and airplanes he had flown, parked in far-off places; pictures of Jim and his horse, standing around and in action; pictures of Jim and his parents with an elderly black couple. He moved along the wall and saw pictures of Jim and a pretty little black girl, some with their horses and some with them among other people, people of all ages.

A framed collection of sayings by Benjamin Franklin, artfully printed, hung on the wall.

One today is worth two tomorrows.
Would you live with ease, do what you ought and not what you please.
Better slip with foot, than by tongue.
Light purse, heavy heart.
Great talkers, little doers.
Look ahead, or you will find yourself behind.
When you are good to others, you are best to yourself.
Well done, is better than well said.

From the Franklin quotes, Harry's eye moved to an enlarged photo of Jim and the same black girl in the other pictures. They were with about a dozen other youths and adults inside a pretty picket fence under a striped awning—the setting seemed to be a horse show. A fine motor home—a Bluebird, Harry noted with envy—made one side of the fenced-in area. Painted on its side and on the horse trailer attached to it was "Screech Owl Ranch~Dime Box, Texas."

There was a picture of Jim and his father, along with two black men next to a little trailer attached to a gray and red Ford tractor, the three of them were acting up, as if involved in a joke.

Harry pointed to another picture and laughed out loud. "This is a swell picture," he said. "Surprise attack from the rear."

Jim joined in his laughter. "Gee, Uncle Harry. That's a perfect name for that picture. Mom took that at just the right time, didn't she?"

In the photograph, Jim's arm was stuck out as far as he could reach as he offered a range cube to a shy cow. He held a fist-full of range cubes behind him in his other hand. Unknown to Jim, another cow had crept up behind him and her long tongue was about to filch a range cube from his hand.

"Her name is Friendly Red," said Jim. "She *is* friendly, too. She'll come up and sniff your pocket if you have a range cube in it." He pointed out another picture of Friendly Red. In it she stood casually before Jim with his hat on her head.

Harry grinned approvingly. His gaze took in the rest of the room. There were a lot of built-ins; a display case on the wall held at least two dozen trophies; a large bookcase was filled with books. Next to the bookcase was a neatly-kept desk on which was a computer monitor, a keyboard, and a printer. To the left of the keyboard were two open books, one on top of the other. The visible book showed many underlined passages. A speaker phone with a cordless receiver was on the right side of the monitor. Underneath the desk was the computer case on a shelf just above the floor. On the wall above the desk was a shelf with some computer-program manuals on it. The secretarial-type chair was of good quality—Harry had bought enough office furniture to be able to see that. A similar chair sat beside the desk.

It could have been the home office of a busy executive, Harry thought. His eye fell on some titles in the bookcase. There was a string of the Hardy Boys adventures, *Silver Chief of the North*, *Gulliver's Travels*, *Sea Wolf*, *Call of the Wild*, a beat-up old copy of *Treasure Island*, *Mutiny on the Bounty*, *The Book of Key Facts*, *The World Almanac*, *The Old Man and the Sea*, *Charlotte's Web*, *Steaming to Bamboola*—

"Quite a variety in your library, Jim," said Uncle Harry. "I see you must like biographies, too." Among the many: *Jane Goodall, Friend of the Chimps*; *Bully for You, Teddy Roosevelt*; *Alexander the Great*; *Ferdinand Magellan*; *Captain James Cook, Explorer of the Pacific*. Uncle Harry recalled a discussion with Jim a few years back and smiled with satisfaction at the sight of *Eli Whitney, Great Inventor*.

"I see you have Eli Whitney's bio, Jim. Quite a man, wasn't he?"

Nodding, but with a pained expression, Jim said, "Yes, sir, he sure was, but he had the worst luck. I got it right after you told me about how he invented the cotton gin. You were right; he didn't make any money on it for years and years. People built gins and used them without paying him a cent, even though he had patented his invention.

"And he had a lot of other bad luck. His cotton gin factory burned down. The parts for a lot of gins and even the machinery for making them was ruined. But he always lifted his spirits up and made a comeback. I learned a lot about sticking to things from that book. In fact, a lot of men who did great things had to overcome big setbacks."

Smiling broadly, Uncle Harry said, "Got a Whitney question for you. What was Eli Whitney's greatest achievement?"

Jim knew. "He figured out the way to make parts for guns so much alike that a part for one would fit in any other—" he squinted his eyes, stuck for the right term to use.

"You got it—mass production with interchangeable parts," said Harry helpfully.

"Yeah," Jim smiled his thanks. "And he did it first on a new gun he designed for the government—they called them muskets. He made thousands of them, and a part for one musket would fit any other. At least his gun factory was a big success after he finally got it going. It went on making guns for a hundred years."

Harry went on looking at the volumes in the biography section of Jim's library. There was *Maxwell Perkins, Editor of Genius*; *Jules Verne*; *Lewis and Clark*. "John M. Browning, is this the guy that invented the Browning automatic shotgun, Jim?"

"Yes, sir, along with about eighty other guns. He invented the Colt forty-five pistol used by the U.S. military in World War One and ever since. He invented all of the shotguns and rifles made by Winchester for I don't know how many years—his lever-action carbines are still made by Winchester today. They have a statue of him in a factory in Belgium, FN, they call it—his small pistol designs put them on the map. Then they made the Browning shotgun, that was after Winchester turned it down flat—Remington made it in the U.S. later, and now Browning Arms is making it. John M. Browning invented most of the light and heavy machine guns used by the military in both world wars, and the airplane machine guns. He was the greatest gun inventor that ever lived."

A flicker of mirth flashed in Jim's eyes as he looked up at Uncle Harry. "Do you know how come he was able to do all that?" Uncle Harry shrugged and shook his head. "He wasn't allowed to watch

TV," Jim declared triumphantly.

Uncle Harry laughed roundly and whacked Jim on the back. "You know, you might have the right idea about TV. See, we didn't have television when I was a kid—like Whitney and Browning didn't have, either. We didn't have to make a choice, like you do. I think you got the right idea. I'm sure proud of what you know at your age, Jim. You've figured out how to amount to something."

Harry pointed out a biography of Alexander Graham Bell. "I was in a house in Washington, D.C. that was his. It's occupied by a trade association now, but it still showed the ritziness of its day, and right in the middle of town. He started working on the phone because he was hard of hearing, you know," Harry mused.

Jim nodded. "Do you know the first words ever spoken on the phone?" he asked with a twinkle in his eye.

Sensing a trap, Harry nodded, but was reluctant to try a direct quote. "Bell called his right-hand man and asked him to come to his office, or lab, didn't he?" Harry said.

"Yes," Jim said. "Watson was in the next room, and Bell said to him on the phone, 'Watson, come in here. I need you.' What most people don't know is what Watson said," Jim commented in an off-hand way.

Harry looked at him for a moment. "Well, what did he say?"

Jim smiled. "Watson said, 'Boss, can you give me a minute? I'm talking to my wife on my other line.'"

Harry guffawed. "Hey, that's good! I hadn't heard that one."

"You couldn't have," said Jim proudly. "I made it up when I was reading Bell's biography. Watson would have given Mr. Bell a smile, if he'd thought of saying that."

Harry nodded. "Old Alex would have fell off his chair laughing, I'll bet, and he'd have told it a thousand times." His eyes wandered over the titles. You really have the biography books, Jimmy. How many would you say you have here? Got any idea?"

"I can tell you exactly," said Jim, turning to his computer. His hand fell on the mouse and the pointer flew across the screen, pausing here and there as he clicked on menu items, causing the image on the monitor to change rapidly. When the screen he wanted appeared he rapidly typed a few strokes. In no more than one second a screen appeared with the heading "Jim's Library: Bios" followed by columns of titles. "I have ninety-two biographies," he said, pointing to a number on the screen.

"Wow! And are you going to tell me you read all of them?"

"Sure. I read every book I get. That's why I get them. But a lot are kid's books—they aren't very thick, the type is big and they have lots of pictures. So it doesn't take long to read one. I bought most of them at used book sales for almost nothing."

"What's that?" Harry asked, nodding toward the monitor.

"I have a database to keep track of the books in my library. I built it using Microsoft Access." He tapped some more keys. "That's how I keep track of books I've loaned out." He stood up and extended a hand toward the computer. "Access is part of a set of programs Dad got me—Microsoft Office Pro. I'm just learning Access, but I know Microsoft Word really good. That's what I did with the time I would have spent watching *Lonesome Dove* on TV. I learned Word."

From a shelf above his desk Jim took down a massive book titled *Mastering Microsoft Word* and thumbed through it. Harry could tell from the wealth of underlined and highlighted text that the book was well-used, as thick as it was.

"Word is a word-processing program, Excel's a spread—but you know all about that stuff, from running a company." He looked up at Harry.

"Yaaaa. I know what they are, spreadsheet, database, word processing, invoicing. Annie, my office manager, could make those things do magic, but I stayed away from them computers. Of course, we had computerized machine tools, and I liked programming *them* to do jobs." He brightened and looked at Jim with an intensity that he rarely displayed. "Boy, oh, boy. What a difference they made in the machining industry. Gads!" He was as near to being excited as Uncle Harry got, Jim thought with an inner grin.

"You had to learn how to use programs then, didn't you?"

"Yeah, and it was the dickens at first. I thought I would *never* get that first machine to do one dadgum solitary thing. But I finally caught on."

"Well, that's using computer programs," Jim said with approval. "You could learn this kind, too, if you needed to." He turned his attention back to the book in his hands. "Dad got me this book. And then a friend of his came over and gave me some tutoring, to introduce me to the program, so I wasn't completely green when I started studying. Then, every night when *Lonesome Dove* came on I studied Microsoft Word. When the *Lonesome Dove* series was over I was halfway through the book. Then I kept going, and now I know Word pretty good, *real* good. So I began tutoring other people that can't learn from a book. *There's* where you really learn something, teaching other people."

"Amen," said Uncle Harry, nodding his head emphatically. "I'll be the first to say knowledge is valuable, but you still have to admit you're out whatever it cost to rent the *Lonesome Dove* video, when you could have watched it free on TV," he concluded, but without conviction.

Jim tossed a devilish glance toward Harry. He replaced the reference book and took a ledger down from the shelf. He opened it to a marked page, half-filled with neat rows of entries with names, dates, time spent, material covered, amounts charged. He turned back a page and glanced at the total at the bottom of it, and turned again to the page that was not complete, and therefore not totaled. He studied for a minute, calculating in his mind. "Up to now," he said, pausing for some consideration, "I've made something over one thousand, eight hundred dollars tutoring Microsoft Word. Whatever it would be, its really four dollars less, because I paid for the *Lonesome Dove* video rental."

"That's a whole lot more than a plugged nickel," said an amused and defeated Uncle Harry. "You really called my hand on that one."

WHEN JIM AND UNCLE HARRY RETURNED to the others, Norma was saying to Aunt Hazel, "What we have that lots of other wives don't have is husbands who stick by us through thick and thin. I bet you can't remember when dear Harry wasn't by your side, can you?"

"Mmmmmm. Well, no, but I can't remember anything. So he might be off somewhere without me knowing about it."

"Here he is right now, Aunt Hazel. You can see for yourself." Harry entered the room and Norma nodded toward him. "Aren't you lucky? A lot of women don't know where their husbands are. I don't, for one." She laughed. "He'll call from, say, Calgary, Canada. Then in a day or two he might call from Washington, maybe Mexico City. I don't know where in the world he is tonight."

"Oh Harry," Aunt Hazel said upon seeing him. "I'm sorry, Harry. Did I make you sad? I don't want to make you sad."

"Naaaa. You didn't make me sad, Honey. I was just in Jim's room. Norma, that's some statue that artist made of Jim and his horse. Top of the line. I never seen anything better than that."

Norma's soft gaze fell on Jim. "Nor I, Uncle Harry. It's the most beautiful sculpture I've ever seen. It was such an incredibly generous thing for Andrew to do. He has people beating his door down, people who are eager to pay big money for his work, and he took time to do that, for Jim. I cried when I saw it. And Andrew, he was so humble in his praise of Jim, and so proud of that piece—he says it's his favorite of everything he's ever done. 'My heart was in that one,' he said."

"Jim must have some stroke with that guy," Harry said. "He thinks he might be able to introduce us. I hope so. Norma, I'm hungry, and I don't mind telling you what I'm hungry for tonight—I'm too tired to go out for dinner. All the way from New Orleans I thought of those big, juicy hamburgers from Charlie's Hamburger Joint. I hardly eat hamburgers anymore because I can't find any that measure up. I'll buy if we can have a Charlie's hamburger."

Norma agreed to the plan. "I'll go pick up some Charlie's burgers this minute."

"Get me two. I have some catching up to do," he said.

Norma left, and a small smile played on Harry's face. He said, "Let me see your hands."

Jim held out his hands.

"No, turn them over so I can see your fingernails."

Knowing what was coming, Jim laughed and turned his hands over.

"Hmmm. No black fingernails. Must be getting more accurate with that hammer. I told many a guy about you always having a black thumbnail and at least a couple of black fingernails on your left hand from whacking them with a hammer. That reminds me, you haven't had a car door slammed on a finger lately, have you?"

"No, *sir*. I sure don't want to do that again."

When Jim was about seven his mother had driven him and some friends somewhere and on getting out of the car one of them slammed the door on Jim's finger. Uncle Harry came to visit a few days after that accident, when Jim's finger was still in a big bandage with a metal guard around it. He'd winced at the sight of the bandage and asked Jim how it was feeling. "It doesn't hurt too much, now," he'd said.

"I'll bet it hurt like blazes when it happened, didn't it?" said Harry sympathetically.

Harry would never forget Jim's answer. He chuckled now at the recollection of it. Jim had thought hard a moment and his face assumed a dreadfully painful expression. "It felt just like a *tiger* bite!" he'd said. Harry laughed; the statement was a presumption that *anybody* would know how much a tiger bite would hurt.

"I told the guys at the shop about your tiger bite, too," he said with a big smile and a gentle whack on Jim's arm.

Norma bustled in and announced, "Okay everyone, Charlie's hamburgers are served. Come to the dining room."

Jim and Norma overheard Hazel telling Harry she needed to put on her shoes. Norma called out, "You don't need shoes, Aunt Hazel. You're only coming in here."

"I need my shoes on," Hazel said. "I might decide to go see my mother."

"Hazel," Harry sighed, "your mother has been dead for twenty-five years."

"Dead? My mother dead? How did my mother die and me not know about it?"

"You knew about it, or you wouldn't have gone to her funeral. They don't have dry runs or rehearsals for funerals—it's always the genuine thing. Yep, she died, sure enough. Here, put your foot in this shoe. No, the other foot—well, let me get the other shoe. Here—now you changed *feet*. You always stick out the wrong foot—well, keep it there and I'll change shoes. Now, here. *No*, Hazel, now you changed feet again. Okay, then we'll try this shoe. Come *on*, Hazel, how am I going to—"

Hazel said heatedly, "That's what I hate about you, Harry, you can never make up your mind!"

"Jim—" Uncle Harry pleaded.

Jim came running. "Sure, Uncle Harry. I'll help her with her shoes." Jim dropped to his knees in front of Aunt Hazel. Whichever foot she stuck out, he grabbed the shoe for it and on it went.

"Here, Aunt Hazel, I'll help you up."

"Aren't you nice, Jim," she said as he brought her smoothly to her feet. He was glad to be Jim again, and not Bobby. He held her hand as they walked into the dining room. After he positioned her at her chair, he stood by as she slowly, deliberately let herself down. Her purse straps had moved down to her wrist, and with a practiced action she shoved the purse back up to her elbow.

Seated, she opened her purse and dug around inside it. Satisfied with the purse and its contents, she snapped it shut and looked up at Jim. "Aren't you nice. Did they teach you such nice manners in the Navy?"

"Yes, ma'am," said Jim with a grin.

Harry looked up, a big smile on his face. "By golly, Jim. I ought to take a page out of your book. It sure cuts down on the hasslin'."

Aunt Hazel leaned down and for a few seconds worked away at something under the table. Presently she straightened up, holding out her right shoe. After looking at it from every angle, she placed it on the table by her plate. She looked at it, head cocked critically, then moved it ever so slightly one way, then another until it was positioned to her satisfaction.

Harry gasped, "What are you doing, Hazel? Your shoe belongs on the floor!"

She looked down at her left foot, which had a shoe on it, and tapped her heel on the floor to provide audible evidence that she was wearing a shoe. "My shoe *is* on the floor," she said indifferently. "Where else would it be?"

"That's your other shoe, Hazel, right in the middle of the table where we're eating. You should put it on your foot, or on the floor, at least."

"It's okay," said Norma brightly. She waved her hand and made a little expression that brought discussion of the shoe to a close.

A few minutes into the meal Harry noticed that Aunt Hazel had not taken a bite. She sat patiently with her hands folded together in front of her, looking alternately at Harry and Norma, and at Jim on her right.

Harry mumbled, "Eat your hamburger, Hazel."

"Why would I want to eat *your* hamburger? I want to eat my own hamburger."

Jim sensed the meaning of "your" as it was handled by her mind. He nudged her hamburger plate an inch to draw her attention to it and said, "Eat *my* hamburger, Aunt Hazel."

"Oh, there's my hamburger. I was wondering when I was going to get *my* hamburger."

Harry noticed the way Jim handled the matter. A studious expression appeared on his face.

Aunt Hazel had eaten half of her hamburger when she stopped abruptly. She folded her hands in front of her and assumed a finished, resolute look.

"Aren't you hungry, Hazel?" Harry asked, indicating the hamburger.

"Yes."

"Then why don't you eat that hamburger?"

She looked at the half-eaten hamburger, and then with sadness in her eyes she looked at every face around the table. "I don't have the heart to eat a hamburger with my mother missing."

Harry reached over and tenderly took her folded hands in his. He said softly and with compassion, "Hazel, honey, your dear mother isn't missing. She's been dead for twenty-five years. You can eat your hamburger because she's not missing. She's in her grave, where she's supposed to be."

Hazel sat bolt upright and looked straight at Harry. "Twenty-five years?" She twisted her shoulders in a display of disbelief. "Not twenty-five years. I don't think she's even been dead a year yet," she said with finality.

As earnestly as any words were ever spoken, Harry said, "Well, she has been. And even if she wasn't even dead a year yet, once you're dead, you're dead. And there's no use going looking for her. So eat your hamburger, Hazel. I mean, eat *my* hamburger." He glanced at Jim.

She looked at the remains of her hamburger and said, "How many times do I have to eat it?"

"Just this last time, Aunt Hazel," said Jim.

She glanced warily at him, picked up the hamburger, and finished eating it.

Harry looked longingly at her plate. "Are you going to eat that pickle?"

"What pickle?"

"The one on your plate."

"What plate? I don't see a plate."

"Hazel, the only thing in front of you is a plate—except for your shoe—and the only thing on that plate is a pickle."

"Where's a pickle? I don't see a pickle."

In a swift move Harry reached way over, snatched the pickle, and plopped it into his mouth. "Norma, are you going to show us those towns you wanted us to see last time but didn't?"

"Yes. I want you to see the old mansions in Rip Ford, and the quaint old downtown square there; it's been restored and there's a statue of Rip Ford, the legendary Texas Ranger that the town's named after. Dime Box isn't too far, and there are some pretty restored homes to see there. Washington on the Brazos is a must. They've done wonders with it."

Hazel said, "I thought, uh, I thought—I forget."

Harry said considerately, "What did you forget, Hazel?"

She looked studious for a moment, and then waved a hand in the air. "I forgot what I forgot."

CHAPTER 28

"You know, folks, I just can't remember from one year to the next what a wonderful place you have here," exclaimed Uncle Harry, busily looking left and right. "It's like something out of a picture book." He had driven everyone down to the bottom pasture in his motorhome and now they were all standing on the natural bridge. The sunshine on this Saturday morning slashed through the trees, striking like orange flares against the white limestone creek bank, the trees, the ferns. A light mist still hung in the air, invisible except where the sunshine cut through.

"A little piece of paradise," he said. "Ain't it pretty, Hazel?"

"Yes, it is. I like it here. I wish we could bring my mother to see it. Could we sometime, Harry?"

Harry's immediate expression was one of pained exasperation, but then he glanced at Jim and his face assumed a pleasant, tolerant demeanor. "We ought to do just that, Hazel."

She smiled gratefully at him. "What are those white flowers, Norma?" she asked.

"Dogwood. Aren't they pretty? They only seem to grow in the shade of these big trees, and there are no more on the place except right along the creek, here."

Aunt Hazel asked, "Can we see some baby calves?"

They certainly could, and they made their way to the motorhome, with Norma frequently getting Aunt Hazel back on course. Harry drove them across the bottom to where the cow herd was grazing.

Norma made the discovery.

"Matt! Jim! Everybody, look! Friendly Red has a new calf, and it looks just like her."

Friendly Red was unmoved by their excitement. She lay there chewing her cud, her newborn baby contentedly curled up at her side.

"Here comes Old Black to see what's up," said Jim as he watched the horse approach.

"About time I got to see that famous horse," Harry said. He watched as Old Black came up to Jim, and as Jim scratched the horse's chin and around his ears. He laughed as Old Black pushed his face into Jim's chest and shoved him backwards, as two frisky friends might meet and test each other. Harry walked around Old Black slowly, thoughtfully. "He's a mighty fine horse, Jim. That was a lucky day when you found him—and I bet if he could talk, he'd say it was his lucky day when he found you. He couldn't hardly live on a better place, or have a better master, either."

Jim smiled his appreciation and nodded in agreement. "I'm showing him again. I haven't asked him to go flat out yet, but we took first place in western riding and western pleasure two weeks ago, and thirds in reining and pole bending."

"I'M BEGINNING TO SEE HOW COME so many people have these motorhomes, Harry," said Matt as the big vehicle rolled smoothly along a country road. "You see a lot of them at the horse shows. Most of us can't afford to have them, though, so Jim and Norma and Alexandra make friends with some of the people that do have 'em."

They were returning to the Bradley ranch after a day of sightseeing. Aunt Hazel was perched in her seat on Harry's right where she usually rode, taking in the scenery. Matt sat on the end of a couch right behind Harry. Norma and Jim occupied big easy chairs further back.

"Yaaaa," said Harry. "They're the way to travel nowadays. We even have a washer-dryer back there, so we're a completely self-contained unit—don't have to use washaterias, even."

Harry had noticed some newspaper boxes beside some of the mailboxes along the road. Most of them had the names of local papers on them, such as *The Brentwood Banner*, but now and then he saw a box for *The Houston Sun*.

Perhaps for want of something else to break the silence with, he said, "Matt, I see that people get the *Sun* way out here in the country."

Hazel came bolt upright and stared at Harry for a long time. "Boy are you dumb, Harry," she declared emphatically. "The sun shines all over the world."

JIM CAME IN THE FRONT DOOR AND LOOKED in the living room, then went into the kitchen where he found his mother. "Where's Aunt Hazel, Mom?" he asked. "I want to show her something funny. Mehitabel was moving her kittens from the attic and Sam picked one up and is sitting by it a ways off from the others. She's trying to get the cat to play with her, so she's holding a kitten hostage."

"I think she went to the bathroom—"

"Eeeeeek!" Aunt Hazel's scream came from the bathroom, but in seconds she appeared in the hallway, pulling her panties up under her dress. "There's a *snake* in the bathroom!" she exclaimed.

Jim ran for the bathroom. Matt and Harry had heard Hazel's scream from outside and rushed into the house. A search of the bathroom turned up no sign of a snake.

Harry shook his head with grave concern. "I hope we don't get into a phase where she starts seeing things like snakes and green monsters."

Matt said, "I don't see how there could have been a snake in here. But I could tell she really believed she saw one."

Jim went into the kitchen and said to Aunt Hazel. "We can't find a sign of a snake. Where was he when you saw him? Did he wiggle across the floor?"

"He wasn't on the floor," she said. "I turned around and there he was, looking me right in the face."

Jim pondered the answer. It seemed so illogical that a snake could have been on top of the commode tank, where it would have had to be to look her in the face. Maybe Uncle Harry's fear was right, that Aunt Hazel was seeing things.

By the time he got Aunt Hazel outside to see the drama involving Sam and the cat, it was over. "Shucks, Aunt Hazel, I wanted you to see that. Sorry that snake messed everything up. Would you like to meet Charlotte, our spider?"

Aunt Hazel laughed. "You have a pet spider?"

"Sure," he said. He took her hand and led her through the barn into the corral. "She eats flies and bugs and kind of cleans up the place. She builds pretty webs, too."

Harry and Matt were on the porch, engaged in idle conversation, when they heard Aunt Hazel's robust laugh and the animated, cheerful tone of her talk with Jim.

Harry said, "Matt, it sure is good that Hazel gets to spend some time with you folks. It's about the only time I ever see a smile on her face. Poor thing just sits around looking at nothing all day long, probably thinking about her mother or somebody else she can't ever see anymore."

They could hear Hazel laughing merrily. "I don't buy that baloney," she said. "That spider doesn't understand you, Jimmy. You can't fool old Hazel. I think she was going to walk off that way without you telling her to do it. But it's a good trick." She laughed heartily, from deep down and for a long time.

"For a kid, Jim has an unusual tolerance for old folks, don't he, Matt?" Harry said.

"Well, I wouldn't say it's a tolerance, Harry—it's more a genuine affection. He truly likes you both. You should see how excited he gets when he learns you're coming. Jim likes everybody. And he presumes everybody likes him, until he gets a rude awakening now and then."

Matt related the incident at Richter's store about Old Man Skinner's hateful treatment of Jim, as told to Matt by Andrew Meridith.

"I hope you gave the old goat a piece of your mind," said Harry heatedly.

Matt smiled. "There was a time when I would have done that. But Andrew said he was telling me so I would know that Jim had weathered a rocky road like a gentleman. He also told me how he and his wife had schooled their daughter to ignore taunts. 'You can't go through life getting into a fracas every time somebody calls you a nigger,' he tells her. So when somebody tries to get her goat, she just flashes them her biggest smile and lets it all roll right off her back. Jim's really learning a lot from that girl—and from her parents, too."

"This artist is black?" Harry asked, the surprise evident on his face.

"Sure. I thought you knew that. He's Oscar and Ruby's son-in-law—married to their daughter. They have about as much class as you're ever going to encounter—in blacks, whites or any other color. The sky's the limit for Alexandra. Smart, personality plus, speaks with pure eloquence—she even has Jim cleaning up his speech. We're going to drop in on them for a few minutes in a while. Jim wanted you to get to meet them."

Aunt Hazel and Jim had concluded their visit with Charlotte. Jim left her with his father and Uncle Harry and went back into the bathroom and made another search for the snake, worried about the phase Uncle Harry had spoken of. There was hardly a place for a snake to hide. He picked up the paper Aunt Hazel had been reading in the bathroom. It was open at the funnies. He went to the kitchen, a humorous scene forming in his mind.

His mother saw the gleam in his eye and the gathering smile before he said a word. She waited for whatever was forthcoming with a little smile of her own.

He glanced cautiously toward the living room, where Aunt Hazel was sitting. He said in a low voice, "Hey, Mom. Get this. Aunt Hazel is sitting on the commode reading the funnies. She starts to turn a page and a snake that's been reading over her shoulder gives her a tap and says, 'I'm not through with this page. Could you hold up a minute?'"

Norma laughed with him. "I do hope it's not going to be a frequent thing with her. It would be awful to think you really were seeing snakes. Poor Uncle Harry. He seems a little intolerant sometimes, but he's so good to Aunt Hazel. He makes her life as good as it can be."

ON THE WAY HOME FROM THEIR VISIT WITH THE MERIDITHS, Harry said, "You're right about those folks. Fourteen karat. I couldn't have enjoyed anybody more. That little gal tickles my insides the way she smiles—conducts herself like a genuine little princess. *Gorgeous*, ain't she?" He smiled. "Some barn he has there, and that studio! You can tell he's into the big bucks, but he's not one bit ostentatious about it."

Sitting in the back seat between the women, Jim was relating a funny incident about a scorpion that had got up his dad's pants leg and stung him. The merriment behind them gave Harry a chance to speak confidentially to Matt. "I asked Andrew about casting that statue in bronze," he said. "Told him I'd be more than delighted to pay for it if he would do it. He said it was already being *done*. Did you know that?"

"No, I haven't heard anything about it."

Harry glanced behind him and was reassured that his words were being covered by another burst of laughter. "Being a metals man, I found it interesting that they could use acids and heat and other techniques to give a century's worth of age to a bronze. I sure am anxious to get a look at the real McCoy."

The sun was a hand's breadth above the horizon when they arrived home. "We're going to Richter's store, Jim," Matt announced a few minutes later. He said to Norma. "Harry wants to have a beer and sit in on Saturday Night Live. He says it's better than a Broadway play, listening to those fellows gab. There ought to be a pretty good gathering, this being a nice evening. Want to go?"

Caring little for the chatter at Richter's, she didn't. Old Man Skinner would likely be there, embarrassing the black men with his talk about how the "nigras" were better off when they knew their places—why didn't he just go ahead and say "niggers," she wondered; "nigras" was such an offensively begrudging substitute. She also wondered how he avoided getting punched in the nose now that the sheriff was no longer a crony of his.

Matt was amused at the way she'd once needled Old Man Skinner after suffering a few of his sessions in silence. Finding him the only customer there when she and Matt had walked in, she'd gone on a stealth attack. She circulated around him, animated and smiling her best genuine artificial smile. She talked about how much they enjoyed socializing with the blacks in the community. "We were visiting with the Meridiths! Don't you just love little Alexandra, Mr. Skinner? She is *so* smart and talented. And they have such a *beautiful* place—of course, Andrew is *very* rich!"

Skinner's sullen silence allowed her to ramble on. "Do you know Ruby and Oscar Jackson, Mr. Skinner?" she asked, as if it was possible that he did not. "Oh, good. I wasn't sure you had met them. We had them over for dinner last night and you couldn't *imagine* a better time. Have you ever had them to dinner? No? Well, if you want a delightful evening. . . Ruby is *so* gracious and entertaining—and *Oscar!* A walking encyclopedia on Winchester County." She took a long breath to let Skinner squirm and sulk a little more.

"Oscar can tell you the most exciting history! Did you know, Mr. Skinner, that our dear old Rosenbaum place was part of a league— Oscar says that's three square miles of land, and that's why League Line Road is three miles long." She clasped her hands together and assumed an expression that marveled at the logic of it. As she spoke she twisted her body and indulged in little curtsies of expression.

Matt prowled the shelves nearby, listening and stealing peeks at her performance. Reinhard Richter relaxed on his nail keg with his pudgy fingers interlaced across his ample tummy, smiling complacently at the performance.

"*Our* place was part of a league granted by Stephen F. Austin, the father of Texas, to a Mr. Arthur McCormick on August seventh, eighteen-twenty-four," Norma gushed. "Oscar said old Mr. Rosenbaum bought it from the McCormicks sixty years later, in eighteen-eighty-four. Isn't it exciting to know that only two families stand between our place and *Stephen F. Austin?* Anytime you want to know any history about Winchester County, Mr. Skinner, you should ask Oscar.

"Ruby and Oscar Jackson," she said with a sigh. "The finest people one could ever meet. We're so lucky to be their friends!"

She turned away and said, "Well—" as if she was finished. Then she quickly turned back and said, "If you want to know the history of *your* place, Mr. Skinner, Oscar can tell you. Maybe your place traces close back to Stephen F. Aust—" She stopped abruptly, frowned and seemed reluctant to go on. "Oh, dear. *That's* right," she said with a tinge of regret in her voice, "your place was part of that big ranch subdivided by a Houston developer, who bought it from the bankruptcy auction of the Houston oil man that bought it from the insurance man that went broke." Then she brightened, "But maybe it had real roots before all of those people got involved. You should ask Oscar."

Ever since that day, Old Man Skinner was no more anxious to encounter Norma Bradley than she was to see him, but she wasn't sure she could play the role successfully a second time.

Norma shook her head. "No, I don't want to visit the Theater in the Round unless you can guarantee that Old Man Skinner isn't starring. Anyway, Aunt Hazel and I are going down to visit Ruby and Oscar."

"That's good. We won't stay too long—depends on what's showing. I hope Harry has some luck. The last time I took him to Richter's, Old Man Skinner hogged the show, talking about his theory of democracy. I told you about that . . . I can't believe I didn't tell you about it. You recall it, don't you Harry?"

"Sure do. But the part I liked best was what Jim said on the way home."

"Tell me," she demanded.

Matt said, "Well, you know how Old Man Skinner thinks a democracy should work—that only certain people should be allowed to vote, that they should have to measure up to some standard before they could vote. Voting would be restricted to property owners, which would cut out a lot of 'nigras,' Skinner said. Voters should be *responsible* citizens—whatever he meant by that he didn't say. So we just listened, and on the way home we were all quiet, thinking our own thoughts.

"Suddenly Jim leans over the seat and says to me and Harry, 'But who would decide?' I had forgotten about Skinner. I asked him what he meant. He said, 'Who would decide whether a person gets to vote or not?'"

Harry laughed. "Old Jimmy ain't so dumb as Skinner figured his audience to be. He'd found the fly in Old Skinner's ointment right off. Who decides? That's the *key*. Skinner would naturally see *himself* as the grand master deciding who can vote and who can't. His plan is nothing but a dictatorship, and little Jimmy here smoked it out just like that." He snapped his fingers.

When the trio arrived at Richter's Store, the sun, looking red-orange to Jim, and to Harry like a glob of red-hot iron ready for the forging hammers, was resting on the horizon, slightly flattened into an oval by its apparent encounter with terra firma. A few black men occupied the benches on either side of the front door. They all spoke greetings to Matt Bradley, sincerity showing in their faces; two spoke directly to Jim. Both Matt and Jim responded warmly; Harry greeted them with a smile and a nod. There were enough pickups and cars parked outside to show that a good little group was inside.

"I don't see Old Man Skinner's pickup," Matt said happily.

Inside, Matt waved to Reinhard Richter. On seeing Uncle Harry, Reinhard came bustling out from behind the counter, wiping his hands on his apron and beaming his good nature upon him. After they exchanged greetings Richter spoke a few words of welcome to Matt and Jim and returned to his padded nailkeg.

"Get a soda, Jim. On the house," Richter called out. Jim took a Coke from the crushed ice and went to the counter to thank him. Richter got up and put some cracklings in a bag. "That's for you and your dad helping me get that hay in awhile back. I'd of lost a hundred bales for sure if you hadn't helped me get it in."

Jim expressed his thanks and said he was glad they were passing by that day so they could help. He didn't bother to remind Mr. Richter that he had already been given at least a half-dozen sodas and as many bags of cracklings as thanks for his part in that deed. Then he went to a nook beside the old wood stove that heated the place in the winter, the most out-of-the-way place he could find.

Matt and Uncle Harry had selected beers. The men inside nodded cordially to Harry and most of them spoke a greeting to Matt. Harry said to nobody in particular, "I like to try local beers when I can, and when I'm in this neck of the woods I'm anxious for some of this Shiner Bock." Some heads nodded in polite approval.

Harry strolled casually about the store, marveling with an occasional silent chuckle at some of the age-old advertising and some of the merchandise. The splendid old post office in the corner, no longer used, could be part of a movie set, he thought. His eyes roamed over the intricately designed oak woodwork beside the counter and even below it. The words "Post Office" were carved in the arched facade, which was ornamented with a row of nicely turned oak spindles, closely set in a carved molding that followed the arch up, over, and back down the other side. His fingers caressed the worn oak counter with its finely carved edges.

He moved on to a faded advertisement for *VISTA* car wax and moved a few items so he could read it. The proud owner of a red Rambler American was looking down the side of his car, admiring its gleaming shine. The poster described a contest with the grand prize a 1959 Rambler American sedan with a suggested price of $1,845, delivered at Kenosha, Wisconsin.

On the wall were posters advertising Old Gold and Fatima cigarettes, and one for a special Christmas carton of Philip Morris cigarettes with pictures of Lucille Ball and Desi Arnaz, accompanied by the little bellhop, Johnny. The copy said, "Something <u>wonderful</u> happens when you give Philip Morris."

In a glass paneled display case was an Adam hat, the kind worn by George Raft in fifties movies, sitting jauntily on a dummy head. The price tag was $4.99. A camera was on display: an Argus C-3 with flashbulb attachment, complete with a carton of Sylvania Blue Dot flash bulbs. Alongside it were two razors, one a Sunbeam Shavemaster electric, the other a *Gem Feather Weight single-edge razor, including a free ten-blade Push-Pak of Amazing Gem Duridium blades and crystalline case: All for only 98¢. A $1.80 value!*"

Harry's eye fell on a stylish Shaeffer's TM pen and pencil set— "TM," said the card beside it, meant "Thin Model." Imaginative, Harry thought. The set included a handsome black and silver Snorkel-model fountain pen and a matching mechanical pencil. The hood over the penpoint was stamped "14K." The price tag for the set said $27.50.

"Reinhard," Harry called in a low voice to the proprietor, seated on his padded nail keg. "Is this fountain-pen set for sale?"

Reinhard laughed. "It sure is. It's the last of the bunch. I stocked up on them things for Christmas—let's see," he screwed his face up in a contemplative expression, "it must have been along about fifty-two I got 'em. Make you a deal, a dollar off just to get rid of it."

Harry nodded his acceptance and said, "Sold." Then he lovingly removed the pen from the little elastic band that held it in the case. He took off the top, which had been placed over the non-writing end to allow display of the attractive, expensive-looking point. Then he twisted the end and out ran the snorkel, which allowed filling the pen without dipping the point in the ink. Harry smiled at the distant recollection of receiving a gift set just like this one from Hazel, a birthday present in—could it have been fifty-two? After replacing the pen in the case he closed it and put it in his pocket with the warm feeling of having made a precious purchase. He stopped by the counter and pocketed his change.

"Thanks," said Richter. "I'll make you a deal on that hat, too."

"Thank *you*," said Harry. "The hat's a beaut, but the wrong size." He strolled around the fringes of the group and found himself a place to stand and drink his Shiner Bock.

Jim had noticed with some nervousness that the very first time he took a crackling from the bag, Mr. Mehlmann's eyes hungrily followed his hand, and from time to time thereafter as he ate them. He chewed with as little movement of his mouth as possible. Feeling of his bag told him he still had plenty of cracklings; he almost wished they were gone.

He looked up when Reinhard called across to Uncle Harry, who stood on the far side of the group from the counter. "Harry, did Matt tell you I almost had to shoot him awhile back?"

"No, he didn't say anything about that."

Matt laughed heartily. "I sure should have told you that one, Harry," he said. He looked across the men who were sitting on boxes, upended wooden soft-drink cases from years gone by, and other makeshift seats, since there was not a chair or bench in the place. "Fellas, don't ever do anything to make Reinhard think you might be a little tetched," he tapped his head, "or he'll blow what's left of your brains out."

Reinhard's chuckles had him bouncing up and down, and Harry noticed for the first time that an old double-barreled shotgun leaned against the wall beside him.

Jim, who had been present when it happened, said in a soft voice, "Tell Uncle Harry, Dad,"

"Okay." Matt spoke to everyone in general. "I left the farm one evening late and went into the garage off the barn where I keep the little Ford tractor—the one you overhauled, Walter," he said to Walter Mehlmann. "I forget what I was after, but I had to squeeze between the tractor and some tow sacks stacked in there. Then Jim and I came to Richter's to get a soda before heading home to Houston.

"He's sitting here all by himself, right there like he's sitting now, rared back on that nail keg." Richter began chuckling all over again at the memory of that event.

Matt continued, "I was standing in front of the counter—I forget what I was talking about, but I had become kind of excited in the telling of it, waving my arms. And just then a scorpion that I must have picked up when I went by those tow sacks popped me right below the knee. See, he probably got on my pants, and during the ride up here he crawled up my pants leg."

Jim was laughing quietly.

"I let out a whoop and a holler I must have guessed immediately what had stung me—and started jumping up and down, trying to dislodge the thing and get him out of my pants leg. It stung me again and I hollered and jumped higher. Finally I saw that scorpion there on the floor, and I stomped him into the next century. Having killed him, I stopped jumping around to tend to the bites. I get my little Cutter snake bite kit out of my pocket, and for the first time notice that Reinhard has his shotgun in his hands, holding it at the ready.

"I hadn't seen what he was up to while I was fighting off the scorpion, but evidently he thought I'd gone stark raving mad. He looked at me, then he looked at the gun in his hands. 'I thought you'd lost all your marbles, Matt,' he said. I tell him it's a heck of a note when a guy that gets stung by a scorpion gets shot over it, too. Good grief . . ." he said wiping tears of laughter from his eyes.

There was a period of laughter and comment, followed by a pause in the conversation, as it often happens when the fire under a good subject has gone out.

Ralph Edelbrock, a tall, skinny, redfaced man who seldom talked and never joked, was sitting on a beat-up Grapette case, leaning forward with his hands clasped, his forearms resting on his knees. His stern eyes stared at his beer, sitting on the floor. Apparently he had been absent from the group for a while and as he cleared his throat to speak, some there hoped his absence would be explained. He took a swig of beer and set the bottle on the wooden floor, being careful to put it precisely on the wet ring left there when he'd picked it up. Without looking he said, "Hoop snake almost got me about a month ago."

"Hoop snake?" asked Lester Myers.

Edelbrock's expression was as serious as one can be. Without looking up he said, "Deadliest snake in America—North, South or

Central America. The highbrow Latin name for it is *serpens contortrix anularius.*"

With a tinge of skepticism, Lester asked, "Now how would you know something like that, Ralph?"

Ralph gave him a piercing look. "You'll learn a whole lot about the hoop snake, and mighty quick, if you ever have a brush with one, Lester. *If* you live to tell about it."

"Yeah, yeah. I suspect you're right about that, Ralph," Lester quickly, humbly agreed. "Deadly, huh? Glad you came through it, Ralph. How'd it come about?"

Ralph still stared at the floor, as if reliving a terror almost too horrible to recall. The men were tolerant of his need for patience, and they waited.

"I had gone down to clean out a stopped-up ditch that drained a little pasture down at the bottom of my east slope. So I'm walking up the east slope with a grubbin' hoe in my hand."

He shook his head and squinted his eyes, as if having to brace himself before continuing. His expression was intense. He glanced up and his eyes quickly swept the group. "Y'all know what a hoop snake is, don't you? They're rare as all get-out. Well, they are now, but they won't be rare for long." Before anyone could answer, his eyes dropped once more to stare morosely at the floor.

After an interval, he said, "A hoop snake works his way to the top of a hill, then he takes his tail in his mouth and starts to writhe until his contortions—that's where *contortrix* comes in—his wiggling gets him up. Right away he's rolling like a hoop—*anularius,* or 'ring.' I don't guess they had actual *hoops,* such as barrel hoops, back in them Latin days. Once old hoop snake gets rolling, he can go so fast while darting this way and that you can't hardly get out of his way. *Blinding speed!*" Ralph shivered noticeably.

Expressions of deep concern, fear of even the *thought* of such a marauder, however rare, could be seen on the faces present.

"So I'm coming up the east slope with the hoe in my hand, and I see him—a *hoop snake* coming down the hill like a runaway wagon wheel and headed right for me."

When Ralph raised his head he had a wild look in his eyes; his red face was a picture of fright. There was an air of brittle tenseness about the men, all transfixed on Ralph.

Lester could no longer stand the slow pace of the story. "What did you *do?*" he asked.

"There was only one thing *to* do," Ralph said. He surveyed the men with a fateful, dogged look, lips drawn back to reveal his yellow teeth. "I stood my ground until he was just about on me," he snarled. "Then, I jumped aside and stuck my hoe out as a decoy. He bit my hoe handle as he went by—teeth like an *alligator*—and boys, you've never seen nothin' like the effects of the venom of a hoop snake."

"Dog*gone!*" Lester exclaimed. "Good thinking, Ralph. *Dang!*" He smacked a fist in a palm. "Little Jim here was telling me once about a cottonmouth bitin' his bandanna, and he was scared the venom might've poisoned it. But it didn't, right, Jim?"

Surprised at being drawn into the drama, Jim's only response was his head bobbing quickly up and down.

"I never heard of this here hoop snake," Lester said. "How come something like this could be around and me not hear about it?"

Ralph studied the floor and then nodded in a display of understanding. "They haven't been here long. According to the Department of Agriculture investigators—I read this in the County Agent's office just a week or so ago—a pregnant female hoop snake came in with a load of exotic wood from East Africa. A rich guy from Houston—" He glanced at Matt. "No offense, Matt."

Matt flashed a big smile. "No offense taken. I'm the *poor* guy from Houston."

"A rich guy from Houston that bought the Winklemann place was redoing the house. You know how they do, spend more remodeling than a new house would cost. His wife just *had* to have a special exotic African wood stairway bannister and U.S.D.A. thinks that pregnant hoop snake from Africa wound up at the old Winklemann place and had her babies there."

"Hot *dang!*" Lester cried. "That's at William Tell, only five miles from this very spot!" He looked from one man to the other. All were nodding, displaying their own fears of the hoop-snake threat.

Ralph looked up at Lester and jerked his chin aside in acknowledgement. "You ain't wrong, Lester. Agriculture Department says in a few years this here hoop snake's gonna make fire ants and killer bees seem like pets by comparison. First place, the snakes *we* know eat rats, fish, and things like that. They only bite humans out of fear. Except the copperhead—he's just hateful through and through. But the *hoop* snake, he considers humans a delicacy. Second, where cottonmouths and rattlers at least try to get out of your way, a hoop snake can see a man from a mile away, smell him from two miles downwind, and he'll work his way uphill from where the man is, or where he's headed, stalking him, just to get a crack at him."

Someone whistled low. The men looked at each other and shifted uneasily. Everyone there had paid part of the price of the invasion of fire ants, and most were aware they were believed to have entered the country in a load of lumber from South America. It had taken forty years for fire ants to migrate from Mobile, Alabama to Winchester County.

"Look how fast those killer bees come up from Brazil," said Tommy Thompson from the back fringe of the group. The severity of his expression was plain. "I read that twenty-some queens escaped from a laboratory down there and in just a few years here they are, jumping on people right around here, and out of pure meanness." He shook his head sadly, "Now we got something that didn't get loose in Brazil, or even Mobile, but right here in Winchester County. We'll be disgraced across the country, once word gets out about this hoop snake."

Milo Mangrum, whose farm was in the flat of the Brazos River bottom, was staring with the narrowed eyes and tilted head of one who has detected a ray of hope. "What if he can't get uphill from you, Ralph? On account of they ain't no hills."

Ralph threw him a serious wink and a look of encouragement. "That's where you got a chance, Milo," he said.

Milo sighed hopefully and some of the tenseness left his face.

Ralph added, "Yep, that's where you got a chance. On flat land a hoop snake can't make his hoop, and he can only crawl about ten miles an hour."

Milo's face remained composed for a long time before it once again assumed a confounded expression. "*Ten miles an hour!*" he cried. "You can't outrun something for very long that can travel a steady ten miles an hour!"

Ralph threw his hands out in a defeated gesture. "I guess that's why the inhabitants of the country where this thing comes from have to live elsewhere," he said with authority.

Lester's hands were fists, drawn up at his sides. "And you already *seen* one! A *grown* one! Dog*gone!*"

Ralph's gaze again became morose and he resumed staring at the floor. Some of the men began to relax, appearing as it did that Ralph's recitation of his experience was over.

"By golly," said a man heatedly, "I'm getting ahold of Phil Gramm's office tomorrow—well, Monday. They got to get the Agriculture Department on this right away, if it ain't already too late. Matt, I bet you know Bill Archer. . . . Dick Armey? They're the kind of heavyweights we better get working on this thing."

"Good idea, Smitty," said another. "Senator Gramm would be one to call. He'll go after something this important. I'll get ahold of him, too. And Archer and Armey for sure. We better remind them about how the Department of Agriculture could've held fire ants right there in Mobile and gradually exterminated every last one, but they didn't."

One of the men stood shaking his head and looking at the floor. "They said fire ants would never get far from Mobile. They said they could hold the killer bees in Central America where the land gets skinny. Now this."

Ralph, almost forgotten, sitting low on his Grapette case, cleared his throat again and added, almost as an afterthought, "Boys, you ain't never seen nothin' like the power of that hoop snake venom." He threw a long, significant look at his audience, and here his narrative shifted into high gear.

Speaking at a rapid clip, he said, "As soon as that sucker bit my hoe handle, it started swelling up just like that!" He snapped his fingers. "It was swelling up so fast, by the time I hit the house I was *dragging* it—and barely able. In no time it was as big as a log and still growing. I called Brentwood Lumber to come out, and they picked it up with a pole trailer. By the time they got it to the mill, that hoe handle had swole up so big that the lumber cut out of it was enough to build a barn. So I built a new barn and everything was fine until I painted it. Not knowin' that turpentine is the only antidote for the venom of a hoop snake cost me a barn. Naturally, I painted my new barn and when that turpentine in the paint started neutralizing the venom, the wood started shrinking until—well, there wasn't enough wood left to make a hoe handle out of it."

Ralph's forlorn expression changed only slightly to a wry smile. He took a swig of his beer and listened as isolated embarrassed laughter broke out, followed by booming guffaws as backs were slapped and arms were punched in good humor. He'd had them hooked right up to the last line, and his pleasure showed in his face.

Lester alone did not smile. He laid an icy look on Ralph and grumbled, "Well, that was a good story, Ralph. I won't lie, you had me fooled right up close to the end. But you won't fool me no more." He stood slump-shouldered, hands in his pockets, looking down at Ralph with disgust. Then he slowly turned away, throwing one last contemptuous glance over his shoulder.

Ralph looked at Lester's back and his smile broadened. "It was worth it to fool you just once, Lester," he said.

The wind was out of the group's sails for a long time except for relieved chuckles and occasional exclamations. "Hoop snake! Baloney." Somebody said, "Contortrix whatchamacallit! That was the tipoff right there." Another man said, "The inhabitants of the country where the hoop snake comes from have to live elsewhere? *That* should have woke me up!"

Finally, Swede Christensen broke the long silence, one broken now and then by a chuckle, a laugh. "Wasn't that a surprise about Henry Rosenberg?" Most of the heads nodded. Matt looked at Swede with a curious expression, but he wasn't going to bite.

"Yeah, Matt," said Swede. "Henry Rosenberg died day before yesterday. He had got his first social security check that day, went to town and cashed it, bought a few things and came home. That evening he's sitting in his rocker having a bowl of ice cream. His wife comes into the living room and there he sits, the ice cream bowl in his lap like he just set it there, looking like he'd fell asleep. He was dead as a mackerel. Heart attack."

Matt looked suitably sorrowful over the news but, still wary of taking a baited treble hook, said nothing.

"Yeah, I heard. But that's the way to go, ain't it?" said a voice from the group. "No pain, no worryin' about old man death looming nearer every day."

A murmur of agreement arose.

Walter Mehlmann, a modestly fat man of about seventy, cleared his throat as a mischievous smile played on his face. "Now, I don't know so much about that," he said. "There's something to say about getting some notice, like old Smithfield did a couple of years ago. His doctor gave him a year after he found that cancer, and he died right on schedule. He wasted that year, though, moaning and groaning about having to die, and him being only seventy-nine. I got to where when I saw him coming in Brentwood, I'd just cross the street or go in a store to keep from having to hear his whinin'. In the first place, he'd already outlived most people. In the second place, did he think he wasn't never gonna die?"

"What do you mean by saying he wasted the year?" asked one of the men. "What could he've done about it?"

"What could he've *done?*" boomed Mehlmann in a voice reeking with astonishment. "What could he've *done?* I'll tell you what *I* would've done. First, when Doc Reynolds gave me the news, I'd pat him on the back and tell him—smiling real nice so he'd know there wasn't no hard feelings—I didn't want no more of his advice.

"Then I'd beeline it over here and tell Reinhard there to sack me up a big bunch of Mrs. Winklemann's fresh homemade cracklin's, and not to tie the sack up like he always does, because I want 'em *now!* I'd tell him to be sure to pick out the fattest cracklin's of the bunch." He glanced again at Jim, whose hand had just dipped into the crackling bag.

Jim stopped in mid-move, reluctant to take out a crackling, or even to withdraw his hand from the bag. At the first opportunity, he surreptitiously hid the sack behind the smokestack of the old wood stove. He'd eat them later in privacy, he thought.

Walter Mehlmann waved a fat arm in Reinhard's direction. "I'd ask Reinhard to give me the best and biggest stogie he's got in this place—no, the whole box. And that evening I'd go to Mrs. Schumann's Cafe and order the biggest chicken-fried steak in the house, and tell her not to scrimp on the cream gravy, neither. And I'd salt the heck out of it, too, using my own Celtic Sea Salt that I'd brought along—saw it talked about in the paper just the other day. And I'd hope Doc Reynolds happened to be there to see me. Ha! I'd take a pinch of that salt out of the little wood box and just before sprinkling it on my steak, I'd wink at Doc. Then I'd top that off with apple pie with vanilla ice cream on top—*two* scoops. After that, I'd stop at Hugo's bar and have a manhattan—*two* manhattans. Walter was beaming. "What do you think my place would bring, Reinhard?"

"Oh . . . two-seventy-five, maybe three hundred."

"Okay," said Walter, "Say three hundred thousand for the farm, maybe fifty grand for the shop and tools—the business has to have some value. So say I walk with three-fifty or so. I sell the farm with a lifetime tenancy—wouldn't be hard to make that deal, with Doc Reynolds certifying that my days are numbered. When all the money is in the bank, I go tell Lee Roy on the QT that I want it all out in cash. Give him a few days to get it together, because I wouldn't want to sop up all his check-cashing cash. But he's got to keep quiet, I tell him, because I don't want to get robbed—that's what I *tell* him, but that ain't the only reason.

"See, I don't want the IRS snooping around any sooner than they would be anyway. Lee Roy has to report that withdrawal, so they'll know soon enough. Before I even talk to Lee Roy I make reservations for a week in Vegas. As soon as I get the money, I hide about seventy, eighty thousand somewhere, then divvy up the rest between my kids. I tell them each one to keep mum about it, and don't make any big deposits and don't buy anything expensive, or the IRS will get suspicious." He gave out a robust laugh as his plan continued to unfold.

"Then I'd go on that trip and make sure I was noticed. I'd make some big bets at the crap tables at several places and make a nuisance of myself so they're sure to remember me. But I really don't lose more'n maybe ten grand—who knows? I might even *win* some dough.

But instead of staying a week I come home a couple of days early, to make it look like I went broke."

Walter laughed heartily at his flourishing ingenuity. "Then I sit down and write a letter to the IRS and tell them I'm glad I don't have to worry about them anymore because I went to Vegas and squandered all my money." His full face was red with laughter, his eyes barely visible through slits. The idea of putting one over on the IRS sent a wave of glee through the entire group.

"Then right soon I would get a few of you guys together and we'd go to Zihuateñejo, Mexico. I was talking to a rice farmer that had a tractor in my shop. He went down there and chartered a fine fishing boat for a week. Him and his five buddies caught marlin and whatever else big fish you catch in the ocean down there. Had a heckuva time, and only spent a few thousand." He looked around at the faces, each now glowing with the presumption of being one of the lucky sport fishermen, forgetting the theoretical aspects of the event. "Wouldn't that be a swell time?" Enthusiastic agreement erupted all around.

Mehlmann stepped up to the meat case with an exaggerated movement of body and arms. He looked over his shoulder at his audience. "Then I'd come in here and say, 'Reinhard, see those two pork chops there?'" Reinhard got up and opened the case. His fingers hovered over the row of chops, favoring the lean chops on one end. "No, no, no," said Mehlmann impatiently, "the *big* ones down there. The ones with the thick fat around the edge." Reinhard held one up for inspection by the congregation. It must have weighed ten or twelve ounces. "I'd buy those two chops to have with my fried eggs in the morning. With my grits, with a puddle of butter in the middle. With my little box of Celtic Sea Salt handy, because you need a lot of salt with a fine breakfast like that."

He pointed at the slabs of bacon hanging from the ceiling joists. "I'd need a slab of that bacon about every week or so; keep a couple of cases of Shiner Bock in the fridge at all times—" a glance at Uncle Harry "—and a few cases in reserve so my pals will be more apt to stop by and shoot the breeze. Since I'm not working anymore, I got a lot of time to shoot the bull.

"And Reinhard, you'd need to start stocking those good, marbled strip steaks you can get from KC Meats. The ones with plenty of yellow fat running through 'em and on the sides, because that's going to be my steady diet when I'm not eating chicken-fries at Mrs. Schumann's."

Harry's laughter over the macabre drama unfolding of its own accord before his very eyes had escalated to breathless squeals and was as provocative as a school of sardines under a flock of hungry gulls. It had taken a while for the level of hilarity to rise to its rightful zenith, but now it was at its peak. Reinhard Richter sat bouncing on his nail keg, his apron pressed against his eyes with both hands. The contagious laughter smothered the subject and they would learn no more about Walter Mehlmann's theoretical last days. The group began to break up.

A big man sauntered casually over to the counter. He spoke quietly to Reinhard and tapped emphatically with a straight forefinger on one end of the meat display. Reinhard opened the display case, placed the two fattest pork chops on a piece of paper on the scale, wrapped them up and tied the package up with string. The man paid for them—and, of course, the generous amount of heavy paper they were wrapped in—and with lowered head glanced quickly and self-consciously left and right. Then he tucked the package under his arm and left without a word to anyone.

Lester stopped at the counter, said good night to Richter, and then, with elaborate casualness, said, "Reinhard, give me a couple of those cigars—no, the big, black ones. I know a guy who would love to have a good smoke, and I'll just stop by and give them to him on the way home." Reinhard did not comment on the fact that nobody lived between the store and Lester's place.

Walter Mehlmann was almost past the counter when he leaned way over close to Reinhard and said in an undertone, "Reinhard, give me about a pound of those cracklin's. I'll drop 'em off to Ben on the way by his place. He always liked cracklin's—*fat* ones, Reinhard, he likes fat ones."

Another man stopped at the counter as Walter walked away. "Give me a dozen of those jumbo eggs, Reinhard, and a pound of bacon and a pound of butter." He placed a box of grits and a package of pancake mix on the counter. "Lessee," he added, "you better give me a half-pint or so of that heavy cream."

Walter was barely out of the door when he tore the string off the crackling bag. Jim felt a measure of redemption to see him holding a big, fat crackling high, examining it in the poor light. Then, smiling broadly and with a small, elegant flourish of his hand, he gracefully placed the crackling in his mouth. From behind the stovepipe Jim retrieved the bag containing his own few remaining cracklings. He could eat them now without feeling guilty.

"ALL RIGHT, AUNT HAZEL AND YOU GENTLEMEN just in from the theater," said Norma, "dinner is served in the dining room. A one-course dinner—Louisiana shrimp-and-oyster gumbo. Well, two dishes, counting the rice." As they filed out of the living room, Norma said quietly to Aunt Hazel, "Are you having a good time? You haven't said a word."

Aunt Hazel's mind was obviously still visiting the Jacksons. She said softly, "I was just watching your friends, Ruby and—uh, well— they are so nice. I didn't have anything to say, so I just watched." Norma squeezed her hand and helped her to her place at the table.

Harry was still wearing a big smile. "You gals should have been there tonight. My sides are aching from laughing—" He snapped his fingers and said, "Oh, yeah! Wait till you see what I bought at Richter's." He produced the Shaeffer pen and pencil set, opened the satin-lined case with a flourish, and displayed it first to Norma, then to Hazel. "*Exactly* the same set you bought me for my birthday over thirty years ago, Hazel. See that price tag? Richter gave me a buck off because it was the last of some stock he bought in fifty-two!" He laughed until his eyes were slits. "Had 'em since *fifty-two* and the price tag still holds. No inflation at Richter's."

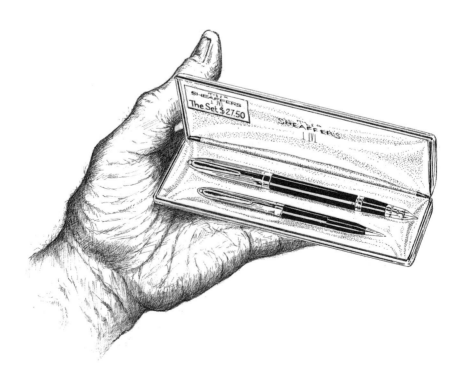

CHAPTER 29

A cool front had come through during the night, leaving the morning air laced with a welcome nip. Jim slipped out early and gave Old Black his treat. He caught a few flies for Charlotte and complimented her on a nice web. Way off to the southeast he saw the deep dark blue trailing edge of the front. It had brought no rain but left a high, thin overcast behind. He conversed with Old Black for a time, and then sounds in the house told him others were stirring. He was just about to step in the front door when he heard a piercing scream. Rushing inside he almost ran into Aunt Hazel, who was shuffling swiftly along with her panties around her ankles, her face contorted with horror.

Matt came running out of his bedroom clad only in pants.

Aunt Hazel pointed toward the bathroom and gasped, "The snake! I saw the *snake!*"

Matt rushed into the bathroom, followed by Jim. They made a hasty search but found nothing.

"Jim," said Matt, "we have to take this room apart. I'm going to go outside and look under the house. You look through the cabinets." He stopped and looked around thoughtfully. "I can't believe she would have hallucinations only in here. We have to believe she really saw a snake."

Harry had entered the room and was standing quietly off to one side. He looked skeptical.

"Dad, Aunt Hazel said yesterday that the snake was looking over her shoulder. Do you think maybe—" They both looked at the commode water tank. Matt stepped over and removed the lid. There, coiled up on the mechanism inside, above the water line, was a menacing, agitated snake, long enough to make a couple of coils around the inside of the tank.

"Doggone, Dad!" Jim exclaimed, jumping back.

Harry threw up his arms and recoiled several steps.

"Is it deadly?" asked Jim.

Harry pointed a chubby finger at the snake and exclaimed, "*That* thing's gotta be a *killer!* We're lucky poor Hazel is still alive."

The mottled-brown snake's head was weaving and thrusting menacingly. It was hissing in a loud and hostile way and striking out with a sinister, black forked tongue. To further add to its deadly appearance, its head spread out to form a hood behind its cold eyes giving its head a shape like a cottonmouth.

Jim noted a small smile growing on his father's face. "No, it's not deadly, not even poisonous," Matt said. "It couldn't hurt you, but it could sure make you hurt yourself. Poor Aunt Hazel. She must have heard this guy hissing over her shoulder and looked around to see it maybe only a few inches from her face. Golly, when you think of suddenly, here in the bathroom, turning around and he's looking you right in the face." Matt shuddered.

"What kind of snake is it?" asked Jim, not entirely at ease, considering that the snake was technically still on the loose.

"It's a hognose snake, sometimes called a spreading adder, but it's not an adder. Boy, it sure looks deadly, doesn't it? But it's harmless, has no venom at all. Since it has no other defenses, nature gave it that scary hiss and ferocious behavior."

Matt pointed out a half-moon-shaped opening in the rim of the water tank near the wall. "The overflow, that's how he came and went. And he had to stick his body out of that hole when he was making his appearance to Aunt Hazel. Harry, how would you like to turn around and see that fella looking over your shoulder?"

Redfaced, with both hands doubled up into big fists, Harry trembled at the thought. A small smile began to play on his face. "At least—" he began, suppressed a laugh and jabbed a finger at the toilet seat. Eyes twinkling, he blurted out, "If I was ever going to have to look *that* thing in the eye, that would've been the right place for me to be sittin' when I seen it!" Harry's strong, deep laugh boomed out, rattling the china in the kitchen cabinets.

Norma stopped dead still in her preparations for breakfast and turned quickly toward the sound, listening, then rushed out of the kitchen to see Jim stumbling into the hallway, doubled over in convulsions of laughter and feeling his way, blinded by tears and incoherent as he fought to catch his breath. She turned on her heel and walked fast to the bathroom. Wary, she saw first the open top of the toilet, then the snake.

She was recoiling from the sight of the snake when she came to realize that Harry was leaning in his corner not from fright but for support while he caught his breath to continue a fit of uncontrolled laughter. Matt was sitting on the floor in a corner with his legs stretched out, his body racking with spasms while he wiped at his eyes with his handkerchief, totally overcome by the most sustained and idiotic laughter Norma had ever heard.

Could it be the fabled *laughing* snake whose victims laughed themselves to death? She stepped back even farther out of range of the bobbing, weaving, hissing snake, his tongue flashing out like ominous, black lightning strikes. She shrugged and left the room, hoping that whatever they had wasn't fatal. The sight of two grown men and a boy in such a stage of mirth did have its effect, however, and she was laughing to herself with head bent toward the floor when she returned to the kitchen.

"What is it, Norma?" said Aunt Hazel.

"Oh, nothing, Aunt Hazel." She was reluctant for the snake's victim to discover that there was indeed a most hideous snake in the bathroom, and in a hissing rage. And to see *every* man on the place helplessly convulsed in laughter. . .

Matt got an ice chest from the back porch and used it to take the snake way out back and dump it in the wild. That activity and being separated from Jim and Uncle Harry allowed him to compose himself. He went to Aunt Hazel and explained that they had found a snake, a completely harmless snake, "But anyone in your—your situation would have been scared—" He deliberately avoided the phrase "anyone in your *position*." Somehow, he managed to keep a suitably grave face. "Aunt Hazel, I'm mortified that I didn't find that snake the first time you saw it." He patted her hand and saw that she was no longer shaken. "You were braver than I would have been." She smiled. "Seeing that snake over my shoulder would have scared the *heck* out of me," he chuckled, reminded of a statement by a Louisiana pilot who had described an encounter with especially severe turbulence. He said, "Yeah, boy! That would have scared the *heck* out of me, and I ain't afraid of *nothing*."

"WHERE'S JIM?" NORMA CALLED. HE FOLLOWED the sound of her voice to the living room.

"Jim, don't forget that Sheriff Martinez is coming this morning with his family," she said. "You could have Old Black saddled in case any of the children want to go for a ride." She held up a hand in understanding. "I know you won't let another hand touch his mouth, but I mean if they'd like to ride with you."

He had no sooner finished grooming and saddling Old Black when he saw the sheriff's squad car coming up the lane. He rode a short distance down the lane and escorted the car to the house.

With the sheriff were Sonia Martinez and their five children. Sonia Martinez was as bright and cheerful as could be, as she had been on every previous occasion they had seen her. She hugged Norma warmly, hugged Matt, and then hugged Jim, *squeezed* him a long time, then shook hands with Harry and Hazel.

Jim was very happy to see Sheriff Martinez. When he'd seen him shortly after their adventure, Martinez's leg was in a cast, he was much thinner, and he'd had a grayish, sickly color to his lined face. He had thanked Jim as sincerely as words can convey feelings, and just as sincerely had asked about Old Black.

Jim had also seen him at the Meridith's when the sculpture was presented. He'd looked great then; he said some grateful words about Old Black but he'd said nothing about the intrigue following the incident at Klanke's Mill. Rumor around the county was that there were some big changes in the works, but rumor had been the extent of it.

Today, as Jim watched him in this relaxed setting, thrusting his arms with athletic vigor as he spoke and moving with a light step and a spring in his walk, he thought the sheriff might be just like Old Black, stronger than ever.

During past visits by Mrs. Martinez and the children, Jim and the boys had engaged in simple, fragmentary conversations in Spanish. Mrs. Martinez provided strong encouragement to him. "If you know even five words, Jim, use them. Soon you will know six." So he used the words he knew, improved on their pronunciation and indeed learned new words. Now the group of children were happily engaged in a Spanish conversation of sorts. Jim appreciated their tolerance, for they allowed him time to grope for words, which encouraged him to feel free to make mistakes. Each time he'd been with them his Spanish had improved markedly, and he was now using it with Hispanic kids at school and at horse shows.

Sheriff Martinez had been engaging in light, animated conversation with Matt, Harry, and Norma. Aunt Hazel stood by quietly, as she tended to do in the presence of strangers. Mike Martinez looked toward the corral, where Old Black was standing saddled and tied to the fence. He went up to him and spoke to him in a low voice, holding his head in both hands. Soon he was followed by the other adults.

He smiled at Jim and said, speaking with humility, "Jim, I know you and Old Black don't want to be thanked for saving my life every time we meet. But I haven't thanked you *properly* yet. I'm back in shape now. In fact better than new it seems to me. And I want to say once more how grateful I am to you for getting me out of that well and taking such good care of me until help got there."

He reached up and scratched Old Black on his poll. "It took everything both Jim and this mighty horse could put out to get the job done that day. It was divine providence for me that the only team that could have saved me came along, out of nowhere it seemed to me."

He looked around at the other faces. "I don't know how much Jim told you, but we were beginning to wonder if maybe our rescuers weren't going to show." He slapped his leg. "I wouldn't have this leg if Jim hadn't taken care of it the way he did. I probably, well, there's no probably about it, I would have died of gangrene if he hadn't made that tourniquet and worked it all afternoon."

He squinted his eyes and looked out over the beautiful scenery to the northeast. "I feel like you ought to know why we couldn't seem to get a grip on that dope gang. It was because my chief deputy was in with them up to his armpits. I knew Swagger was involved, but I thought he was only taking payoffs to look the other way. I was not the least suspicious he was in with them all the way. I kept him on the force because I could watch him better than I could if he wasn't there for me to keep an eye on. In the end, with all of his buddies killed, there was nobody to testify against him.

"There had always been a lot of old-time political support for Swagger, support from some powerful people who could work with him but not me, and I needed to give him enough rope to hang himself. I gave it to him, and he did. Even if he almost hung me first." He grinned sheepishly.

"Then I fired him—as you've probably heard. He moved out of Winchester County. He had drawn Deputy Grimshaw in with him, so Grimshaw's gone too. For the first time in over two years as sheriff, I can say we have a totally loyal and competent department. And now we're going to work at improving it.

"Jim, I could go on living without being sheriff. But I couldn't go on at all if I hadn't got out of that fix you found me in. So it's thanks to you that I'm still around. And my family still has a provider, my children still have a father, thanks to you." Jim's face was heating up. He looked down at his boot toe as it busily arranged a small mound of dirt and then flattened and rearranged it. "As for Old Black here, well, I have a hunch he instinctively knows how I feel." His hand had been on Old Black's neck, rubbing under his mane as he spoke. Now he roughly rubbed the horse's nearest ear. Sure enough, Old Black tossed his head and pushed against the sheriff's chest.

THE BRADLEYS WERE PREPARING TO DEPART for Houston, leaving Uncle Harry and Aunt Hazel alone at the farm.

Norma gave Harry a hug. "Uncle Harry, it always seems like you've just got here before the visit's over. Please don't wait a year this time. Would you come back in six months, or sooner?"

He held her at arms' length so he could look into her eyes. "Norma, I was thinking the same thing. No reason we can't come by here, rather than somewhere else. We'll come by in about three or four months. It's good for Hazel. You're about the only folks she has any fun with."

He smiled to see Hazel involved in some humor with Matt and Jim, all laughing heartily. "He's some boy, Norma. And Matt's some guy. You've just gotta be so proud of them."

She nodded, and watched as Harry took Jim aside.

He took Jim by both shoulders, held him at arm's length, and looked at him for a few seconds. "Jimmy, I doubt you realized it, but you gave me some tips about handling Hazel to keep from agitating her. You showed me some ways to raise her spirits when she's glum. I'm going to keep working on those techniques I saw you using. Next time we come I hope you'll see a happier Hazel, like she is right now." He glanced toward where Hazel was laughing and talking with Matt and Norma.

Big, rough-hewn Harry P. Beams, retired machinist and not a candidate for President of the U.S., had a small tear in his eye when he extended his hand to little Jim Bradley, certified hero, championship competitor, and psychologist. They shook hands warmly and then Uncle Harry wrapped him up in a big hug.

CHAPTER 30

Norma Bradley sat in a lawn chair reviewing the course descriptions while Jim vigorously brushed away at Old Black's glistening coat. In the distance, Alexandra could be seen approaching at a brisk pace.

"Jim," she called out, laughing and holding up a piece of paper. "Look at *this!*" she said when she came up to him. "They have Old Black listed in the aged gelding halter class. Isn't that funny? I checked to make sure they didn't leave you out of some performance class or another, thinking it was a swap of entry forms, but you're okay in all of them. I wonder how that happened. They'll refund your entry fee—it's surely their mistake—"

"I entered him," Jim said quickly. "I got to thinking that he's come back so strong and young-looking that he might have a chance. And I don't want Old Black thinking—" A frown crossed his face and was gone. "Anyway," he said, "I studied the rule book and his scars and that knot on his knee are supposed to be disregarded by a halter judge. Everywhere else he looks great."

He smiled. "I sure don't expect him to beat Gorky or Applejack or the other front-runners, but he could place somewhere out of nine, don't you think?"

Alexandra looked stunned. So did Norma Bradley.

"Well—uh," Alexandra's smile flickered, then widened. "Sure. *Sure!* He could place . . . I don't see why not. I was just surprised because you'd never shown him before. I was thinking they had made a mistake. Sure, he could place."

"Look at him, Alexandra," Jim said eagerly, "he's got all his weight back, his coat shines real bright, and look how he stands so straight." He moved to the halter, jiggled it, and Old Black immediately became untracked. The old horse knew this was an inspection, and he stood straight and proud, his nose thrust out to reveal a touching dash of audacity. Jim stepped aside to allow an unrestricted view.

"Don't he look fine? Have you ever seen Old Black looking any better? Of course I haven't put the dressing on his hooves yet."

Alexandra looked at the heroic champion's large feet. Nothing could mitigate the conformation faults of large feet, a rather large head, and a cresty neck. Not to mention that even a youthful nineteen-year-old would have a hard time placing against an arena full of top-notch halter horses in their prime. She said in all honesty, "I would swear on a Bible that I've never seen Old Black look any better than he does this minute. I'd be proud to be holding his halter lead any time, Jim."

OLD BLACK DID NOT PLACE THAT DAY. But he won three trophies along with the blue ribbons that went with the first-place wins, plus two second-place red ribbons. Jim returned home happy, as usual. "You can't expect every judge to see horses the same, Mom," he reasoned.

Norma smiled in agreement. But she felt as uncomprehending as she knew Alexandra had been. Old Black didn't have a prayer in a halter class, period. They had known that from the first, and there had never been the slightest intention to enter him at halter, not even when there were fewer than nine entries, when ribbons went begging for any old plug that would have showed.

Show after show came and went with Old Black consistently getting the gate in the halter classes. When Norma asked Matt about it, he could only say, "I don't know what Jim's thinking, Honey. It must somehow be connected to the incident at Klanke's Mill—a new perception Jim has of him. Or maybe Jim worries that Old Black's feelings might be hurt if he doesn't show him. But the way he gets so enthused that every show is *the* show where Old Black is going to win a ribbon at halter—that tells me he believes he's really got a chance."

"I don't know what to do," Norma said with uncharacteristic gloom. "And that awful Ricky Hoffman rubs it in so hard, as if he's extracting vengeance from Jim for taking over in performance."

Matt put his arms around her. "Well, you know he *is* extracting vengeance," he said, laughing. "And halter is the only vengeance left for him to get. What do we do? We don't do anything. It will have to take care of itself. So don't worry. We'll just watch him lead Old Black into those halter arenas, and watch him lead him out. Then we'll watch him kick the pants off the halter champs in the performance classes."

ALEXANDRA WISHED FOR ONE OF THE good old days, when there were a lot fewer entries in the halter classes, but the classes seemed to be getting bigger all the time.

Then one day as she and Jim were looking over the entries, she saw that only ten horses were entered. If she scratched Applejack, she reasoned with mounting excitement, Old Black couldn't fail to win a ribbon in a nine-horse class. As soon as she could do so without arousing Jim's suspicions, she went to the registration booth and scratched Applejack from the class.

When the class was called, the nine geldings that made up the class were assembled at the gate, ready for the class ahead of them to conclude so they could enter the arena. Jim looked around for Alexandra and Applejack and idly wondered what could be keeping them. It was only as they were entering the arena that she came up and explained that Applejack had bumped his hip on the trailer and was favoring his right hind leg.

"I don't want to lead a limping horse in there just to get the gate," she explained.

Sitting with the Bradleys in the stands she watched as the judge examined each of the nine horses. All three of them felt the same wonderful sensation, the *relief*, that Old Black was not to be denied a ribbon today.

The judge began positioning his horses, taking them from the short lineup and putting them head to tail in the order of his placings. As always, Ricky Hoffman's Gorky was first.

When eight horses had been so positioned, Old Black still stood, alone, where the original lineup had been standing. The judge and ring steward approached him. The judge spoke to Jim, then bent down and ran his hand over the knot on Old Black's left knee. Jim said something, his expression lively and pleasant. The judge spoke again and Jim's face went dark.

Matt read his lips: "Yes, sir." Jim pulled the brim of his hat down and marched out of the arena, Old Black stepping as proudly as if he had received first place. There could be few people who participated in the circuit of youth horse shows in which Jim Bradley exhibited who didn't know Old Black from his performances in the shows *and* from his deed at Klanke's Mill. A warm round of applause arose from the stands, causing the judge to turn around and look with some curiosity at the boy and the horse he had just excused from the arena. The ovation did nothing to temper Jim's somber expression as he walked the length of the stands on his way to his trailer.

Matt ached with sadness for his son. A stinging sensation crept deep in his face and jaws, and he hoped he would not have to go for his handkerchief, as Jim's mother had done already. Watching blurry-eyed as Jim marched out of the arena while the judging was still going on, Matt remembered the fleeting moment of humor that he had indulged in once long ago—about the horse that was so ugly it couldn't win ninth place in a nine-horse class.

Jim had put his horse up and now, his face expressionless, came up the steps of the stands and sat down on the row in front of his parents. Alexandra joined him, a somber expression on her face. Jim leaned close to Alexandra and said something to her. She clapped a hand over her mouth to suppress a giggle but was not entirely successful. Then she shot an elbow into his ribs, laughing, in a way that said, "Behave!" Matt and Norma looked at each other, curious over their levity following his expulsion from the arena.

NORMA BRADLEY HAD TAKEN OFF WORK and was anxiously waiting for her husband to get home. She had decided not to leave a message at his airport office. She never did that, and Matt would read positively awful implications into a call-home message.

When she heard his car drive up she rushed outside. He got out of the car all smiles. "What a welcome surprise. After a hard day in the sky, here's my dutiful wife waiting at the cottage to—What's wrong, Honey? Something's wrong! Jim okay? You—"

Her face was gray and lined; her eyes were red from crying. "Matt, Ruby Jackson's had a heart attack. Andrew called day before yesterday when they took her to the hospital, and Oscar called last night to tell me that it looked like it was a minor heart attack, and they were expecting to bring her home, maybe tomorrow. But, Matt you know how serious *any* heart attack is."

"Have you talked to anyone today?" he asked.

"No. I called the Meridiths but there was no answer; they must be at the hospital. And Mrs. Mabel doesn't answer. I called the hospital and talked to the chief nurse of the ward where Ruby is, and she said Ruby seemed to be doing fine. But I couldn't get her to go to the waiting room to ask if anyone from the family was there I could talk to."

"Do you have the hospital's number?"

Matt learned from an officious nurse that Mrs. Jackson was doing very well and receiving selected visitors, but that any further information would have to come from friends or relatives. He tried

Andrew Meridith's number and the line was busy. It would probably stay busy now, he thought. Then he called the Winchester County Sheriff's Department. Matt explained to Millie Thatcher what he wanted.

"Yes, sir, Mr. Bradley, I'll take care of it," Millie said.

In ten minutes the phone rang. It was Andrew Meridith. "A deputy of Mike's came up and said you were trying to get in touch. I apologize for not calling you, Matt."

He said Ruby was indeed doing very well, and was expected to go home the next day, barring some reversal of her improving condition. Nevertheless, Matt asked if the three Bradleys would be permitted to visit her. They would, Andrew learned after a few minutes. "We'll be up there about three, Andrew, if that's all right."

They took Jim out of school on the way. Norma was very careful to tell him that their worries had been lessened considerably by Matt's conversation with Andrew.

"She is expected to be taken home tomorrow," Norma said, "and she'll have to take it easy for awhile. But it looks like one of those warning heart attacks, the kind that encourages people to change their diet and work habits to prevent a worse attack in the future. Doctors say that people who survive a warning heart attack are very often likely to live longer than they might have without the warning."

Jim nodded his understanding.

"MOM," HE SAID ON THE WAY BACK TO HOUSTON, "I'm sure glad we got to go see Mrs. Jackson in the hospital. If this was tomorrow, we couldn't see her because she would have been sent home."

"Well, we could have visited her at home, then," Norma said.

"Yeah, Mom, but I'm glad she knows we like her enough to come see her in the hospital even if she *is* going home tomorrow."

"Yes . . . Yes, I see what you mean," Norma said. "I truly see what you mean, and I'm glad too." She looked at Matt. "He makes a very good point, doesn't he?"

"Yes he does. And our coming was good for Oscar's feelings. God knows what he's gone through. This has been a shock to me too—I've always regarded the Jacksons to be as eternal as the countryside, but now we find they're mortal, too." He shook his head.

In the back seat, Jim was going through some agonizing thoughts of his own. He could not imagine their life at the farm without Ruby Jackson. "But if they send her home, won't that mean she's getting well?" he asked.

"It's a very good sign, Darling," said Norma. "A very encouraging sign. We'll see her again day after tomorrow. Yes, Jim, I'm like you—I'm very glad we came."

THE PHONE CALL FROM ALEXANDRA'S MOTHER came just after six the next morning. Ruby had died during the night. When Matt wandered into the kitchen, he was shocked at what he saw. Norma was standing with tears streaming down her face, pressing a hand to one flushed cheek. She took an uncertain step and turned toward him, her other hand pressing hard against her mouth. Her face was red and she was shaking visibly.

"Oh, Matt, Matt" she cried, flinging herself into his arms. "Ruby died last night. She had another—"

With his own eyes full of tears, Matt took her close in his arms and let her cry. He heard Jim singing a little ditty as he came cheerfully from his room. There seemed no way to soften the crushing news, and no time to do so, for Jim's face registered recognition the moment he realized his parents were crying.

"Jim, Son, Ruby died last night," Matt said. Tears sprang from Jim's eyes with such suddenness that they almost squirted. He fell to his knees at his mother's feet, crying as his father had never heard him cry before. Norma took him in her arms. There was no abatement of the sobs that racked Jim and his mother as Matt's arms encircled them both.

They went to the country that afternoon in gloomy silence.

Presuming that Oscar would be at the funeral home where Ruby would be lying, they stopped first at the Meridiths and shared their grief with them for a while. Jim and Alexandra went off by themselves, and it appeared to Matt that it was Alexandra who was consoling Jim.

Just as they were getting ready to leave the Meridiths, just as it seemed that they had become composed enough to comfort Oscar at the funeral home, Jim grabbed his mother around the waist and broke into spasms of crying, his head buried in her chest. It was a long time before he brought himself under some control.

"What's Mr. Jackson going to do without her?" he asked.

"We'll be by Daddy's side every minute, Jim," Alexandra's mother said quickly. "He'll be in a bad way without Momma, but one of us kids will be with him every minute for however long it takes. And if I know you, Jim, you'll help him through these hard times, too."

But how *could* poor Oscar Jackson exist without his beloved Ruby? At the moment, his time was filled with visitors at the funeral home, hundreds of them, for Ruby Jackson was the most beloved black lady, the most beloved *person*, in the north end of Winchester County. Oscar was provided with sedatives by a doctor so he could lose himself in sleep at night as the love of his life lay in her casket until her funeral on Monday afternoon. The funeral would occupy that day. But Jim's question tormented Norma Bradley—what was Oscar Jackson going to do without Ruby?

THE LITTLE CHURCH WHERE OSCAR had been a deacon for so many years sat in a grove of big pine trees right on League Line Road. It was already surrounded by a sea of cars and pickups when the Bradleys arrived. They had come to the funeral quite early to make sure they could get in, but many others had had the same idea. A line that must have numbered in the hundreds extended from the door, more than the possible capacity of the church. After they had taken their places at the end of the line, Matt looked around and was gratified to see two sheriff's department squad cars parked among the others. They were there not for traffic duty but to pay their final respects, as they were not occupying privileged, easy to-exit-places. It was a thoughtful courtesy by Mike Martinez, Matt thought. Parked on the road for escort duty were two deputies with motorcycles.

As he was thinking about this, a little girl in a yellow dress, perhaps seven years old, came and spoke shyly to Norma and took her by the hand. Norma reached out for Matt and Jim, and the three of them were led inside.

They were taken to the casket, where they viewed Ruby for the last time. Poor little Jim was so shattered by grief that he was almost unable to stand, and he unashamedly allowed his parents to assist him. Their little escort in her yellow dress stood by until she astutely observed a cue of some kind that they were ready to move on. Then she led them to where Oscar sat with his large family, including the Meridiths. He sat plain-faced, looking stunned and no doubt in deep shock. Both Matt and Norma hugged him and said some consoling words, but Jim was the only one he seemed to recognize. Oscar gave him a small smile and shook his hand. Then the little girl led them, threading her way through standing people, to where three seats on the end of a pew on the front row had been reserved in the certainty of their coming.

There was not another empty seat in the church. The windows were open, and through every one could be seen people gathered and watching from outside.

A quiet hum of conversation accompanied the piano, forming a serene and peaceful murmur from the grieving friends of Mrs. Ruby

Jackson. With tears in his eyes, Matt surveyed the faces visible to him. Across the room, beyond Ruby's casket, sat Sheriff Martinez and his family, grief evident in their faces. On the same bench sat a black deputy and his family. With the exception of the Bradley and Martinez families, there was not another white face to be seen. He knew from local legend that Ruby was as close as there was to a nurse in the north end of the county—she had nursed countless whites as well as blacks through some grave illnesses. He wondered how many dozen white babies Ruby Jackson had brought into the world when no doctor could get out to the country in time. He thought of Reinhard Richter and many others who he thought to be lifetime friends of the Jacksons, but curiously absent from Ruby's funeral. In his opinion, there could be no civilized answer.

Matt had no idea, as he pondered the absence of other white friends of the Jacksons, that the death of Ruby would end an era of the most wholesome social fellowship he had ever known. He and Jim would still occasionally join in the crowd at Richter's on a Saturday night, but just occasionally. They had enjoyed their last hog killing. There would be no more happy dinners with the Jacksons, and they would gradually come to a realization that something that could not quite be grasped, but some essential vibrant element of their part of Winchester County had died with Ruby Jackson.

The minister, who had been talking to Oscar and others in his immediate vicinity, turned and stood up. He walked to the pulpit, a sign that the service was to begin. He opened by recalling Ruby's devotion to her community, God and the church, her sixty-one years of wedded bliss to her faithful husband Oscar, her generosity, and her fine sense of humor. It was a pleasant and consoling service, but it could not console them for long, or account for the absence of the white community that Ruby had so willingly served for so long.

Knowing that Oscar would be surrounded by family, the Bradleys left the church and headed directly for Houston. They were quiet, absorbed in their own thoughts. They had cried until there were no more tears to cry.

Jim had been considering the inescapable reality that he would never again see Ruby Jackson. He gave conscious thought to his failure to realize that although both Ruby and Oscar Jackson were old, he had never considered a world without them—without Duffie, or Rufus, or Mr. Richter. He recalled talking to Mr. Jackson about living on the farm if he went to college at A&M, and how he could see the Jacksons all the time. But he was only eleven now, and it would be a long time before he would be in college, a *long* time, and Ruby was already gone.

Jim tried to think of what it would be like at the farm without ever seeing Mrs. Jackson waving a dish towel again, her semaphore flag announcing a message. He thought of the hog killings, their dinners together, and all the warm times they'd had. Would Mr. Jackson ever be happy again? Would he still want to sit on the tailgate of his pickup in the bottom and talk to Jim about the old days, and bounce up and down while he chuckled at a joke on himself? The Oscar Jackson who sat in that church pew looked as if all of his joy had evaporated, never to return.

His thoughts went to the beautiful day he rode over to show off Old Black to the Jacksons. He recalled Oscar's genuine praise of the horse, the saddle, and Ruby's conviction, however unrealistic, that Old Black was the prettiest horse in the world. He thought of his discovery that Oscar was a good calf roper. That was their way, the Jacksons—interested in you, not themselves.

Remembering the way Ruby had made him quit hoeing and "gab" brought an inward smile. He could still feel her arm around him as she tucked him against the softness of her body, the warmth of the sunshine as they sat on the stump that had been the head-chopping block for hundreds of turkeys. He thought of her simple logic on the nature of happiness: you go out of this world like you came in, naked and with nothing to your name except your report card of life. Yes, a good report card made life more pleasant on earth even while it was earning you a place in heaven.

With pride he recalled Mrs. Jackson's praise of his hoeing in her garden, the way he skimmed the hoe just under the crust of the loamy soil, cutting every weed and never, *ever* cutting down a young vegetable plant, once he got the hang of it. She had introduced him to her hoe when he was five, and even though she lost a few plants in the beginning, she always bragged on his work and he improved rapidly.

"Turn Buddy loose in that garden," she'd said with disgust when he was seven, and old enough to do good work, "and we would be in the Salvation Army line at Christmas, lookin' for a handout."

Somehow, he knew that Mrs. Jackson's garden would never again feel the gentle, loving cut of a hoe; her garden was finished. Would it still be all right for him to go over there the way he always used to and just walk up on the porch, sure of being invited in? "In" would no longer be the joyful atmosphere, the pleasant old scents of the Jackson house mixed with the nice smell of Oscar's pipe and the delicious aromas that always wafted from Ruby's kitchen. Whatever the answers to his questions, Jim knew that a curtain had come down on a wonderful time of his life, and that a new and uncertain time was beginning. He'd loved the Jacksons more than anybody else but his parents. He was glad Mr. Jackson had made him promise to "use every day—shucks, even every *part* of every day—like they was as valuable as diamonds."

A more comforting line of thought beckoned, and Jim found it easy to indulge in it. Nobody could deserve to go to heaven more than Ruby Jackson. During her funeral, he'd thought that she probably had gone to heaven the moment she died in the hospital, and that her spirit—or whatever went to heaven, he just couldn't seem to grasp that part of it—was looking down, her hands on her hips and smiling broadly, a hint of pretended reproach in her expression, and thinking of how silly they were to be sitting there crying in that church, with her up in heaven.

He leaned close to the car window and looked up at the pretty blue sky, decorated with a few big, bulging cumulus clouds. He was not really expecting to see a vision of Ruby Jackson up there, but he would not have been so very surprised if he did, and he looked a long time, even trying to find a cloud that might look a little like her. His face began to ache.

After a long silence, speaking in level tones and without emotion, he said, "I just made Mrs. Jackson a promise. I promised that for the rest of my life, when I'm about to do anything that ought to be thought about, I would think of her and Mr. Jackson like they were looking over my shoulder. And if I thought they wouldn't like for me to do it, I wouldn't do it. And if I thought they wanted me to do it, I would do it. That was part of my promise."

Norma's eyebrows raised as she waited for the other part.

"I promised her, too, that I would think of you, Mom and Dad, like you were looking over my *other* shoulder."

CHAPTER 31

"Okay, Black, we're here!" Jim said as he opened the door of the horse trailer. He zipped up his mackinaw and turned the collar up against the cold north wind. A glance down confirmed that his exhibitor's badge was fastened to his breast pocket.

"Feast your eyes, Black old boy," he said. The horse was turning one way, then another, taking in the scene. Directly ahead Old Black saw a sea of trucks, horse and cattle trailers, pickup trucks, cars, travel trailers, and motorhomes. Beyond them lay the sprawling Astrohall, thirteen acres of indoor exhibition space. The giant Astrodome, where Old Black had carried Buck Jones to second-place money in their final roping together, loomed off to their left.

Long red and white banners decorated the upper area of the Astrohall. "Houston Livestock Show and Rodeo—March 26th - April 4th," they announced.

Old Black threw his head high in the air. Nostrils flared, he sniffed audibly and then sucked in some deep breaths to savor the intoxicating aromas that he knew so well. He whinnied long and loud, setting off a chain of responses from a number of other blanketed horses being led here and there.

Jim adjusted the stable blanket on the horse's back and smoothed out the wrinkles. On their way toward the Astrohall, Old Black's head continued to swivel first one way and then another, his eyes darting and ears flickering in recognition of the many familiar sights and sounds. He snorted repeatedly to express his excitement, and as he walked he picked his feet up as smartly as if he was on parade.

As they made their way between the rows of trucks and cars, it seemed to Jim that out-of-state license plates outnumbered those from Texas. "Gosh, Black, there's even one from Manitoba. That's in

Canada! People come a long way for this show! But I forgot, you've been to Canada, haven't you?"

Jim's father, who had walked ahead to locate the entrance for exhibitors' animals, motioned with a wave of his arms. In spite of Old Black's excitement, he was moving obediently along on a slack halter lead, his shoulder brushing Jim's.

Inside the enormous Astrohall they fell in behind Matt Bradley, who referred often to a sheet that gave directions to the horse stalls. They walked past pens of calves, cows and huge bulls, past pens of goats, pigs, chickens, geese, turkeys, rabbits . . .

They passed the sheep area, where a teenage girl was sitting on the floor shearing a sheep that lay sprawled across her legs, calmly resigned to losing its coat. The creamy wool cascaded from big electric clippers, leaving nothing but pink skin in the clippers' wake. A man wearing the badge of a show official collected the wool and placed it in a bag, which was tagged with a number for later judging.

The huge hall was alive with activity and the sounds of animals, small vehicles, and machinery. The announcements that came from the speakers mingled with all the other sounds to create an insistent, low-level clamor.

Now they began encountering horses being ridden and led along the wide aisles, and soon they were in an area lined with horse stalls. Old Black raised his head again, whinnied, and glanced rapidly in every direction, as if he was expecting a response from some old equine pal.

In the aisles between the rows upon rows of horse stalls were small red tractors pulling trailers filled with soiled straw bedding; similar rigs were loaded with bales of clean, pale straw and brown prairie hay, which workers were throwing into freshly cleaned, unoccupied stalls. In other stalls, horses lay dozing, nestled contentedly in their fresh, sweet-smelling beds. Others stood alertly watching the goings-on, while still others were standing hipshot and indifferent to the hum of activity. From a distance came the pounding sound of a horse kicking the boarded side of its stall.

Some stalls were decorated with ribbons won in past shows. They saw black horses, browns, bays, sorrels, roans, grays and dapple-grays, duns, palominos, paints, Appaloosas, buckskins, and mouse-colored grullas. Exhibitors lounged on makeshift benches of hay bales placed outside their stalls. Horses were tied in the aisles, being groomed, saddled, or unsaddled. A farrier in his leather apron was shoeing a horse that stood calmly on three legs chewing on a mouthful of hay he had snitched from a nearby bale.

Some riders were dressed English style, in smartly tailored coats and riding breeches, glistening black boots and shiny spurs. Most were dressed western style; the rodeo cowboys stood out from the rest of the exhibitors in their well-worn chaps and boots and their functional coats and jackets. Most of their horses had heavy winter coats.

Matt opened the wide gate of stall H-forty-two and went in. He placed Black's water bucket and the red plastic feed bucket in a corner. Jim draped the halter rope over one of the big steel pipes that made up the front of the stall, leaving the horse standing in the aisle. "Don't you think it's a good stall, Dad?" he asked. "See, we're not near a door, where cold air can blow in on him."

"It sure is, Jim. It's a great location. The stalls here are nice and roomy, too. Black will like it just fine. Looks like the welcoming committee has been here."

Three bales of bedding straw and a bale of hay lay on the clean cement floor. In one corner was a large metal chest with a hasp for a lock. Matt took a lock from a canvas bag he carried, opened the chest and hung the open lock from the hasp. He handed Jim a key attached to a plastic address tag. "Look at this, Jim. This chest will hold the works."

"They think of everything here don't they?" Jim said. "I'll make your bed for you, Black," he told the horse. He picked up a bale of straw, broke it open, and with his father helping began breaking up the bales and building a thick mat on the floor of the stall. When the bedding was arranged to his satisfaction, he picked up the water bucket and went off to find a faucet.

Back in the stall with the bucket of water, he scooped the straw from a corner and placed the bucket on the floor.

Matt took some papers from the canvas bag over his shoulder. "While you're getting Black settled in, I'll find the show office and get the paperwork taken care of."

"Can we have a hamburger when you come back, Dad? I smelled hamburgers when we were walking through and I've been thinking of a big, juicy hamburger ever since."

Matt laughed and reflected that Jim would rather have a hamburger than a T-bone steak. He'd even almost prefer a hamburger over one of Mrs. Schumann's chicken-fried steaks covered with cream gravy. "Sure, Jim. Hamburgers it is. With everything." Taking the map, he went off in search of the show office.

Jim picked up the halter lead and Old Black followed him into the stall. The horse sniffed here and there, making a thorough examination of his quarters. Jim took off the red nylon work halter and placed it in the chest. From the canvas bag he took a variety of supplies and began neatly stowing them in the chest—a container of Animax, some Omolene, a spray can of coat sheen, horse shampoo, hoof dressing, saddle soap, leather dressing, neutral shoe polish for polishing saddle and tack, Absorbine, four rolls of red Vetwrap leg wrap. He set aside a stiff-bristled horse brush, a mane and tail comb, and a hoof pick.

"How about a hamburger for you, Black old pal?" he asked, removing from the red plastic feeding bucket a brown sack that held a feeding of Omolene. He poured it into the bucket, and cupping his hands together, he scooped up some feed and sniffed at it. He liked the aroma. Old Black demonstrated his liking of it, too, by shuffling his feet impatiently. Jim opened the container of Animax and added a scoop of it to the feed. He mixed it in with his hands, then held the bucket under the horse's nose. Old Black shoved his mouth deep into his feed and came up munching with contentment. Jim hung the feed bucket from a hook in a corner.

He took off Old Black's stable blanket, folded it neatly and placed it in the chest. Then he slipped his hand through the leather strap on the horse brush and set about brushing Old Black's coat. He worked vigorously, sometimes using both hands on the brush. When he had finished with one side, he crawled under the horse's belly and brushed the other. When Old Black finished his grain, Jim placed the big feed bucket upside down next to him so he could stand on it to brush his back.

After his neck had been brushed, Old Black lowered his head, tantalized by the anticipation of the part of grooming he liked best. When Jim began gently brushing one of his ears, the horse's head sank until Jim had to step off the bucket. Old Black slowly cocked his head to one side and drifted into a blissful trance with his eyes closed. The old boy was glad he had two ears, Jim imagined. After giving his other ear a good rubbing, he combed the horse's mane, and then his tail. The final job was to clean Old Black's feet.

When his father got back, Jim had Old Black taken care of, all the equipment put away, and the chest locked up. He told Old Black good night and hugged his neck.

Looking at his father, he gleefully bared his teeth and narrowed his eyes in a fiendish expression. Rubbing his hands together, he announced, "Now for the hamburger stand."

The Astrodome arena was so big that several events could be conducted at the same time without interfering with each other. They began in the morning and continued until late afternoon each weekday, then the arena was cleared so it could be readied for the evening rodeo performance.

The spectators occupied only a small number of the seats in the giant stadium. They congregated opposite the events in progress. A group of rodeo cowboys lounged off to themselves in the south concourse. For them, the main attractions were the comfortable stadium seats and the nearby coffee shop. There was always the chance, too, of bumping into old acquaintances.

Each event had its own sound system; the drone of the low-level announcements provided a soothing background for the cowboys' banter; usually they paid little notice of the goings-on in the arena. Today two events were in progress, the flag-race course on the near side of the oval space and cattle judging on the other.

The course for the flag race differed markedly from courses set up in smaller arenas. The greater distance between flags gave fast horses an advantage, but the location of the course in the open arena demanded superior horsemanship. Courses that are laid out along the rail, which are the most common, give horses a reference to key on. Mounts that lack good control are more likely to stop closer to the familiar rail than beside a pole standing isolated in the middle of nowhere.

The group of cowboys seemed to change little in overall number—usually a dozen or more as men came and went. As new faces joined the group they were sometimes greeted with good-natured banter and ribbing, while others joined and departed with little notice other than a wave of a hand, a nod. A tall man of strong build sauntered casually down the stadium steps and joined the group. Unlike the other cowboys, he was smartly dressed, wearing a tailored dark brown suit of western cut. His sharp-toed cowboy boots were shined to a high gloss.

"Hey, if it ain't Randall Atkins," a cowboy wearing a big, pleasant bucktoothed grin boomed to the new arrival. "I haven't seen you since Amarillo. Just figured that you'd dropped out of rodeoing after I beat your socks off in that bulldogging."

Randall Atkins's face lit up. "Listen to Josey," he said, addressing the other cowboys. "He'd had such a long dry spell I was afraid he might be thinking of quitting. I couldn't bear to see him go to work in a filling station, so I thought I'd better let him win one. Then I stayed out of sight for a while to give him some crowing time before I started in beating him again." Chuckles rippled through the group. Randall Atkins and Josey shook hands warmly.

"How have you been, Josey?" Atkins asked sincerely.

"How do you mean, Randy? Health-wise, wealth-wise, or wise-wise?"

Randall Atkins laughed along with the rest of the cowboys. He shook his head, resigned that Josey could not be drawn into serious conversation.

"I'm going for some coffee, Randy," Josey said. "The least I can do is bring you a cup. A demonstration of my eternal gratitude for your sacrifices on my behalf. Who knows, you might have saved my rodeoin' career. How do you take your coffee?"

"Big cup. Three creams and four sugars," said Randall Atkins.

Feigning astonishment, Josey looked at the others and said, "He don't want coffee, fellers, he wants me to make him a puddin'." A hearty round of laughter swept the group.

"Where've you been hiding, Randy?" another cowboy asked, climbing over a row of seats to shake hands with him. "I heard you'd quit rodeoing. Anything to it?"

"A bull got me down in San Antone a couple a years ago. He worked me over pretty good before the clowns could get him off me. While I was on the mend I judged halter classes. It started out as something just to keep beans on the table. Now judging is all I do out-side of my horse raising. I was already an AQHA judge, then I got qual-ified by the Paint Horse Association, then the Appaloosas. And then there are the open shows. I usually judge several shows a month."

Josey was back with the coffee and had stood listening. "Can you make a living at judging, Randy?"

Randall Atkins smiled and sipped his coffee. "You make a good pudding, Josey," he complimented. "Actually, there's been some politicking in the horse shows. A few judges have been known to favor certain people holding the halter ropes, and judge *them* instead of the horses. But there's a lot at stake, considering what halter points mean in the horse industry today. So the AQHA—all the breed associations for that matter—and a big majority of your exhibitors and breeders are determined to get not only unbiased, but qualified judging. By golly, that's what I try to give them."

"Take a look at that chestnut down there, Mr. Quarter Horse Judge," one of the cowboys directed, pointing out a horse that was entering the flag-race starting circle. "He's a beaut in my book. How would he stand in a halter class?"

Randall Atkins turned toward the horse, raising a hand to shield his eyes. The big, stout, glistening animal walked with an easy, flowing motion. Its young rider, dressed out in a western outfit of dark blue gabardine pants, sky blue satin shirt, and silver-belly felt hat, sat the horse confidently in a black saddle ostentatiously adorned with silver. The bridle and breast strap were similarly decorated.

Still watching the horse, Randall Atkins answered, "I can tell you how he has stood when I've judged him in the past. First place in his class a number of times. Grand-champion gelding once or twice. Outstanding horse. That boy's daddy is well-heeled. Bought him that horse to get him away from a bad crowd, and dope. His strategy seems to have worked, too. I heard on good authority that his daddy paid fifty grand for that horse, but if it straightened the kid out it had to be worth it."

Josey said, "The price of that saddle would keep me goin' for a time. I saw that boy warming up a few minutes ago. Seems like a cocky little dude."

"Yeah, he's cocky all right," Atkins said. "But he's okay. And that horse has some real speed to go with his looks. Good blooded, I'll tell you. Nizhny on the top side out of a Sparkling Native mare."

"Nizhny?" said one of the men. "Boy you *are* talking fifty grand for a Nizhny horse. I saw a colt by Nizhny sell for *one hundred grand* at a yearling sale last year."

Clint Barnett held up both hands. "Boys, I got a real good story to tell about Nizhny. Ya'll know about Nizhny, don't you?" Satisfied, he continued, "Nizhny's stud fee is ten thousand." He laughed, and aware that his mirth had drawn curious looks, he explained. "It would take a woman to think of something like this, which is why you should never cross a woman."

"Where does a woman come in?" asked one of men. "Get on with the story if you're gonna tell it."

Barnett said, "Nizhny's owned by that woman breeder out in Roswell, Annabelle MacKenzie, and—"

"No kidding? She owns Nizhny?" asked a voice.

"Yep. Anyway, she had a ranch manager who sold two straws of Nizhny's semen under the table to Seth Hashem—Hashem has a stud he's been promoting. Won a couple a big races with him a few years ago, and then spent a fortune getting him made an AQHA Supreme Champion. He was getting some horses to breed for way more than his stud fee was really worth, considering the horse, and somehow he talked Mike Sanderford—ya'll know who he is, got that big showy place on the Interstate just west of Houston—he conned Mike into breeding two fine running mares to his stud." He looked around the group, nodding for emphasis. "I mean, they were some *fine* mares Sanderford took over to Hashem's. How he came to allow those mares to be bred to Hashem's stud I can't even imagine, because Sanderford is a savvy horse breeder. But he did, anyway.

"Here's where the woman comes in, Charlie. One day this Mexican who'd worked for Annabelle MacKenzie forever came to her with a story. He said he knew she would fire him for telling tales on his boss, but he had to do it anyway. He told Annabelle that her manager had ordered him to deliver two vials of Nizhny's semen to Hashem the next night, and that he was supposed to keep it on the QT.

"Annabelle thanked him for this valuable parcel of intelligence and assured him he was in no danger of being fired. She told him not to say a word to the manager about talking to her about it, but to bring the nitrogen bottle with the semen straws in it to her on his way to deliver it to Hashem. Annabelle got busy on the case, and when her Mexican hand came by with the nitrogen bottle the next evening, she had him sit outside while she made a little swap."

Barnett started laughing, and the conclusion yet to come caused him to laugh until he could hardly go on, much to the impatience of his listeners. Finally he wiped his eyes. "The next year, this very spring, everybody's awaiting the blessed events. Mike Sanderford, Hashem—but Annabelle was the most anxious of all." He irritated his listeners again with another bout of laughter.

"Boys, I want you to know it hit the fan this spring. Within two weeks of each other, Sanderford's prize mares both foaled. But the foals that were supposed to put Hashem's stud on the map were the prettiest little mules you ever saw—a filly and a colt. Haw, haw, haw—

Annabelle had swapped Nizhny's semen for *jackass* semen." As the others began to comprehend the grand scheme, a wave of side-splitting laughter began.

"Sanderford filed a complaint with AQHA and he sued Hashem for a ton. The case hasn't come to trial yet. Hashem is trying to settle, but Mike already has plenty of money and won't settle. He wants Hashem's head mounted and hanging on the wall in his barn, right above the manure pile, he says. Boys, I'm going to tell you, that conniving Hashem has got himself between a rock and a hard place. It came out in the paper that he told the Austin County D.A. that he was only trying to get Mike more than he bargained for by using Nizhny's semen in place of his own stud's, and he told how he paid Annabelle's manager a grand apiece for two straws of Nizhny's semen. No telling where this is going to end. But Hashem's through, in the horse business. Annabelle's crooked manager is out on bail and out of a darn good job. Mike Sanderford says he's going to keep the mules on his place. They got a right to be some *fine* mules."

Barnett concluded in a serious voice. "Boys, don't sneak around and put a burr under a smart lady's saddle blanket. By gosh she'll figure out a way to make you holler calf-rope. See, a man would've flew off the handle, fired his manager, and that would have been the end of it. Even Hashem, the real culprit, would have got off scot-free. But Annabelle fixed everybody's wagon. Mike just kinda got caught in the crossfire; she didn't know whose horses were going to get the jackass semen. But Mike got two fine race mules out of the deal." He chuckled. "He's set, if they ever start racing mules."

There was the period of silence that often follows a good story. Randall Atkins was the first to speak. "That boy, the boy with the Nizhny gelding down there, he can ride like an Indian, but he kicks his horse around some, showing off. I've had some chances to watch him in performance events. It's not unusual to see him in the winner's circle. The only team I know of that poses a *regular* threat to this one is a little feller that rides an old black gelding."

The conversation had drawn the attention of all the cowboys to the chestnut Nizhny gelding, who was going to be the next horse to run the flags. His rider held him in the starting circle for some time, making the horse spring on his forefeet from side to side. The boy surveyed the place, as if to see if he had everyone's attention.

Then he crouched way down over the horse's neck and drove his spurs home. "Ouch!" said a cowboy. The beautiful horse was off like a racehorse out of the starting gate and flew with blazing speed toward the first flag.

Approaching the pole, the rider reined up sharply and the horse planted his hind feet and began a long slide that ended right next to the flag. In an instant the flag was exchanged and away they flew. The horse slid about a yard beyond the second flag, however, leaving it just out of the rider's reach. The boy snatched the reins hard and a few specks of froth could be seen flying from the horse's mouth. He backed up a step, throwing his head around. The exchange was made and he was off to the third flag; this time a perfect exchange. The fourth and fifth flags were executed just about as well. The horse stopped abreast of the last flag, but seemed to have been anticipating the reverse and didn't stop close enough to the pole for his rider to make the exchange. The boy dug a spur in the horse's left flank, apparently intending to make him sidestep closer to the flag, but the horse took a jump ahead, and then backed up.

The mistake consumed only a few seconds, for the horse moved quickly. But the cowboys, who had a keen appreciation for the flying hands of the rodeo clock, knew that mistakes that cost whole seconds could mean losing a place in the money.

The last flag exchanged, the rider spun his horse around, sending the big gelding roaring back down the straightaway. Feeling spurs and whip right up to the finish line, the horse seemed to fly.

"It's going to take a heck of a ride to beat *that* time," one cowboy said.

Even though he had plenty of running room to allow a leisurely stop, the boy pulled his horse up like he was stopping at a flag, bringing him to a sliding, rearing stop. "Doggone, he's rough with that horse," Josey said. "Talk about heavy-handed." Another said, "Could've saved that stop for something useful." Heads nodded.

"He lost some time on two flags, and that caper at the end. But he sure seemed to make it up with speed," said one of the men.

"It was a good run, no question about it," Josey said. "But on the fourth flag he was asking the horse to stop a little early. I noticed he was bouncing his front feet off the ground to keep from stopping short. That horse can really run, though, can't he?"

"Anybody been paying attention to the times posted?" someone asked. "I'd like to see how he finished compared to some of the others." Evidently, no one had.

The announcer, speaking softly to avoid interfering with activity in the other class, said, "The time, twenty-nine point two eight. That's a new best time by two-point-one-three seconds. Good run, Ricky."

"I guess that answers my question," said the cowboy.

None of the next dozen or so contestants posed a threat to this time. Soon the cowboys lost interest in the flag race and resumed their conversations.

Suddenly one of them pointed out a horse in the arena. "Hey, Butch," he said. "See that black horse down there? The one with the kid in the white shirt, talking to the gal on a sorrel gelding. No, Butch, way down there. Look for the black gal in the yellow outfit."

The cowboys were all searching the arena when the man named Butch located the black horse. "Yeah, Slim, I see him, now. What about him?"

"That horse looks real familiar to me. Mighty familiar. Haven't you seen him before?"

The boy riding the black horse reached up and touched his hat brim to the girl and gently picked up his reins. He leaned ever so slightly and the horse rolled back in a delicate and graceful movement and began a lively walk down the arena in the direction of the starting circle. Walking on a slack rein, the horse carried his head level with his shoulders and nodded gently in rhythm with his easy stride.

"Now, ain't that pretty, the way he rides that horse so easy," said Slim. "I'm sure I seen that horse before."

Another cowboy said, "You know who that looks like? Now I'd swear it, seeing him move. That horse is the spitting image of Old Black. Remember? Buck Jones's roping horse?"

"It sure does look like him," said someone else. "I know how to tell for sure if it's Old Black. Just watch him run. I'd know Old Black's running style, that's for sure." He chuckled.

Slim agreed. "Yeah, if it's Old Black he'll be running hell-bent for election and looking like he's dragging an anchor. But by golly he got the job done anyway, didn't he? Did any of you guys see Buck's run at Butte, when he set the record?" Several heads were nodding emphatically. "Was that a run or wasn't it? And the way Old Black threw that calf right in Buck's hands just when it looked like he'd busted out. That was the overall best run I ever seen."

"It was in my book, too. You bet," said the other cowboy. "I was glad I already made my run when I seen it, because I knew there wasn't no use in anybody else trying for top money at that rodeo."

Randall Atkins had been listening, and watching the horse. "That's the kid and the old black gelding that I spoke of a while ago," he said. "The one that beats the chestnut with the silver mounted saddle. If this kid hasn't already run, you guys're in for a real performance demonstration. You never *saw* a horse try harder. He's just *determined* to win for that little fella. He's not all that fast, but he *never* makes a mistake. The boy handles him with kid gloves, too. There's something about that pair, a closeness between them. You'll see the kid talking to the horse sometimes. Not just a few words of encouragement, but a real conversation."

Atkins laughed. "The boy will be talking away, then he'll chuckle, like he's told his horse something funny. Then once in a while, the horse will reach around and tap his leg with his muzzle, like he's telling the kid in a friendly way, 'Don't feed me that line.'"

A tall black cowboy descended the steps and joined the group. He shook hands all around.

"Well if it ain't Andrew Meridith, widely acclaimed sculptor and exhibitor of top-notch cutting horses," said Slim in his announcer's voice. Meridith was popular with the other horsemen. His nickname was Mud, arising from his artistic use of it.

He went to the rail and leaned quietly there, watching the activity in the arena and listening to the conversation going on behind him.

The boy on the black gelding sat his horse easily. He was considerately well clear of the area to give the competitor on the course plenty of room at the finish. When the race was over and the time announced, the announcer droned, "The next contestant will be entry number thirty-seven, Jim Bradley riding O-o-ld Black."

One cowboy smacked his palm with a fist. "I'll be danged. It *is* Old Black. And still performing. I'll betcha he's old enough to vote. Randall, you said that kid beats the dude sometimes?"

"Not just sometimes, *most* of the time," said Randall Atkins. "Who'd you say the horse is?"

"He's a roping horse, Randy," Josey said. "That's a rodeo event where you have this long rope that has a loop at one end of it, see. The object is to rope little cows, then get down and tie 'em up." He turned to the others. "He's a steer wrestler and a bull rider, you know, boys. Don't compete in nothing else, so you have to explain technical things to him." He chuckled at his own humor. "His name is Old Black, Randy," Josey said with a genuine air of reverence. "That there horse holds the world record in calf roping. He was rode all his life by a fella named Buck Jones. You know him, don't you? I thought everybody knew Buck Jones. You heard about Buck didn't you, boys? About him having bone cancer?"

Heads nodded solemnly.

Andrew Meridith was watching Slim and Josey intently, a mild look of wonder on his face.

Entry number thirty-seven was still standing outside the starting circle. The announcer said, "Folks, we're being held up a few minutes while we reset a couple of flag stands. There will be a short delay."

Slim resumed observing the black horse, who was now walking away from the starting circle. "Old Black. I'll be," he said softly. "He still holds the calf-roping title, Josey. I saw it, and I can't see how a calf could ever be roped in less time."

Andrew Meridith was searching the faces of the men one by one with a look of curious surprise on his face. "Come on, boys. Sure, that's Old Black. Is his calf-roping fame all you know about him?"

"Well—what else is there to know, Mud?" Slim asked, abashed.

"That's the horse that pulled our sheriff out of the well after some dope smugglers tried to kill him." Meridith said. "He almost killed himself doing it, too."

"Naw, naw!" Slim exclaimed, rising up straight in his seat. His manner reflected not disbelief, but surprise. Sitting bolt upright, Slim stared at the black horse now approaching the starting circle.

"Naw, Mud," he said again. "Sure, I heard all about that. Saw it on TV—all the fireworks and everything. Looked like something out of Vietnam. But I didn't hear about Old Black having a hand in it."

"The kid riding him is Jim Bradley. His dad has a place in Brentwood, not far from us. My little girl and him are good friends— our families are good friends all around. I guarantee you that's the horse, and that's the kid: the pair that saved Sheriff Mike Martinez.

"Old Black would never have made it at halter, even in his heyday, and the boy knows it—well, he *did* know it. And he never showed him until lately. Until after the episode with the sheriff at Klanke's Mill. Alexandra, my daughter—she's the girl in the yellow outfit on that sorrel gelding, down there in that group where Jim Bradley is—Alex thinks the reason Jim started showing the horse at halter was to keep him from getting the idea Jim doesn't think he's pretty." He laughed.

"Jim knows Quarter Horse conformation better than some judges, but he started showing a horse that didn't have a prayer at halter even in his prime. And the horse keeps getting the gate. Alexandra says she'd give anything to see Old Black place in just one halter class.

"She came home from a show one day kind of red-eyed. I asked her, 'What's the matter, Honey, get the gate?' She just started bawling. Said the judge had given Old Black the gate even though there were only nine horses in the class. Disqualified him, she said, because of that knot on his knee. Everybody knows a healed injury isn't a cause for disqualification.

"I've got to tell you this part. Alex was telling me all this, crying so hard it was about to break my heart, too. Then, all of a sudden, with tears still streaming down her face, she broke into the *biggest* grin—took me completely by surprise—and said, 'Daddy. Do you know what Jim did after getting the gate?' She said he took Old Black to his trailer and tied him up. Then he came to where she was sitting in the stands with his folks. He sat down with her and said 'Boy. I sure am getting to know my way out of that gate,' and she said they laughed and laughed over that."

The announcer said in a low, conversational voice, "Okay, Jim. We're ready when you are." Then, in a more formal voice he said, "The next contestant is entry number thirty-seven, Jim Bradley, riding Old Black. Good luck, Jim." Old Black was in a brisk walk toward the starting circle.

Randall Atkins moved uncomfortably in his seat. The disqualification of Old Black had occurred when he was just beginning to judge. Andrew Meridith was right, he reflected with regret. The knot on his knee was not grounds for disqualification. But when he discovered that, the show was over, and the denial of that ninth-place ribbon was sad history.

Old Black entered the starting circle and stopped. The cowboys in the stands were quiet now, watching. "Sit down, Andrew," said one, "you must have been drinking muddy water, because I can't see through you." Andrew sat down.

Every one of the youth contestants was watching. Old Black stood leisurely as Jim tugged his hat down tight. A boy standing in the circle handed him the flag he would swap at the first pole. He snuggled down into the his big roping saddle, untracked Old Black, and without further fuss the pair stormed out of the circle on their way to the first flag.

"Go, Black, go," yelled one of the cowboys. The entire group had become Old Black's cheering section, and people began to turn and look at them.

"That there's our Old Black!" cried Josey. "Look how he tears up the arena, and strung out there like he's reaching for the wire. *Gooooo, Black*," he yelled.

Old Black went into a tail-dragging slide only yards from the first pole and slid to a stop with Jim exactly on target with his leg almost touching it. Jim made the swap in a cloud of dust and was out of the cloud and on the way to the next flag almost before it seemed possible.

"Yaaaa-hoooo!". . . "Go Black go!". . . "Yeee-haaa!". . . cried the cowboys, two dozen strong. Every flag change was made with the same precision. At the last pole, Old Black spun into a rollback to his left and began the run for the finish.

"Go! Go! Go! Go!—" they chanted in unison, on their feet now, waving their hats as horse and rider charged down the long run for the finish. There was no kicking or whipping, Jim just leaned far forward and let Old Black run on a loose rein.

The other contestants and the knots of spectators in the stands all became wrapped up in the excitement, cheering, clapping, pulling for the old horse with the animated running style.

Passing the finish, Jim relaxed in the saddle and Old Black gradually slowed, making a large circle until he came to a stop near the announcer's stand.

Almost everyone stared at the riotous cowboys, whose cheering had not yet died down. As the announcer leaned toward the microphone, Ricky Hoffman stood up in his stirrups and cocked his head, listening closely.

"Well," said the announcer, "we have a new leader by about a second and a quarter. Twenty-eight seconds flat. Great run, Jim."

Ricky Hoffman dropped heavily into his saddle. Brisk but polite applause rolled from the spectators and competitors. The cowboys, though, erupted into another round of cheering that went on for some time. Andrew Meridith stood waving his hat, hoping to catch Jim's attention, but he saw that Jim was a bit shy about looking in the direction of his unknown cheering section.

"Hey, kid," Meridith called to a boy on a horse within earshot. "Son," he said when the boy arrived at the rail, "would you ride over and tell Jim Bradley, the kid that just rode, to come over here?"

They watched as the boy loped over to Jim and spoke to him. At first he just sat on Old Black looking toward the cowboys, not comprehending. Then he noticed Andrew Meridith and put Old Black into a snappy lope. "Hi, Mr. Meridith!" he said riding up with a big smile.

"Hey, Jim. Heckuva ride. Took the lead, and I don't want to yank fate's leadrope, but I bet it stands. Jim, there's some guys here that want to meet you. This here's Hank Josey—" Meridith introduced them, each one, and they all shook Jim's hand and received a sincere, "Glad to meet you" from him.

Andrew stood quietly, watching with a good feeling as the boy rode away at a slow walk, heading to the sidelines where the flag race was still being conducted. Well off to the side, he saw Ricky Hoffman sitting on his horse and staring at Jim, his body slumped over in a dejected slouch. But as he watched, Ricky straightened up, and in a moment put his horse in a trot on a course that would intercept Jim.

He rode up and said a few words—friendly words, Andrew presumed, because he was smiling a real, down-to-earth smile. Jim responded to him with congenial animation on his face, his hands expressive. Ricky Hoffman extended his hand and leaned way over toward Jim. They shook hands for several seconds, and then Ricky threw Jim a respectful wave of the hand and rode away. Andrew smiled, nodding thoughtfully.

"Homo sapiens ain't necessarily beyond redemption," he said to himself.

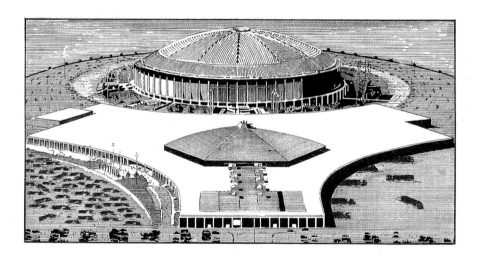

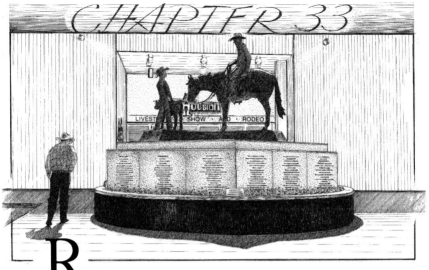

andall Atkins zipped his quilted jacket up against a nippy breeze and tugged his hat down against the brightness of the day as he strode down the long ramp leading from the Astrodome's south concourse. His eyes were adjusted to the light as he approached the huge bronze sculpture outside the entrance of the Astrohall that led to the permanent offices of the Houston Livestock Show & Rodeo. He admired the sculpture with new appreciation each time he saw it.

He was congratulating himself on his good luck. He very badly wanted to talk to Sheriff Martinez, and when he'd privately asked Andrew Meridith if he would introduce him on the phone, Meridith had responded, "I ought to be able to do better than that. He's here, with his mounted posse. I'll have him tracked down and put you two together." Meridith had arranged a lunch meeting in the Corral Club.

Inside, he made his way to a door marked "American Quarter Horse Association—Show Office." When he entered, a woman seated at a desk covered with stacks of forms and file folders put her hand over the telephone mouthpiece and said pleasantly, "Hi, Mr. Atkins." Then she resumed talking without missing a beat. Her fingers hovered over the papers on her desk and homed in on one of several wooden clothespins, each holding a stack of pink message forms. She handed the messages to him and kept the clothespin. He went through them rapidly, sorting as he went, and put them in his jacket pocket. He looked at the woman, who said into the phone, "Hold, please," punched a button and gave him her attention.

"Mrs. Reynolds, could you get me the roster for the aged geldings class in the youth division. It's this afternoon and I want to check it for an entry."

"Sure," she said, rising from her chair. "It's a big class. Over fifty horses." In a moment she returned with the list. Randall Atkins sat in a chair by her desk and proceeded to go through the entries. Mrs. Reynolds, whose telephone buttons were all lighted and blinking, picked up the receiver, pressed a button, and resumed a conversation in mid-sentence.

Randall Atkins moved a finger down the list, turning pages as he went. His finger stopped on entry thirty-nine, "Buck's Old Black, Exhibitor: Jim Bradley." He pursed his lips and began drumming his fingers on Mrs. Reynolds's desk as he stared at the line on the page. He looked at her. She said to the telephone, "Hold, please," and looked at Atkins with raised eyebrows.

"Mrs. Reynolds, would you see if Brock has a few minutes? I need to see him about this class," he said, tapping the list with a fore-finger. Bill Brock was the highest ranking official of the American Quarter Horse Association at the show.

She tapped in a number and spoke for a moment. "He can see you right now, Mr. Atkins. His office is on the other side, across the hall."

Bill Brock was standing when Atkins walked into the room. "Howdy, Randy," he said cordially. They shook hands. Brock led him to a sitting area, some comfortable stuffed chairs arranged around a coffee table. He poured two cups of coffee and pushed the cream and sugar in Randall Atkins's direction. Atkins spooned three sugars and poured a generous amount of cream into the steaming cup of coffee.

"This is the biggest Quarter Horse show ever, Randy. Well, not just for Quarter Horses, either. I had breakfast with Joe Payne this morning. He said paint horse entries set a record, too. Ready for two days of tough judging? I guess you know we had to change arenas for your Quarter Horse classes. Just got too big for the show ring."

"Yeah, I got the word. Three days of judging," Atkins said. "I'm judging Appaloosas too. You guys at AQHA should be happy with the way things are going for Quarter Horses. I was watching some youth performance classes over in the Astrodome this morning. I have to tell you, there's some mighty handy cowboys and cowgirls in those classes. And some tough horses." He took a long sip of coffee, then looked up at Bill Brock.

Problems abound at big livestock shows, and Bill Brock was faced with new ones every day—like the change in arenas for the halter classes. Every exhibitor in every class had to be notified, which meant pinning messages on their stalls. He asked, "Something on your mind, Randy, a problem of some kind?"

"No, Bill. No problems. But I want to talk to you about a departure from the judging procedure in the youth aged gelding class today." He waved off Brock's immediate show of concern over things likely to create problems. "It's something that will take some doing, no question about that. But I think you'll see that it'll be worth the effort. Let me explain what I want to do, and why."

Almost a half-hour later, Randall Atkins stood shaking Bill Brock's hand.

"I'm going to have to talk to Amarillo, Randy. This is a headquarters decision. But I'm of a mind they'll go along with it. No points are being handed out, and he's not a breeding horse. And an honorary award shouldn't offend people with earned awards. Who would be opposed to it, and on what grounds? I'm glad you thought of it—an excellent way to recognize the horse, not to mention the Quarter Horse breed. I promise I'll give it my best effort. Let you know by two at the latest."

Randall Atkins was once again at Mrs. Reynolds's desk. "Mrs. Reynolds, I need a trophy. A special trophy, and I need it engraved by four o'clock. Is that possible?"

"Call it done, Mr. Atkins. It's the impossible that takes time around here." Atkins admired the way the staff maintained such calm efficiency in the midst of the chaos that seemed to reign everywhere during the show. "What kind of trophy, and how is it to be engraved?" Seeing his look of indecision, she opened a drawer and produced the catalog of a trophy company. "If you'll pick one and write out what you want engraved on it, I'll have it to you easily by four."

He pulled thoughtfully at an earlobe. "I guess once it's engraved, we've bought it, huh?"

"Yep."

"Well, let's go ahead anyway. There's another thing—I hate to give you a request like this, Mrs. Reynolds, and I wouldn't if it wasn't important. But I also need an award certificate, the kind with the gold seal of the AQHA and a purple ribbon with gold letters. Is that a possibility?"

She laughed. "Mr. Atkins, we do dozens of those every day. Who'll supply the information to go on it?"

"I will."

"Okay, I'll tell Ronnie Sue to be expecting something from you. She also does the calligraphy—the fancy writing."

Atkins began slowly leafing through the catalog, occasionally pausing to study a trophy. At last he said, "This is the one I want.

Now, let me sit down over here and work out what I want to say on it. And please make a note that I'm paying for the trophy and the engraving, not AQHA. I'd like everything sent along with the other trophies to the aged gelding class in the youth show."

He looked at his watch. It was fifteen minutes before twelve. Maybe Meridith would arrive early with the sheriff. "Mrs. Reynolds, if anyone needs me I'll be in the Corral Club until about quarter to one. Then I'll be in the arena. My first class is at one."

SHERIFF MIKE MARTINEZ WAS A BIG MAN, physically hard and capable of taking care of himself, Atkins observed. He liked the sheriff's direct and firm eye contact that seemed to peer pleasantly right into your mind. Those eyes might hold a different expression for a criminal, he reckoned. In his snappy tan and brown uniform, Martinez looked like a casting director's creation of the All-American Sheriff.

Andrew Meridith had left them at the Corral Club bar after making the introductions. "Sheriff," Randall Atkins said, "could we go over to that table in the corner?"

He put his elbows on the table with one fist cupped in the other and leaned toward Mike Martinez. "Sheriff," he began, "I wanted to get some factual information about that day when you were rescued from a well by the boy and his horse. I was talking to some cowboys over in the Astrodome this morning and Andrew Meridith was the only one there who was aware that the horse was Old Black, a roping horse. Some of those cowboys have known the horse for a dozen years, even longer. But it was a bolt out of the blue to them, like it was to me."

Martinez's brown eyes gazed into Atkins's without revealing anything whatever. Atkins continued. "All I can remember from the TV news is burning buildings, flashing lights, colored smoke and flares and the sounds of machine guns blazing away. And of course we saw the helicopters flying around. I also read about it in the papers. But if either the boy or the horse was identified, or if they showed a picture of them, I sure missed it."

Sheriff Martinez's face took on a small smile. "Don't feel bad, we all missed it, just like we were supposed to. The *Brentwood Banner* finally ran some stories, but I don't know if any other news people did."

Atkins nodded. "The horse is here in the show and I'm judging him at four o'clock. I've judged him before. Never used him in a class because he just doesn't measure up conformation-wise to these younger, top-bred horses. I even—" Randall Atkins swallowed hard and decided not to go into the nine-horse-class affair.

The sheriff shrugged indifferently, his strong shoulders filling his shirt to capacity. "With all that Old Black has done in his life, I can't imagine that he needs to win a beauty contest to prove his abilities, or his heroism either. But Andrew says it's come to mean a lot to Jim."

Atkins swallowed again and nodded.

"He's a good man, Andrew is," the sheriff said softly. "He made the most beautiful sculpture of Jim and Old Black. You ought to see it. Andrew thinks it's the best thing he's ever done, his magnum opus. Worked real hard to make it just perfect, and at a time when people are beating his door down to get pieces they were paying big money for. But he put everything on the back burner until he finished it. He captured those certain somethings you see in the horse and in the boy. He signed it and gave the plaster version to Jim."

With a fingernail, Sheriff Martinez embossed a design in the tablecloth. "But before he gave the plaster casting to Jim, Andrew had two bronzes made of it. Just two. I can't imagine what it must have cost him, but he wouldn't let me or anyone else chip in, either. Andrew has one for himself, and the other one is for Jim—when Old Black dies, Andrew's going to give him the bronze and take back the plaster. How about that?" A smile that had come suddenly went away. Martinez added almost inaudibly, "I'm not anxious to see that presentation."

After a silence, Atkins said, "Sheriff, it seems incredible to me that a horse as well known as Old Black is still anonymous to the world in terms of what he and Jim did to rescue you that day. We live in a world of total media blitz. How do you explain it?"

Sheriff Mike Martinez looked thoughtful for a time before he answered. His eyes had taken on a hard glint.

"Old Black is the horse," he said sharply. "And Jim Bradley is the boy. Man, I should say. More of a man than you're likely to find walking around in big pants. Now I'll tell you why nobody outside of a hundred miles of Brentwood ever got the story."

Sheriff Martinez delivered his crisp recitation as if he had prepared for it.

"That's it, Atkins," he said when he had concluded. "And the reason nobody outside of Winchester County ever got the whole story was because the news people accepted the concoction that Deputy Swagger gave them. He staged the whole scene like a movie production, which is why it took so long for our guys to come to the rescue. And once his version of the story had been smeared all over the country, backed up by live films, they sure as hell weren't going to do a

Sixty Minutes exposé on themselves. Why should they advertise that they were to be taken in like that? But looking at their side of it, Swagger's version was all they had. The only insiders, me and Jim. were incommunicado.

"Swagger heard my radio call to base. And what does he do? First, he calls up the TV people! To make sure that when he charges courageously into battle he's got his war correspondents along. Then he puts in an emergency call to the D.E.A., people who crave publicity almost as much as he did. So here *they* come with helicopters, rockets, flares, more machine guns. And, naturally, their own TV cameras. Then, because he was *chief* deputy, he took over the operation.

"The reason all you can remember is helicopters and burning buildings and tracers lighting up the scene is that he went out there to give the TV people a documentary of himself in action. There was no need to burn down everything combustible on the place. Even if they were old and deserted, those buildings had value. But raging fires look great on TV. The most imaginative part, I thought, was Cecil B. de Swagger's foresight in filling all the machine-gun magazines with tracers. Have you ever seen them shoot anything but tracers in a Rambo movie? They burned up the barrels of every one of our submachine guns." The sheriff laughed to himself.

He pursed his lips, scowled and closed one eye. The expression was deadly. "While we're cowering in that grove of trees, poor little Jim is going out of his mind. Here is a kid whose biggest previous personal calamity was getting his finger squashed by a car door, and look what he's got on his hands—a man bleeding to death, his beloved horse gasping what might be his last breath, and he's having to fight off our attackers with a twelve-gauge shotgun."

He laughed. "I laugh about it now, but that shotgun was loaded with three-inch super-magnum buckshot loads. They kick so bad they're almost as brutal to the shooter as to the guy getting shot. Jim's shoulder was a mess. Blood poisoning was even a concern, Doc Smith told me." He looked hard into Atkins's eyes. "Little Jim Bradley killed two of those outlaws. Deputy Swagger killed the rest of them. It's true: dead men tell no tales.

"On TV, you saw Swagger on camera and my entire force behind him at a respectable distance so nobody's even recognizable but him. I'm on an operating table. Old Black's still where he dropped in his tracks. Jim's by his side with Doc Smith. And Swagger is telling the cameras that he's rescued the sheriff from the well. 'I commandeered a horse and pulled him out,' he says, like the horse had just wandered by, gladly helped hoist me out under Swagger's expert guidance, and then was turned loose with a pat on the rump to go off and graze.

"The first knowledge I had that something was just a tad off kilter was when I came around enough to understand the spoken word. My wife is there by the bed crying tears of joy and thanking God for giving Swagger the strength to save her husband.

"Then she tells me she'd made his family a big platter of her hot tamales that he loves so much, as an unworthy but heartfelt token of her eternal gratitude. I swear to God, when I began to get a bead on what had come down, if I could have moved I would've tracked him down and blown him to kingdom come. It's a mighty good thing I was trapped in a hospital for two weeks, because that's how long it took for my rage to die down. When I did get around to him, I didn't kill him, I just fired him and ran him out of the county.

"Now, Mr. Horse Judge," he said, pushing his hat up and exposing his untanned forehead. "You're asking for some kind of expert testimony that will help you see Old Black's fine qualities. I know horses. Been around horses all my life. Just by looking at that horse today I can see all the things that say 'champion.' World Champion is sure in the record books someplace, never mind what he did that day on the Brazos.

"The horse is a senior citizen. He's been around. So he's a tad beat up. And he's come back from death's door. But when I look at Old Black today, I don't have one bit of difficulty seeing the blue blood in that horse.

"But Old Black has something else, Mr. Atkins. When you look that big, old, wonderful horse in the eyes, you can see right down into his soul. There's a fire down in there that burns in only the purest of the very purest of champions. It's as rare as the Hope Diamond, in man and horse, but in Old Black that fire is there and it's as obvious as can be."

Randall Atkins leaned on the table toward Sheriff Martinez and spoke softly for a few minutes.

Sheriff Martinez stared into Atkins's eyes. "Okay, I'll do it for Jim, and I'll do it for that valiant horse. You've got me in a trap, because I'd do anything . . ." He took a deep breath. "Jim's a hard case when it comes to showing him any gratitude. He idolizes certain people. Like Andrew. And me—well, idolizing Andrew is pretty easy to do. But he seems to be totally unaware of his own greatness. Maybe that's what real heroism is all about."

Sheriff Martinez stood up. "So, yes, I'll participate. I want to talk to Andrew about it, too. And I have a suggestion about who ought to present the trophy."

CHAPTER 34

The low and almost unceasing drone of the loudspeakers merged harmoniously into the mix of background sounds in the Astrohall. "Attention sheep exhibitors. Judging of breeding dams will begin at four-fifteen in the west show ring. . . . Will Bill Richardson please come to the show office. Bill Richardson to the show office please. . . . The capon auction will begin at four-thirty in section J-twelve, that's section J as in Juliet-twelve. . . ."

The speakers were quiet for a moment and then the monotone resumed. "Attention exhibitors in the youth Quarter Horse show. Judging of class four, American Quarter Horse Association registered geldings over four years old, that's the aged division, will commence in fifteen minutes. Horses may enter the central arena at this time. That is the central arena, *not* ring number four. I repeat, all AQHA halter classes have been moved from show-ring four to the central arena. Judging of aged Quarter Horse geldings will commence in fifteen minutes. You may take your horses to the central arena at this time."

Jim finished a last-minute buffing of Old Black's hooves and stood back, examining his work with immense approval. "How's he look, Dad?" Without waiting for an answer, he exclaimed, "Boy, howdy, Dad, he looks the best ever. I think he has a chance to place, even if it is a big class. Mom?"

Norma forced a smile, hoping she seemed enthusiastic, "Jim, I've never seen him looking better." She turned away as her smile faded. "I'll put the trophies in the locker. We can leave the ribbons on display. They'll be all right, won't they, Matt?"

Jim stepped in front of the horse, a time when Old Black always lowered his head, just in case Jim had in mind giving him an ear-rubbing. Jim did so. "I'll tell you, Black, if we don't win something, don't you be ashamed, because I sure won't. There are a lot of good horses in this class, and they come from all over. You saw those license plates from everywhere you could think of. But even if the judge decides he can't use us, I'll bet he'll have a hard time making up his mind."

An ache arose in Norma's face, her throat tightened. She turned away and busied herself with tidying up some things.

Matt felt it would be safe to leave the ribbons won in performance classes pinned to the stall's back wall. Before snapping the lock on the chest, he asked. "Do you have everything you need, Jim?"

"Yep," Jim said brightly, "You and Mom should go on ahead and get a good seat. It'll take us a few minutes to get to the ring and be checked in, with all the horses in this class."

The Bradleys were seated and watching the gate when Jim entered the arena leading Old Black. Norma's eyebrows were knitted, giving her a troubled look, and she spoke in a worried tone. "Matt, Jim knows what it takes to place, even in our local shows. In *this* kind of competition . . . he just *has* to know Black doesn't measure up. Has he developed some kind of parental blindness to Old Black's faults? Why do we let him keep punishing himself like this?"

Matt patted his wife's hand. "Don't worry, Honey. I don't know what drives him, either. But it's not going to be the end of the world for him to get the gate one more time. He'll get the gate in this class, that's for sure. And he'll come out of that ring with his hat pulled down to hide his disappointment, and he'll cover it up by talking about his wins in the performance classes."

He looked at his watch. "I'll tell you what, when we get back to the ranch we'll put Old Black up and go to Mrs. Schumann's for dinner. One of her chicken-fried's will do the trick. And tomorrow Jim'll be telling the kids at school about the trophies and belt buckles he won. He was especially proud to win the flag race with Andrew and his friends watching. This has been the best show ever for him and Old Black."

The ring steward was still rearranging the rows of horses. Fifty-four horses was a crowd even for the central arena. There was some pushing as two exhibitors maneuvered for the first position in the first row. Some still believed—or hoped—that a judge might have better recall of the first horse he laid eyes on in a class. A girl leading a sorrel gelding won the coveted position. The class was arranged in three rows.

The speakers came to life. "Folks, this is the youth division of the Quarter Horse halter competition. The horses entered in this class are registered Quarter Horse geldings four years and older. This class is sanctioned by the American Quarter Horse Association, the world's largest equine registry with about two-and-a-half million registrations. Your judge today is Mr. Randall Atkins of Abilene, Texas. There will be nine placings in this class."

The announcer covered the microphone with his hand while Randall Atkins spoke to him. "Exhibitors, Mr. Atkins has asked me to announce that he will conduct the judging in two phases because of the size of this class. In the first go-round, he will select the horses he wants to keep for a second round of judging. The exhibitors of those selected will be asked to form a new line facing the east rail. That's the rail on this side, near the officials' table here. When he has the horses he wants, those remaining will be excused from the arena. Will all three rows move back to make room for a row along the east rail, please."

Judge Atkins entered the arena. He spoke briefly to the ring steward, who made a note on his clipboard. With the ring steward by his side, he walked briskly to the sorrel gelding and stopped directly in front of him. He nodded to the girl exhibitor and lifted his hat in a gesture of courtesy. The exhibitor quickly moved a step away from the horse to offer the judge an unobstructed view, expertly holding the halter lead high to keep her horse's head alertly upraised. As he moved to examine the horse from the left side, she stepped briskly to the horse's front, out of the judge's way. The judge's eyes did not leave the horse as he moved on to examine it from the rear, quickly taking in its features. Then he viewed the right side and strode quickly to the front of the next horse. The examination had taken less than thirty seconds.

The girl wondered if her horse had been cut from the class without even being judged on the way it traveled.

The judge nodded a greeting to the boy who was exhibiting the next horse in line. The first exhibitor was relieved when the next one was not asked to travel his horse. That would come in a second inspection, she realized.

Old Black stood in the third row. Judge Atkins examined him with the same brisk appraisal given the other horses, with two exceptions. After examining him from the front, he took a step closer and peered for a moment into Old Black's eyes. Then, although he had not spoken more than a one-word greeting to any previous exhibitor, he turned to Jim, smiled warmly, and said, "You have a fine horse here, son."

Jim mumbled a surprised "Thank you." He did not succeed in his effort to suppress a quick smile.

Norma Bradley nudged her husband with an elbow. "What do you suppose he said to Jim, Matt? From Jim's expression, it must have been something complimentary."

"I can't imagine," he said.

Seated on the top row of the stands was a large woman. Her cold eyes bored in on Old Black through narrow slits. She had just taken a big bite from a hamburger when the show judge spoke to the boy exhibiting entry number thirty-nine. She was a veteran observer of halter classes and had noticed with curiosity when the judge stepped forward and paused a moment at the head of the black horse.

What had caused her to freeze in wonder was the smile that flashed across the face of the boy exhibiting the old horse. She placed the half-eaten hamburger beside the two remaining in the cardboard tray in her lap and turned to the man seated beside her.

"The only reason the judge could have for saying anything to that kid is pity. That nag must be on his last legs. He shouldn't even be allowed in a halter class. But did you notice that he took a close look at the horse's face just before he talked to the kid? And the kid looked like he heard good news. If that horse is still in the arena after the cut I'm going to throw a fit!" The man merely shrugged his bony shoulders. His wife had been known to throw a fit at a horse show for a lot less.

The woman's indignant stare became a pleasant maternal gaze when it fell on her daughter, who was holding the halter lead of the first horse seen by the judge. A tight smile of confidence brightened her face. "Picking up a blue in this class would really rack up the halter points," she thought. Her unbiased opinion was that her daughter's horse had an outstanding chance to win first place, and a good shot at grand-champion gelding, which would make the haul from Cincinnati well worth it. She retrieved the half-eaten hamburger from the tray.

Thirty-four minutes after entering the arena, Judge Atkins was once more looking at his first horse. He stepped behind the sorrel gelding and asked the girl to show her horse's walk. She walked the horse forward a suitable distance, turned him around and walked back. The judge asked for a trot and the girl complied. He went on to the next horse. The girl wondered if the judge would examine the way of traveling of each horse in the class before he started sending keepers to the front. Her mother was curious about that as well.

Mother and daughter learned the answer to that critical question when the judge sent the fourth horse to the front rail. Mother's eyes were afire with rage. Her daughter's were downcast and swimming with tears. Mother's frail husband rolled his eyes toward the ceiling in an expression of impending doom.

By the time Judge Atkins got to Old Black he had selected twenty-two keepers. The woman on the top row wondered if crowding, made worse by a horse that should never be allowed in a halter arena, could have contributed to the judge's inability to see her daughter's horse in the proper light. "Can you imagine why the judge would even give the old black horse a second glance?" she asked her husband, then absently began eating her third hamburger.

Jim walked and trotted Old Black as directed by the judge. When the judge put his hand on the boy's shoulder and pointed to the front rail, the woman on the top row gasped and was seized with spasms of choking.

Jim was unable to contain himself. He struck out victoriously with a little left hook, a huge smile on his face. He jogged up to the row of keepers with Old Black trotting smartly beside him.

Norma jerked upright as if she had received an electrical shock. "Matt! He made the first cut! The judge is keeping Black in there."

Matt was even more dumfounded than his wife. He sat frozen, his hands gripping the bench.

Furious, the woman on the top row snatched the tray from her lap, which still contained two hamburgers, a jumbo Coke and some french fries, and threw it into the air behind her. The debris rained down on people strolling in the aisle behind the stands. Their amazement and their anger went unnoticed by the woman; she was on her feet, throwing a fit.

"Matt, in Jim's mind that's as good as a win!" Norma said excitedly. "Just to stand there for the final round will be as good as a win to him." She looked heavenward and sighed.

The ring steward gave a signal to the announcer. He leaned forward to put his mouth close to the microphone on the table before him. "The horses remaining in the three original rows are excused from the arena. Thank you very much for your participation." The audience thanked the losers with a long period of applause as they filed out of the gate. A feeling of solemn, empathic compassion swept through Jim's being as he watched them go.

Judge Atkins instructed the ring steward to assemble the remaining twenty-three horses in one row down the center of the arena. He then began the second phase of judging the class. Occasionally he would ask to see a horse's way of traveling again. Up and down the row he went, occasionally speaking to the steward who made notes on his clipboard. As he approached Old Black, the judge spoke to the ring steward. The steward stepped behind Jim to see the number bib on his back and made a note on his clipboard. Finally, the judge began to select horses, sending one, then another to the front rail. The sparsity of his selections revealed that he was picking, not culling. The horses he was sending to the front were those that would place in the class.

The ring steward walked rapidly to where Jim stood and spoke to him. Norma saw a curious expression come over Jim's face.

"What could that be about, Matt?" Norma asked, a knuckle pressed against her upper teeth.

He shook his head.

The woman on the top row leaned forward in a menacing attitude, her left forearm planted on her knee, her clenched right fist jammed into her ample hip. She had absolutely no interest in watching any halter class in which her daughter was not present, and on any other occasion she would have returned to the stall, offering consolation to her daughter in the form of criticism of the judge or grave suspicions of crooked show management. But this—this was *scandalous!* And she was going to sit right here and see this thing through.

After nine horses had been selected, the steward signaled to the announcer, who said, "The horses remaining in the back row are excused from the arena. Thank you very much for your participation in this outstanding class."

Jim's parents were thrilled that Jim had at least been spared from getting the gate with the first cut. It was when they looked for Old Black among the horses now leaving the arena that they realized he was not among them. The ring steward was standing in front of Jim, talking and making motions with his clipboard. Jim moved Old Black to the back rail while the judge repositioned the winners to reflect the final order of the aged gelding class. First place went to the chestnut who had lost to Old Black in the flag race.

In this, the world's largest youth Quarter Horse show, every winner was awarded both a ribbon and a trophy. After the brief awards ceremony, the horses filed out of the arena with the blue-ribbon horse leading the parade. Only Jim and Old Black remained, standing alone at the back rail. Some of the spectators were beginning to wonder what this was about. Horses that would be in the class that followed this one began to crowd the wide aisle leading up to the gate, their exhibitors craning their necks to see what was going on.

Jim stood militarily straight, his expression blank. Old Black's stance was erect and proud. With ears perked and his nose thrust forward, he appeared almost defiant; not a muscle moved, not a hair twitched.

Norma was clutching a handkerchief in her hand. "Matt, if this is something that's going to embarrass Jim, I don't think I can stand it."

Matt laid a hand on hers and squeezed. "Honey, these people would never single out any youngster for abuse or ridicule. In fact, I'm beginning to have a feeling that Jim or Old Black, or both of them, are going to get some kind of recognition."

Judge Atkins concluded a discussion at the officials' table and strode back into the arena, this time carrying a cordless microphone. He blew into it, cocked an ear, then blew into it again. "Can you hear me?" he asked softly, looking toward the officials' table. Several heads nodded.

"Ladies and gentlemen," Atkins began in his pleasant, resonant drawl, "I'm going to take a little time this afternoon to make a special presentation. Although this is a departure from the agenda, the award I am making has been approved by the American Quarter Horse Association and will therefore go into the record book." He had motioned to the steward to put Jim and Old Black in the center of the arena, and he met them there.

The judge stopped a few yards from Old Black, viewing him from the side opposite Jim. Jim stood stiff and expressionless. Past experience told him this could not be anything good.

Atkins again lifted the microphone. "Superior conformation is a guide, often reliable, of a horse's potential abilities. Over a few centuries of observation, man has learned to look for the physical features that horses need to do certain jobs and do them well. Plow horses and wagon teams can't do their jobs if they're built like Quarter Horses or Thoroughbreds. The early speed needed to work cattle and the strength to jerk a ton of beef to the ground demand physical conformation that the eye can see. Good temperament is desired in all horses, and whether they have it or whether they're cranky can be determined by observation."

People in the audience began to ask each other what this could be about. Some were referring to their programs. Most of the spectators were people who could see with their own eyes that the horse in the arena was not a threat in the show ring. But this judge clearly liked him, and seemed to be intent on holding him out as some kind of example. So why hadn't he used him in the placings?

"Over the last hundred years or so, the American Quarter Horse has been selectively bred to perform many duties. The Quarter Horse is a cutting horse, a roping horse, a trail horse, a race horse, and a horse that can carry his master to town, to church, to school, or across the state. The Quarter Horse must be able keep a cool head in the midst of all kinds of commotion. And quite obviously to everyone here, the Quarter Horse is an ideal youth's horse.

"A characteristic we hope is there in every horse is courage. Unfortunately, there is no way to determine whether courage is present at all, much less to what extent. It's the same with man. Courage can only be demonstrated in circumstances that demand it, and we can't simulate those conditions. The most unlikely people have on occasion shown exemplary courage on the battlefields and elsewhere, while some presumed to be courageous have collapsed with fright under pressure. Since we can't test for the presence of courage, we have to just hope that it's there, in horse and in man, when courage is demanded.

"Halter classes are a means of selecting superior horses that *appear* to possess the most desirable physical attributes of the breed. Theoretically, a halter champion would likely be a performance champion. But like the marvelous physical specimen who can't fight his way out of a paper bag, an occasional halter champion won't make it in the performance arena, on the ranch, or on the race track.

"To further prove the superiority of outstanding individuals, AQHA has promoted competitive events in rodeos and horse shows. A special class—AQHA Champion—was established for horses that have prize-winning conformation and in addition have shown superior performance in competitive events. The all-around best of the best of the champions are the AQHA Supreme Champions."

A bustle of conversation hummed among the spectators. Some were returning with cardboard trays filled with soft drinks, hot dogs and hamburgers. The interest of the crowd was ebbing, but Randall Atkins seemed not to notice. Jim and Old Black stood as still and erect as before.

The facial expression and body language revealed that the woman on the top row was becoming ferocious. She was considering what kind of a disturbance would be appropriate if *this* judge awarded *this* old nag the title of AQHA Supreme Champion. She was capable of creating just about any level of disturbance such an occurrence might demand. She considered placing a telephone call to AQHA president Don Franklin, something she'd been known to do before in even less critical situations, but rejected the idea in favor of staying at her post. She wagged a snakeskin-booted foot to the beat of a quick, metronomic cadence.

"Once in a while," Atkins continued, "a horse comes along that doesn't quite measure up to the conformation standards necessary to win blue ribbons in the halter arena, but demonstrates that he or she is capable of performing right alongside recognized, decorated champions. Once in a lifetime or so, a horse without the visual excellence so desirous in the breed proves himself to be so vastly superior as to become legendary.

"Go Man Go was one that comes immediately to mind. The black gelding standing in the arena right now is another horse of such rarity. He has proven by deeds throughout a long lifetime that he stands squarely along with the handful of the greatest horses that ever lived. His registered name is Buck's Old Black; he's more commonly known as just Old Black. According to AQHA records, he's twenty years old. He hasn't come through his years of giving his best unscathed, so you can maybe understand why I couldn't use him in this class of over fifty outstanding horses, probably none of them even half his age."

A hush had fallen on the spectators. The audience was now riveted on the trio standing in the arena.

Norma sat straight and stiff, a hand over her mouth and tears of joy welling up in her eyes. The knuckles of the hand that held Matt's were white. Matt was smiling; he turned and winked at her.

"Which brings me to the subject of the special recognition being belatedly awarded to this horse today. Those of you who are rodeo fans undoubtedly recognize Old Black. He is the world champion calf-roping horse. He won the title four years ago in Butte, Montana and it still stands. He took second place right here in the world's largest combined rodeo and livestock show two years ago."

Applause rippled through the stands. The woman on the top row did not applaud.

"His championship performance may never be beaten, but even if it is, Old Black will forever remain the Babe Ruth of calf roping. Old Black has also won for his former owner more money than any other roping horse, living or dead—another record. Upon his retirement from the rodeo arena, Old Black was up there among the oldest roping horses in regular competition.

"Two years ago, when he was eighteen, Old Black embarked upon a new career as a performance horse in the youth arena. True to his proven reputation, he began taking his new master to the pay window with predictable regularity.

"Today, I watched a tremendous physical match between a young, superlative specimen of the Quarter Horse breed—the horse that just left this arena with the blue ribbon—and this veteran campaigner. Old Black was up against a much younger opponent who possessed superior speed and conformation. The young horse was ridden with great skill, as was Old Black. Old Black won that flag race event, and he won on guts, heart, brains, and a determination to take his master to the pay window—something he is famous for doing.

"Old Black has also shown a level of courage superior to that of any horse I've ever heard of, superior even to horses who lived only in fables, where their courageous deeds could be wholly invented. But Old Black is not famous for his courage. Outside of his home town of Brentwood, Texas, he is the living essence of unsung heroes.

"I am certain that many of you heard of the deed performed by this horse not even a year ago, during which he demonstrated his boundless courage, because it was headlined in news stories across the country. But not many of you could have learned the details of that deed, simply because the details were unknown until the story was stone cold. To refresh your memory, a Texas sheriff had been thrown down a well by a gang of drug smugglers, and he was left there to die. There was a big firefight that you saw on TV, and it was mentioned that the sheriff had been rescued from the well; a horse pulled him to safety with rope. How many of you heard about that? Can I have a show of hands?"

A swarm of hands flew into the air. Randall Atkins pointed to a woman in the stands. "You, ma'am, where are you from?"

The woman cupped her hands and shouted, "Sandusky, Ohio."

"Did you see a picture of the horse or hear his name?" The woman shook her head. "This is the team, Old Black and Jim Bradley, that labored so long that day to pull Sheriff Mike Martinez out of that well and then drag him to safety, and keep the critically injured man alive until help came."

Thunderous applause broke out. Matt glanced sideways at Norma as she stood applauding, laughing and crying at the same time, oblivious to the tears streaming down her face. In the arena, Jim's expression was as straight as if the judge was talking about someone else. But Old Black seemed to know that the applause was for him, for he was throwing his head up and down. A wave of laughter swept through the stands.

The woman on the top row still held the same threatening posture, but her head was cocked aside; her furrowed brow and a squinted eye revealed an emerging but still skeptical interest.

Atkins went to stand beside Old Black, took hold of a lock of his mane. "What you saw on television and read about in the newspapers was the finale of a real-life drama of agony, courage and pure determination that almost cost the lives of this boy and his horse. If they had not succeeded, Winchester County Sheriff Mike Martinez would be dead, too.

"He had been bashed in the head, thrown into the well and left for dead. A leg was broken in the tumble down the shaft. Bleeding profusely from his torn leg and from head wounds, he was certain to die. But what can only be described as divine providence intervened. Jim and Old Black were out exploring that fateful day. Jim just happened to have a lariat, and on top of that it was an extra long heeling rope. Even so, it was just *barely* long enough. Providence!"

Now the only sounds audible in the place were cattle bawling in the distance, horses whinnying, chickens cackling, radios playing from afar . . . Small tractors and golf carts purred here and there. The entire area had become packed with passersby, drawn by the fixed, silent attention showing in the faces of the spectators. Jim and Old Black stood as before. The woman on the top row was now sitting straight upright, both arms stiff by her sides, and hands grasping the bench.

"Jim heard Sheriff Martinez call for help. Then he and Old Black began a rescue operation that would last from two in the afternoon until after dark. During the long ascent from the well, there were times when the horse had to stand there holding a steady strain on the lariat with over two hundred pounds on the end of it.

"Straining against that load without relief was taking a serious toll on the horse. Toward the end Old Black began to tremble with weariness, but he hung on. It took over two hours to get the sheriff out of the well, and when that part of the job was done Old Black was on his knees, trembling uncontrollably, sweating profusely, and frothing at the mouth.

"But his work wasn't over. The sound of the drug smugglers' speedboat was heard, approaching from downriver.

"Sheriff Martinez couldn't walk, of course. He couldn't even crawl, and was desperately weak from exertion and loss of blood. Forty yards away was a wooded area where they could hide; it was where Sheriff Martinez had concealed his patrol car. His pistol had been taken off him, but he carried a shotgun in the patrol car. If they could get there before that boat landed they could radio for help, and they could try to defend themselves until help arrived.

"Jim rigged up a makeshift sled using a sheet of roofing tin and his lariat, and he had to ask Old Black to help pull the sheriff to the woods. Somehow, the horse found another warm coal deep down inside, but when they finally reached the woods, he collapsed in his tracks. He would not be able to move a muscle for the next twenty-four hours, and it was some time before the vets could say the horse would live."

White handkerchiefs and colored bandannas could now be seen dabbing at eyes among the spectators. The woman on the top row was now sitting straight upright and very still, both hands covering her mouth in an expression of pure astonishment. Norma Bradley had abandoned her attempts to wipe away the tears and just allowed them to flow freely down her face, a face lifted high with pride.

"The smugglers had indeed returned and Sheriff Martinez, Jim Bradley, and Old Black were the targets of a frantic search. Then Jim was called on by the sheriff, who was unable to rise, to defend them with his shotgun. This Jim did, ending the lives of two brutal criminals who had previously killed a State Trooper and had attempted to kill Sheriff Martinez."

Judge Atkins turned from the sea of faces to Jim and Old Black. He stood looking at them for many seconds, then turned slowly back to the audience. "Perhaps the most essential of the providential happenings that day at Klanke's Mill was that it was *this* young man and *this* horse that happened by. Considering the seeming impossibility of the job they undertook, I personally wonder if any other team imaginable would have got that job done.

"And for some time only two people knew the real story. Sheriff Martinez was unconscious on an operating table, and Jim Bradley, completely done in, was at the side of his mortally exhausted horse."

Atkins motioned to the officials at the desk. There was a period of total quiet, and then came the sound of scattered clapping that rose steadily until it reach a din. The lady on the top row was standing, and with hands held very high she was clapping with animated enthusiasm. She looked down, grabbed her husband's coat by the shoulder and snatched him to his feet.

The gate opened and the crowd watched as a girl of about fifteen, elegantly dressed in a satiny yellow western outfit with red and green embroidery, was escorted into the arena by a ring steward who carried a big silver trophy. Hardly able to believe his eyes, Jim moved for the first time. With a thumb he pushed the front of his hat up an inch and broke into a smile almost as big as the one that sparkled before him. He could see both rows of Alexandra's teeth. Tiny quivers gave away the nervous giggles she was trying to hold back.

Then through the gate strode the strapping uniformed figure of Sheriff Mike Martinez. He stopped at Alexandra's side.

Judge Atkins faced the stands and raised the microphone. "Ladies and gentlemen. Winchester County Sheriff Mike Martinez will make a presentation on his own behalf and read the citation for the special award being made by the American Quarter Horse Association. Miss Alexandra Meridith will present the trophy." He handed the microphone to the sheriff and stepped aside.

Sheriff Martinez spoke in a strong, deep voice with a trace of a Mexican accent. "Folks, after our adventure out there at Klanke's Mill, I decided to deputize Old Black and Jim Bradley. They will be genuine deputy sheriffs, as authorized by a special amendment of the articles under which the office of the Winchester County Sheriff's Department is established, approved by the Commissioners' Court." He withdrew from his shirt pocket a little white Bible and handed the microphone to Atkins.

He looked from Jim to Old Black as he spoke in a low, personal voice without the microphone. Soon, Jim raised his right hand. He looked at Old Black, then back at the sheriff and shrugged. How could a horse raise his right hand? he seemed to ask. A small smile brightened Martinez's solemn expression. Jim put his left hand on the Bible and after a moment appeared to say "Yes, sir." He then tugged on the halter lead and Old Black threw his head up and down. The crowd roared with laughter.

Sheriff Martinez put away the Bible and took two badges from his shirt pocket. He pinned one on Jim's western vest, the other to Old Black's halter. Then he stepped back and saluted smartly, first to Jim, then to Old Black. Jim returned the salute and, as if on command, Old Black threw his head up. From the stands came a wave of laughter and a roll of applause. Speaking into the microphone again, Sheriff Martinez read from a scroll Judge Atkins had handed him.

"Old Black, for service in the line of duty you have earned the title of World Champion Calf Roping Horse, thereby bringing high honor and esteem to yourself, your master, and the Quarter Horse breed. For service far above and beyond the call of duty, you have glorified horses of every breed, most particularly the Quarter Horse. You have shown that you possess the physical ability sought by Quarter Horse breeders everywhere; you have displayed boundless courage and determination. In recognition thereof, you are hereby awarded the title of Honorary AQHA Supreme Champion. Signed, Don Franklin, President."

A new crescendo of applause arose as the ring steward held out the purple ribbon for Jim to inspect. Then he attached the ribbon to Old Black's halter.

Sheriff Martinez allowed the paper to re-roll itself and handed it to Jim. He shook Jim's hand warmly and said a few private words. Then he stepped up to Old Black and stroked the horse's chin. Old

Black raised his nose, his eyes closed in ecstasy. Sheriff Martinez took Old Black's head in both hands and kissed him on the nose. Then he raised the microphone. "I am deeply and eternally grateful to you both, Jim and Old Black." He looked at Alexandra and said, "Alexandra Meridith will present the trophy."

In the moment it took Alexandra to step up, Jim turned to Old Black and hugged him tight. When he released him, Old Black playfully tipped Jim's hat with his nose and it fell to the ground. Laughter drummed through the crowd. Then applause began as Alexandra held the trophy out to Jim.

He took the trophy and held it high so he could read the engraved words. Then he showed it to Old Black and spoke to him. He looked again upon the positively luminous face of Alexandra. Sheriff Martinez stepped forward and took the trophy from Jim. Beaming, Jim grabbed Alexandra around the waist and, holding her tight, turned around and around with Alexandra's tiny, booted feet swinging free. When he came to a stop and observed the sea of faces watching, he picked up his hat and clamped it on his head to hide his reddened face. Applause, cheers, and piercing whistles were reverberating through the Astrohall as the group walked toward the arena gate. It did not even enter Jim's mind that this was the first time he had ever led Old Black out of a halter arena with a prize.

It was taking some time for Jim, Alexandra and Old Black to work their way through the throng of well-wishers, out of the gate and into the broad open area fronting the arena. Hundreds of hands caressed Old Black's coat as they crept along, reminiscent to him, perhaps, of that triumphant day in Butte, Montana.

Meanwhile, back at stall H-forty-two, people had begun to gather; preparations were busily under way for a celebration. Mrs. Martinez and several others worked around a table, putting out bowls of chips and dips and dipping vegetables. Oscar Jackson was there, busy and smiling and looking almost like his old self. Oscar and the oldest Martinez boy took a large bronze statue from a box braced with wooden corners and carefully placed it on the table. Tied to the rail was a big, beautiful chestnut gelding with a blue ribbon pinned to his black, silver-mounted halter. The boy who owned the horse was energetically helping in the preparations. Andrew Meridith, just arriving from the stands with Matt and Norma Bradley, announced, "They're on their way, folks, but fame makes for slow going."

WITH JIM LEADING OLD BLACK AND ALEXANDRA carrying the trophy, they threaded their way through well-wishers who were crowding the aisle. They spoke and smiled their thanks and slowly inched toward the corridor that would take them to stall H-42.

Just as they passed the back side of the spectators' stands, a tall, lean man dressed in western attire stepped out from among the other bystanders. His face was slashed by a broad vee-shaped smile that showed a lot of teeth. Displaying a noticeable hitch as he swung his right leg, he walked up, slapped Old Black on the neck and rubbed him briskly. "Hi, old pal," he said in a strong, warm voice. "Still in there winning, ain't you, boy?" His eyes roamed over the horse. "Never seen you looking better—nope, not ever." Then he turned his smile on the boy.

Jim jerked back with a start. "Mr. *Jones!*" he exclaimed. "Look, Black, it's Mr. Jones!" He smacked a fist smartly in a palm and raised a knee in a small crouch of joy. "Gee—gosh—Hi, Mr. Jones!" he cried with unrestrained delight.

Buck Jones seized Jim's shoulder in a congenial grasp and extended his hand. Jim took it, squeezing with as much grip as he could muster for this man who had praised his handshake so long ago. Buck held the hand up for inspection and saw that it was no longer that of the child he'd met two years back; it was longer and more muscular, a small version of a working man's hand. A solemn and reflective expression flashed across his face and was gone.

Buck cocked his head and laughed. He pointed a teasing, accusing finger at Jim and turned to Alexandra. "I can see one thing clear as a bell, Miss. I'd better keep an eye out or this cowboy's going to steal all my thunder, the way him and Old Black are carrying on." He punched Jim playfully on the arm.

"Naw, Mr. Jones," Jim said with evident embarrassment. He turned and put his arm around Alexandra. "Mr. Jones, this is my best friend, Alexandra Meridith. You know her father, Andrew. Alexandra, this is Mr. Buck Jones. He raised Old Black from a colt and made him the world's champion."

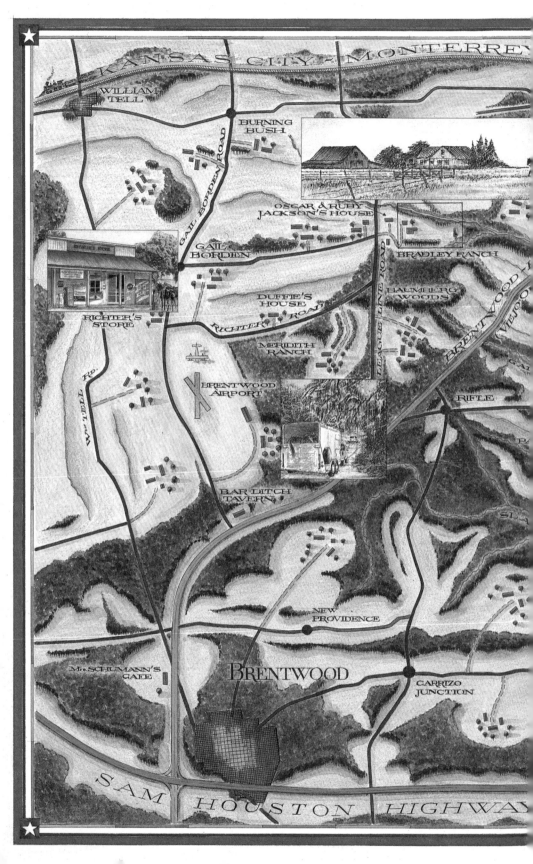